About the Author

Claire Leggett has loved dragons, magic and everything fantastical since she read The Enchanted Wood by Enid Blyton. As a child she used to sneak to the bottom of the garden in the hope of finding fairies. Alas she never found any, so she brought them alive in her own imagination. Her stories are full of magic, adventure and escape.

When Claire's not writing she can be found creating her own handmade journals, swinging on a sidecar, or in the garden attempting to grow something other than weeds.

Claire lives in Western Australia with her husband, who loves even her most annoying quirks, and is currently learning how to crochet.

You can connect with Claire by joining her reader group. http://www.claireleggett.com/reader-group/.

Also by Claire Leggett

Fantasy
The Emperor's Conspiracy
The Daughter's Duty
The Assassin's Gift
The Healer's Curse
The Servant's Grace

Claire also writes contemporary romance and romantic suspense under the pen name Claire Boston.
www.claireboston.com

The Healer's Curse

The Emperor's Conspiracy

Claire Leggett

First published by Bantilly Publishing in 2020 originally under the pen name Claire Boston

The Healer's Curse: The Emperor's Conspiracy 2

EPUB format: 978-1-925696-54-7
Mobi format: 978-1-925696-55-4
Print: 978-1-925696-60-8
Large Print: 978-1-925696-61-5
Hard Cover: 978-1-925696-62-2

Cover design by Lana Pecherczyk
Edited by Ann Harth
Proofread by Teena Raffa-Mulligan
Map by Shona Husk

Our greatest glory is not in never falling, but in rising every time we fall.

Confucius

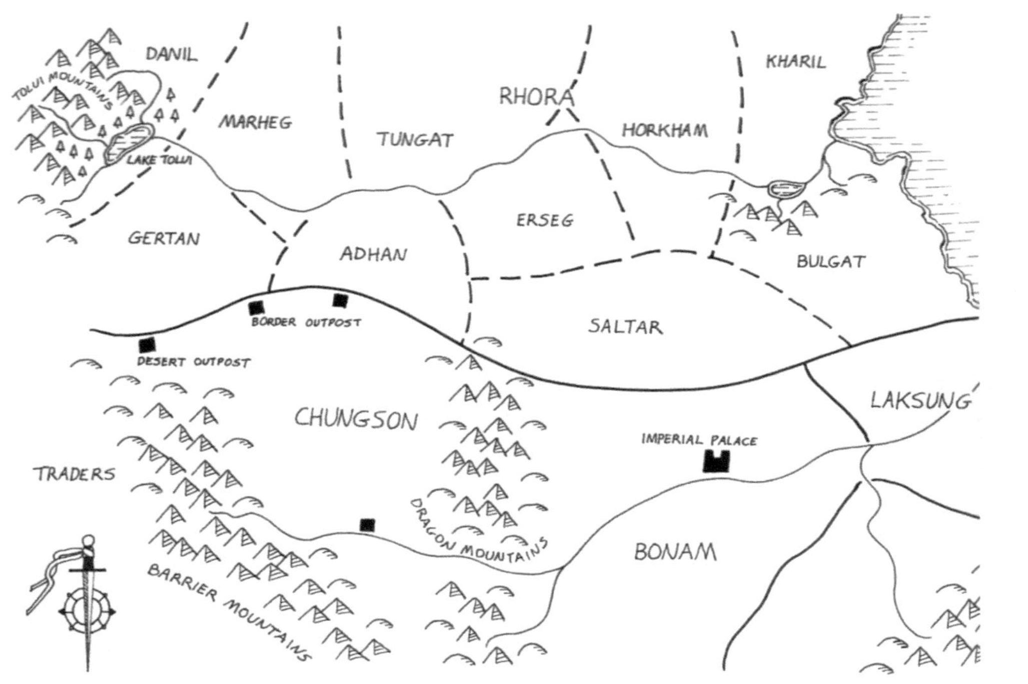

TOLUI MOUNTAINS
DANIL
LAKE TOLUI
MARHEG
TUNGAT
RHORA
HORKHAM
KHARIL
ERSEG
GERTAN
ADHAN
BULGAT
BORDER OUTPOST
DESERT OUTPOST
SALTAR
CHUNGSON
LAKSUNG
TRADERS
IMPERIAL PALACE
DRAGON MOUNTAINS
BONAM
BARRIER MOUNTAINS

Dedication

To all doctors, nurses and other health care professionals who work so tirelessly to care for the sick, injured and unwell. Thank you.

Chapter 1

Geriel wandered the well-trodden dirt between the white yurts. The evening quiet suffocated, pressing on her chest as if smothering her, and yet murmurs from inside the yurts grated like an out-of-tune morin khuur. After the excitement of the past few moons, the mundanity of camp life was stifling.

She had finished in the healing tent for the day and was in no rush to return home, where the yurt would be full of her brothers and sisters all wanting to talk. That wasn't the type of noise she wanted. Geriel missed the thunder of riding across the steppes with the Rhoran warriors, missed the sense of purpose training with Lien had given her. But there was no longer an urgent need to learn everything her adopted sister could teach them. The secret bodyguard and Lien's old assassin master were all dead.

Until only a few days ago, all ten Rhoran tribes had filled the camp with laughter and celebrations. Something was always happening, and there was always someone new to meet. But the tribes had finally gone their separate ways, taking their share of the treaty reparations with them. Geriel's tribe felt smaller now than it ever had. She knew every person in every yurt and longed for a diversion beyond daily healer training and family chores.

Geriel wandered to the horse yard, scanning for her own brown steed, Khulan. She sighed. Perhaps she should ride across the steppes, clear her mind, stop wishing for more from life. The sun would be up for another hour at least.

"Why the big sigh, child?"

Her heart swelled with love at her father's voice, but as she faced him, guilt swamped her. Sukh was her rock, the man who was always there for her, who gave her confidence and a sense of purpose. Geriel had failed him. She'd been unable to heal him. She'd been useless at the one thing her tribe expected of her.

He waited for her answer, his shoulder-length brown hair in need of a comb and his eyes patient.

"No reason." She couldn't tell him she was stifled here, that she needed to escape from the expectations of the tribe, the ones she'd already failed.

"Would you like to ride with me?"

She smiled. He read her mind. The solution to all her father's problems was a ride on the steppes, a way of clearing his head and opening it to new possibilities and options. "Yes, please."

As she answered, Khulan lifted her head and trotted over. Her father's ability to communicate with horses could be useful. "I'll get my saddle," Geriel said.

He chuckled. "It's right here." He shifted and next to him on the fence were both saddles.

"You knew I would say yes."

"I had a hunch." He passed her the saddle and they prepared their horses.

She hadn't ridden Khulan much since she'd returned from helping the injured Rhoran the Bonamese emperor had released as part of the peace treaty. She'd left the difficult healing—those that required use of her gift—to Amslan and had concentrated on the normal healing processes; bandages and ointments, tinctures and tonics, with the occasional stitch thrown in. She couldn't tap into her gift with any regularity no matter how many times she practised the meditation Lien had taught her. She felt utterly useless when she failed to heal. Her gift had been discovered at sixteen, far later than usual, so she hadn't had a chance to develop it properly.

It was probably too late now.

"Come, child. Your thoughts are cloudy. Let the steppes blow them clear."

Geriel mounted Khulan and kicked her into a canter, letting the cool wind on the steppes blow past her. She closed her eyes, trusting her horse to follow her father, and tried to release the tension, the dissatisfaction with her life.

She should be happy.

Her people had just defeated the Bonamese emperor, had stopped his invasion, had prevented him from seizing an artefact which would have destroyed them. The treaty had returned all their missing tribe members, had given them a new batch of silks, rice and other goods and had seen the dragons reclaim their rightful land in the mountains that bordered Bonam and its vassal state Chungson. It had been a rousing success.

But taking part in the attack, even on the outskirts as a healer, had opened a new world of travel and adventure to Geriel. She wanted to experience life outside her tribe, wanted to explore the world.

Her mother and the spiritual leader wanted to find her a suitable husband.

She grimaced. That's not what she wanted, not yet.

She still didn't know who she was, or what she wanted out of life. Having to consider another person would stifle her further. She was grateful the emperor invaded when he did. The Rhoran tribes had gathered for the khan's wedding, and her mother had decided it was the perfect opportunity to find Geriel a husband. But then the camp was attacked and all focus turned to defeating the emperor. Lien made certain Geriel went with the army and Geriel was so incredibly thankful for the opportunity.

Her father called out and she opened her eyes, found him circling around and slowing. She followed suit and ended up next to him, on the top of a rise, looking over the endless expanse of the grassy steppes. Before her was the way to the rest of the world; the emperor's land of Bonam, its neighbouring state, Chungson and beyond the mountains were the traders' lands and people she had yet to meet. She inhaled deeply, smelled the grass and her horse's sweat, smelled home. Summer was almost at an end.

"Will you talk to me, child? Tell me your troubles?"

Geriel closed her eyes. Normally he was the one she confided in, but how could she tell him she was dissatisfied with her life? "Why do you think I'm troubled?"

"Because you have been quiet since we returned. It was your first campaign; do the memories haunt you?"

She couldn't lie to him, even though it would be the easier option. "I was prepared for the fighting. I've healed warriors before, I knew what injuries to expect."

"Then what?"

Her throat closed. She swallowed hard. "How are you, Father? Your injury was quite severe." She winced at the phrasing. Nothing *quite* about it. He would be dead without Amslan.

"I am healthy. I'm sorry for scaring you so."

She turned away and he touched her hand. "I am well. Don't blame your sister for not defeating the enemy faster."

Her eyes widened. "I don't. Lien fought hard for us."

"Good. Perhaps you could tell her that. She still blames herself, all these moons on."

Lien had no reason to blame herself. Geriel nodded. "I will."

"Did I thank you for saving my life?"

Geriel gritted her teeth. "I didn't." She nudged her horse with her heels to move away from him.

He followed. "Of course you did. You were the first to reach me. I felt your healing."

She wanted to kick Khulan into a gallop and leave her father behind, but he would continue the conversation when he caught up with her. "No. I did almost nothing. Amslan was the one who healed you. I was useless." A heavy weight pressed against her chest making it difficult to breathe.

"That's not true," her father growled. "Amslan said I would have died before he arrived if it wasn't for you."

"He was being kind." The piercing horror of seeing the knife sticking out of her father's chest was still sharp. The hot flush of fear.

Her father grabbed her arm. "Amslan never says things he doesn't mean, and he definitely doesn't pander to anyone." He shook her arm as if trying to shake some sense into her. "If he said you saved my life, then I believe him."

"No. Amslan saved your life, I just prolonged it long enough for him to arrive."

"That counts, particularly to me, to your mother and your siblings. If you hadn't, Amslan would have found me dead."

That wasn't the point. He didn't understand how desperately hard she'd tried to reach her gift and heal his heart, but she could only brush the power with the edges of her consciousness. Her panic had almost consumed her. It wasn't until Amslan arrived to show her what to do that she'd been any use.

"Your gift is powerful."

Anger rose in her. "But I am useless. I can't access it when I need it, I can't control it. When it works, it's luck."

Her father raised his eyebrows. "I didn't teach you to give up."

Frustration welled in her and she shouted, "You don't understand. Your gift has always come easy to you."

He laughed, a loud, raucous sound, and some of her anger eased. It was impossible to be mad around such a joyous noise.

"Child, we all struggle. My parents thought I was crazy when I first communicated with horses. No one had done it before and I made mistakes, misunderstanding what they meant. It took a long time to convince anyone I wasn't making it up."

She frowned. "I never realised."

"I don't like to talk about it. The tribe treated me differently and it was very lonely. It took time to earn both the horses' and the tribes' trust and to understand how my gift worked."

"How did you?" Geriel asked.

"Trial and error. I had no one to teach me, so I tried different things, hoping one day I'd be able to prove myself. Then one of the mares went into labour and I knew she was having trouble. I heard the foal struggling and I told the man in charge of horses what to do.

After he tried everything else, he listened to me and I saved both the mother and foal. The tribe believed me after that."

Her father had always been respected and admired for his work with horses. She couldn't imagine a time when he wasn't.

"You need to discover what works for you and your gift, but ignoring the problem is not the solution," he said.

Shame filled her. He was right. His near death had caused her to lose focus, to indulge in self-pity. "Thank you, Father." Now that life had returned to normal, she would take Amslan aside, ask him to help her master her gift. There would be further battles with the emperor and she wouldn't allow herself to be as useless next time.

He smiled. "You're welcome. I'm always here to help."

"I know." She wanted to wash away her doubt for the day. It would return, but for now she would enjoy the ride with her father. "Race you back to camp?" She didn't wait for his answer. She kicked Khulan into a gallop and grinned at her father's whoop behind her.

~*~

The next morning, Shuren's quiet chatter woke Geriel early. She opened her eyes to see her youngest sister on the other mattress playing with the wooden horse their brother had made. Pale morning light peeked through the central flap of the yurt.

Her sister, Checheg, groaned beside her. "Go play outside, Shuren. We're trying to sleep."

"I was whispering," Shuren yelled.

Geriel shook her head. She wouldn't get any more rest. "Let's go outside and play." She stepped over

Checheg and pushed aside the curtain that separated their sleeping quarters from the communal quarters. Her parents' and brothers' curtains were still in place, though they would have all heard Checheg's complaint. She was used to the lack of privacy, but fondly remembered the quarter moon when she'd stayed in Lien's yurt before Lien had married and it had been just the two of them. They'd had so much space and peace. A luxury.

She changed into a dress and pants and followed Shuren outside. The cool air was fresh with the scent of grass and colour hadn't returned to the land yet. Everything was grey as the sun rose slowly in the sky. "This way." She gestured towards the horse herd. Hopefully it was far enough away from the yurts for them not to disturb anyone else.

"Checheg's so mean," Shuren said, her bottom lip sticking out.

"She goes to bed later than you, so she needs a little more sleep."

"Jochi gets to stay up later than I do."

"When you're eight, you'll get to stay up later too."

"But that's two more years!"

"It will pass quickly." A distraction would be good before Shuren got really sulky. "Look, there's Lien." Their adopted sister, and Tribal Mother stood at the edge of the camp running through her morning patterns. She moved with such grace, posture straight, her movements fluid and balance absolute. Her long black braid barely moved and her yellow belt was exactly centred around the waist of her blue dress. Geriel would never be that perfect.

"Lien!" Shuren yelled and ran to her.

Geriel winced, hoping Shuren hadn't woken those in nearby yurts. Lien finished her pattern as they approached and bent to hug Shuren. "Little sister, you're up early this morning."

"That's because Mother makes me go to bed too early."

Lien smiled. "I'm sure she knows best." She hugged Geriel. "Sister, how are you?"

"I'm well. I hear there's to be a tribal council today."

Lien nodded. "We need to discuss our trip to Chungson."

Geriel's heart skipped a beat. "I'd still like to go with you." They had recently discovered Lien's brother was still alive and hiding in Chungson. The emperor had arranged the death of his predecessor—Lien's father—and her brother had been thought dead as well.

"I'll discuss it with Temur and Father."

Shuren gaped at her and tugged on her hand. "You can't leave again. It was awful with you gone. I was so worried."

Geriel squatted closer to her sister's height. "This trip won't be as dangerous as the last one. We'll be travelling in secret, and not going anywhere near Bonam."

"I don't like it. I'll tell Father not to let you." Before Geriel could stop her, Shuren ran off.

She sighed and stood, resisting the urge to chase her. "The attack on the camp really frightened her."

"She witnessed a lot of death and destruction," Lien said. "I believe Father will let you go. The dragon sanctuary has a lot of rare plants in it. My father spent some time studying there before he was killed. We need to take a healer with us to discover new plants."

Geriel's heart leapt and danced. Her parents couldn't refuse if it was for the good of the tribe.

"Would you like to have breakfast with us?" Lien asked as she walked back towards the yurts.

"Yes, please." Of late the noisy dinner table at home stressed her.

They moved through the camp, greeting more early risers, until they reached the khan's tent in the centre. Lien walked in. "Temur, we have a guest for breakfast."

Geriel hung back until the khan said, "Who is it?" Then she stepped through the door. She'd always been a little overwhelmed by Temur, though she didn't let it show. He was their khan of all of Rhora, not just their tribe, and was confident and assertive. He'd achieved much at such a young age.

"Geriel." He opened his arms to welcome her. "Come in."

She sat on one of the cushions while Lien served the food.

"Are you well?" he asked.

"Yes. Thank you." She longed to put her case forward to accompany them to Chungson. "And you?"

He grinned, his face lighting up as he glanced at his wife. "I've never been better."

His love for her sister warmed Geriel. Before they married, Lien had been worried. She was an outsider, a Bonamese princess given to the khan by the emperor who had wanted to get rid of her. Their courtship had been tumultuous, but now they were in love.

She wanted that with whomever she had to marry— hopefully in the distant future.

"I'll stop by the healers' tent this afternoon," Temur said. "How are our patients?"

"Their injuries are healing." Geriel lowered her eyes. Their souls might take longer. Some of them had been prisoners of the Bonamese for years, subjected to brutal conditions.

Temur nodded. "We'll make the emperor pay for what he did."

The first step was to speak to Lien's brother, Bao, the rightful heir to the Bonamese throne.

Temur handed her a bowl of soup. "Amslan tells me your gift isn't getting any stronger."

She winced and sipped the soup. Temur waited for an answer. "It came to me late, so perhaps it won't."

Temur shook his head. "Amslan believes you're blocked. We need to work on it. The conflict with the emperor has shown me we need more healers with the gift."

Geriel stared at her bowl. She wanted to improve but Amslan was right. She couldn't grasp her gift. "I will continue to try."

"I'll ask Solongo if she can help."

Geriel stifled a groan. The last time she'd seen the spiritual leader, Solongo had raised the case for her marrying soon. She would rather not remind her of that conversation.

"Geriel could come with us to Chungson," Lien said. "She would be the perfect person to study the plants in the dragon sanctuary."

Temur frowned. "Perhaps. We need to keep one gifted healer with the tribe and I wanted Amslan to join us."

Dread lodged in Geriel's stomach. She couldn't argue her case against Amslan's. Not only had he saved her father's life, but he'd also saved Lien's life several times and his own wife as well. He was so much stronger than she, and also Temur's best friend.

Lien gave her a sympathetic smile. "We'll discuss it at the tribal council."

She had no hope. The elders of the tribe would all agree to Amslan going to Chungson. She'd be stuck here, unable to properly heal anyone. Her appetite left her and she stood. "I must go. Thank you for breakfast."

She left the tent, despair threatening to overwhelm her again.

Chapter 2

Geriel strode away from Temur's tent, nausea swirling in her stomach. She couldn't do anything right. Leaving so suddenly would have annoyed Temur, and shown she lacked the maturity to go with them. She sighed, stopped walking and smoothed the loose hairs back towards her braid. Too late. So what now? Going home would mean dealing with the noise and demands of her siblings who would still be eating, but she wasn't due at the healers' tent until later. She used to love going there, full of a sense of purpose, a knowledge that she was helping her tribe. Now guilt and reluctance were her constant companions. Still, wandering the camp aimlessly would only lead to someone asking what she was doing.

Keeping her steps small and slow, she walked towards the larger tent. At the door, she braced herself before pushing it open. The sharp scent of herbal disinfectant oil tickled her nose, wafting from the oil burner. She greeted the healer who had cared for their patients overnight and was now making bandages from silk.

"You're here early," he said.

"Shuren woke us. How is everyone?"

"Healing," he answered. "A few can go home today as long as they don't do anything strenuous. Their bruises will heal in time."

Amslan and Geriel were the only ones in the tribe to have the gift of healing and the tribal council had decreed they should only use their gift for life-threatening injuries or to mend broken bones. The gift had limits and it drew on the healer's energy until nothing was left. Geriel shuddered. Then she really would have failed. Amslan often ignored the danger, using more of his gift each time. Though he seemed to be getting stronger.

"Aside from that, it's the usual work."

That meant changing bandages, feeding patients and examining tribe members who were unwell. Geriel accompanied the healer around the tent, talking to patients, giving some leave to return to their yurts and taking note of who needed their bandages changed. By the time he left, she had five patients to help.

The Bonamese had badly beaten Unegen and he had scars and cuts all over his body, but his worst wound was a deep cut across his arm that had required more than two dozen stitches. She unwound his bandage, the stinky, sweaty smell telling her the wound was infected before she revealed the red, pussy injury. Goat dung. "It's a little infected." She prepared a bowl of water with some herbs in it. Carefully she cleaned the wound until no more pus came out. She hesitated before reaching for the dressing. An infection could turn life-threatening if she wasn't careful.

She would examine him. Nerves humming along her skin, she placed her hand over the wound, closing her eyes.

Geriel inhaled slowly, visualising her peaceful place,

a small hill on the steppes where she could sit and view the grey shadow of the mountains in the south. She exhaled and connected with Unegen, her consciousness sinking into his body around the wound and reaching for her gift. At once she felt the infection, dark and thick, hovering around the area, waiting for her to leave so it could attack the cut again. It struggled, trying to hide, but she circled it like the tribe circled animals on a hunt, moving as fast as she could so none escaped, gritting her teeth at the exertion. As the circle joined, she visualised the infection dissolving, dissipating. Slowly, it did as she wanted. She panted, and when the infection finally disappeared, she pushed her consciousness further, examining the surrounding arm to ensure she had it all. Geriel withdrew and opened her eyes.

Dizziness hit her and she swayed, clutching the blankets until it stopped. Geriel forced a smile. "The infection is gone."

"Thanks," Unegen said.

She wrapped the wound and then slowly stood, in case the dizziness hit her again. It was ridiculous that something like this should hit her so hard. She mustn't be doing it right. Amslan had healed wound after wound, injury after injury, barely breaking a sweat. No matter what she attempted, she couldn't heal one thing without wanting to vomit from the strain.

Moving on to the next patient, she let the normal tasks soothe her. She might not be able to tap into her gift easily, but the daily tasks of a healer came naturally to her. Her knowledge of ointments, tinctures, teas and other treatments was strong, and she made a point of always speaking with the healers of other tribes whenever she could. She pored over any books she found and added her own concoctions to their body of knowledge.

As she finished treating the last patient, the door opened and Berke stumbled in. Geriel raced to help the warrior to his feet. His body was wet with sweat and behind him his wife, Sarnai looked on worried.

"This way." Geriel led him to a spare bed away from the other patients, carrying most of his weight as he leaned heavily on her. "How long has he been like this?" she asked Sarnai.

"He woke up like this," she said. "Complained his head and body ached and he had a fever."

Geriel wet a compress and laid it on his forehead.

He panted. "I ache everywhere."

"We'll make you feel better." She rested a hand on his arm. "How were you yesterday? Any aches and pains, stiffness?"

"Yeah, I've been sore for a couple of days. I thought it was muscle ache from moving all the emperor's reparations from the wagons into the tents."

"Let me see what I can find." Her heart raced as she closed her eyes and visualised the mountains. She entered his body and flinched as the cause of his symptoms swarmed through his bloodstream, shiny and oily, invading every part of him. Her chest squeezed. There was too much. Where should she start?

She opened her eyes.

"Can you heal him?" Sarnai asked.

Berke stuck out his tongue as if he tasted something bad. Red spots coated his tongue.

Her heart leapt. "Wait. Let me examine your mouth." Geriel counted a dozen small spots. Not good. Anything with spots was generally highly infectious. "Stay there."

She washed her hands, and then rubbed a disinfectant oil in before she hurried to the bookshelf and flicked through the book she needed, praying this wasn't what she suspected. Her throat closed as she read the entry. Please let her be wrong. She read a few more pages, found some other potential diseases and exhaled.

Returning to the couple, she said, "I need Amslan to confirm what this is." And had to talk to the older healers, find out if they knew of a cure if it was the worst possibility. Nothing had been recorded in the book.

"He's in the tribal council," Sarnai said.

Of course. Disturbing the council because she wasn't capable of healing Berke wouldn't look good. And she might be wrong.

The door opened and Shuren entered the tent. "Wait there, Shuren." Geriel hurried to where her sister was pouting. "Can you fetch Tuya for me?"

"I hurt my finger." Shuren held it up to show a minor cut.

Geriel stifled a sigh. "I'll wrap it."

"No, heal it for me." She jutted out her chin, a precursor to a tantrum if she didn't get her way.

Shuren really was becoming difficult. Geriel would talk to her mother about a way they could help her. "All right." Geriel knelt, covered Shuren's finger with her hand and accessed her gift, dipping into its well to draw it out. It took little effort to heal what was nothing more than a scratch, but Shuren beamed and hugged her. "Thanks, Geriel." She headed for the door.

"Shuren, don't forget Tuya. I need you to ask her to come to the healers' tent immediately."

Shuren nodded. "I'll do it now." She ran off.

Geriel let out a breath and turned back to her patient. "I haven't seen anything like this before, but Tuya might have. She can advise how to progress."

Geriel was probably overreacting. She prayed to Qadan it was one of the lesser diseases.

Sarnai squeezed Berke's hand.

It seemed to take forever for Tuya to arrive. Geriel monitored Berke, whose skin glistened with sweat. Occasionally a violent tremor shook his body. Finally the door opened. Tuya strode to Geriel's side. "What's wrong?"

"Berke is unwell with fever and aches and has red dots in his mouth. I've not seen anything like this before." Geriel fisted her hands together, trying to remain calm.

Tuya's face paled and she stepped back, away from the bed. "Open your mouth."

Berke did as she asked.

"Traders' Curse," Tuya breathed.

Geriel's chest tightened. She'd been right. Traders' Curse caused the patient to break out into pustular rashes and scabs. It was highly infectious and the last time it had ravaged a Rhoran tribe, it wiped out a quarter of the population. Those who survived were horribly scarred. Nausea rose. Its incubation period was up to three-quarters of a moon which meant Berke could have infected all the other tribes or caught it from one of them. She had to warn them.

Tuya stared at Berke for a moment and then snapped out of it. "They both need to be isolated immediately. I'll arrange a tent." She stepped further away, glanced around. "Has he come near any of the other patients?"

"No."

"Have you treated any other patients since he came in?"

Geriel froze. "Shuren." Children were most at risk of dying from the disease.

Tuya frowned. "All right. Stay here. Don't let anyone in or out. I'll get Amslan." She ran out the door.

Sarnai sobbed, hugging her husband, probably infecting herself.

"Sarnai, you shouldn't touch him." Geriel pulled her away and led her to another bed. "I'm sure Amslan can heal him." She prayed she was right. "Let me check you for signs." She closed her eyes. Sarnai's skin was cold, but it warmed under Geriel's touch as Geriel searched Sarnai's blood. There. Not as pervasive as Berke's case, but it was there and multiplying. She exhaled and looked at the woman.

Her eyes were wide with fear.

"I'm sorry. You have it too, but it's not as bad as Berke's."

"Can Amslan fix me?"

Geriel nodded, her mind whirring. There were steps to take when they had an outbreak of something infectious. Isolation was the first step. The second was figuring out who else could be exposed. She grabbed a piece of paper from the table.

Across the tent, Unegen stood. "I'm leaving."

Geriel rushed to block the door. "Wait. Please. You can leave as soon as we check you. We'll take you to another yurt." He was a big man and could easily push her out of the way.

"Why don't you check me now?"

She held up her hands. "I've touched Berke. I might have caught the infection as well."

Unegen sprang away from her, moving back to his bed. She would have laughed at how quickly he moved if it weren't such a serious matter.

The door opened behind her and Amslan walked in. He had such a presence about him, a lithe, fit body with lethal grace. His dark eyes challenged and judged her, and seemed to find her wanting. He strode to Berke and, without a word, touched his arm, closing his eyes. The strain on his face was instantaneous. Geriel hovered next to him, waiting for him to speak.

Eventually he sighed and opened his eyes. "Show me your tongue."

Berke opened his mouth.

The red spots were gone. Geriel grinned, relief flooding her. "You've healed him."

Amslan shook his head. "Not yet. It's too much. I've only reversed some symptoms." He turned to her. "You've touched him?"

She nodded. "And the disease is in Sarnai."

He glanced at Berke's wife and let out a deep breath. "All right. Let me check you first." He placed his hand on Geriel's arm and closed his eyes. A warm tingle spread through her as he scanned her and the wait seemed interminable but eventually he looked at her. "You're clear."

She sighed. Thank Qadan.

"Connect with Sarnai when I do. I'll show you what I did with Berke."

Her chest squeezed as she moved around the bed to where Sarnai lay. She knelt across from Amslan and visualised her mountains. As she connected with Sarnai, she gasped. "It's multiplied quickly."

Amslan grunted. "That's what I was afraid of. We need to herd it together and surround it with a wall." He demonstrated what he meant. It was tricky. The disease slid around the wall she built like noodles from a spoon. She made her wall bigger, only letting Sarnai's blood filter through and eventually she met with Amslan's wall. Her breath came in gasps and her muscles strained. She couldn't hold it for long.

"Let me." Amslan took over and sealed the disease

together like corralling horses. He withdrew his consciousness and Geriel followed suit.

She swayed, and Amslan's face was pale. Food would help her recoup her energy, but she didn't want to seem weak in front of him. "Would you like something to eat?"

"In a minute." He squeezed his eyes shut, panting.

Fear froze her. He was drained. That wasn't good. He was their best healer. For him to be so exhausted from this one healing… and they hadn't cured Sarnai.

"Is she all right?" Berke asked.

"It's contained for the moment," Amslan answered. "When we've eaten, we'll get rid of the disease and concentrate on you."

"What about us?" Unegen demanded.

"As soon as there's somewhere safe for you to go, I'll check you," Amslan said. He gestured Geriel towards the door and lowered his voice as she approached. "We need to know everyone Berke and Sarnai have encountered during the past moon. Also where Berke has been, what he has touched. This had to have come from somewhere."

"Maybe one of the Bonamese prisoners was infected." Berke had guarded the Bonamese army after they had surrendered.

Amslan's eyes narrowed. "Berke, did you notice any of the prisoners with rashes or spots?"

Berke shook his head.

Amslan washed his hands. "Wash your hands after you've touched either of them, and check the book for other ways to stop the spread. I'll be back." He strode out of the tent.

Geriel cleaned her hands again before she read the details of the disease. The author had noted the disease appeared to lay dormant for up to three-quarters of a moon, but wasn't as contagious at that stage. However it spread by touching something an infected person had touched, or through the air from coughs and sneezes. That wasn't good.

They had to isolate people now.

She tied a cloth over her mouth and nose, and then handed cloths to the other patients in the room. "Put these on."

They obeyed without question.

Berke and Sarnai were quiet when Geriel rejoined them with a piece of paper and a quill. "I need to know everyone you've seen since you returned from guarding the prisoners."

"There're too many," Berke said.

"Our children!" Sarnai wailed. "Qadan, please don't let our children be infected."

Geriel wrote them down, her mind whirling. Their children were friends with her brothers and sisters, and the whole group of children often played together. They would have gone home to their parents and their parents would have interacted with friends. At this rate, they'd have to quarantine the whole tribe.

"I delivered the reparations to each family."

Dread lodged in her stomach. This was disastrous. She inhaled deeply. Don't panic. "Let's start with who helped you do that."

Berke went through the list, shivering and shaking as he did. As he finished, Amslan returned.

"We've set up a quarantine tent on the outskirts of the camp," he said. "I'll take you two there now."

"What about our children?"

"Tuya is fetching them. They'll meet you there and I'll check them." He turned to the other patients in the room. "As soon as we've moved them, we'll check you. Don't leave." His face was grim.

Unegen nodded.

"Take everything they've touched out onto the steppes and burn it." Amslan handed Geriel a pair of leather gloves. "Wear them. Temur is organising a bonfire."

She waited until Amslan left with Berke and Sarnai before slipping on the gloves and gathering the sheets. She scanned the room. The door had to be scrubbed and the floor, and she should probably burn her clothes too. But not until she cleaned everything.

Before she left, she asked her patients, "Does anyone need anything?"

"Go," Unegen said. "We'll be fine. This needs to be stopped."

She nodded and carried the sheets outside. The camp was practically deserted. Lien and Temur stood talking to Tuya, but they must have ordered everyone back to their yurts.

Her stomach swirled. She'd thought all the battle injuries had been bad, but this was worse. The insidiousness of it, not knowing who had the disease and who didn't.

She frowned. They'd guarded the Bonamese army for more than a moon before the peace treaty had been signed and the soldiers were allowed to return home. It was plenty of time for the symptoms to appear and no one had noticed anything. Perhaps the warriors hadn't cared if the Bonamese were ill.

"Geriel, put the bedding in the fire." Temur pointed to a bonfire out on the steppes. She did as she was asked and by the time she returned, Amslan had joined them. She walked over.

"How is the healers' tent?" Lien asked.

"I need to scrub the door and the two beds should probably be burnt as well," Geriel replied.

"I'll help you with it," Temur said.

"No," Lien said. "You can't risk being infected."

"I can manage on my own." Geriel understood the risk that came with being a healer. "What's our plan?"

"Have you got the list of names?" Amslan asked.

She handed it to him.

He whistled and shook his head. "We'll separate those who worked with Berke first."

"When that's done," Tuya continued, "we'll check everyone for the disease. Amslan says you can sense it?"

Geriel nodded, her chest tightening. There were a lot of people in the camp. She would have to use her gift for each one, and blocking Sarnai had left her light-headed. "What about the other tribes?"

"As soon as Amslan clears some riders, we'll send them to each tribe, warn them," Temur told her.

This was a nightmare. "I'll finish the healers' tent." At Temur's nod she walked off, her heart beating heavy in her chest. A disease like this could wipe out half the tribe.

She'd been scared for her people when the Bonamese invaded, but it was nothing compared to the fear that gripped her now.

They had no known cure and chances were high every single tribe was infected.

She wanted to be sick.

This would be a tougher foe than the Bonamese by far.

~*~

The camp reacted quickly. By the time Geriel had cleaned the healers' tent and examined the patients inside, riders had been cleared and sent to the other tribes.

All the patients were uninfected, which wasn't

surprising since they'd been in the tent since they'd been freed by the Bonamese. Geriel ate some dried curd for energy, marked the door with a black circle to show it was clear and went to find Amslan. He was in the yurt with some of the people who had come into contact with Berke.

Amslan looked up as she walked in. "The healers' tent is clear?"

"Yes. What do you need?"

"Come here. First we want to identify anyone who is infected. You know how to?"

She nodded.

"If they're clear, they are to go next door. I don't know whether what we see in their blood is the earliest sign." His concern was clear by the furrow on his forehead.

In other words, the disease might not be evident in the early stages.

"And then what?" one of the men asked. "How long are we going to be quarantined?"

Amslan scowled at him. "As long as needed. We've hopefully caught this early enough that it hasn't spread far."

He was trying to keep people calm, but if it had been dormant for twenty-one days, it was likely everyone had encountered the disease.

Geriel sat at the opposite end of the table to Amslan and gestured to the man who was their best fletcher. "Sit down."

He sat, worry in his eyes, his thumb rubbing over a few cuts on his hands. Geriel focused and touched his arm, diving into his bloodstream. There. The infection wasn't as thick as Berke's but worse than Sarnai's. She opened her eyes. "I'm sorry. You're infected."

"Then heal me!" He squeezed her arm.

She winced and yanked it out of his grasp. She glanced at Amslan. It had been hard enough to contain Sarnai's infection, let alone heal it.

"Not yet," Amslan said. "We need to figure out who's infected first. Then we can deal with the infection."

"That's goat dung! You're healers, you're meant to heal."

Amslan said something to the woman he was with and then walked over, towering above them. "What we're meant to do is ensure the whole tribe is well," he said, his voice low with a hint of danger. "Geriel and I are the only ones who can identify the disease before you get symptoms. We must protect those we can before we heal the infected." He glared at the man as if daring him to disagree.

Geriel wouldn't cross him.

The man growled and stormed off to the other side of the tent. Geriel exhaled.

Amslan looked around. "Does anyone else have a problem with that?"

Silence.

Geriel forced a smile. "Who's next?"

Chapter 3

Geriel stumbled out of the last tent, gripping a piece of dried curd in one hand and a stick of charcoal in the other. She caught her balance and leaned against the door until the dizziness subsided. Thank Qadan no one was around to see her weakness. With a deep breath, she carefully marked an X on the door. Everyone inside was infected. She forced herself to chew on the dried curd and leaned back against the door, her medicine bag resting against her leg. The sun was sinking below the horizon, bathing the camp in the last rays of light.

What a day.

At each home, she'd eaten something to build her energy stores, but it was no use, they depleted as soon as she scanned the family. If the whole family was clear, she marked a circle on their door. If anyone was infected, she sent them to the quarantine area and marked a cross on the door. There were far fewer circles than crosses.

No one was allowed out until Temur gave them permission.

One more home to go, the one she'd been dreading, the one she'd deliberately left until last—her own family. Pushing herself off the door, she staggered to the next yurt. She adjusted the scarf over her face and then opened the door. Her mother pushed some cheese into her hand, wrapping her arm around her and leading her to the cushions by the table. "Sit, child. You're exhausted."

Geriel didn't deny it.

"How bad is it?" Sukh asked.

She closed her eyes as she chewed and then swallowed. "About a third of the tribe are infected, another third have family members who are infected." Mostly warriors who had fought Emperor Xue.

Her mother gasped. "What will we do?"

"There's a tribal council tonight. I'll know more after that." Amslan would tell her what to do. She reached for a piece of meat, restoring her energy and delaying the inevitable. So many families had been divided already. Those who were clear were fearful for those who had the disease. People had sobbed, yelled at her, pleaded and begged for her to heal them. Her continual denial made her sick. The truth was, she couldn't heal them, could barely control her gift enough to scan them.

Now it was her family's turn. Checheg sat across the table from Geriel next to their two brothers, Nekhii and Jochi, while Shuren sat on one of the beds, playing with her wooden horse. Her father stood, hands behind his back, watching her.

Her stomach a swirling mass of nausea, Geriel removed her glove and placed a hand on her mother's arm. "Stay still for me." The visualisation came easily now, but diving in was harder, as if her gift was at the far end of her reach. Slowly she scanned her mother's body and relief filled her as she opened her eyes. "You're clear."

She swayed as her mother stood and Checheg sat.

"Have some tea." Her mother pushed a cup into her hand.

She curled her fingers around the cup, but as her mother let go, she didn't have the strength to hold on. It fell from her hands, spilling on her top. The heat barely registered.

Checheg pulled Geriel's top away from her and cool air hit her skin.

"What's wrong with her?" her mother cried.

"She's exhausted," her father answered. "Get her a dry top."

Geriel wanted to reassure them she was fine, but the words wouldn't form. Her brain was still foggy. She ate the meat Checheg pressed into her hand, the chewing motion all she had energy for. Her mother stripped the damp top from her body and replaced it with a fresh one. This was what a rag doll must feel like. Her arms moved only when Checheg moved them.

"We should get Amslan," her mother said.

"No." They couldn't leave the tent. With a great deal of effort, she said, "Let me finish eating. I'll be fine."

She hadn't convinced anyone, but at least they didn't leave. She continued to eat, her eyes closed. When her mother pressed a cup to her mouth and said, "Drink this," she obeyed.

It was a sweet tea with a mixture of restorative herbs. Her body responded, energising a little and she opened her eyes again. "Thank you."

Sukh frowned. "You've done too much today."

"It was needed." They all understood the importance of the tribe.

She drank two cups of the tea and then placed her hands on Checheg. Inhaling deeply, she scanned her sister, pronouncing her clear and then scanned

Nekhii—also clear.

Relief filled her as Jochi took his place. She sipped more tea, ate a piece of lamb from yesterday's meal and then scanned him. She frowned. Something strange was in his blood. It wasn't the disease, but it wasn't normal either. She opened her eyes and her parents stared at her.

"I'm not certain," she said. "I need Amslan to check. There's something there, but it's not the same."

Her mother put a hand to her mouth and Jochi's eyes widened. "Am I going to die?"

"No." She wouldn't let that happen. "I'll get Amslan to examine you when I've finished with the others."

Her mother moved to help him and Geriel held out a hand to stop her. "You shouldn't touch him. Not yet, not until we know for sure."

Her mother snarled. "No one will stop me from comforting my child."

Geriel dropped her hand and blinked. She resisted the urge to respond, to tell her she risked her own life. Her mother wouldn't care. She sighed. "Shuren. Your turn." Geriel washed her hands and rubbed oil into them.

Shuren stood on the other side of the tent, her arms hugged around her. "I don't want to."

"You have to." Geriel glanced at her father. She didn't have the energy to deal with Shuren today. He approached his youngest child.

"Why don't we do it together?" he said.

She shook her head and stepped backwards.

Geriel continued eating while she watched the dance between her father and Shuren.

He crouched. "Child, everyone in the tribe has to do this. It's our duty."

"What if I'm sick?"

"Then Geriel will fix you."

Fear stabbed Geriel. What if she couldn't? Her father had so much faith in her and she would disappoint him again.

"And you'll do it with me?" Shuren asked.

Sukh nodded and held out his hand. "Come on." He led her to the table and she sat in his lap.

Geriel took a deep breath and prayed to Qadan for her family to be safe. She placed a hand on Shuren first and slowly scanned her. Then she checked her father. Fear curdled in her stomach and slowly she opened her eyes. She swallowed hard.

"Well?" Her mother asked.

She exhaled. "They're both infected."

~*~

Geriel swayed as her mother cried out and Shuren burst into tears. Sukh gathered his youngest child in his arms and soothed her, glancing at Geriel.

"What now?"

She loved how brave her father was, how he didn't dwell on the horror, but searched for a solution. She had to follow his lead even though inside she quailed in fear. "Now you need to come with me. We've set up tents to house anyone who is infected. We'll take Jochi as well so Amslan can examine him." She was proud at how even her voice was. If she let her fear show, she would scare her family further. "The others will stay here and be monitored. We'll clean or destroy anything the three of you may have touched—clothes you've worn, bedding. Tuya says the disease can lay dormant for up to three-quarters of a moon. After that, if there's no sign of the curse, you'll be allowed out."

"So we might still catch it?"

Geriel nodded. "We don't know how contagious it is

before symptoms show, or if what I can sense is the first indication of the disease."

"And what about them?" her mother demanded. "Can't you heal them now? They're your family."

Guilt strangled her heart, but it was her father who responded. "She's exhausted, love. She can't do any more today. I'm sure we'll be fine in a few days."

Geriel said nothing, but took more food from the table and climbed to her feet. "We should go now."

Her mother stepped forward to hug Sukh and he put up a hand to stop her. "No, love. Best you don't get too close. Know I love you and I'll take care of our little ones. We'll see you soon."

Tears ran down her face and Shuren still sobbed in Sukh's arms. Checheg also cried and Nekhii had his arm around her. At least they had each other.

Geriel focused on the floor, her steps small so she didn't lose her balance. Even with the restorative tea, her whole body was wobbly. She used the door to redistribute her weight as she marked an X on it and held it open for her father and youngest siblings. "This way."

The camp was deathly silent. There weren't even the soft murmurs of conversation. She'd give anything for the boring quiet of yesterday, rather than this chilling stillness. The quarantine tents were on the other side of the camp and it took an age to reach them. Temur and Amslan stood outside talking. Amslan watched as she approached, a frown on his face. He could tell how exhausted she was, but he didn't look much better himself. Dark rings surrounded his eyes.

"These are the last ones?" he asked.

She nodded. "I'm not certain about Jochi. There is something odd about his blood."

Amslan rested his hand on Jochi's arm, closed his

eyes. His frown deepened and then he grinned. "He has the gift." He looked at Temur. "It's immature at this stage, but we might need him to heal."

Geriel's heart jolted. Jochi was only eight. Far too young to deal with the emotional side of healing.

"Teach him," Temur said. He smiled at Jochi. "You'll be a great help to us."

"So, I'm not sick?" Jochi asked, his eyes wide.

"No," Amslan replied. "You and Geriel can stay with Erdene and me so that we can teach you."

It was probably best she didn't stay in her yurt. There may still be infected items in there and she couldn't afford to get sick. Amslan's wife, Erdene was kind. She would be a buffer to Amslan's terseness.

"We need to get to the tribal council," Temur said. "Say goodbye to the others and come with us, Geriel. You're needed."

Her eyes widened. "Yes, Temur." She'd never been invited to a tribal council before. Though she longed to hug her father and sister goodbye, she resisted and showed them into the tent where they'd be staying. Then they took Jochi to Erdene and Geriel hugged him. "I'll be back as soon as I can."

His serious wide, brown eyes stared at her as he nodded. "Everything will be all right."

If only she could be so certain.

The council was held in Temur's yurt because the gathering hut was being used for quarantine.

Inside were remarkably few people: Lien; their spiritual advisor, Solongo; Tuya; Temur's father, Mongke; and one of Temur's advisors, Chinua. Chinua hugged her. "How is your family?"

Tears pricked her eyes as she squeezed him back. He was one of her favourite people in the camp. Their families had always been close. "Father and Shuren are infected."

His eyes filled with tears. "Saran too."

Geriel swallowed hard. Saran was Shuren's best friend. Both were far too young to deal with a disease like this.

"Please sit," Temur said.

Geriel sat at the table and Lien handed her mutton and noodle soup, and milk tea. Geriel let out a quiet breath while Temur called the meeting to order.

"First, I'd like to thank Geriel and Tuya for identifying the curse so quickly," he said. "Quarantine has been set up with only a minimal amount of fuss. Amslan, what are the final numbers?"

"At least half of the warriors who fought the Bonamese," he said. "Most of their families as well." He shook his head. "I can't see how we missed the infected soldiers. We had them in the camp for more than a moon."

"What are you saying?" Solongo asked.

"Maybe our books are wrong," Amslan said. "Maybe the curse can lay dormant for longer."

"I wrote those entries." Tuya crossed her arms. "It's what we observed the last time we dealt with the curse."

"Then maybe it's changed," he said. "We have a third of the camp who have interacted with the infected, so we'll keep them quarantined. Geriel and I will have to scan them every couple of days to discover if they have the curse."

Her chest tightened. It would be difficult to scan so many people as well as treat those who had the disease. If ever she needed to master her gift, it was now.

"Finally there's probably another third who haven't come in regular contact with an infected person and who are clear. We'll monitor them too, but less regularly."

"So can you heal everyone?" Temur asked.

Amslan was silent a moment, studying Geriel and Tuya. "No," he said. "There're too many and the disease is too aggressive. Geriel and I are exhausted from dealing with Berke and scanning everyone."

Nausea swirled in her stomach.

"What do we do?" Lien asked.

"I've divided the infected into tents based on the severity of the infection. Those who have only the beginning signs in their blood, all the way through to those who will break out into visible symptoms soon. We need to choose who to treat first."

Solongo stroked her long plait. "Is there nothing the other healers can do?"

Tuya answered. "There's no known cure. We can make people comfortable, but they'll either recover or they won't."

"What are their chances?" Mongke asked.

"A quarter of our people died during the last recorded outbreak," Tuya said. "Children were the worst affected."

Which meant if Geriel couldn't heal her, Shuren might die.

"How hard is it to heal?" Chinua asked.

"It's slippery," Amslan said. "Some diseases and infections clump together, making it easy to get rid of them, but this one is like oil, difficult to clasp. It takes a lot of energy to contain it. I haven't attempted to remove it yet." He sipped his tea. "Sarnai was moderately infected and it took both Geriel and myself to contain the disease. It might be best if we attempt to heal those only mildly affected first, before it gets worse."

Temur turned to Chinua. "When do you expect our messengers to return?"

"Not for a half moon at least. I told them to wait at the camp and find out how many others are infected, before they returned."

"They'll need to wait until symptoms present themselves," Amslan said. "There's only one other who has the healing gift."

Tuya nodded. "It's going to get much worse before it gets better." She sat a little straighter. "There was a rumour of someone being cured during the last outbreak." She pursed her lips. "When trade began again, one of the traders said a person in the mountains had been cured, but we all thought it a lie because no one could say what cured them."

"The dragons mentioned that my father had gone to their sanctuary looking for new cures," Lien said. "Not long after, he was murdered by my uncle."

Tuya frowned. "When was that?"

"Eighteen years ago."

"That's around the same time."

Maybe the Bonamese knew of a cure. Though they weren't likely to share it, maybe their neighbour would. "Can we ask the Chungson?" Geriel asked.

"Maybe." Lien turned to Temur. "It's worth investigating."

He nodded. "We can't send as many people as we'd planned."

"I can go on my own." Lien sipped her tea.

"No." He was firm.

"A healer should go as well," Amslan said. "To talk to the dragons and the healers of Chungson."

"Tuya?" Temur said.

She shook her head. "I don't travel as fast as I used to. We should send Amslan or Geriel and perhaps one of the infected. That way they can test any cures on them immediately to make sure it works."

Geriel cringed. A day ago she would have jumped at the chance to go to Chungson, but now, with her family ill, she didn't want to leave.

"Don't we need them both to heal those already infected?" Mongke asked.

Amslan caught Geriel's eye. They both knew they couldn't cure everyone. They hoped they could prevent as many as possible from dying. "I discovered today Jochi has the gift," he said. "Though he is young, he can probably take over scanning people which will save me energy. Then Geriel can go with Lien."

She clenched her teeth. She didn't want to leave knowing her father and Shuren were ill. But they were in far better hands with Amslan than they would be with her. Her gift wasn't strong enough. What if she couldn't contain the disease as they travelled? What if she killed whoever she took with her? What if she couldn't find a cure?

"Who else?" Temur asked.

"Sukh," Amslan suggested. "He's mildly affected and Geriel should be able to keep the disease contained."

Mongke frowned. "Is it wise to send an infected person with them? The disease could spread to the Chungson, or whoever goes."

Lien nodded. "I agree. We'll take one of our fast, healthy riders with us. The Adhan tribe is closest to the border and the rider can take any cures to them to test."

"All right," Temur agreed. "Lien, Chinua and Geriel will leave at first light tomorrow to find a cure. Amslan will train Jochi and focus on healing those least affected first. Tuya will lead the healers in caring for those who are the worst affected. Agreed?"

Everyone nodded though Geriel's chest tightened painfully. She wasn't up to the task. She would fail her family and her people because she didn't have control over her gift. She should have tried harder to master it.

The meeting broke up and after giving Geriel another hug, Chinua left to get everything ready for the morning. Lien came over to Geriel. "You can stay with us tonight." She smiled. "I know these aren't the circumstances you would wish for, but I'm pleased you are coming with me."

Geriel forced a smile. "I'll do my best." She wanted to be sick. The exhaustion and fear battled her defences, screaming at her to refuse the decision, and tell Temur she was staying here. Then she could cure her family. She ruthlessly shut the thoughts down. Her duty was first to her tribe, then her family.

After the others left, Amslan joined her.

"You need to believe in yourself," he said. "Your ability is there, it's strong and healthy and waiting for you to access it."

She stared at him. "But I can't."

"You can. I don't know what's stopping you, but maybe the dragons can help. They heal differently from us. One of their healers is Dhalin, and she will help, I'm sure."

She'd heard the stories of how Dhalin had healed some of Lien's injuries after her battle with her former master. But Dhalin hadn't been able to heal everything. Would the dragons be any use to her?

"Keep your energy up," he continued. "Look for anything that might slow the spread, clump the disease, or dissolve it. If you find more greenshade, send that. It will help to soothe the patients when they're covered in spots."

She nodded, her mind whirling. She wanted to shake her head, tell him she was a fraud, that she wasn't up to the task, but he looked at her as if he believed she could do this. The lives of her family, her whole tribe depended on her—she had to try. There was no one else.

"Get some rest." He walked back to Temur.

Lien took Geriel's arm and led her to the bed. "You can share the bed with me tonight. Temur will sleep on the floor."

"What about my things?"

"I asked Chinua to get them from your tent. Mother will pack what is needed."

The draw of the bed was strong. "I should go and see Jochi, make sure he's all right."

"Erdene will take care of him. You can see him in the morning, before we leave. What you need now is sleep."

Geriel hesitated, but Lien was right. She could barely walk unsupported. She lay down, the softness of the mattress cocooning her body, drawing her under. She managed to unwrap her belt, leaving it on the floor next to her.

Then sleep pulled her under.

Chapter 4

Light was beginning to filter in through the top of the tent when Lien shook Geriel awake. Why was Lien in their yurt? Geriel blinked. The curtain was red not blue. She was in Lien's yurt. Memories of the day before came flooding back and her body tensed. Traders' Curse. She had to leave, search for a cure.

"Are we going?" she asked.

Lien nodded. "Soon. Get dressed and I'll organise breakfast." She moved to the other side of the curtain and spoke to Temur in low tones.

Geriel shifted, her body reacting a second slower than her mind, like it didn't really belong to her. Retying her belt required all her focus and the queasy storm in her stomach didn't help. She was so weak, too weak, she should tell them she couldn't go. Any healer could investigate the properties of plants. She'd be more help here in camp, even with her limited skills.

Pushing back the curtain, she found not only Temur and Lien, but also Chinua and Amslan sitting at the table. Chinua grinned at her. "Your mother packed your bag. She said she only packed things she was sure Shuren and Sukh hadn't touched." He gestured to the pack in the corner. "She wishes you a safe journey."

Geriel managed to smile. His easy-going nature would be a blessing on this trip. A couple of years ago, Geriel's mother had hinted about her marrying Chinua, and Geriel had quickly put a stop to that. He was like an older brother to her.

She checked through her bag. It had her clothes, medicine bag, journal and included a small bowl of sweet curd for the journey. Her heart squeezed. How could she leave her family behind when they needed her? She turned back to the others. "I can't go."

Amslan scowled but Temur's gaze was steady as he asked, "Why not?"

"I'm needed here. My skills can be used to help Amslan and Jochi. Any healer can look for plants."

"Aside from Tuya, you're the only other healer who is unaffected," Temur said.

She gasped. She hadn't realised. "We should heal them first then."

"I will," Amslan said. "But the truth is, you're the most knowledgeable about plants and remedies. You'll make connections others won't."

Her eyes widened and her cheeks flushed. She'd always been passionate about learning as much as she could. After she discovered she had the gift and was useless with it, increasing her knowledge had been her way of compensating for her lack of skill.

"Since meeting the dragons, I've suspected we can use our gift in different ways," he continued. "You may find you can scan the plants to discover their properties."

"And you can stop by the Adhan tribe on the way to Chungson and help them," Temur said. "We don't know how many are affected, but you can at least help them quarantine the camp."

His argument was solid. Curse it. She glanced at Lien.

"I will take care of your family," Amslan said.

Part of her fear faded. They would be safer with him. She let out a deep breath and nodded.

Lien handed her a bowl, steam rising from the broth, and Geriel sat to eat while Temur gave Lien and Chinua last minute instructions. After stopping at the Adhan tribe they would travel to the mountains where Chungson soldiers were being trained by Lien's friend, Jie. From there they would send word to Lord Anming of Chungson, and hopefully he would know of a cure.

Amslan sat next to her.

"I meant what I said." He sipped his tea. "You are one of our best healers and when you can control your gift, you'll be better than me."

She stared at him. The circumstances were dire for him to be lying to her.

"You picked up Jochi's gift far earlier than I would have. It is such a faint glimmer I would have ignored it."

"I thought it could be the curse."

"But you knew it wasn't. You're strong, Geriel. You need to have more faith in yourself."

She glanced at the others who were still talking and lowered her voice. "I've been trying for six years."

"Perhaps too hard. You need to surrender to it rather than work it to your will." He sighed. "I'm not a good teacher. I hope I can explain it better to Jochi than I did to you."

She had no words to reply. The fault was hers.

"Are you ready?" Lien asked.

Geriel gulped the last of her broth. It would be days before she would have more than travel rations. "Yes."

She grabbed her bag and followed the others to the

horse yard. Erdene was waiting there with Jochi. He flung his arms around her waist and hugged her. "Do you have to go?"

Her chest squeezed. "Yes. I need to find a cure." She gently pushed him back so she could look at him. "Be good for Erdene and Amslan. Listen to what Amslan says. You have the gift and you can help our tribe. It's an important task."

Fear crossed his face and he whispered, "What if I fail?"

She couldn't let him fear the same thing she did. "You can't fail," she said. "Anything you learn will be a help. At first, all you might do is scan our tribe to make sure the curse hasn't spread. It might not seem like much, but this will save Amslan both time and energy. That's very valuable."

He stood straighter. "Really?"

"Yes. You will be wonderful, little brother." She kissed his cheek and squeezed him. "Have faith in yourself." If only she could follow her own advice.

Jochi nodded. "You too. You will find a cure." His confidence warmed her and she smiled.

"Take care." She tied her bag to Khulan's saddle. They were taking two horses each so they could travel faster. She checked her other horse and then mounted.

Temur and Lien murmured to each other and then kissed, their love clear.

"Ride swiftly," Temur said as Lien mounted her horse.

"We will."

Chinua took the lead and rode out of the camp. Geriel took one last look behind her. Normally there would be far more people waving them away on the start of a long journey, but the four lone figures highlighted how critical the situation was.

She had to find a cure.

Her tribe's survival depended on it.

~*~

They rode fast, thundering over the steppes, only slowing to change or rest the horses. The first night they slept under the stars, stopping only long enough to get some rest.

On the second day, Chinua took them more to the west, following markers which indicated the location of the Adhan tribe. Their leader, Muunokhoi had spent some time in Chungson. He knew the most about where they were going and how best to get there.

Late on the third day, the camp appeared ahead of them. Geriel tied a cloth over her mouth and nose and the others followed suit. A guard stood on the outskirts, and as they rode up, his expression was grim.

"Mother, we quarantined the camp as you suggested," he said to Lien. "Why are you here?"

"We are on our way to Chungson to search for a cure. We wish to speak to Muunokhoi, and Geriel can help quarantine your camp more accurately."

Relief crossed his face. "Welcome. Muunokhoi's tent is in the centre, with the green door."

Geriel hesitated before she dismounted and walked over to him. "Let me check you." She pushed his caftan sleeve up, and lay her hands on his skin. Visualising her mountains, she allowed her consciousness to sink into him, slowly scanning his blood. When she opened her eyes, he watched her. "You're clear."

His breath whooshed out of him. "Thank Qadan."

"You need to stay away from anyone who is, or might be infected," she told him. "No touching them or anything they've touched. We need to ensure this doesn't spread."

"What about my family?"

"I'll check them, and depending on what I find, you might not be able to see them until this is over."

She mounted her horse.

"The quarantine is paramount to stopping the curse spreading," Lien told him. "Our camp is completely segregated, which is difficult for families, but essential."

He grimaced and nodded. "Yes, Mother."

Geriel followed Lien through the camp and when they reached Muunokhoi's tent, Chinua knocked. Muunokhoi's wife opened the door, her face fearful. She slumped in relief when she saw Geriel. "Bless the ancestors." She stepped back. "Muunokhoi has the curse. It's bad."

Across the yurt, Muunokhoi lay on the bed, his face covered in pustules. Geriel gasped. He was far worse than Berke, than anyone in their camp. She wouldn't be able to do anything for him. Her heart ached.

Lien moved to step inside and Chinua held her back. "No, Mother. We can't risk you."

"Who is in charge?" she asked.

"The healers," Muunokhoi's wife said. "Their tent is over there." She pointed.

"We will see them first," Lien said.

"Wait!" Muunokhoi's wife grabbed Geriel's hand. "Aren't you going to heal him?"

Geriel exchanged a glance with Lien. They both knew how bad he was. "I must first assess the whole tribe," Geriel said, her healer training taking over. She placed a hand on the woman. "Stay still." Geriel barely had to look to find the curse had infected her. "Is there anyone else in there?"

"Our children."

"Bring them here and get me some water to wash in."

Whether it was her tone, or the fact she was a healer, the woman rushed to obey, herding her three teenaged children to the door.

Geriel scanned them all, washing her hands between each person, finding only the oldest without traces of the curse. "Come with me," she told the boy.

"Where are you taking him?"

"He's not infected," Geriel said. "It is safer for him to leave."

The woman's eyes widened. "Does that mean the rest of us have the curse?"

She nodded. "I'm sorry. The children are not badly infected, so keep them away from Muunokhoi. I will return when I can." Geriel moved away. The desperation in the woman's eyes was clear. She lunged for Geriel, her grip tight on Geriel's wrist, squeezing. "Heal us now! Muunokhoi is our leader. He is needed." She shook Geriel's arm as she spoke.

Geriel winced, her heart racing. It was impossible for her to heal him. He was too far gone for Geriel's skills. She tried to remove her arm from the woman's grasp, but she clung tight.

"Let go," Chinua growled, stepping forward.

The woman did so, but begged, "Please. You have to heal us. It's your duty to the tribe."

She was right.

Before Geriel could respond, Chinua tugged her back. "Her duty is to the whole Adhan tribe, not just your family. She will return when she can."

Relief filled Geriel as she walked away with the others. Chinua left to care for their horses while Lien and Geriel followed the older boy to the healers' tent. Ten people were inside, half of them lying on beds and half sitting around a table with books spread upon it. Geriel recognised Uranchim, the head healer of the tribe. She grimaced. As part of her healer training, she'd spent a moon in each camp, and Uranchim had been a hard teacher, impatient and exacting, and set in the hierarchy of experience. He hadn't liked that she had the gift. He spun around as the door opened. "What?" he demanded, and then relaxed as he recognised them. "Mother, Geriel, why are you here?"

"We're travelling to Chungson to find a cure," Lien told him. "We've stopped to offer some assistance in quarantining your camp."

Uranchim turned to Geriel. "You can't heal it?"

Shame filled her. "I can sense it."

He tutted as if she'd failed.

Lien spoke. "Geriel's gift has allowed as to segregate our tribe. We hope it will slow the spread. Amslan is healing those he can, but it is a difficult disease to heal."

Uranchim waved a hand to the table. "Sit. Let me get you some food and we can discuss."

Geriel sat. She couldn't let his attitude bother her. He was abrupt and impatient with everyone. "Who has dealt with the curse before?"

A couple of the older healers at the table raised their hands.

"Do you recall any rumours of people being healed?" Lien asked.

"One," Uranchim said. "A trader from across the mountains said one of his men was taken ill and they stopped in the meadows for him to heal. The next day his spots had cleared, but no one knew what had done it." He put a plate of meats on the table and shrugged. "Perhaps the man had simply mistaken a rash for the curse."

It corroborated the rumour Tuya had told them and gave them a place to start.

The healers sat around the table with them, keeping

enough space between them so they didn't touch. Geriel ate and drank the sweet tea Uranchim poured for her.

"How many of your people have symptoms?" Lien asked.

"About a score," he said.

"What are you doing for them?" Geriel asked.

"We've moved them into separate tents, and cleaned their homes."

"We'll separate them further," Geriel told him. She explained the system Amslan had come up with.

Uranchim nodded. "A good system. When will you start?"

She exhaled. "I scanned Muunokhoi's family," she said. "Only his oldest is clear." She indicated the young man. Something tickled the back of her mind, but refused to come forward. There was something odd about Muunokhoi being so badly affected. She'd have to ponder it later.

"We'll take care of your family, child," one of the healers told him.

His face was grim, but he nodded.

Chinua arrived and nodded a greeting. "I've taken care of the horses and set up our camp on the outskirts."

A wise decision. Neither Lien nor Chinua should spend much time in the camp in case they picked up the infection.

"Let me start with you." Geriel placed her hand on the closest healer and closed her eyes. Slimy tendrils floated in her blood. She would likely show symptoms in a couple of days. "You're infected."

The healer's eyes widened, but she stood and moved away from the rest of the table. At least these people understood what had to be done.

Uranchim fetched Geriel some water to wash in and one-by-one the healers came to her to be checked. Uranchim and one other were uninfected. Geriel divided those least affected into a separate group. Could she replicate what she'd done with Amslan? She had to at least try. "I may be able to halt the disease," she told them. "But I need to scan the rest of the tribe first."

"I will join you," Uranchim said.

Geriel turned to the other unaffected healer. "I will need more fresh water and something to mark the tents with."

The woman nodded and left the yurt. Geriel scanned those on the beds, divided them according to the degree of their infection and then went outside with Lien, Chinua and Uranchim.

"Mother, you should go to our camp," Chinua said.

"You both should," Geriel said. "I'll be busy with the Adhan people, I don't need the extra work to heal you."

"I'll stay to protect you from others who share Muunokhoi's wife's opinion," Chinua said. "At least until you find one of the warriors uninfected." His expression brooked no argument.

Geriel's heart warmed. After her experience with Muunokhoi's wife, she would be glad for his support. "All right. Thank you."

Lien opened her mouth to protest.

"No, sister," Geriel said. "Too many of my family are infected. I won't risk you too."

"Temur ordered me to protect you," Chinua added.

Lien sighed. "Fetch me if you need me."

Geriel waited until Lien had left and then turned to Uranchim. "Shall we begin?"

Day gave way to dusk, and dusk to night. Each yurt

blurred together as did the faces of those infected. It took all Geriel's effort to put one foot in front of another and every time she stood, she swayed.

"Time for you to rest." Uranchim led her back to the camp Chinua had set up. Both Lien and Chinua were already asleep. She crawled into her travel bed. The Adhan camp was worse than her own camp, probably because of their inability to identify those who had the curse without showing any symptoms. At least half were badly infected and most would be showing symptoms soon. There'd been panic, but the warriors had stepped in to protect her. There was little she could do.

The next morning she woke late, her head cloudy with fatigue. Gingerly she sat.

"Are you hungry?" Lien asked from where she sat by their fire.

"Yes."

Lien brought over a plate full of dumplings and roasted meat. As she ate, Geriel laid her hand on Lien's arm and checked her again.

Still clear.

She sighed. "Where's Chinua?"

"He's talking to the men who went to Chungson with Muunokhoi."

Gathering the information they would need. Good. They would leave as soon as she finished in the camp. The cure had to be their priority.

After eating, she found Uranchim and continued to scan the rest of the camp. By the time she was finished, only two tents held uninfected people. Nausea was her constant companion. It would be a rough few months if she couldn't find a cure.

She sat in the camp Chinua had erected and ate

dinner while Uranchim and Lien discussed the next step. "I will go with you to Chungson," Uranchim said. "The more people searching for the cure, the better."

"And what of your people?" Lien asked.

"This is the best way to help my people." He glanced at Geriel. "How many can you heal before you leave?"

She gritted her teeth. At the moment her whole body was so lethargic that it was difficult to even chew. Still she attempted to focus, tried to remember how many she'd identified in the early stages of the disease. "I could stop the spread in maybe a score of those with milder symptoms."

"Good."

Geriel forced herself to continue eating. There were so many she couldn't help, so many who would likely die before they found a cure.

"How long will it take?" Lien asked.

She shook her head. "I'm not certain—a morning."

"Then we will plan to leave at midday," Lien said. "It's another two days' ride to the mountain."

Geriel would be glad to leave here, glad not to be reminded how weak her gift was. Hopefully one of the dragons would be able to help her.

She woke early the next morning and went into the tent of those who were the least affected. She'd protect the healers first, so they could help others. Her stomach swirling, she settled on the bed, her legs crossed, eyes closed as she visualised her mountain, the symbol of a wider world. Mastering her gift was the only way to help her people. Amslan had said to stop trying so hard, though it was difficult, the urgency kept pushing her.

Breathing in and out again, she gestured the first healer forward and placed a hand on her arm. Slowly she relaxed into her. The disease was a little thicker today, but not by much. She needed a way to gather it all together like noodles when she stirred a pot.

Maybe that was it. Maybe she should visualise the blood whirling around the body and see what happened. She cautiously tried it. A light touch moved the disease but not the blood. Hope pushed through her nerves. She swirled it faster and faster and the infection drew into a single ball. Now she had to trap it.

She pictured a pot and flowed the disease into it, slamming the lid on it. Then she checked the seal and the blood for any remaining portions.

Clear.

She exhaled and opened her eyes. The usual wash of fatigue wasn't there. "How do you feel?" Geriel asked the woman.

"No different."

She checked her again and the pot was still there, bobbing in her blood stream but contained.

A solution that worked. It might not be a cure, but it would stop the disease from advancing until they found one. She grinned. "Who's next?"

It took only an hour to help those in the tent. Geriel took the food Uranchim handed her, but she didn't need it. Energy coursed through her body and the excitement of finding a solution added to her high. Working with the body, rather than wrestling against it, had worked. She checked the first woman she'd helped and the pot was still in place.

Geriel stood. "Let me go to the next tent."

Uranchim frowned. "Are you certain?"

"Yes." She had to send a message to Amslan, tell him what she had discovered. With her new technique, perhaps he could halt the disease in everyone in camp.

Then he could move on to the next tribe and help them.

She entered the next yurt. Each of the ten people inside sat apart on a mattress. A couple carved wooden statues but most talked to each other. There wasn't much else they could do. Anything they touched would have to be thoroughly cleaned or burned afterwards in case it had been infected.

She sat next to a small boy. If she could, she'd help all the children in the camp. They were the most at risk of dying. Placing her hand on his arm, she dove in, and encountered a thick greasy sludge. She frowned. It hadn't been anywhere near this bad yesterday. Perhaps the disease spread more quickly in smaller bodies. Keeping her touch light, she spun the infection, but it barely moved, taking almost all the space in his body. Nausea welled in her stomach. She couldn't help him. There was too much to contain even if she could lump it together.

She gasped for breath as she opened her eyes. Uranchim smiled at her, but she shook her head, glancing at the boy. "I have done what I can."

The boy stared at her, fear in his eyes. She wanted to reassure him, but she couldn't. She rose to her feet, swaying a little. "Let me check someone else." She had to fight her panic, concentrate on relaxing and staying lightly connected and in the end she helped about half of those in the tent. Geriel stumbled out. There was definitely a limit to what she could do.

Uranchim steadied her. "You need to rest."

She nodded. A short rest and food and then she'd go to the next yurt. Uranchim helped her to where Lien and Chinua waited.

"Are you ready to go?" Chinua asked.

She shook her head. "There are more I can help. I

need to send a message to Amslan about what I've learnt."

"I'll find you a rider." Uranchim left.

"Can you heal them?" Lien asked.

"No, but there is a way of containing it which requires little effort when the disease hasn't spread." It might even be too late for Amslan by the time the messenger arrived.

Lien smiled at her. "It's a start."

When the rider arrived, Geriel wrote instructions and explained what they meant to the warrior. Before he left, she scanned him again to ensure he was clear.

Then she moved on to the next tent. She would help everyone she could before she left.

This tent was worse than the one before. Oily, slimy tendrils were in each bloodstream and it was almost impossible to stir. She helped one person who was the least affected and sat back, the exhausted nausea back with a vengeance. She gasped for breath and took the dried curd Uranchim handed her. Everyone watched her, waiting for her to tell them everything was going to be all right. She couldn't. It was hopeless. She swallowed hard. "I've done all I can for the moment."

Uranchim helped her to her feet as voices complained, and a warrior stepped in front of her, protecting her. Uranchim helped her out of the tent and led her back to Lien. "That is enough. It's time we left."

Her heart was torn. So many people she hadn't helped. "I should check everyone again."

He shook his head. "You've helped more than we'd hoped for. We need to leave." He said to Lien, "I'll get my things."

Geriel turned to her sister. "We should stay another day. There might be a few more I can help."

"Or we can help the many by finding a cure faster."

Lien smiled gently. "It is time to go if you can ride."

Frustration swam through her even as she knew Lien was right. "I can." She could sleep in the saddle if she had to. Riding was in her blood.

Chinua packed their camp while Geriel ate and within the hour they were on the steppes again.

This time no one waved them off.

<h1 style="text-align:center">Chapter 5</h1>

They crossed the border into Chungson on the second day after leaving the Adhan camp. Geriel's muscles tightened. She'd finally stepped foot outside of Rhora. These weren't the circumstances she'd ever imagined in her wishful fantasies. No, in them she was acting as an emissary, or providing Lien emotional support for meeting her brother again. The fate of her people wasn't resting on her shoulders. Now, she'd happily never leave her country if it meant the curse hadn't come.

Chinua raised the white emissary flag in case they came across anyone before they reached the mountains. The alliance between Chungson and Rhora was secret, so if anyone saw them, Lord Anming could claim ignorance about their visit until they arrived. He could blame them for reaching out to him. Chungson wasn't prepared for a full battle with their Bonamese overlord yet and the Rhoran were used to being the enemy.

The flag didn't guarantee them safe passage—the emperor ignored it at his whim—but hopefully any Chungson citizens would respect it. Anyone who attacked them wouldn't live to regret it. Lien was their most elite fighter, gifted with speed so none who attacked her survived. But killing took a toll on her.

The first group of travellers they came across, farmers taking their wares to town, ran into the forest when they spotted the Rhoran, leaving their wagons behind.

Chinua chuckled. "Our reputation precedes us."

Lien smiled. "The Rhoran feature in stories parents tell their children to scare them into behaving."

So sad. They could have a good relationship with their neighbours, share their knowledge, but Xue's desire for power had ruined it.

The next caravan they approached was traders from across the mountains. They wore loose clothing and headscarfs which partially covered their faces. Geriel's heart leapt. Maybe they knew of a cure. She stopped one of the riders who was mounted on a Rhoran horse. "May I have a moment of your time?"

"We have plenty for you to buy," the trader said.

"I'm after knowledge," she replied, noting the way the trader was assessing Khulan. Rhoran horses were sought after in many countries for their speed and endurance. "I seek a cure to a disease called Trader's Curse. Do you know of it?" She described the symptoms.

The trader shifted his horse away from her, fear in his eyes. "I know of it. Who is infected?"

Geriel glanced at Lien. "My tribe."

"I know of no cure, but let me ask the others." He made a wide berth around her and caught up with the caravan. After a few minutes he rode back, stopping at calling distance from her. "No one knows of a cure."

Her spirits fell. "Thank you for your time. Safe travels."

The man cantered away.

By the end of the day, they turned towards the mountains which soared high above them and camped off the road. Lien continued their lessons in speaking Bonamese. Geriel had asked to learn before the curse had broken out, mindful she might need to know it if she was allowed to go to Chungson with her sister. The words twisted her tongue, but she could speak whole sentences now. Enough to be polite and ask questions.

Chinua handed around dried mutton and curd and she scanned him to make sure he was still clear of the curse. They were still too close to the road to light a fire. No point attracting undue attention. That night Geriel took the midnight shift to guard them.

Never had she known such darkness. The trees loomed large above her, constantly whispering, blocking out the starlight and the moon. Only vague shapes could be seen, lumps of branches or bushes crowding around them, a perfect screen for anyone sneaking up. It would be hard to fight amongst the trees and harder to flee. Her skin prickled as in the distance a bird or its prey shrieked. Above and around her leaves rustled, maybe from the wind, maybe from an animal moving through the forest. She clutched her sabre, constantly scanning the dark and moving around the camp. Wolves lived in the mountains too, and snow leopards, big creatures that could be out to hunt tonight.

They should have lit a fire. It would keep the four-legged predators away at least.

Her eyes slowly adjusted to the dark; shapes became trees and bushes, but it was still darker than she'd ever known, even on a cloudy, storm-ridden night on the steppes.

Eventually light crept back to the land, defining the forest and returning colour to its plants. She woke the others and handed out chunks of cheese and dried mutton for breakfast.

"How much further is it?" Geriel asked as they ate.

Uranchim looked up. "We might get there this evening."

Good. She wanted to start searching for a cure. The plants here were familiar to her.

"Is there a road we can follow?" Lien asked.

"There's a trail that leads into the mountains, but I don't know how much it is used," Chinua said. "If we run into villagers, they might panic."

"We don't have much choice," Uranchim said. "The forest is thick and will be difficult for the horses to move through."

Chinua nodded. "We'll deal with anyone we come across."

They travelled through the forest before reaching a dirt trail wide enough for two horses to walk side-by-side. They skirted villages when the forest morphed into rice paddies, avoiding detection, and the ground continued to slope upwards. When the trees occasionally parted, the mountains loomed high above them.

"How far up are we going?" Geriel asked.

"About halfway," Uranchim answered.

"Do you think we'll see Kew while we're here?" she asked Lien.

Lien smiled. "I hope so."

Kew had been Lien's dragon in the imperial court. They had later discovered she had been stolen as an egg. When they'd met with the wild dragons, Kew had chosen to stay and learn from them. In the short time she'd spent with them, Kew had learnt how to mind speak rather than changing her skin colour to portray different emotions and projecting pictures into Lien's mind. What else would she have learnt since then?

Would the dragons be able to help Geriel with her gift?

That night they camped in a clearing near a stream. After Geriel had scanned the others to ensure they were still uninfected by the curse, she squatted on its banks to fill their flasks with its icy water. The cold was so crisp it almost hurt her hands. It must travel down the mountain from the snow peaks.

She examined the plants along the bank, but they were still familiar. Nothing which could be a cure. She noted the direction of the camp so she didn't get lost, and wandered up stream, its gentle babbling music to her ears. She inhaled the rich, damp dense smell of foliage and rubbed her arms as the heat faded from the day. The sun hadn't kissed her skin all day. Instead she'd been shaded by the trees and bamboo, which made it cooler than she'd ever known. There was no dust, no grass smoke, no livestock smell. The scents here were different, strange.

She knelt in front of an unfamiliar bush bearing purple berries. Using her knife, she cut a stem and a bunch of berries, and placed them into the bag she carried at her waist. Her hand hovered over the leaves as she remembered Amslan's suggestion. Could she connect with a plant the same way as she connected to humans? Would they reveal their secrets to her?

Her throat tightened as she brushed the leaf and closed her eyes. She visualised the mountain and reached into the plant. It was strange, foreign with the way it was structured, but she could connect to the leaf, stem, berries and roots. Their properties swam at her— the berries were poisonous to humans but the leaves would work against infection.

She pulled her hand back and stared at the bush. Her

head light, a little dizzy, she cautiously climbed to her feet. If she could sense the properties of the plants, did that mean she'd sense the cure? Would she not have to try hundreds of different concoctions to heal her tribe? She prayed to Qadan it was true and at the same time she prayed she could master her gift. The idea of scanning every plant she came across frightened her. It could easily exhaust her and she would be useless again.

A twig cracked behind her and she spun around. Her heart leapt to her throat. A soldier, his black uniform identifying him as Bonamese, stood only a few yards away pointing a bow and arrow straight at her.

Her hand went to her sabre.

"Don't move." His Rhoran had a tinge of an accent.

She stilled, heart racing. The nearest tree was several feet away, too far. How close was she to the camp? Would Lien hear her if she yelled for help?

Though there might be more soldiers around. She scanned the surrounding forest for movement.

"What are you doing here?" His dark eyes pierced hers, demanding answers.

"Looking for plants," Geriel said. "I'm a healer." Best if she stick to the truth as much as she could. She crossed her arms, her fingers inching towards the knives at her belt.

"Where are you from?"

She almost rolled her eyes. "Rhora."

He scowled. "Which tribe?"

She pressed her lips together. Would it be advantageous if she said she was from the khan's tribe, or would that get her into more trouble?

"Which tribe?" the man demanded again.

"Geriel, where are you?" Chinua's voice, low but coming closer.

The soldier shifted, facing Chinua.

Fear flooded Geriel. "Chinua, run!" She snatched one of her knives from her belt as the soldier turned back to her. She threw it and lunged towards the tree.

Footsteps crashed towards them and Chinua burst into the clearing, his bow and arrow drawn. The soldier whirled to him as Geriel grabbed her other knife. She could distract the soldier and Chinua could shoot him.

The soldier lowered his bow. "You're from Lien's tribe."

Chinua stared at the man. "Jie?"

The man nodded.

Relief washed through her. Geriel exhaled and tucked her knife back into her belt. This was the man they were coming to meet. Why hadn't he said so?

She stepped out and scanned the clearing. Her knife was stuck into a tree behind the soldier.

"I see you've met Geriel." Chinua tucked his arrow back into his quiver.

Jie raised his eyebrows. "Yes." He tugged her knife from the tree and handed it to her. "You telegraph your movement too much. Try a smaller flick of the wrist." His tone was patronising, as if speaking to a small child.

She snatched the knife from him. She'd wanted to distract the man, not kill him. "Perhaps next time you should identify yourself rather than threaten me."

His eyes widened an infinitesimal amount, and the intensity in them deepened. She shivered. Was he upset she'd spoken back to him? He'd learn quickly Rhoran women weren't as submissive as Bonamese women.

"Lien will be pleased to see you," Chinua said. "The camp's through this way."

Geriel turned away from Jie and waited for him to follow Chinua before walking after him. Though they were allies, it was hard to shake the teachings of a lifetime that the Bonamese couldn't be trusted.

Lien jumped up when they walked into the clearing. "Jie!" Her delight was clear as she ran over and hugged her brother's best friend. "What are you doing here?"

"I'm on patrol. We don't want anyone sneaking up on us. How did you find us?"

"Muunokhoi's men told us where you were going," Chinua said.

Jie smiled. "How is he?"

Chinua glanced at Lien. "Not well."

"I'm sorry to hear that. Where's the rest of your party?"

"It's only us," Lien said. "The camp has had an outbreak of Traders' Curse. Everyone else is in quarantine."

Jie took a step back. "The curse?"

She nodded. "We believe some Bonamese soldiers must have been infected."

Jie swore. "So the Rhoran will be unable to help us fight Xue."

Geriel clenched her hands. How dare he? The Rhoran were suffering, possibly dying from this disease and he saw it as an inconvenience. She opened her mouth to tell him what an inconsiderate boor he was, when Lien said, "Only for the moment. We're searching for a cure. There are rumours a plant in the mountains might help and we're hoping the dragons or maybe someone in Chungson know about it."

"I hope so too," he said. "We need your help." He glanced around the camp. "Come with me. It's not far to the meadow. You might as well camp there tonight."

The nagging sensation that had been in the back of Geriel's mind since the Adhan camp strengthened. She packed her things, her mind racing. Jie knew Muunokhoi because Jie had ridden with him to Chungson while the rest of Rhora had ridden into battle against the emperor. Muunokhoi had spent no time with any of the Bonamese soldiers when he'd returned. So why was he one of the worst affected by the curse?

She mulled it over as she followed Lien and Jie, leading her horses. Chinua scowled next to her and Uranchim brought up the rear.

"What's wrong?" Geriel asked.

"It goes against everything I know to trust a Bonamese," Chinua answered. "Especially one who led the attack on our camp."

"He was forced to. If Xue knew Jie had survived the attack, he'd sign Jie's death warrant." She touched Chinua's shoulder. "I understand your concern, but Lien trusts him."

"She also trusted the emperor right until he tried to kill her again," Chinua said.

It wasn't the most reassuring thought. "At least she can protect all of us if Jie turns on us."

"True."

Not long afterwards, the ground flattened and they walked out of the trees into a large meadow. Dozens of dirty grey triangular tents had been set up in neat rows and a few hundred soldiers wearing grey uniforms wandered through the camp. The ground between the tents had been flattened and was more mud than grass, but beyond the camp grew the flowers and plants Geriel was here to study. She prayed the soldiers hadn't flattened too much, else her journey could be wasted.

A soldier shouted in alarm, drawing his sword.

Geriel's hand went to her sabre as Jie gestured for the man to calm. "At ease, soldier. They're friends."

The soldier lowered his sword, but stared at them.

"Who are they?" Lien asked.

"Chungson soldiers," Jie said. "I'm teaching them about the Bonam defences. Follow me."

The soldiers watched them warily as they moved through camp. Geriel kept her hand on her sabre's hilt as she walked past the men, varying degrees of hostility on their faces. They ranged in age from their twenties to their forties, but there wasn't a single female amongst them. Some men stepped back when they noticed her, and others leered or spat.

Her skin prickled. Lien had mentioned Bonam men thought they were better than women and from this reaction it appeared the Chungson were the same—or perhaps it was simply because she was Rhoran. It would be trying if they tried to interfere with her work.

"You can set up here," Jie said when they reached the far end of the camp. The meadow spread out in front of them and a pen of horses was nearby. She smiled as the smell reminded her of home.

Enough of the meadow was still intact, but it had been chopped up around the practice targets.

"When you're ready, come to the red tent in the middle for dinner. I'll introduce you to the Chungson captain in charge." He left.

"Someone should stay behind to guard our things," Chinua said as he unpacked his tent.

Lien frowned. "I hope that's not necessary."

He grunted.

Geriel kept an eye on the camp as she set up the tent she shared with Lien. Soldiers watched her in return, muttering things she couldn't hear to their companions. When she finished, she checked the horses had enough food and then they all walked together to the red tent.

Jie was inside with an older man, perhaps in his mid-thirties. Jie smiled. "Permit me to introduce you to Captain Wei. He is under the direct orders of Lord Anming and oversees the training here."

Wei bowed to Uranchim, the oldest of them and

directed his comments to him. "Thank you for coming. We look forward to working with you."

Chinua laughed. "Direct those thanks at Lien. She's in charge here."

Wei's eyes widened. "I thought the khan was serious about his offer to help. Why didn't he send one of his advisers?"

Chinua rolled his eyes and stepped forward. "Permit me to introduce Lien, formally State Princess of the Bonamese and now Tribal Mother and wife to our khan, Temur."

Lien smiled. "I can make decisions for the whole of Rhora."

Wei stepped back. "I don't know whether Lord Anming will agree to that."

"If he wants our help, he will," Lien said.

Geriel hid her smile. The Chungson were about to get an education in how capable women were. She was looking forward to it.

"Please sit." Jie gestured to the table.

"Our priority is to find a cure," Lien said as she sat. "But Chinua and I will continue to work with you both to plan against Xue." She glanced at Jie. "You've seen Bao?"

He nodded. "I will send word to him you are here. He is looking forward to seeing you again."

Geriel hoped the reunion would be everything Lien dreamed of. Lien had thought all her family were dead for the past eighteen years and to discover her brother was alive and in hiding had come as a shock to her.

"As am I." Lien glanced towards the door. "Are the dragons' nesting grounds nearby?"

"They're higher than us," Jie said. "Riltien visits us regularly."

"Good. We need to ask them if they know of a

cure."

Geriel's muscles tightened. Could they help her with her gift as well? How were her own family faring? Was Jochi coping with his new responsibility, had Shuren or Sukh shown any symptoms of the curse yet? She'd spent far too long travelling. It was time to start working.

They talked long into the night and Geriel's eyes grew heavy. She should conserve her energy for the coming days. A yawn overtook her and she turned away, covering her mouth with her hand.

"Sister, you should go to sleep," Lien said.

"Both you ladies should," Wei said. "It is late. We can talk more in the morning."

Geriel narrowed her eyes. "I am not tired because I'm female, but because I've spent days healing people." How dare he think she was weaker because of her gender.

Uranchim spoke. "I would welcome the break," he said. "It's been a tiring quarter moon."

Lien stood gracefully and bade everyone good night. "We will see you in the morning."

Jie nodded.

Geriel followed her back to the tent they were sharing. Before Uranchim and Chinua said goodnight, they both held out their hands to Geriel so she could scan them. Still clear. As they got ready to sleep, Geriel lay her hand on Lien's wrist and checked her blood. Everything was normal.

The ever-present tension in her shoulders relaxed slightly.

Perhaps tomorrow she would find a cure. There wouldn't be too many unfamiliar plants in the meadow. One of them had to work.

She smiled and went to sleep.

~*~

The tent flat whipped open and the noise startled Geriel awake. She blinked, her eyes clearing and in the dark a large shape loomed over Lien. Her heart lurched. She lunged for the shape. "No!"

She touched cold hard scales as a voice in her head said, *Lien! Geriel!*

Her breath released with a whoosh and she flopped back on her bed. "Kew. You scared the life out of me."

Lien hugged her dragon. "How did you know we were here?"

It had been several moons since they'd seen each other.

Dragons watch the camp.

Geriel wasn't surprised. The dragons had been forced out of their traditional breeding grounds because of the emperor and had only just returned when the peace treaty had guaranteed their safety. The dragons wouldn't be too quick to trust people though.

Kew butted her head against Geriel's and snorted smoke. Geriel laughed. "It's good to see you."

How are our brothers and sisters? Kew asked.

Geriel sobered. "Shuren and father are not well." She explained about the curse.

I'll ask Dhalin to come first thing in the morning, Kew told her. *She knows everything about healing.*

Geriel hoped so.

Kew settled between them and let out a happy snort. *You need to sleep. We'll talk in the morning.*

She smiled. It was still weird hearing Kew talk. Being with the dragons had obviously helped her tremendously. And if Kew could learn so much in such a short a time, maybe Geriel could too.

For the first time, hope surged through her.

She snuggled down and went back to sleep.

Chapter 6

Geriel's tent was empty when she woke the next morning. She frowned. How had Kew and Lien managed to leave without waking her? Maybe she'd been more tired than she'd thought. She cleaned up, braided her long hair and then peered out of the tent. Not far away, her travelling companions sat around a campfire, preparing breakfast and beyond them soldiers wearing crisp grey uniforms wandered around the camp or sat around smaller campfires cooking breakfast. Even if Chinua wore the same uniform as the soldiers, he'd never be mistaken for Chungson. Rhoran skin was much more tanned than that of those who lived in the southern countries.

Geriel retrieved her coat to arm her against the cool morning mountain air and joined her friends at the campfire. She inhaled the woody campfire smoke, so different from the grassy smoke scent on the steppes. A couple of soldiers glared at her and more than one touched the pommel of his sword. Her skin crawled. Surely they wouldn't attack her when it was clear Jie and Wei had invited them here. Maybe she should go back for her knives.

"Good morning, sister," Lien called.

Geriel sighed and continued to the fire. "Morning." She held her hands out to warm them.

"I'll be pleased when Wei and Jie explain who we are," Chinua grumbled. "I'm getting tired of all the stares."

So it wasn't just her.

Lien smiled. "How are you feeling today?"

"Fine." Nerves hummed around her skin. Today she had to find a cure, talk to the healer dragon, Dhalin, and hopefully save her people. Pressure squeezed her chest. She took the bowl of soup Lien handed her and ate, listening to the conversation around her. Snippets of Bonamese conversation reached her and she understood some words, mostly morning conversation about what was happening that day.

Jie walked towards them, greeting his men, his steps confident. He laughed at a couple of things that were said, obviously popular with the soldiers. His face was more relaxed, his expression kind and friendly.

Could they trust him? Kew had vouched for him back when he'd been a prisoner in Rhora and dragons read a person's emotions and thoughts.

He stopped close to Geriel, forcing her to tilt her head to look at him and his expression was back to the reserved mask she'd seen the day before. "I've sent a messenger to Lord Anming and Bao. He will tell them you're here and ask if a cure for the curse is known. We'd prefer you didn't tell the soldiers about the disease as it might cause panic."

Lien nodded.

"Wei is gathering the soldiers together this morning to discuss our plans," Jie continued. "We'd like you to be there so we can introduce you."

"Of course," Lien said. "What time?"

"Now."

Nice of him to give them some warning. Geriel ate a few mouthfuls of her soup. "Give me a second."

"You're not needed," Jie said. "Just Lien and Chinua."

She paused, annoyed at his tone, ignoring the brief pang at being left out. He'd already dismissed her as unimportant.

"You can all come," Lien said. "I need to ensure they understand not to interfere with your work."

Geriel smiled, ignoring Jie. She cleaned her bowl and followed the others to where the soldiers gathered on the meadow. Wei stood on top of a wagon, and Jie and Lien joined him.

Wei called for quiet. "We have new guests." He gestured to Lien. "Tribal Mother Lien is wife to the Khan Temur of Rhora. She has brought the warrior, Chinua to teach us about Rhoran fighting strategies and how best to use the Rhoran in battle."

Geriel smothered her smile. Lien could teach them just as much as Chinua could.

The soldiers murmured as Lien spoke. "Thank you for welcoming us. We look forward to working with you. While we are here, two of our healers—" she indicated Uranchim and Geriel, "will be researching the plants in the meadows to find new cures to help both of our peoples."

Geriel's stomach swirled. The fate of her people rested on her. The longer it took her to find a cure, the more people would die. How many had already died?

No, she had to stay positive, be confident.

"I ask that you do not interfere with their work in any way. If there is an issue, please come to me or Captain Wei."

A couple of men sniggered. One muttered, "Who

would go to a woman for help?"

Geriel sighed. It wasn't her task to educate these men, but perhaps by watching Lien, they would learn some respect for women.

A guard called a warning and Geriel looked up to see two dragons flying in from the mountains, one sandy brown and one green, their wings spread. They were almost twice as big as Kew, about half the size of a horse. She gasped. She'd never seen a dragon flying. Kew's wings had been bound when she was a baby and she couldn't do more than hover off the ground. Geriel frowned and looked at Kew. Her wings were bigger than they had been. Could the effects be reversed?

The dragons landed and strode towards them, their wings folding into their backs and their tails sliding along the ground. Lien stepped off the wagon and went to meet them. She inclined her head. "Riltien, Dhalin, it is good to see you again."

And you, Lien-mother.

Wei continued to speak to the soldiers as Geriel approached the dragons, her stomach churning. Uranchim and Chinua joined them.

"Permit me to introduce my sister, Geriel, and Uranchim, who are both healers. You know Chinua."

The green dragon stepped forward. *I am Dhalin. Kew tells me you have questions for me.*

The dragon healer. Geriel's heart jumped. "Yes. Perhaps we can talk."

Come. We shall speak by the stream.

Geriel and Uranchim followed Dhalin away from the crowd of soldiers to the stream running along the edge of the meadow. A couple of smooth grey rocks lay on the edge and Geriel sat on one. The gurgle of the water was in direct contrast to the storm in her stomach. If Dhalin couldn't help her, what would she do?

You are like Amslan. Dhalin looked at Geriel.

She jolted at his name and then remembered Amslan had healed one of the dragons when they'd been chasing Lien's old assassin master. "He is far stronger than I am."

Uranchim raised his eyebrows.

She shifted. It wasn't a secret.

Show me this curse you wish to heal. Picture it in your mind.

Geriel closed her eyes, and visualised the oily sludge.

Interesting. You both have different thoughts of it.

"Uranchim sees the outer symptoms," Geriel said. "I see what is inside. I can contain it if it hasn't spread too far, but I can't remove it."

I have not seen anything like this before, but I shall ask my fellow healers.

Geriel's shoulders fell, disappointment flooding her. What had she expected—some magical cure? It was foolish and naive. The dragons were different creatures, had different ailments and concerns. But perhaps Dhalin could still help. "Do you have any greenshade in the area?" She visualised it in case Dhalin knew it by a different name.

Dhalin nodded. *In the lower mountains.*

It was a start. The greenshade would help soothe the symptoms of the sufferers.

"We should start collecting it immediately," Uranchim said.

The dragon growled. *You may not take it all.*

"But we need so much!" he protested.

Geriel placed a hand on his arm. He should know better. "We must leave enough for it to regrow."

"You've seen how bad it is," he said. "And that's only two camps. What about the remaining eight tribes? They must be suffering equally."

If she thought about it, the task would overwhelm her. "We will take as much as we can." Geriel let out a breath. Uranchim shouldn't upset the dragons, but she couldn't say anything directly to him. He had seniority over her even though Geriel had the gift. "Why don't you stay with Dhalin and tell her everything you know about the curse?" she suggested. "You have far more experience than I have. I will gather the greenshade today and then we can send it home."

A good suggestion, Dhalin agreed. *Kew can show you where the plants are.*

"Thank you."

Uranchim pressed his lips together but nodded. Not good. She'd have to ask Lien to speak to him about his behaviour towards the dragons. If she attempted it, he would ignore her in his arrogance.

How was Jochi getting along with Amslan? The threat of the curse added a far greater pressure to learning to heal. Had he accessed his gift yet? Was he helping the tribe? She hoped Amslan was being kind to him.

She walked back to the camp. Jochi always threw himself into learning new things with gusto. She wouldn't be surprised if when she returned he was more adept than her. But that would be good for the tribe. And he would help Sukh and Shuren as well.

The soldiers were gathered by the targets and Geriel had to walk behind them. Chinua stood with Wei demonstrating the Rhoran bow.

"You said you were desperate for a woman." One of the soldiers nudged his companion and nodded to Geriel.

"Not that desperate." They both laughed.

"Pay attention." Jie's bark made her jump as he joined her.

Both soldiers stood to attention and nodded.

"It may take them some time to get used to you in camp," Jie said. "Best you do not go anywhere by yourself."

Because these men had no respect for her. "I can protect myself."

He walked too close to her side, heat and confidence emanating off him, his gaze intense. Her body tingled all the way down to her toes. If he wasn't so annoying, it would be attractive. "Do you know where Lien is?"

"She returned to her tent."

"Thank you." She moved in that direction.

"You're young for a healer. Were your male superiors ill with the curse?"

Her mouth dropped open. The partial truth hurt, but she wouldn't enlighten him about her gift. She didn't bother answering, instead she increased her stride and ducked into the tent where she found Lien and Kew.

"Could Dhalin help?" The hope was clear on Lien's face.

Geriel cringed and shook her head. "Not yet. She's going to ask the other healers if they've seen the curse before. She did tell me where we could find some greenshade though. If it's all right, I'll collect it now if Kew can show me where it is."

"Of course. I'll come with you."

Geriel smiled. It would be quicker that way and she enjoyed spending time with Lien. She put the things she needed into a bag and slung her quiver and bow over her shoulders. "Will we need the horses?"

No. Walking will be better.

She handed Lien another bag for the plants. "Let's go."

"I'll let Jie know where we're going."

"Do we have to?" The less she saw of the man the

better.

Lien smiled. "He will worry if I don't."

That was his problem. They were perfectly capable of taking care of themselves.

She followed Lien to where Jie was watching Chinua's training session with the soldiers. "We're heading down the mountain to gather some plants," Lien said.

He frowned. "Who's going with you?"

"Geriel and Kew."

"Which warrior is going with you?" he growled.

Lien chuckled. "Myself, Geriel and Kew."

"I will go."

Geriel didn't want him watching her every move. He made her uneasy, self-conscious. "It's not necessary."

"Sometimes villagers come into the mountains," he said. "They do not know of the alliance between Rhora and Chungson. We cannot risk them attacking you."

Was he serious?

"We can protect ourselves, Jie," Lien said. "Kew will also be with us."

He shook his head. "No. I will come. Which way?" He directed the last question at Kew.

Kew nodded to the south. *He'll learn.* Kew's amusement made Geriel smile and she checked Jie's reaction.

He didn't hear me. I can choose who I mind speak to.

Kew had definitely grown stronger. Geriel almost wished someone did attack them so she could prove Jie wrong. He took up position behind Kew, and Geriel and Lien followed side-by-side. Geriel lowered her voice. "Are you going to tell him about your gift?"

"I find it's better if I show people, don't you agree?" Her smile was a little bit wicked.

Geriel chuckled. The first time Lien had shown the

tribe how skilled and fast she was, she'd shocked everyone silent. Her speed, so fast that she disappeared, was one thing, but combined with her deadly accuracy with arrows and knives, plus her martial skills, put her into the deadly weapon category. She'd saved the Rhoran from attacks from the emperor on multiple occasions.

Jie glanced back at them. "Quiet. There may be villagers around."

She raised her eyebrows. They hadn't been noisy. He thought he was better than them. Never mind. She wasn't here for his approval and she wouldn't let him get in her way.

After an hour, Kew walked into a clearing full of greenshade. Geriel inhaled. Perfect. There was enough here for several tribes, though maybe not all. Some of the plants were even still in flower. She'd gather some seeds for the Adhan and Saltar tribes. They had access to the most fertile soil on the steppes and they grew commonly needed plants where they could.

The plants clumped together and were easy to split. "Take every third plant," Geriel said. "Roots and all."

Jie held out a hand to stop her from moving forward. "Let me scout the area first."

There is no one around.

Jie frowned. "I'll still check."

Geriel hid her grin. "Go ahead. We'll start."

He glared at her as if that would frighten her into obeying him. He had a lot to learn about Rhoran women. She demonstrated to Lien how the plant was to be plucked. She almost missed his quiet growl as he stalked away.

Lien smiled at her. "Don't be too hard on him, sister. He comes from a different culture to you. He has been constantly told women are weaker and need protection. It will be hard for him to change his mind."

Geriel nodded. "I know. It's kind of fun though."

"I'm surprised you weren't harder on me when I arrived at camp," Lien said.

"I felt sorry for you. You were clearly unprepared for life on the steppes and you had no choice in your situation." She dug up another plant. "None of us wants to be forced into marriage."

Lien hummed in agreement. "Mother never found you a suitor, did she?"

"No, thank Qadan. With all the fighting and unrest, marrying me off was the last thing on her mind." She attacked the ground a little too hard.

"I'm glad. I'll talk to her about it if you'd like."

"If we don't find a cure, it might not be an issue." Her chest squeezed. She dug faster, as if that would make much difference. The greenshade was a stop gap, not a solution.

"How are the plants used?"

"Its leaves are boiled and used on the skin to soothe the pox. The roots are used in a tea to reduce the fever." There could be thousands of people affected. Until she knew, it was impossible to tell if this patch of plants would be enough. "How are we getting the plants home?" she asked. "It will take too long for Chinua to ride to all the tribes, and our people won't react well if a Chungson soldier rides into camp." Not to mention it wasn't wise to teach them how to find the tribes on the steppes.

I will talk to my kin, Kew said. *Maybe we can take them. It will be faster that way.*

Lien grinned at her. "That would be perfect."

Kew turned blue in satisfaction as Jie stepped into the clearing, moving silently. "Neither of you was on guard while I was away," he said. "Chungson is not like the steppes where you don't have to worry about other people. You need to be constantly aware."

He treated them like children. "I thought your job was to check the surroundings."

"I might have been captured."

"We will be more alert in future," Lien said quickly, shooting Geriel a look to be quiet. "Will you guard us now?"

Jie straightened his stance. "Of course."

Right. Lien was making him feel useful. Geriel turned her back on him and continued gathering the greenshade.

The morning passed quickly, and as Geriel reached the end of her section, she wandered towards the stream to investigate the plants there. A few were familiar to her, but she brushed her fingers along those that weren't and connected to them. It was difficult, dragging her gift to the surface and then connecting with the strange structures, but she recognised their properties and picked some leaves and flowers so she could draw them and add them to her book when she returned to camp.

She moved to the next plant, closing her eyes to focus more easily and collected samples of it as well.

A branch cracked. Her pulse jumped and she looked up, searching. The sound came from directly across the stream from her. She eased to her feet, her eyes on the opposite bank and stepped back. It could be an animal or a person and she wanted to meet neither.

Another noise, footsteps through the forest. The nearest tree was several yards away. She hurried backwards, her eyes scanning the forest, and a young boy about Jochi's age stepped out of the trees across the stream, holding a bucket. His eyes widened with fear.

She smiled, hoping not to scare him further. "I won't hurt you. I stopped for water. I am lost." The Bonamese still felt clumsy on her tongue.

Slowly the boy stepped back. He pointed. "Rhora is that way."

She nodded. "Thank you."

Jie walked out of the forest, his bow and arrow drawn, pointing directly at her. The fierceness in his eyes made her heart lurch. "On your knees, Rhoran scum." The hatred in his tone made her flinch.

"Now!"

She dropped to her knees, eyes wide. What was going on? Had he turned on them? Had he managed to catch Kew and Lien off guard and hurt them?

"You're the last one." He glanced at the child. "Boy, don't worry, you're safe." He turned back to her and winked. "Lie on the ground."

He was acting. The relief made her pulse thump in her wrists and Geriel slowly did as she was told, the terror leeching from her pores. He would be a vicious opponent.

Jie lowered his weapon and grabbed some rope from his belt. He knelt on her back. "Don't tell anyone," he called to the boy. "We don't want to worry the village." He wrapped the rope around her wrists.

"Yes, captain."

"Get your water and go."

The boy hurried to obey, his footsteps crashing through the bushes. Jie waited until they faded before he removed his knee from her back. "I told you to be on guard. You shouldn't have wandered so far."

Geriel let out a breath and moved her hands, trying to loosen the rope. It was tight. She shifted into a seated position. "You were convincing. The boy will think you defeated me."

He raised his eyebrows. "I did defeat you." He scowled. "We need to go before he tells people and villagers scour the area. They'll notice where you dug the plants. They'll know someone was here."

He was right. Though it pained her to say it, she said, "I'm sorry." She stood and turned so he could undo the ropes.

"I'm tempted to keep you tied," he murmured as his fingers brushed her wrists. "You'll be less trouble that way."

A warm tingle swept through her body as his breath tickled her ear. She inhaled sharply. She shouldn't be reacting like this. She didn't even like him. With her wrists loose, she stalked back to the clearing where she'd left Lien and Kew.

Lien glanced up as she returned. "Who was it?"

Geriel frowned. Kew must have warned them. "A boy. Jie pretended to capture me."

"We should move," Jie said. "He won't stay quiet for long. Get your things."

She glanced around the clearing. They had picked as many plants as they should. The rest would be left to renew the population. "Kew, is there more greenshade in the area?"

I'll ask.

They climbed back up the mountain and it wasn't long before Geriel's calves and thighs burned. The steppes were deceptively hilly, but they were nothing like the steepness of the mountains. Her breath came in little gasps and she was relieved to see Lien was similarly affected.

"We can rest here," Jie said after they had walked for about half an hour.

Lien smiled at him and sank to the ground. "I am not used to mountains."

Geriel stayed standing, refusing to let him see she needed the rest, but she leaned against one of the trees, its rough bark massaging her back.

"You are fitter than I expected, Kixi," Jie said. "Time with the Rhoran has been good for you."

Geriel glanced at Lien. She didn't seem offended by the name, so perhaps it was affectionate.

Lien grinned at him. "It has."

He glanced at Geriel and then walked closer to Lien. "Do they truly treat you well?" he asked in Bonamese.

Geriel snorted. "Better than your people did."

He scowled and Lien placed a hand on his arm. "They are my family and my people now," she told him. "Geriel is my adopted sister. Her family took me in and cared for me. Her father taught me how to ride and her siblings reminded me what it was to be loved."

Geriel's heart swelled.

Jie's smile was genuine and it softened his features, made him more approachable. "I am glad." He scanned the clearing, ever watchful. "If you have rested enough, we should keep moving." He glanced at her.

Geriel's legs ached, but the longer she stood here, the more they would cool and stiffen. "Let's go."

She wouldn't give him an excuse to feel superior to her.

Chapter 7

When they finally reached the camp, Jie left Geriel and Lien with Uranchim and Dhalin who were still sitting by the stream. Geriel waited until he walked away before sighing in relief and settling next to Uranchim. Her legs rejoiced at the rest.

"Did you find it?" Uranchim asked.

Geriel patted the bags. "Yes. There's enough for a small amount for each tribe. I'll divide it into ten packages." She glanced at Dhalin. "Do you know where we can find more?"

I believe there is more, higher in the mountains. Let me ask.

Dhalin fell silent and Uranchim helped Geriel sort the plants into piles.

"Is this it?" he asked.

"Yes." It was pathetically little for each tribe. But they weren't certain every tribe had been affected by the curse. She prayed to Qadan some had been saved.

There is more greenshade further up the mountain, Dhalin said. *I can show you where tomorrow.*

"Thank you." They should wait until they gathered more before they sent it.

Could our kin carry the plants to the Rhoran tribes? Kew

bowed low to Dhalin as she asked.

I will ask.

Geriel hoped so. It would take days to reach each of the tribes by horseback and they might not have enough healthy men in each tribe to do it.

Dhalin walked over to her. *You can sense the curse before the symptoms show.*

"Yes."

Show me what you do.

Geriel braced herself, closed her eyes and then touched Uranchim's arm. As she ran through her meditation, Dhalin gently pushed into her mind. Then she scanned Uranchim's blood.

Geriel's heart stopped. No. It couldn't be.

She focused on the small spot she'd discovered in his blood.

Is that it?

Dread pooled in her stomach. "Yes."

Ah, I believe I'll be able to identify it now.

Geriel paid no attention to the dragon. She visualised the container and slammed it around the disease before she slowly scanned his blood for any more signs. The rest of his blood was clear. How had he been infected? It had been days since they'd left the Adhan camp and she'd been scanning him every evening. She stared at the older healer. "You're infected."

His mouth dropped open and Lien gasped.

Geriel scrambled to her feet. "What did you bring with you?" It had to be something he'd touched since leaving the camp.

Uranchim was quick to recover. "Food, clothes."

"Show me." They had to get him away from the rest of the camp. She might have caught it early enough, but she wasn't taking any chances. It was lucky he'd been away from people all morning.

She followed Uranchim to his tent next to Chinua's, Dhalin and Lien keeping pace with them. "Find Chinua," Geriel told Lien.

Lien hurried away.

Chinua had been working with the Chungson men all morning. If he was infected too… it didn't bear thinking about.

Geriel waited outside the tent while Uranchim gathered his things and then showed her his bag.

"Where did the silk come from?"

"The bounty from the Bonamese."

All at once everything clicked into place. None of the Bonamese men showing signs of infection, Berke being the first affected, Muunokhoi infected despite spending no time with the Bonamese army. The infection had come from the goods the emperor had sent as reparations, not from the men.

The emperor had deliberately infected them.

Horror flooded her. It meant people could still become infected despite the quarantine. The goods had been shared evenly between each tribe and each family. "Burn it," she ordered. "Anything that came from the Bonamese and anything it has touched. Then move your camp to the opposite side of the meadow."

"You've contained it, haven't you?"

She nodded. "But we can't risk it."

He began to break down his tent. Lien returned with Chinua.

"What's going on?" he asked.

Geriel lowered her voice. "Uranchim has been infected by the curse."

Chinua swore and then held out his arm. She washed her hands and then closed her eyes, scanned him little by little, not wanting to miss any sign he too might have the disease.

Clear.

She breathed out. "You're clear, but you'll need to stay isolated for a few days." They couldn't risk it. He had shared a tent with Uranchim on the journey. She placed her hand on Lien's arm and scanned her. Also clear.

"I need to train the men."

Lien shook her head. "I will."

"They won't take orders from you," Chinua said. "They question why you're here."

"I'll talk to Jie." Lien walked off.

"Wait." Geriel called her back. "We need to get word to the tribes. The curse didn't come from the army, it came from the reparations Xue sent."

Chinua swore and Lien's face paled, horror in her eyes. "How do you know?"

"Uranchim was clear until today, but his silk came from the reparations," Geriel said. "It explains why Muunokhoi was so badly infected when he hadn't been near the soldiers, but he travelled back with the reparations."

"I never thought my uncle would be so dishonourable." Lien walked off.

I need to talk to my kin, Dhalin said, her tone concerned. *I will be back.*

Chinua clenched his fists. "What do I have to do?"

Geriel scanned the camp. They couldn't keep him here in case something was infected. "Collect more greenshade in the mountains." She glanced at Kew. "Could you go with him, show him where it is?"

Kew nodded.

Chinua scowled. "All right."

Uranchim and Chinua moved across the meadow and set up two separate camps. Geriel checked to ensure they left nothing behind, her muscles tight. The only positive from this situation was at least now she could test her treatments on Uranchim.

When Lien returned with Jie, his expression was bleak. "No one is to know Uranchim is infected," he said. "People will panic. We need to come up with an excuse."

"Uranchim needs quiet to work on a cure," Geriel said. "Chinua is helping us gather plants."

"The men will think it odd that a warrior is doing women's work. He's supposed to be teaching us Rhoran techniques."

Why did the Bonamese insist on dividing tasks into men's and women's work? "Lien can do that."

He laughed. "She can't have learnt much in the time she's been with you."

Geriel looked at Lien. "You should show him." Jie's prejudices were getting in the way.

She nodded. "Let's find somewhere private." Lien collected her weapons from the tent and they moved away from the camp and into the forest.

"Kixi, I know you mean well, but a few moons of training doesn't make you an expert."

Geriel smirked, some calm and light sweeping over her. She was really going to enjoy this. Maybe it would help dull the horror of her discovery.

"How about twelve years?" Lien asked.

He frowned. "What?"

"I've been training since I was eleven," Lien said.

He gaped at her.

"Attack me," she said.

Jie stepped back. "I'm not going to attack you."

"Fine." She turned to Geriel. "Attack me."

Geriel chuckled. "Be gentle." She threw a punch, but the space where Lien had been standing was empty and suddenly Geriel was on her back, staring at the sky.

Jie blinked as Lien helped her up. "How?"

"The emperor discovered I had the gift when I was eleven. Ying trained me to be fast and trained me to fight."

"Ying? As in the general in charge of the Office of Internal Scrutiny?"

She nodded.

"You can't be serious. Ying is the most vicious general Xue has."

"Had." She corrected him. "I killed him." Lien grabbed Jie, threw him over her hip and he landed with a dull thud on the ground.

Satisfaction filled Geriel as Jie stared at Lien as if he'd never seen her before. Lien helped him stand. "I'm faster and more lethal than you can imagine. When your men attacked our camp, I killed two-thirds of them."

The blood left his face. "So when you said you could have killed me…"

"She was being honest," Geriel said.

He swallowed hard. "All right. Show me."

Geriel had to give him credit, he accepted it quickly and with grace. She stood back while Lien demonstrated her skills with the bow and arrow, her knives and then her speed. It was probably wrong of her to take such pleasure in watching Jie's mouth drop open and his eyes widen. He'd learn not to underestimate Rhoran women.

When Lien finished, he said, "You could take on the whole Bonamese army by yourself."

Lien shook her head. "The gift is limited. I can only use it for so long before it runs out and I'm exhausted. We also don't know whether Xue has any more gifted warriors. Ying was one, as were Fen and a couple of Xue's concubines, but they are all dead now."

"First Princess Fen was one?" Then he shook his head. "They're all dead?"

Lien's expression sobered. "I killed them." Her voice was flat.

Geriel squeezed her sister's hand.

"All right." He nodded and pressed his lips together. "The men may have a problem with you teaching them at first, but they should come round after they've seen what you can do."

Kew trotted into the clearing. *Dhalin wants to see you.*

Geriel hoped she brought good news.

They made their way back to the camp. Uranchim and Chinua had isolated themselves across the meadow and Dhalin was waiting for them nearby.

We will inform your people about the emperor's treachery, she said. *At the same time, we'll carry the greenshade to your tribes. Kew will take Chinua to collect more of the plant.*

Geriel sighed. "Thank you. How far away is it?"

A distance.

"Can you sense the curse?" Geriel asked Kew. Just because Chinua was clear now, didn't mean she hadn't missed some part of it.

I will check him daily, Dhalin replied.

Relief filled her and she glanced at the descending sun. "Should he leave now?"

Yes. He will reach the location before dark.

Geriel glanced at Lien. "Are you happy with that?"

Lien smiled. "Little sister, in the matter of finding a cure, you are in charge."

Fear hit her. She didn't want to be in charge, it was too much responsibility. She glanced around the meadow as if that would give her an answer and caught Jie watching her, waiting for her to crumble. She would not let him think less of Rhorans. She swallowed. "Chinua can gather the plants we know will help and work with the dragons to get them to our tribes," she said. "I will monitor Uranchim and we will both search for a cure." She glanced at Jie. "How long will it take for your message to get to Lord Anming and to receive a response?"

"A quarter moon."

She was tempted to ask Dhalin if the dragons could get a message to him, but the appearance of a dragon in Chungson would cause too much of a stir and word would get back to the emperor. He couldn't know the dragons and Chungson were working together.

"I will train the Chungson soldiers," Lien added. "And Jie, Wei and I will discuss our next steps in relation to defeating Xue."

They had a plan of sorts.

Geriel walked away, but her shoulder blades itched and her chest was tight.

Everyone was watching her, and their expectations weighed heavy.

~*~

Three days of searching for a cure and Geriel had nothing. She'd scanned the properties of plenty of plants, making potions, teas and concoctions to test on poor Uranchim, but the curse kept growing in its little pot. Each time Geriel released it from its container to test potential cures, it grew larger and more difficult to contain.

The only bit of good news was the dragons had taken the greenshade to the tribes and they'd discovered the Danil tribe in the north was unaffected. They had the furthest to travel and hadn't unpacked any of the reparations. As soon as they'd heard where the curse had come from, they'd burnt the whole wagon. Dhalin was flying there today to check their blood and confirm there were no traces of the disease.

The rest of the tribes already reported multiple people badly affected, covered in pustules. The greenshade had been welcomed. Only one other tribe had a gifted healer and he was as exhausted as Amslan. The dragon who had gone to Geriel's tribe had reported Jochi was learning fast and helping to scan the tribe. It lightened Geriel's heart, soothed one of her worries.

Geriel made sure she had all the tools she needed and went to find Lien at the main fire. Soldiers stared at her as she walked by. She ignored them. She'd been here days, and still they treated her as an oddity. What was wrong with these people? They'd accepted Lien teaching—particularly after she'd defeated several of them during exercises—but they still eyed Geriel with suspicion. Not only was she female and Rhoran, but she was also a healer.

At first she'd attempted to speak to them, and one day when she'd returned to camp early, she'd offered to spar with someone who didn't have a partner but had been laughed at.

She hadn't bothered to show them her skills. Changing long-held beliefs about her people was not her task here.

Geriel's footsteps slowed. Lien was speaking with Jie. Geriel had hoped he would already be busy with something else by now. She'd avoided him, and the rest of the soldiers as much as possible, but mealtimes were difficult because Lien always ate with him. Geriel tried not to let it bother her, but something in the way he looked at her—as if she wasn't quite right—disturbed her. She'd taken to sitting on the opposite side of the table to him and listening to them talk about Lien's brother. Most days she was too tired to do more than chew her food anyway, scanning the plants having taken its toll.

Lien glanced up. "Are you heading out?"

Geriel nodded. "I'm heading higher into the mountains, following the stream."

"Who's going with you?" Jie's dark eyes demanded an answer, peering deep into her soul.

She squirmed under his gaze and made herself stiffen. "No one." Dhalin was flying to Danil today.

He frowned. "I'll go."

Her muscles tensed. "That's not necessary."

"You will be focused on plants and not your surroundings, and many dangerous animals stalk these forests."

"I don't need a guard." Geriel glanced at Lien, hoping she would back her up.

"He's right, sister. Someone needs to go with you in case you are injured."

Geriel narrowed her eyes. "Why not send one of your men?"

Jie's lips quirked upwards. "They're not my men to order. I will get my things and then we can go." He left before she could protest.

"You'll be safe with him, sister."

That wasn't Geriel's concern. She hated the way he made her so self-conscious, as if she was a creature to be studied and understood. But part of her was drawn to him too, and that was even worse. She still remembered the brush of his fingers against her wrists when he'd tied her up.

Nothing good could come from her attraction. He was Bonamese, much older than her, and all her focus had to be on finding a cure. He was also so much more contained than Rhoran men—quiet, intense, showing little emotion unless something made him laugh. The difference was intriguing—and unsettling.

Jie returned to the fire with his bow and quiver, a sword strapped to his waist and carrying a bag which she assumed contained food and drink. They would be gone all day.

"Safe journey, sister," Lien said.

She forced a smile. "I'll see you when I return." She moved towards the stream, Jie falling into step beside her, not too close to touch, but close enough for her to be aware of his every movement. Her skin prickled. Should she make conversation? No, silence was best.

The rocky ground on the edge of the stream allowed her to concentrate on her footing, moving as quickly as she dared past the area she had already searched. She still panted, but climbing was easier than it had been a couple of days ago. She was getting used to the mountain's slopes.

Jie followed her without a word. She'd expected him to take control, to tell her what to do and where to go. It was nice he didn't.

She stopped a couple of times to scan plants she hadn't seen before and the second time she did, Jie asked, "Why do you close your eyes before you pick the plant? Is it some kind of prayer?"

Geriel glanced at him. She'd forgotten they hadn't told him about her gift. Lien had decided to keep it a secret in case word spread and the soldiers wanted her to heal any injury they had no matter how minor. She hesitated. He should understand the reasons not to tell everyone. "You've seen Lien's gift of speed," she said. "I have a gift of healing. I can connect with plants and see their healing properties and I can heal some injuries." She didn't have time to go into detail now. "Let's keep going."

After an hour or so, she slowed. She didn't recognise

the plants clumped together under a large tree. She sipped from her water flask and took out her knife.

"You climb well." Jie's voice made her jump.

She raised her eyebrows. "Thank you?" What did he expect her to say?

A slight quirk to his mouth. "I'll check our surrounds." Then he moved quietly into the forest.

She let out a breath. If nothing else, he was a good warrior, moving silently through the trees. She'd observed him with the other soldiers when she'd arrived back in the evening. He fired his arrows fast and accurately, and his sword work was impressive.

She squatted to study her first plant and braced herself to access her gift. She'd watched Amslan get stronger and stronger over the past few moons as he used his gift more frequently, but each time she used hers, it dwindled and became harder to access. She'd asked Dhalin about it, but the dragon was waiting on advice from other dragons.

Slowly Geriel scanned the first leafy plant. How many plants had she already scanned, how many samples had she picked? It was a never-ending task and taking far too long.

No, better she did *something*. But the problem was, each plant could be prepared in a multitude of ways; raw, boiled, baked, ground, and the cure might be found in its roots, leaves, flowers, stems or seeds. Perhaps the person had been cured in spring when all the flowers bloomed and if the cure had come from the flowers, then she wouldn't find it now, not when autumn was near and many flowers were no longer blooming.

She needed more information about the rumour. Hopefully a response from the lord of Chungson would come soon.

Geriel placed the plant in her bag and sat back on her heels. A movement across the stream caught her attention and the hairs on her arms stood on end.

Wolf.

It stared at her, amber eyes, white chest, straggly grey fur and its ribs prominent. Hungry.

Slowly she stood. Wolves rarely travelled alone, but for this one to look so starved at the end of summer might mean it had lost its pack.

The stream wasn't a large barrier for the wolf. It could jump it or wade through easily enough. She'd left her bow and arrow resting against a tree behind her and though she had her sabre at her waist, she didn't want the wolf close enough for her to use it.

She stepped back, continually scanning her surroundings to make sure other wolves weren't flanking her. Where was Jie? Loud noises wouldn't scare the wolf, not if it was desperate for food. She wanted her weapon in her hand before she attempted anything.

The wolf stepped forward.

Another three steps before she'd reach her bow. She took another step.

So did the wolf.

If only she was as fast as Lien, then she wouldn't have a problem. But she wasn't. She had to scare it.

She raised her hands above her head as she stepped closer to her weapon, making herself as big as possible. "You don't want to attack me." Her words sounded loud in the stillness around her, but weren't loud enough to scare.

The wolf's ears flicked at the noise.

She waved her hands at the wolf.

Instead of scaring it, the wolf crouched and then pounced, jumping across the stream. Too close for her bow. She unsheathed her sabre as the creature leapt at her, mouth open, teeth sharp.

She sliced the sabre upwards as the wolf's body hit her, claws slicing into her arm. Red hot pain seared her and she yelled.

The wolf jerked twice, its jaw close to her neck and then went still, its weight pinning her to the ground. She pushed hard, and the wolf shifted, but not enough. Blood made her hands slick and the stench of its innards spilling out on top of her made her retch.

"Geriel!"

Relief filled her at Jie's voice and seconds later the wolf was shoved away from her body.

"Are you hurt?" Jie jerked her to a seated position and she hissed as his fingers pressed into the deep scratches on her arm.

"I'm fine." Two arrows pierced the wolf's body. If her sabre hadn't killed it, Jie's arrows would have. Warm blood seeped through her clothing. Ugh.

"I told you to stay aware of your surroundings," he said.

She glared at him as she got to her feet. "I was." She stumbled towards the stream, the adrenaline pumping through her body making her a little light-headed.

Jie steadied her. She snatched her arm back. "Check if there are any more."

"They would have already appeared if there were," he said.

She hoped he was right. Kneeling at the edge of the stream, she washed her hands and then splashed water on her face, scrubbing the blood off it. She bled through the ripped edges of her dress sleeve. She might need stitches.

Geriel unwound her sash and pulled her dress off, dumping it on the ground next to her.

"What are you doing?" Jie gasped, his eyes wide. Quickly he averted his gaze.

"Examining the injury," she replied. "Does my partially naked body offend you?" She wore silk bindings around her breasts so her modesty was covered but the Bonamese were sensitive about propriety. She splashed water on her arm and gritted her teeth at the cold and the sharp sting in her wound. Definitely some stitches. The gashes ran from the top of her shoulder, halfway to her elbow.

"Let me see." Jie dropped to his knees beside her and pried at her wound.

She tried to pull back, but he held firm. "That hurts."

"You need to get all the dirt out so it doesn't get infected."

She almost laughed. "I know. I'm a healer, remember?"

He met her gaze, and for a second his cheeks flushed, but then he said, "Right. I'll get you a bandage."

She washed her dress in the stream and then used an edge of the fabric to thoroughly clean her wound. When she was satisfied, she let Jie wind the bandage around her arm. His touch was light, his movements sure. This wasn't his first time helping an injured person.

"Thank you."

He nodded. "Can't you heal yourself?"

"No. My gift doesn't work like that." She was the only person she couldn't heal—assuming she could access her gift.

"We should get you back."

"No. Lien can stitch it together this evening. The bandage will be fine until then."

She finished washing her dress and spread it out over a rock to dry. The air was far cooler in the mountains, but she'd warm up as soon as she continued scanning.

"Are all Rhoran this stubborn?" Jie's question made her blink in surprise.

"It's not stubbornness. I'm capable of continuing my work. It's only a scratch." A scratch that continued to throb and pull, but she wouldn't tell him. Instead she returned to the plant she'd been examining and Jie disposed of the wolf.

She worked through until midday when Jie pulled some dried meat out of his bag and handed it to her. "You need to eat."

She bit into it. He was right. Though she didn't use much of her gift at a time, the constant use wore at her. She sat with her back against a tree and studied him. He'd been silent since the attack, occasionally patrolling the area, but never far from her.

It was strange to work in such complete silence. Her tribe always talked to each other when they worked, discussing tribal matters or simply catching up. The silence made it far easier for Geriel to concentrate.

"How does it work?" Jie sat across from her.

She frowned. "What?"

"Your gift. How does it work?"

Geriel hesitated. Though Jie was an ally, and Lien trusted him, it was weird to confide in a Bonamese. "I can connect with a person's body and heal it."

The scepticism on his face was clear.

"Shall I demonstrate?"

"On what?"

She smiled. "You." She pointed to his hand which he'd scratched at some time during the morning.

He shuffled closer and held his palm out. She placed

her hands around it. "It will get hot for a moment." She closed her eyes and ran through her meditation, her muscles tight. A scratch was normally easy to fix. She connected with him, felt his interest in what she was doing. Her face heated. Somehow it was so much more intimate to heal him. Perhaps because she was so aware of holding his hand. She drew her gift from its well and focused on the cut, pictured it healing, the edges of the skin coming together. She brushed her thumb over the area. When she opened her eyes, Jie stared at his hand and then at her.

"You didn't believe me," she said.

He shook his head. "I've never heard of such a thing. Having a healer like you in battle could be a tremendous advantage."

She nodded. "To a certain degree. We only have a set amount of energy before we must rest. If we use too much, we can lose the gift entirely." She still held his hand, brushing her thumb over where the scratch had been. Her face heated and she let go, placing her hands in her lap. "It's one reason your attack on the camp didn't kill many. That and Lien fighting with us."

"How many healers do you have like this?"

"Four. When we're not at war, there's little need for them, so others use their gift for different things. My father can communicate with horses." Pain pierced her. Was he still alive? She had to get back to work. The longer she sat here, the more ill her father became. She ate the rest of her food and got to her feet.

"Is there anything I can do to help?" Jie asked.

"Do you know much about plants?"

"I know some basic remedies. I was posted out to the desert border outpost and we didn't have a lot of supplies. We had to make do with what we could find."

Curiosity stirred. "Tell me about them."

Jie described the plants he'd used for different ailments as Geriel worked. He told her only the pertinent facts, describing the plants. A few descriptions she recognised, but not all. Each time she scanned a new plant he fell silent, as if he realised her need to concentrate, and then helped her collect the samples. She hadn't had such an engaging conversation in a long time.

As the temperature dropped and the sun sank lower in the sky, Jie stood. "It's time to get back."

She fetched her dress from where it had been drying. Her nose wrinkled at the dampness, but she put it on anyway and tied the sash.

Both she and Jie carried a bag of plants as well as their weapons.

"Lien seems happy living with your people."

Geriel glanced at him. His expression gave nothing away. "I believe she is. My tribe welcomed her when she arrived."

"And your family adopted her?"

"Yes. Rhoran wedding traditions state a man must fetch his bride from her parents' yurt. No one wanted to return to the imperial palace after the emperor tried to kill her, so my parents offered to adopt her. Father had already spent hours with her, teaching her how to ride, and Mother taught her about home life." She smiled. "Lien slowly showed her true self in those moments when she was enjoying herself and not thinking about how she should behave."

"Thank you." He turned to her. "She was like a little sister to me, but I wasn't allowed to visit her. I worried about her, as did my parents, but we couldn't go against Xue. I observed her becoming the perfect imperial princess at ceremonies and not the high-spirited, fun child I remembered."

"The high-spirited child is still with her. You should see her ride across the steppes. She's incredible."

He smiled and became so much more approachable. "I'd like to see that."

Her heart skipped a beat and she glanced away. "I'm sure you will."

"You two make enough noise an army could sneak up on you."

Geriel gasped and Jie whirled around so fast, sword in his hand, he was almost a blur.

Chinua. He carried two large bags with him and glared suspiciously at them. "Shouldn't one of you be alert for danger?"

Jie grunted and lowered his sword, stepping back behind Geriel as Kew trotted up to him, her skin flushing pink in happiness.

Geriel hid her smile. "Have you finished collecting greenshade?"

Chinua raised the bags he held. "This is the last batch. The dragons have taken most of it to the tribes already."

She placed a hand on his arm. "Let me check you." She swayed a little at the effort and Jie placed his hands on her hips to steady her. The warmth distracted her and it took her a minute to refocus. Chinua was still clear. She exhaled and opened her eyes again. "You're fine."

She stepped back, colliding with Jie who held her steady again. "Sorry." Her face was hot as fire. Chinua narrowed his eyes. She didn't need him getting protective of her. "Shall we go? One run in with a wolf a day is enough for me."

As she hoped, the mention of a wolf distracted Chinua. "What happened?"

She showed him the tears in her tunic and explained

as she walked next to him. Jie dropped behind them and she missed his presence, but felt him watching her. She refused to look back. What she'd felt today—the camaraderie—was simply joy at sharing knowledge with another person. She was doing what she could to improve relationships between their two countries.

But that wasn't true.

She couldn't pretend her hips didn't still zing from his touch. She'd never been this intrigued or attracted to a man before.

She would have to ignore it. There were far more important things she had to do right now.

Like finding the cure.

Chapter 8

Geriel rose early the next day and headed to Uranchim's camp. Though exhaustion fogged her mind and her arm throbbed from the wolf attack, she was eager to test the plants she and Jie had gathered. Lien had stitched Geriel's wound the night before, and Geriel had gone to bed early, needing the rest and the distance from Jie.

She shouldn't be thinking about him.

Uranchim sat by his fire, heating a pot of water. "Morning."

She placed the bags of plants down and smiled at him. "How are you today?"

He held out his hand and she scanned him. The pot still held.

"I found a few new plants yesterday. One has clumping properties which might make it easier to control the disease."

Uranchim nodded. "Good. It's about time we found something useful."

The comment stung, though he didn't seem to mean it as a dig at her ability. She passed him the cloud flower. "Make it into a paste." It would be easier to swallow than chewing on a bunch of the plant.

He got to work, while she recorded the information in her book. Preparation and testing were the only thing Uranchim could help with. He couldn't record the information in case the disease was transferred to the things he touched.

There was a whoosh of wind above them and Dhalin landed next to the camp.

Geriel's heart leapt. "How did it go?"

The Danil tribe are free from the curse.

Uranchim whooped and Geriel grinned. "That's such good news!"

Dhalin inclined her head. *Batzorig burnt everything from the Bonamese and has sent his healers into their mountains to gather plants they believe may help. He and his tribe are available for anything you need of them.*

"I'll tell Lien. Thank you for your help."

Falin told me how effective the quarantining has been in the Erseg and Adhan tribes, Dhalin continued. *I have asked the elders whether I may teach more of our healers how to identify the curse and send them to the remaining camps to segregate them.*

Falin was one of the dragons who'd carried the greenshade to the tribes. Hope bloomed in Geriel's heart. "That would be a great help."

I will tell you their answer. She examined the plants Geriel had gathered. *We use that for infections in the blood.* She nodded to the cloud flower.

Geriel made a note. "What else do you use these plants for?"

Dhalin settled next to her and began to teach.

Late in the day, Lien hurried to Uranchim's camp, concern clear on her face. Geriel stood and met her across the meadow, not wanting her to get close to Uranchim. "What's wrong?"

"Wei broke his arm during training. Can you heal it?"

"Do you think it wise?" She could imagine the soldiers' responses if they knew what she could do.

Lien nodded. "It's a bad break. If he's not healed, he may have to return home and we'll have to deal with someone new."

Someone who might not be as accommodating. "All right. Where is he?"

"In the infirmary."

Geriel blinked. "They have an infirmary?"

Her sister grimaced. "Apparently. Jie said their doctor refused to have anything to do with us and so they thought it prudent not to mention it."

Unbelievable.

Dhalin joined them. *May I watch? I would like to learn how you heal bones.*

Geriel nodded as nerves coalesced in her stomach. It had been a while since she'd healed a broken arm and she was still tired from using her gift yesterday. Would she have enough strength to heal him? Bones required far more energy than tissue to heal.

Three men were inside the infirmary. Wei's broken arm was in a sling and the man Geriel guessed was the doctor was cleaning a nasty gash on another soldier's head.

"What happened?" she asked.

The doctor scowled at her and Lien. "What are you doing here?" Then his eyes widened. "Dragon."

None of my kin did this.

The man nodded. "Sorry, no, you surprised me." He cleared his throat. "He didn't block an attack fast enough."

May I see if I can help?

The doctor frowned and Lien said, "Dhalin is a

healer. She can heal some of our injuries, but not others."

Geriel glanced at Lien who gave a small nod. Right. She was hiding the fact Geriel was the healer.

The soldier with the gash appeared a little concerned but nodded.

Geriel, place your hand on his arm.

She smiled at Dhalin. Maybe they could teach each other.

She touched the man and closed her eyes. Dhalin's consciousness inspected the swelling and bleeding in the man's head. The dragon tried to drain the swelling away, but her technique wasn't quite right. *Show me how you do it.*

Dhalin's voice must be only in her head. Geriel hesitated. She was meant to heal Wei not this soldier. Would she have enough strength to do both? She hoped so. Slowly she drained the swelling and fixed the cut.

I see. Your technique is different. You do not use much of the power inside of you.

Geriel shook her head and opened her eyes. She couldn't ask what Dhalin meant with the others here. Instead she asked the soldier, "How do you feel?"

"Great."

The doctor stared at the dragon. "The cut is gone."

Dhalin inclined her head. *We shall examine Wei next.*

Wei had come over to watch and now he went back to his bed. "What do I need to do?"

Relax.

Jie entered the tent and Geriel's heart jumped. She didn't want him here. He was too much of a distraction.

"How are you?" he asked Wei.

"Broken arm, but the dragon is going to fix it."

Jie raised his eyebrows, looked at Geriel, but stayed

silent. At least he wasn't giving away her secret.

She placed her hand on Wei's arm. The break was clean and the doctor had aligned it well.

I could not fix Lien's bones after she was injured by Ying. Show me how.

Geriel drew on her gift, pulling it from the well. Then slowly she fused the broken bones back together. Her body strained as she pulled on the gift, knowing her well was almost dry. She had to be careful not to empty it. Her hand shook and she gritted her teeth.

Don't strain so. Dhalin's essence fed her.

Easier said than done. She fought to drag the gift from the bottom. With a last burst of energy, she healed the remaining break and drew back, out of Wei's body. Her head spun and she gasped, her body damp with sweat. As she shifted away from Wei, she swayed and fell right into Jie's arms.

~*~

Something cold and wet pressed against Geriel's forehead. "Wake up, sister."

The idea of opening her eyes seemed like too much hard work. Geriel's whole body was lethargic, heavy, and ached.

"Open your eyes!" The male voice barked the order with such authority that she frowned and obeyed, the bright light making her blink, and the shapes above her came into focus. Lien and Jie.

Lien sighed. "Are you all right?"

"What happened?"

"You fainted after Dhalin healed Wei," Lien said.

Dhalin? No, the dragon couldn't heal bones. She shifted her head. Wei and the doctor stood off to the side examining Wei's arm. That's right. They couldn't know she was the healer.

Get her a drink. Dhalin stood at the end of her bed and Jie hurried to fetch it.

Strange he would be so quick to obey the dragon.

"How are you?" Lien asked.

"Tired." Sitting was too much hard work. "How long was I out?"

"Only a few minutes."

Jie brought a cup to her and gently helped her sit. She leaned against him, not having enough energy to sit on her own. She inhaled deeply and his masculine scent stirred something inside of her. He placed the cup to her lips and she sipped the revitalising tea. Dhalin placed her nose against Geriel's skin and sent her a boost of energy.

We should talk about what happened.

Geriel nodded. Maybe the dragon could help her.

As her strength returned, she still leaned into Jie, his arm around her waist, her head resting on his shoulder. It was a nice place to be. Comforting and warm.

Geriel moved away. She shouldn't be getting strength from him. Her face flushed. "Thank you." She glanced at Wei. "How is your arm?"

"Healed." He shook his head. "I never knew the dragons were so powerful."

She smiled.

Lien handed her some food. "Eat, sister and rest a little while."

She didn't want to stay in the infirmary. "I'm fine." She braced herself to stand and Jie touched her arm.

"Rest." His eyes dared her to disobey him.

She wasn't quite that strong yet. With a sigh, she settled back onto the bed.

"There's no need for everyone to stay," Lien said. "I will sit with my sister until she is well enough to move. I'm sure you have other things to do."

Jie scowled, but Wei nodded. "We should discuss tomorrow's plan. Jie, why don't you come to my tent?"

"Don't let her move until she is well," Jie said as he left the tent.

"I won't." Lien smiled. "Jie seems quite protective of you."

Geriel's face flushed. "He knows what I can do," she said. "I guess he wants me to find a cure."

Lien grinned. "Maybe."

Geriel turned her attention to Dhalin. "Did you understand what I did?"

Dhalin nodded. *Your bone is different in structure to ours. Now I understand, I can heal it in future.*

Good. They would need all the help they could get when the war against the emperor started.

Why visualise a well and not a river?

Geriel blinked. "I was taught the gift is finite. If I draw too much I could lose it."

Dhalin snorted. *I don't know enough about it, though my kin might. I shall ask. Next time visualise drawing from a river. It might not exhaust you so. A river runs endlessly.*

Here in the mountains it did. On the steppes in summer they had to be careful as the level of the riverbeds fell. If she lost the gift, she would be useless to her people. That couldn't happen. She asked Lien, "What do you visualise?"

She shrugged. "I don't visualise anything. My meditation centres me and I pull it from where it lives." She pursed her lips. "Perhaps I'll try a river next time."

The food had given Geriel enough energy to stand. "Let's go. I need to check Chinua."

Lien shook her head, but helped her to her feet. "Do it in the morning. Tonight you will rest."

Lien was right though Geriel didn't want to admit it.

I shall return tomorrow, Dhalin said.

Geriel smiled. She prayed Dhalin's kin would know more about the gift and help her.

The dragon flew away and Lien took hold of Geriel's arm. "Let's sit by the fire."

As they walked, a couple of Chungson soldiers called out a greeting to Lien, though they still looked at Geriel with disinterest. At least Lien was changing their opinions on what women were capable of.

"How is the search for the cure progressing?" Lien asked as she sat by their fire.

Geriel's pulse skipped a beat. "We found a plant today that helps to clump the disease. It will make it easier to control and seal it." It was a small step in the right direction. "It's not a cure, but I sent Chinua and Kew to collect more of it. If the dragons agree to their healers going to the camps to help quarantine the disease, it might really help. Particularly if Dhalin can teach the dragons how to clump and seal it."

"You've done well to find that in such a short amount of time."

A quarter moon wasn't short. Not when the curse could advance quickly. "Any news from Chungson?"

Lien shook her head. "I hope we'll receive a response tomorrow."

Geriel prayed the Chungson knew of a cure, but it was unlikely. Information on cures tended to spread quickly throughout the land—even to Rhora. Traders travelled from far lands to swap their goods for Rhoran horses and brought their knowledge with them.

She yawned.

"You should retire early today," Lien said. "You've been working hard for days now."

A good night's sleep would help. Geriel had prepared all the potential cures for today and there was nothing to do until tomorrow, when it was light. She stood as Jie walked over.

"Wei would like to speak to you, Lien."

Lien nodded and stood. "I'll go now."

Jie turned to Geriel. "How are you?" He examined her as if looking for signs she would faint again.

Her body warmed. "Tired. I am going to sleep now."

"Let me help you."

Her muscles tensed. "That's not necessary." It wasn't far at all.

"It wouldn't look good if you fainted again." He took hold of her arm, effectively cutting off any argument.

She was too tired to argue with him, and the warmth of his hand on her arm soothed her.

In only a few steps he stopped outside her tent. "You healed Wei, didn't you?"

She nodded. "Dhalin didn't know how to. Their bones are different from ours."

He frowned. "Should it affect you so badly?"

No point telling him she hadn't mastered her gift. "I've been using it constantly over the past few days. Healing the soldier's head and then Wei's arm used the last of my reserves."

"We must make sure no one finds out what you can do. There are too many minor injuries in camp for you to heal."

"That's why we didn't tell Wei."

He nodded in agreement. "Good. Rest well." He stared at her for a moment longer before he turned on his heel and walked away.

Geriel exhaled. What was she meant to make of the man?

~*~

The next morning Dhalin arrived as Geriel finished her breakfast. A thrill spread through her at the sight of the dragon's large wingspan and the smooth way she glided into land. Impressive. Kew snorted.

"Your wings are bigger than they were," Geriel said to her.

It is a long process. Dhalin can help them grow but it tires me, and there is so much else I need to learn.

"Will you be able to fly one day?" Lien asked.

I hope so.

"What are you learning?" Geriel asked.

The mind speak is the most important. Choosing who can hear me takes practice and concentration. Also how to scan my surroundings for threats. I am not strong enough yet to do both with any regularity. I miss things. Kew flapped her wings in irritation. *And there is so much I have to learn about dragon society and etiquette. I feel like a baby when younger dragons can do so much more than I can.*

Geriel could relate. "I'm sure it will come in time. You've only been with them a few moons."

Kew sighed.

Geriel cleaned her bowl and gathered her things, then both dragons accompanied her to Chinua's camp. Geriel stopped briefly by the horses to check them. Lien let the Chungson ride them during training so they were getting some exercise, but there had been no point riding them on her journeys into the forest because she'd be constantly mounting and dismounting. Khulan nudged her shoulder wanting attention and Geriel spent a few more minutes with her horse before reaching Chinua.

"What do you want me to do today?" he asked as she scanned him.

I have spoken to my elders, Dhalin said. *They will send one dragon to the tribes and help them isolate the curse. He can carry the cloud flower.*

Geriel's heart leapt. "Thank you." That could make all the difference.

Chinua straightened, hope on his face. "Is it a cure?"

She shook her head. "It will slow the spread though."

His face fell. Both their sisters were infected. "Do you need me to collect more of it?"

"Yes. We need about the same amount again. Kew can show you where it is."

He nodded. "What will you do?"

"Dhalin and I will continue to search."

Chinua stood. "I'd better go. The sooner they get the plant, the better."

Dhalin was silent a moment and then said, *Another of my brethren wishes to join us. We believe we can learn a lot from you.*

"Of course. They are most welcome." She wanted to repay them for their help. "I need to check Uranchim."

They walked to his camp to find him huddled around his fire, face pale and damp with sweat. Geriel's heart raced as she squatted next to him. "You're ill."

"Tried a new concoction. It doesn't agree with me."

Foolish man. He wasn't meant to try anything by himself, it was too dangerous. "What?"

"Egg leaf tea."

She knelt beside him, placed her hands on his skin. His whole being looked murky. She tried swirling the murkiness but unlike the oily feel of the curse, this was more like smoke, dissipating and reforming. She didn't know what to do, how to fix it. She wasn't strong enough.

Calm yourself.

She exhaled, Dhalin's voice soothing her. She wasn't alone in this.

Egg leaf can be counteracted by elm's bark.

Right. She should have thought of that. She dug into her medicine bag. She was relying too heavily on her gift, not on her knowledge. Foolish. Quickly she made a tea with the elm's bark. Uranchim shook.

Reining in her panic, she poured the tea into a cup and blew on it to cool it. Then she held the cup to his mouth. "It's hot. Drink slowly."

The man did as he was told, spilling some, but swallowing most. He closed his eyes, still shaking, but the colour in his face was better.

"Lie down."

She helped him to the ground and then she cleaned up, washing her hands thoroughly. It was impossible to avoid touching Uranchim entirely.

Slowly the shakes stopped and his skin dried. He sat up. "Thank you."

Geriel huffed out a breath and glared at him. "Don't experiment alone again!"

He nodded. "Will you check me?"

She placed her hands on his skin. The murky cloud was gone, but so was the seal she'd put around the curse. The oily substance spread through his body. "We need the cloud flower." She fetched the remaining sample they had and pounded it into a paste. "The egg leaf dissolved the container holding the curse."

Uranchim grimaced.

She handed him the paste. "Eat it."

He did as she ordered and she waited a few minutes before she touched him again. It was working. The curse was slower, sluggish and clumping together. She visualised a deeper well this time and drew on her gift, swirling Uranchim's blood around until the curse came together in a single lump and then she sealed it in a pot.

She opened her eyes, fatigue not hitting her as

quickly this time. The flower helped her do her work.

"Is it done?" Uranchim asked.

She nodded.

"Thank you."

A grey dragon landed across from them.

This is Falin.

Greetings. Falin bowed his head.

"Welcome," Geriel said. "Thank you for joining us."

Geriel just healed Uranchim. Watch. Dhalin replayed the events through Geriel's mind.

Interesting. Falin tilted his head.

Desperation clawed at Geriel, wanting him to know a cure. She blocked the thought, hoping the dragons couldn't hear it. "Uranchim, you should rest for the morning. Don't take any more concoctions on your own."

He nodded.

Come with us, Dhalin said. *We wish to show you something.*

She followed them away from the camp, and they led her deep into the forest, away from the stream. Many of the plants she recognised, but she stopped occasionally to gather those that were new to her. Geriel was careful not to trip over the lush undergrowth, though the pace the dragons set made it difficult for her to keep up and she panted. After several hours the path they took became less overgrown—not quite a trail but the plants were more ground covers than shrubs. Finally a hushing noise reached her ears and she strained to recognise it. Was it water?

The noise grew louder and she followed the dragons into a clearing. The sun shone above and sparkled on the surface of a large pool of water surrounded by rocks, some with a smattering of green moss on them. A waterfall cascaded from an overhang into the pool below. Brightly coloured flowers carpeted the flat ground around the rocks and Geriel inhaled the damp sweet scent of fresh water. "What is this place?"

Our learning place, Dhalin said. *Drink the water and then find a place to sit.*

Nerves filled her stomach as she stepped forward, careful where she trod, not wanting to squash anything or show she had been there. Her boots slid a little over the smooth rocks but she caught herself and then squatted by the crystal-clear water. Rocks shimmered on the bottom of the pool and she caught a glimpse of her own reflection. She'd lost weight since she'd been here, her face thinner than it had been and dark rings circled her eyes. Sweat plastered the bits of her dark hair that had fallen out of her braid to her forehead. She looked a mess. Why hadn't anyone said so?

She splashed her face, the cold water soothing the heat from her body, and then she cupped her hands and drank.

So fresh, so clear, the water re-energised her like nothing ever had.

She drank some more, careful not to overindulge and then scanned the area for a place to sit. She wanted somewhere comfortable, but the whisper of the waterfall falling into the pool and the light spray it gave off was soothing. Crossing her legs, she sat on the rocks on the edge of the pool, placing her hands on her knees.

Good, Falin said. *You already feel a connection to the water. That will help.*

Concentrate on the sound, Dhalin said. *Block out everything except the water falling into the pool.*

Geriel closed her eyes. As she focused, the noise became louder and louder, filling every sense until she didn't feel the hard rock under her, or the cool spray on her face, and inside her mind was the water falling in an endless stream.

Yes. Falin's voice. *It is endless, just as your gift is. This is what you should visualise when you heal.*

He was wrong. The dragons didn't know enough about it, didn't really understand it. She pulled back, the rock digging into her bottom and the spray cold and unpleasant.

Relax, Dhalin said. *Do not fight it. I have been studying your gift, studying you. Your power is much like mine, a muscle to be trained, to be stretched and strengthened, but your fear won't let you do more than simple exercises.*

Every muscle in her body tightened and she shook her head. "I was always told the gift is limited. If I lose it, I'll be useless to my tribe."

Dhalin's touch on her mind was gentle. *It is not true. Even if you were to lose the gift, your knowledge of healing is the best—far deeper than Uranchim's and more than Amslan's. He relies on his gift, rather than learning more techniques.*

Geriel had no words.

You have the ability to be the strongest healer of your people, Falin said. *You need to work past your fear. Focus on the waterfall again.*

The idea of being so powerful, so essential to Rhora was terrifying. It meant she had a far higher place to fall from when she failed.

You will not fail, Dhalin said. *We will not let you. Close your eyes.*

She had hoped the dragons could help her. She had to accept their help. Geriel shut her eyes, allowing Dhalin's faith to give her strength. Soon the soothing shush of the water filled her senses again.

Good. Reach your right hand to the side and place it on the ground. Feel the moss. Connect with it.

Her fingers brushed the soft, spongy moss.

What do you sense?

Geriel connected to it, let its essence flow through her. There was no strain, no difficulty, it was as if the moss wanted her to know everything about it. "It will heal headaches and other minor pain."

Yes. Now touch the plant on your left side.

Her fingers brushed a leafy plant growing abundantly in the area. "This is edible."

What else? Falin asked.

She reviewed its properties. "It will fight infection." Could it fight the curse as well? She'd have to try it. She opened her eyes.

How do you feel?

Energised. As if she'd slept for a moon and could ride for days. As if she could scan all the plants around the pool without any trouble. Hope blossomed in her.

Show me.

Slowly she stood. Worry tried to push its way in, but she deflected it. This was her time, her chance to master her gift. Geriel focused on the waterfall, visualised it in her mind and touched the pretty pink flower poking up in the reeds between the rocks. Its perfume would calm the mind. The ground cover near it would disinfect cuts. Elation filled her and she grinned. She would find a cure.

When she finished scanning all the plants in the clearing, she didn't need food or rest to energise her. She'd found one plant which could perhaps break down and dissolve the curse. She picked a couple of samples and placed them in her bag. Her whole body was light, her brain clear and her heart full of hope. "Thank you." She wanted to hug them both, but she wasn't certain it would be welcomed.

Dhalin exposed her teeth in a smile. *Watching you has*

helped us. You must remember how to do this.

Falin tilted his head. *Chinua has sprained his ankle. Kew says he'll need help getting back to camp.*

It sounded serious. "How far away is he?"

We can reach him by mid-afternoon.

Which didn't give them much time to get back to camp before dark. "Can you heal him, Dhalin?"

This will be a good test for you, Dhalin said. *Let's go.*

Geriel bit her tongue. Now wasn't the time to argue that she had to keep searching for a cure. The dragons were taking the time to help her and Dhalin was right, she should practise, make sure she could use what she'd learnt with people.

The trek was a lot harder, moving further up the mountain, a steeper slope and a rougher path. At one stage both dragons left her to fly over a difficult pass while she climbed a small rock face. By the time she found Chinua sitting with his back against a tree, her breath was coming in gasps and her muscles ached.

"Geriel, thank Qadan." Chinua's hair lay damp against his forehead, his face was red and he grimaced in pain. His foot and ankle had swollen to almost twice their normal size.

Geriel winced. "What happened?" She knelt next to him, placed her hands lightly on his foot.

"My foot slipped off a rock and twisted."

The pain pulsed at her, making her grimace. Pushing past it, she scanned his foot, saw the ripped tendons and muscles. He'd made a real mess of it. It was far worse than anything she'd healed before. Amslan would know what to do.

Hear the waterfall, Dhalin said. *Kew, watch what she does. You should learn too.*

Dhalin's voice soothed her. Taking long, slow breaths, she felt the panic recede as she brought the sound back to her ears, let the shush soothe and focus her. First she took away some of Chinua's pain. Next she examined the rips and tears, untangling them. She visualised how the tendons and muscles should go together and then one-by-one, she knitted and fused them so they were whole again, reaching into the waterfall to get her gift when she needed it.

When she opened her eyes it was almost dark. "That took longer than I thought," she said. "How do you feel?"

Chinua rotated his ankle and grinned. "Feels like new." Slowly he got to his feet and tested its strength. "That's perfect. Thanks." He hugged her and then studied her closely. "How are you? Do you need some food?" He reached for his sack.

"I'm a little hungry." But only because she hadn't eaten much today. Her energy levels were low, but not exhausted. "We should leave now to make it back to camp before dark."

Better you stay here and return in the morning, Falin said. *I will tell the camp.* He took to the air.

Chinua nodded. "It's a tricky path down."

The wolf attack played across Geriel's mind. "We should build a fire." Though she'd never built a fire with wood and twigs as a base.

We will monitor the surroundings, Dhalin said.

Together Chinua and Geriel gathered wood and found a slightly bigger clearing to spend the night. Chinua had brought gear with him because he'd been planning to spend more time in the mountains.

"Did you find much cloud flower?" Geriel asked as they settled next to the fire for the night, Kew by her side.

"Yeah. One of the dragons took the first batch to the Gertan tribe. He was going to quarantine them better and use the cloud flower to stop the curse spreading."

They were making slow progress.

There is more cloud flower higher in the mountain, Kew said. *But Chinua hurt himself before we could get to it.*

"I found another plant today that might cure the disease," she said. "I'll test it on Uranchim tomorrow."

Chinua gave her a long probing look. "Is it too late now? So many people are infected, can anything we find reverse the effects?"

Her chest squeezed. "I don't know. I can't give up."

He shoved a log on the fire, his movements jerky. "Will we even have a tribe to come home to?" The pain in his voice tore her heart.

"I'm doing everything I can." At least searching for a cure kept her busy. Chinua had days of gathering plants when his mind could wander to all the possible horrible outcomes.

"I can't understand how you can be so calm," he growled. "Doesn't it eat you up that our families are suffering, that they might be dying while we're hunting for a mythical cure on a mountain?"

She flinched. "Of course it does! The whole fate of our people is resting on my shoulders." Tears pricked her eyes. "I'm terrified of failing." Curse him for making her admit it.

Chinua swore and dragged her close to him and hugged her. "I'm sorry. I'm so frustrated. I keep picturing Saran covered in pox like Muunokhoi. Her little body couldn't cope with it."

A lump blocked her throat. She'd avoided picturing such scenes involving Shuren.

"Maybe we should go back," he said. "You healed my ankle without any problem. Surely you can heal people with the curse now you've learnt so much from the dragons."

She opened her mouth to protest and then remembered how easy the waterfall made healing. No. It was still too new. It might not be as easy without Dhalin by her side. Besides, Dhalin had said she relied on her gift too much. She was learning about new plants that would help them every day. She shook her head. "I'm one person. By the time I can visit all the tribes, we'll have so many losses. At least the plants we are sending are doing some good, are slowing the progress of the curse and soothing the effects."

"It's not good enough!"

Kew growled softly and Chinua swore again. "I'm sorry. I can't understand why there's been no word from Amslan or Temur. Surely they should have sent an update with the dragon who delivered the greenshade."

She'd been so busy searching for a cure, she hadn't considered that. No news generally meant bad news with Amslan. Her skin prickled. "You're right. We'll ask the next dragon to get us an update."

Kew lifted her head, looked over at Dhalin.

Geriel froze, fear in her heart. "What aren't you telling us?"

Nothing that would be productive, Dhalin said.

What was that supposed to mean?

"You know what's happening in the camps, don't you?" Chinua said. "You've been keeping it from us." He placed his hand on his sabre.

Geriel reached out to him. "Chinua, calm down." The last thing they needed was for the dragons to rescind their help, but nausea curled in her stomach. She didn't want the truth, but now the thought had entered her head, she had to know.

Chinua is correct, Dhalin said. *We have not updated you, because it made no difference. You are doing everything you can to find a cure. Knowing the number of infected and dead will not help.*

A stone fell into Geriel's stomach. "Dead?" She'd known it a possibility, but she'd thought with the plants they were sending they were keeping on top of it, beating the disease back.

"How many?" Chinua demanded.

It does not matter.

This time when Chinua drew his sabre, Geriel didn't protest. "Who?"

Dhalin was silent a moment and then puffed smoke out of her nose. Berke and Sarnai, Muunokhoi—

Geriel gasped. "But we sealed the disease. They should have been safe."

The container only holds for a few days, Dhalin said. *Then the curse grows too big for it. It may not have been the egg leaf tea which caused Uranchim's container to break.*

Dread filled every inch of Geriel's body. They would never get on top of it. They needed a cure. Amslan couldn't possibly help the infected and remove the curse if he used his energy containing it.

"Who else is dead?" Chinua's voice was flat.

Saran.

Chinua wailed, his voice full of pain. Kew hurried to him, placed a paw on his leg. Chinua pushed her off and got to his feet. "I will kill the emperor for this." He stalked into the darkness.

I will watch him. Kew followed him.

Geriel wanted to be sick but she was frozen in place. The beautiful little girl, Shuren's best friend, was no longer alive. She was almost too scared to ask the next question. "What of my family?"

Amslan holds by his oath to keep them safe.

She let out a breath. Was that fair to everyone else?

"How bad is it?"

You are doing all you can.

"I can do more." She could check all the plants in the vicinity instead of sitting here by the fire.

The plants you send are helping, but we estimate about one-third will die at the current rate, which is why we agreed to send one of our healers with the cloud flower.

Geriel's breath left her body. One-third. This time she retched, unable to keep the nausea down. When her body had finished heaving, she stood.

She had to find a cure. She placed her bow and quiver on her back and walked into the forest.

Sleep was a luxury she couldn't afford.

Chapter 9

Geriel stumbled back to camp around midnight, her eyes heavy, her heart low. With Dhalin's help, she'd found a few more plants, but nothing which gave her any great hope for a cure. Chinua slept by the fire, Kew next to him.

Sleep, Geriel. You will find a cure.

Kew's confidence didn't help. Geriel lay staring at the tops of the trees, listening to the rustles and shrieks of the forest, sounds that eventually lulled her to sleep.

In the morning, Chinua was up at dawn, packing the camp.

Geriel wiped the sleep from her eyes, wishing she could wipe the fatigue away as easily. She sat, watched him for a moment before asking, "How are you?"

He glanced at her, his expression hard. "I'll get more cloud flower today. Are there any other plants you need me to collect?"

"I'm so sorry, Chinua." Her voice cracked and she swallowed hard.

He shoved his sleeping mat into a bag and then his anger became grief. His face crumpled and he bit his lip. Geriel jumped to her feet, wrapped her arms around him and he clung to her, shaking.

Tears streamed down her face as she offered what little comfort she could.

Finally he stepped back and sniffed. "I don't blame you, Geriel. I..." He threw his hands in the air as if everything was hopeless.

She understood. "I know."

He continued packing the camp.

She sighed. "I'll tell you if I find any other plants for you to collect."

He nodded and left with Kew.

Geriel turned to Dhalin. "We should get back to camp to test these plants on Uranchim."

Dhalin shook her head. *Not yet. We are close to another meadow. It is near our breeding grounds so you must be careful, but I have received permission to take you there.*

The story of Lien's father searching for a cure involved a meadow near the breeding grounds, but there were so many plants from yesterday that still needed preparation.

Falin can take them for you.

The grey dragon landed nearby. "Thank you." She handed him the bag, told him how to prepare the plants. "Tell Uranchim I will be back this evening so he can test them."

Falin nodded and flew away. Geriel turned to Dhalin. "Let's go."

They reached the meadow mid-morning and they stretched out in front of her, a sea of grasses and flowers. Butterflies fluttered in the air and small birds darted this way and that. She inhaled, a sweet scent from one of the flowers soothed her.

I have announced your presence, you may begin.

So many unusual plants she'd never seen before. Too much choice.

She knelt beside a long yellow tubular flower and brushed her fingers over its soft petals. Closing her eyes, she connected to the waterfall, but visions of Saran and Muunokhoi crowded her mind instead. They begged her to find a cure and berated her for not saving them. The urgency tightened her skin, dogged her mind and the waterfall wouldn't form.

Relax.

It wasn't possible. Not when the fate of her people rested on her. She pictured her well, forced the gift to the surface, scanning the plant and found nothing of use. She continued to the next one and the next one. Each time her muscles strained and it was harder than the one before. She couldn't stop. She had to find a cure.

Stop. Dhalin stuck her face in front of Geriel, preventing her from continuing. *You are not relaxing, not connecting properly. You will exhaust yourself.*

"You told me my gift couldn't be exhausted," she countered.

The way you are doing it now will exhaust you. Go back to your waterfall.

"I can't. I don't have time."

You can and you do. Dhalin's tail slowly moved back and forth. *Either you return to your waterfall, or you leave the meadow.*

Geriel gaped at her. "But the cure might be here."

Exactly. Dhalin waited patiently.

All at once the stupidity of what she was doing hit her and her shoulders slumped. Dhalin was right. She was panicking again.

Closing her eyes, she blocked all other noise, focusing on the shush of the waterfall. Every time the thought of Saran came into her head, she sent her love and pushed her aside to refocus, go back to the water, its sound, its smell, the way the mist cooled her skin. Eventually Saran left her alone and Geriel touched the next plant.

The ease of scanning gave her hope and she hurried through the meadow, testing each plant. There were so many which could be used for other ailments and she itched to write them all down, but there was no longer time. She would ask the dragons' permission to return after the cure had been found.

It was evening by the time Geriel walked into the main camp, exhaustion dogging her steps. Checking Uranchim was her first priority, and then testing the bag full of plants she had gathered. Lien strode over to her. "How did it go? How's Chinua's ankle?"

She couldn't tell Lien about the deaths. Not now. "Dhalin and Falin have taught me more about my gift and I have found many plants which may help. Chinua's ankle is healed and he's gathering more cloud flower." Dhalin had told her the next batch was being delivered to the tribes today.

"But no cure?"

Geriel shook her head. "I won't know until I test them."

"We will find one."

The rasp of swords being drawn at the edge of the camp drew their attention. Geriel's eyes widened and she ran after Lien. A group on horseback stood surrounded, but weapons had been sheathed and Jie and Wei were bowing to the newcomers. One man's tunic was a rich green and of an expensive cloth which identified him as a lord. Around him sat his men, all in the grey uniform of the Chungson army.

"Bao," Lien breathed. She stepped forward, staring at the manservant behind the lord, and Geriel grabbed her arm.

"You can't run over there," she whispered. "No one can know he's your brother." It pained her to hold Lien back. It had been eighteen years since Lien had last seen her brother, but the soldiers all knew Lien had been a Bonamese imperial princess. If she hugged a Chungson manservant, people would ask why. Word could not get back to Xue that the true heir was alive.

Lien stepped back, her eyes still glued to her brother. The lord must be Lord Anming, the ruler of Chungson. Why had he come all this way? Did he have a cure for them?

Jie caught her eye and gestured towards the command tent.

She tugged Lien's arm. "We'll wait for them inside."

Lien let herself be led away, but once inside the command tent she paced. "I can't believe he's here." Tears glistened in her eyes. "He has Mother's eyes and Father's cheeks."

The only other time Geriel had seen Lien this worked up was when Sukh had been stabbed. It was disconcerting. Geriel stepped in front of her sister, clutched her hands. "Calm yourself. Everything will be all right, but you must wait until you see who enters the tent with them."

Lien sighed. "I know." She breathed deeply, closed her eyes and when she opened them again she was calm.

If only finding calm was that easy for Geriel. Lien controlled her emotions, rather than letting them rule her. Geriel had never been so controlled.

The tent flap opened and Wei walked in, followed by Lord Anming, Jie and finally Bao. Jie grinned, his smile wide, taking his expression from serious to joyous. Her heart raced.

Lien squeezed her hand, stealing her attention.

Lien's brother stared at his sister, eyes wide, disbelief on his face. "Kixi." He used the same nickname Jie did.

"Bao." Lien flung herself into her brother's arms, hugging him, tears running down her face.

Geriel's heart swelled. She swallowed hard, wiping her eyes. Anming and Jie both grinned.

Wei frowned. "What's going on?"

He didn't know who Bao was. Would that be a problem?

"Sit, please." Jie gestured to the table and Wei and Anming sat. He glanced at her. "You too, Geriel."

Her muscles tensed. She'd been too busy to take part in any discussions before, and she should get back to Uranchim, but she wanted to support her sister. And maybe the newcomers had news of a cure. She pulled out a chair as Lien and Bao spoke quietly to each other.

"Would you like to explain, my Lord?" Jie asked.

Anming cleared his throat. "Wei, this information cannot be revealed to anyone."

Wei nodded.

"Bao is Lien's brother, thought dead for the past eighteen years. He is the son of Emperor Huang and the true heir to the Bonamese throne."

Wei's mouth dropped open. "Your manservant is a prince?"

Anming chuckled. "Yes. It was imperative to keep it a secret so Emperor Xue did not find out. These training exercises are to prepare the men to attack Bonam and achieve our freedom, but we also aim to replace Xue with Bao."

Bao and Lien joined them at the table.

Wei closed his mouth and shook his head briefly. "When do we plan to attack?"

It was impressive how quickly he processed the information and moved on. She would have had a million questions.

"It depends on the Rhoran." Anming glanced at Geriel. "I understand the tribes have been infected by the Traders' Curse."

She nodded. "We are searching for a cure, but we hoped Chungson might know of one."

"I asked my healers before I left. One of them accompanied Emperor Huang when he came here to search for plants, but he couldn't recall finding a cure."

Geriel's heart fell. "Did they document anything?"

"Yes. Those records are at the library in the imperial palace."

Which made them inaccessible. The emperor wouldn't let them anywhere near the palace. Despair threatened to overwhelm her.

"Perhaps I should go," Lien said.

"It is far too dangerous," Bao said.

Geriel studied her sister. A few moons ago Lien had rescued Rhoran prisoners from the palace from under the emperor's nose. If anyone could get into the library, it was her. "Can you get in unseen?"

Bao glared at her. "My sister is not a soldier."

Lien placed a hand on his arm. "Much has changed since we saw each other last. This is Geriel, my adopted sister."

He studied her, suspicion still on his face.

"I've heard a lot about you." Geriel smiled.

"What do you propose?" Jie asked, taking Bao's attention from her.

"You can't be serious," Bao said.

"Trust me." Jie nodded for Lien to continue.

"With no more gifted women at the palace, it should not be difficult. I can wear a disguise to get into the main courtyard and then sneak into the library and go through the books until I find the right one."

"That could take months," Anming protested.

"No, the library is well organised," Jie said. "The librarian has an index of all the books contained within. If Lien can get inside, it shouldn't take her more than a couple of nights to find the right one."

"You're still suggesting my sister go alone to the palace where Xue is—the man who tried to kill her multiple times."

"Perhaps you should show him what you can do," Jie suggested.

Wei nodded. "Lien has been training all of our soldiers for the past quarter moon. She's formidable."

"Not against a whole palace of guards," Bao protested.

"Who will teach the men Rhoran tactics while she is gone?" Anming asked.

"Chinua should be available in a few more days," Geriel said.

"What has he been doing?" Wei asked.

"Collecting plants which slow the spread of the disease and soothe the symptoms," Geriel told him. "The dragons have been transporting the plants to the tribes and one of their healers is helping to isolate people who aren't infected from the rest."

"Isn't it too late?" Jie asked

"It depends on how well they separated people," she said. "They might also stop the spread, even if they can't remove it entirely."

Bao frowned. "How badly are the tribes affected?"

"We have one tribe unaffected," Lien said. "The rest have about half infected at last count."

"We can't risk it spreading to our men," Anming said.

He was right, but he needn't sound so callous about it. "Our fastest solution is to go to the palace, and find the cure," Geriel said. "It could take me moons to find a cure through trial and error."

Bao frowned. "How are you testing them?"

Lien and Geriel exchanged a glance. They shouldn't tell him about Uranchim. They didn't want to cause a panic.

Bao laughed. "Kixi, you still get the same guilty expression when you're planning to lie about something."

Lien sighed. "After arriving here, we discovered Uranchim was infected with the curse." The men swore and she continued. "We isolated him immediately and burned his possessions. We believe Xue deliberately infected the reparations he gave us."

"Since Chinua had spent the most time with him, we isolated him as well. He isn't infected yet."

"How did you know? Uranchim has no symptoms," Wei said.

They had to be truthful, at least with these men. "I can sense it," Geriel said. "I have the gift of healing. I repaired your broken arm, not Dhalin."

Wei gaped at her.

"Demonstrating both your skills will be quicker." Jie took a knife from his belt and drew it along his palm, cutting it open.

Her heart leapt. So quick to trust she could fix it. She didn't deserve such faith.

Jie wiped at the blood and showed the others how deep the cut was. Then he held his hand out to Geriel. She placed her hand over his palm and closed her eyes. Fatigue hovered around her, but she visualised the waterfall, and drew from it. She connected with Jie and focused on knitting the skin back together. It slid into place slowly. She opened her eyes and removed her hand.

Jie handed her a piece of cheese and then showed his hand to the others.

Bao stared at her. "Mother could do that." He shook his head. "I always thought I remembered it wrong, or changed it in my childish imagination, but she often fixed minor cuts and bruises for me."

It made sense. The gift was passed from mother to child so if Lien had the gift, the empress had to have had it, even if she hadn't been fully aware of it.

"Why don't you heal everyone with the curse then?" Anming asked.

Her chest squeezed. "I can't. The disease is oily, hard to contain and even harder to remove. It took both myself and Amslan to contain the curse in one person. Some of the plants we've been sending might help Amslan heal people, but it won't be fast enough."

Anming turned to Lien. "Why do you believe you can sneak into the palace unnoticed?"

Geriel sat back, sipped the tea Jie had placed in front of her.

Lien smiled. "Because no one will see me. I can remove an arrow from your quiver without anyone stopping me."

He laughed. "I'd like to see that."

Lien moved so fast Geriel missed it. One second Lien was empty-handed and the next she twirled an arrow in her hand. The only man without his mouth hanging open was Jie.

Geriel grinned and bit into her cheese.

"How?" Wei asked.

"I'm fast," Lien said. "That's my gift. I freed prisoners from under Xue's nose because he didn't see me. I also trained under General Ying, from the Office of Internal Scrutiny."

"She's almost unstoppable," Geriel added. "We tried

to devise a solution because Ying had the same gift but we didn't find anything effective."

"Much *has* changed since the last time we saw each other," Bao said. "Does your speed have limits too?"

Lien nodded. "I still believe I can sneak into the palace."

"I can help," Anming said. "When I was last there, the emperor spoke about a marriage between myself and Princess Fen. Since her unfortunate accident, he wishes to marry my sister to Prince Kun."

"What did Xue say happened to Fen?" Geriel asked.

"She was attacked by highway men on the way to the summer palace and killed."

Lien frowned. "I killed her. She had the same gift of speed and the emperor sent her into battle when he invaded Rhora. I couldn't allow her to live when she could wipe out much of my tribe."

"Then I should thank you," Anming said. "Marrying that spoilt, selfish child would have been hideous."

Lien's smile was small. Fen's death still disturbed her.

"How many have you killed?" Wei asked.

"Too many." Her voice was flat, and invited no further questions.

Anming nodded. "Then we should discuss how we will get you into the palace."

Geriel shifted. Lien could easily handle these men. Finding a cure was the best way to help her tribe right now. "If you don't need my help, I need to discuss the plants I found with Uranchim," she said to Lien.

Lien smiled. "Of course. I will see you later."

Jie stood at the same time as Geriel. "I will accompany you."

She frowned. The camp was safe, no need for him to go with her. "You have important things to discuss."

He smiled. "It won't take long."

She sighed and left the tent. Outside, he said, "When Lien goes to Bonam, you will be the only female here. I will ask Anming to send a female servant to the camp for you."

Geriel laughed. "That's not necessary. I don't need another female around in order to function."

"I was thinking of your safety."

His concern was sweet, but he'd still learnt nothing about her. "Why would I be safer with a Chungson servant? Are they trained to fight?"

He shook his head.

"Then how will she be of use?"

"The men won't get any ideas if she sleeps in your tent."

"If any man was to enter my tent, they'd quickly learn I can protect myself." He was scowling so she added, "Chinua will be back tomorrow and I can ask Kew to stay with me."

"Do that."

She paused on the outskirts of Uranchim's camp. Jie was from a culture where women were considered weak. She had to be patient with him. One day when she had time, she would demonstrate her skills. "Thank you for your concern." She joined Uranchim by his fire.

~*~

By midday the next day, Geriel and Uranchim had a collection of concoctions to test. It was difficult to guess how long to wait between trialling a new one, but Geriel monitored Uranchim carefully to make sure he didn't get worse. Movement across the field caught Geriel's attention. Lien was approaching Uranchim's camp, so Geriel got up to meet her.

"Any luck?" Lien asked.

She shook her head, the familiar failure squeezing her chest. "How are things with Bao?"

Lien's smile was small. "Good, but he doesn't quite believe I can protect myself at the palace."

"He doesn't want his sister in danger, especially since he's just got you back."

Lien nodded. "It is nice to have him concerned."

"Have you finalised your plan?"

"I am leaving with Anming this afternoon," she said. "We will travel to the palace to negotiate the betrothal of his sister, Daiyu to Prince Kun."

Geriel frowned. "What's Kun like?" His bodyguard had been involved in an altercation with Lien and then he had fought Temur when the Bonamese had invaded, but it didn't explain what kind of person he was. She didn't want Anming's sister in danger.

"He can be kind," Lien said. "He always encouraged me when I was training and people spoke highly of him. He's a fierce fighter and always obeys the emperor." She sighed. "Still we hope to remove the emperor before the wedding takes place. We will have several moons."

By then the curse would have run its course if they couldn't find a cure, though whether the Rhoran would be in any shape to actually help the Chungson fight was another issue.

"Bao is staying here. He will work with Jie and Wei to train the men. Anming has given him a command position so the men learn to obey him." She smiled. "I told all of them you have my full support and not to interfere in your work in any way."

Geriel stared at her.

"Little sister you are far more capable than you believe. If you need something, ask for it. Finding the cure is our priority."

"But will they listen?"

"I have told them Rhora will not help defeat the emperor if they do not listen to you."

She froze. Such power, such responsibility. "Thank you."

"I have seen you with Jie. Stand up to the others like you stand up to him and you'll be fine." She turned back to the camp. "Come with me now so I can repeat my orders to them with you present. That way there can be no confusion."

They walked back to the camp and into the command tent where Anming, Jie, Bao and Wei were eating. Anming looked up. "Are you ready to go?"

Lien nodded. "If you have any questions about Rhora while I am gone, Geriel can help. She can teach you battle techniques when she's not working on a cure and when Chinua returns, he can help as well. She has my full support and the full power of the khan behind her. Her priority is finding a cure and if she asks for anything, know she is asking as the representative of the khan."

Wei grimaced.

Lien raised an eyebrow at him. "Do you have a problem with that, Wei?"

"She is a woman."

Lien frowned. "As am I."

Wei lowered his head. "You are a warrior. She has done nothing but collect plants."

"She was not prepared when the wolf attacked either," Jie said.

Geriel's mouth dropped open as hurt pierced her. How dare he? "I sliced it open."

"But it still hit you. My arrows killed it."

She battled to keep the anger at bay. Arguing would get her nowhere. "If you want a demonstration, it needs to be now, so I can return to my work."

Jie nodded. "Let's go then."

She gritted her teeth. He truly didn't believe she was capable. "Let me get my weapons." She strode out of the tent, allowing her thoughts to rage. All Jie's kindness, his accompanying her across to her tent, wasn't to spend more time with her, it was because he thought her weak. She'd show him. She needed the men's respect so they would listen if she needed help. She retrieved her bow, a quiver full of arrows, and her sabre and met them on the outskirts of the camp where the meadow stretched out in front of them. "What do you want to see?"

"How accurate are you with the bow?" Wei asked.

"I can hit anything you point at."

"Standing or on horseback?" Jie asked.

"Both." She'd missed riding her horse, but had spent a few minutes each day with her.

"I'd like to see on horseback," Bao said.

Targets were already set up across the field. She whistled, loud and shrill and Khulan's head perked up. She trotted over.

Anming held up a hand. "I can get one of my men to saddle it while you show us something else."

Geriel laughed. "I don't need a saddle." She stroked Khulan's neck, murmuring to her, "We need to show them what we can do."

Khulan snorted and bumped her head against Geriel. Geriel swung onto her back and using her knees, nudged her into a slow walk while she took her bow off her back and readied the first arrow. Then she kicked Khulan into a gallop, riding past the group and onto the field, heading for the first target. The thunder of Khulan's hooves against the hard ground was music to her ears and the brush of air against her face brought her a peace she hadn't had in a long time.

The targets were close together and at the speed she rode, she had to fire fast. She released the first arrow, not pausing as she grabbed and released a second, then a third and a fourth. She continued along the line of ten targets and then slowed her horse and cantered back to the men.

Anming, Bao and Wei all looked shocked but Jie crossed his arms. "Shall we check the accuracy?"

Why was he challenging her? She smiled sweetly. "Yes, let's." She nudged Khulan into a walk to help her cool down, stroking her neck. She leaned forward and murmured, "Good job."

Jie inspected the targets. Each arrow was within an inch of the bullseye. She was a little out of practice.

Jie was silent so she said, "Have you seen enough?"

He glanced at her, smiled, though it didn't reach his eyes. "How good are you with a sword?"

"I prefer a sabre," she replied. "Or my knives." Lien had taught her how to throw knives. They were small enough to hide on her body and just as deadly as the sabre. She had two tucked into her sleeves right now— not that she would tell them.

"That's enough, Jie," Lien said. "Geriel has more important things to do than prove to you she's capable. If she has the time and energy after it is dark, she can show you some more."

"I'll take care of Khulan." Geriel clicked her tongue and rode Khulan back to where the other horses grazed. She brushed her and Lien came over with her saddle.

"I'm leaving soon." She placed the saddle over her horse's back.

Geriel's chest squeezed. "Take care of yourself," she said. "There may be more gifted people at the palace you don't know about."

Lien nodded. "I will be. I'll send word when I find the information."

When, not if. It gave Geriel hope. "As will I." She hugged Lien. "Safe travels. May you travel without notice."

Lien smiled. "May you have success with your quest." Around them other men saddled horses and Bao came to say goodbye to his sister.

Fear and guilt mixed in Geriel's stomach. If she'd found a cure, this wouldn't be necessary. Lien and Bao could have had a longer reunion.

She gave Khulan one last pat and headed back to Uranchim.

Chapter 10

Over the next couple of days, Geriel worked for longer and longer. Several of the plants she'd found had the ability to soothe symptoms and Chinua dutifully picked them in bulk and Falin took them to the tribes. With each new batch, she asked for an update and he brought back tales of death, scarring and misery.

So she worked harder.

In the evening, she took a little time for herself before dark to ride Khulan around the meadow. Although the field was large, it still felt small after the endless steppes. Riding around in circles represented the hopelessness of her situation. She wasn't getting any closer. Trial and error meant it could be the next plant she found or the hundredth plant.

She grew increasingly short-tempered. Uranchim stayed clear of her as much as possible, creating concoctions and testing them. Chinua spent most of the time in the mountains, collecting plants with Kew, returning only to sleep.

At night Geriel stayed by her own fire, close to her tent and continued working, preparing the plants in different ways. Sometimes Falin flew the concoctions to

Amslan to test, but the answer was always negative. No cure.

Bao brought his dinner to her fire and sat next to her.

"How did you go today?"

"I found something which will keep the fever down." She continued stirring the mixture in the pot. He came every night to ask her about the Rhoran, and to talk about Lien. She gave him an hour, because Lien would have wanted it and they needed to forge a strong relationship with him. When he became emperor, he could stop the conflict between Bonam and Rhora, the conflict Emperor Xue had started in his quest for more land and more power.

"That's great."

"It's not a cure."

"No, but those people suffering from sweats and shivers will be incredibly grateful for it."

His words made her pause.

He was right. She'd lost sight of that in her quest to find a cure. Yes, she hadn't found it yet, but the plants she had discovered would make the patients more comfortable, might even help their bodies recover enough so they could fight the disease more effectively, become less run down. "Thank you."

"I have to remind myself what we're doing here, improving relations with the Rhoran, learning about Bonamese defences, will all help in my long-term plan to regain my throne. It's frustrating to wait. I've waited my whole life for this and it feels so close now."

"Why did you wait so long?"

"Chungson hasn't got the strength. Xue made sure of it, splitting up companies, moving soldiers and generals all over the place, changing tactics and strategies so the men are more confused than anything.

Though some of Anming's men have been reaching out to the neighbouring vassal states, we didn't dare do more than whisper rumours of resistance."

"Your men must have a wide range of skills then."

"You're right." He changed the subject. "What was Lien like when she first arrived in your camp?"

"I thought her ever so regal," Geriel said. "Her black hair was so glossy I could almost see myself in it, and her erect posture made me think she might break if she fell." She smiled. "She'd been injured and I tended her, but she showed no pain, no emotion at all. I thought her odd." She laughed. "When I brought new clothes to her, she sat on the bed, waiting for me to dress her like she was a child. I knew then she would get a huge shock when she left her yurt and learnt how to live with us, so I decided to do everything I could to help her. I felt sorry for her being forced to move from home and marry a stranger."

"She would have accepted it was part of being an imperial princess," Bao said. "What do Rhoran do about marriages?"

"Sometimes they're arranged and sometimes they're a love match. Generally most of the arrangements happen when we get together in summer for the great hunt. It's a great opportunity to meet people from the other tribes."

"At what age do you marry?"

"Around my age." She grimaced. "With the emperor invading, my parents were too busy to find me a suitable match."

He raised his eyebrows. "You don't want to marry?"

"I would like to find a love match," she said. "But there is still so much I need to learn about being a healer and a husband would get in the way."

Bao frowned. "Aren't Rhorans more progressive?

Surely a husband wouldn't stop you from learning."

She shrugged. "I'm not ready to marry." Time to change the subject. "What about you? When you take back the throne, you'll be expected to marry immediately, won't you? You'll need heirs."

He nodded, his expression sombre.

"Is there anyone you want to marry?"

"I may have no choice. I may have to marry a lady from one of the vassal states to ensure they support my claim to the throne." He stared into the flames.

Geriel's heart went out to him. "But there is someone, isn't there?"

He shrugged. "No one I can have."

"Why not? You'll be the emperor."

Bao looked around, made sure no one was within earshot. "It is not appropriate."

"Does she know who you really are?"

Bao shook his head. "Only Anming does, and his father before him."

Until she'd met Lien, she'd thought royalty had an easy life, but it seemed though they had wealth, they were constrained by expectations. Like Anming's sister having to marry Prince Kun. "What's your opinion of Prince Kun?"

"He was a sensitive child, always scared of doing the wrong thing and making his father angry. He used to tag along after Jie and me, and we always got into mischief, much to his horror." He laughed. "One day it rained so hard that an area of Father's garden turned to mud. We had the best mud fight, Kun, Jie, Lien and I. When we went back inside, Mother sent us all to wash, but Uncle Xue caught us." Bao sobered. "He banned Kun from playing with us anymore and slapped him so hard it knocked him unconscious."

Geriel's mouth dropped open. "The poor boy. How

old was he?"

"Nine. I overheard Father reprimanding Xue about it. Only a few days later, we travelled to Chungson and my parents were killed." He sighed. "The one good thing about the mud fight was Lien became sick and my parents left her behind to heal."

And so Lien had survived.

Bao was silent a long moment. "It's ironic. We were going to Chungson so I could meet Anming and his sister, Daiyu. Father wanted me to have a close relationship with all our neighbours. He hoped it would ensure peaceful relations into the future. Anming's father was one of my father's best friends." He stood, his expression pensive. "I'll let you continue your work." He walked off.

He'd been a kind boy. Not every child had the patience for younger cousins or siblings. He reminded her a little of Chinua who used to let her tag along after him when she was young. Someone with that compassion would make a good ruler.

The pot hissed in front of her and she turned her attention back to the potion.

~*~

Geriel stretched her back, groaning a little as the muscles pulled. It had to be close to midnight and Bao had left hours ago. Silence had drifted over the camp and occasionally a sentry walked past. She poked at the paste she was cooking. The smell wasn't pleasant, which was a good sign. All powerful medicines smelled terrible.

"You're up late." The voice out of the darkness made her jump and the pot tipped towards her, spilling its contents over the coals. She swore, grabbed the pot to tip it upright and burnt her fingers on the hot clay.

Ignoring the pain, she managed to save a little of the mixture.

"You've burnt yourself." Jie squatted next to her, taking her hand.

She snatched it back. "You sneaked up on me." Hopelessness filled her and she lashed out at him. "Do you know how long that's been cooking? I might not have enough to test."

"I was standing there for a few minutes."

"I'm busy." Her fingers throbbed. She should soak them in the stream but the pain reminded her of her failure.

He took a flask from his belt and opened the cap. Then he took her hand back and poured the liquid over it. It soothed. But she didn't need his nurturing.

"What do you want?" she demanded.

"I haven't seen you in a few days. I wanted to ask if you needed anything."

"I need a cure," she snapped.

Sympathy crossed his face. "Is there anything I can do to help?"

She blinked. It was the first time he'd offered to help her. "Won't that diminish your standing with your men?" she snarled. She couldn't be civil. Not with the frustration and pain swirling inside her, desperate for a way out. She poked the pot, not looking at him. There might be enough for a sample.

Kew lifted her head. *You're being mean.*

Geriel sighed. Kew was right. "I'm sorry. I shouldn't take my frustration out on you."

His lips turned up slightly. "You've been working hard. Perhaps you need to sleep."

She shook her head. "Not until I've made these last few things." It would take her most of the night and then she'd sleep a couple of hours before heading out to find other plants.

He looked at her for a long moment and then settled next to her. "All right. What can I do?"

She stared at him. "You want to help?"

He nodded.

She wasn't foolish enough to refuse. The disease contained within Uranchim was getting bigger not better and he grew more and more tired each day. "Get another pot and the yellow plant over there."

He did as she asked and some of the weight lifted from her even though it would be a long night.

At least now she wasn't alone.

~*~

Geriel squinted at the bright light as she woke the next morning. She sat bolt upright in bed. How late had she slept? Kew wasn't there and warmth suffused the tent. She threw her blankets off and hurriedly dressed.

Falin should have come first thing to pick up some concoctions she and Jie had stayed up preparing until the early hours. She had real hope for a couple, but she wanted to give Falin a few extra instructions before he took them to the Adhan tribe.

She raced out of the tent, glanced around for the pile of treatments. Gone.

Where were they? Had she missed Falin?

Across the field, the Chungson trained on horseback. Jie sat in front of the men, instructing them. He should have woken her before he'd started training. He knew how important it was for her to find a cure. She started across the field.

"Geriel!"

She turned to Bao.

"Falin arrived this morning to take the treatments," he said. "He took a couple to Uranchim and the rest to one of the tribes. Jie thought it best if you slept longer."

She narrowed her eyes. "I don't see him sleeping."

Bao grinned. "The same rules never apply to Jie."

Well she had a few things to say about that. "I wanted to give Falin some extra instructions."

He shrugged.

At least the medicine was on its way to camp. She glanced at the sun. Mid-morning. She'd wasted hours asleep. "Where is Dhalin?"

"Jie told her to come back at midday."

Oh, she definitely had a few things to say to him. She stormed across the meadow to where he taught. A small smile played on his lips as she approached him. He ordered the men to practise and then rode to her. "You're looking better today."

She glared. "What gives you the right to tell Dhalin to come back later?"

"Lien asked me to take care of you while she was gone."

"She also said my research had priority and I can't work while I'm asleep."

"You would have woken earlier if you'd needed less rest."

"That's beside the point," she growled. The man was infuriating. "I need to find a cure."

"Something you worked on last night might be it. Falin will be back in a couple of days to tell you."

"Or nothing might have worked." He made her so mad she couldn't look at him. Instead she observed the men shooting arrows at the targets from horseback. She shook her head. They had no idea. They sat so stiff in the saddle, didn't feel the horse under them and as a result the horses' gaits weren't consistent.

"You don't like what you see?" Jie asked.

"They're hopeless. We'd beat them easily."

He frowned. "That's a big statement."

"True too." It was almost painful to watch. Their aim bobbed all over the place in time to the horses' movement and the horses went wherever they liked, causing the rider to stop aiming and pull the horse back on track. "Didn't Lien show you what to do?"

"She taught us tactics. Perhaps you'd like to show us."

She stared at him. "You're asking for my help?"

He shrugged. "If you think you know better."

She did, but she didn't have the time. One of the soldiers fell off and landed with a thump on the ground. A scream of pain echoed in the air.

She ran over, assessing him as she did. His shoulder was dislocated but he might have broken bones as well. She dropped to her knees beside him. "Where do you hurt?"

"Shoulder."

She placed her hand on his arm and he jerked away, swearing. "What are you doing?"

"I'm a healer," she told him.

"Let her examine you," Jie said.

The man scowled but brought his hand back.

Connecting to him, she scanned him quickly for any other injuries other than the dislocation. The shoulder and some tendons. She visualised the waterfall. "This may hurt a little." With a twist, she relocated his shoulder and with her hands still on him, she healed the tendons. Then she opened her eyes. "How does it feel?"

He rotated his shoulder and his mouth dropped open. "There's no pain. What did you do?"

Good. "It was just dislocated. You should be fine to continue." Better he believe the pain came only from the dislocation.

A shout and another man fell off his horse not far away. She shook her head as he got to his feet, nothing injured but his pride. She turned to Jie. "Let me show you how it's done." If she didn't show them the correct technique, she'd be healing them all day.

He smiled. "What do you need?"

She preferred to use her own horse but his would do. "Your horse and your bow and quiver."

Jie called the men to attention and then dismounted. "Geriel will demonstrate the correct technique."

A couple of men grumbled, but not too loudly. They should know better after witnessing Lien's skills. She mounted Jie's horse, the saddle still warm from him, and nudged it towards the men. "You need to relax more, be one with your horse. I want you to lower your weapons and ride using only your knees to the other side of the meadow and back."

"You're supposed to be teaching us how to fight."

"You need to learn how to ride first," she retorted.

The soldier's face reddened and Jie said, "Could you demonstrate for us?"

She kicked his horse into motion, keeping her hands out to the side and using her feet and knees to direct it to the other side of the meadow and then return.

Jie smiled at her. "Impressive."

"Not really. A six-year-old could do it."

He laughed. "I'll keep that in mind."

He gestured for the men to do as she asked and they rode, the horses almost crashing into each other at times as they attempted to go where the soldiers inadvertently sent them.

She sighed. This would take a lot of work. She glanced at Jie. "Until your men can master riding, they won't be able to fight from horseback. I can give you some exercises to practise and when they're ready, I'll take them to the next step."

"They can all ride."

She shook her head. "Not well. They need to respect their horse and have the horse respect them. They need to direct their horses without using their reins."

The soldiers returned and Geriel took them through some exercises, teaching them how to communicate with their horses through touch—things she'd learnt before she could walk. Then she dismounted and handed the reins back to Jie. "I'll return this evening and check their progress."

Geriel strode back to her tent and gathered her things. Today she'd go lower down the mountain. Bao had joined Jie, so she didn't bother telling anyone where she was going. Dhalin would find her. She'd avoid the area where she'd run into the young boy when they'd first arrived, and instead travel closer towards the Rhoran border.

For the first time since she'd arrived, she was truly alone. She breathed deeply, enjoying the cool air of the forest. She'd missed her solitude. Strange how at times she'd thought the Rhoran camp was suffocating, but it wasn't true. She'd been able to ride almost every day by herself and seek peace from the steppes and the view of the mountains in the distance. Since leaving Rhora, she'd been constantly surrounded, and the expectations on her had been never-ending. She prayed to Qadan that one of the treatments she'd made last night would work. She had a good feeling about the paste which had been knocked over.

Her steps led her away from the camp, and she marked her path by memorising the different shapes of trees. If she got lost, she'd never hear the end of it from Jie. Most of the plants she walked past were familiar. She was running out of options.

A snap of a twig had her instantly alert. She swung her bow from her back, drew an arrow from her quiver and scanned the trees. Another snap, closer this time and the quiet shush of someone walking through the undergrowth. She eased behind a tree. It had to be a villager because they were coming from down the mountain and Dhalin would have let her know if it was her.

Geriel's ears strained as she picked up more sounds, more footsteps, more than one person.

Her chest tightened. She didn't want to kill anyone but couldn't let anyone spot her. Only the soldiers in the meadow knew Chungson was working with the Rhoran. Anyone else would be scared the Rhoran were invading and would inform their local constable. Word would get back to the emperor they were there. Slowly she peered around the tree and her heart stopped.

Two soldiers dressed in black.

What were Bonamese soldiers doing in the mountains of Chungson? Anming couldn't know about them, otherwise he would have warned them.

Her skin prickled. The soldiers wouldn't let her go if they found her, and it was too late to run. They would spot her.

She had to kill them. She squeezed her eyes closed.

Were there only two?

"This had better be the last day," one said.

"Seems stupid to search the mountains because a kid thought he saw a Rhoran," another man agreed.

Geriel's gut clenched. It was her fault they were here.

"Kun's getting a little obsessive," the first man said.

"Shh, don't say that too loud or you'll lose your head."

Maybe there were only two of them. She could kill

them both before they could sound an alarm. She slid another arrow from her quiver and held them both in her right hand. She hesitated. Eventually someone would notice they were missing and realise something was wrong. If they found the bodies, they'd know she had been there. Instead of stopping the search, they would expand it.

She couldn't allow them to see her at all.

Her muscles tense, she waited, her back pressed against the rough bark of the spruce tree. A shout in the distance.

"What was that?"

"Let's check it out. Maybe Kun has called off the search."

Was Prince Kun with the men? That could be extremely dangerous. He couldn't find Bao. The footsteps faded away. Geriel waited for a moment longer and let out a slow, quiet breath.

She peered around the tree. The forest was still.

Time to go. The others had to be warned.

She moved silently back the way she'd come, going from tree to tree, constantly scanning, her bow in her hand. Suddenly she stepped around a tree and came face to face with a Bonamese soldier.

His eyes widened and he opened his mouth to yell.

Geriel's heart skipped a beat, but she acted on instinct, the same as if she'd come face to face with a wild boar. She brought her bow up, notched the arrow and shot.

Her arrow pierced his heart and his shout was cut off.

Horror filled her, but she couldn't stop, couldn't think about what she'd done. Keep moving in case someone had heard his shout. She took two steps away and someone else shouted. She turned, found a

Bonamese soldier pointing his bow at her almost twenty yards away. She leapt out of the way as the arrow fired and narrowly missed her. Around her people crashed through the forest, converging on her.

Run.

She ran forward, not up the mountain, but across it, hoping to outrun the men behind her. Her heart pounded in her chest and she took no notice of her path, her only goal to get away and not lead them straight to the camp. An arrow whizzed past her and she ducked.

Turning, she fired back in quick succession, hitting one soldier and missing the next. Almost a dozen men chased her.

Keep moving.

Stealth was impossible and in her quest for speed she left a trail of broken plants behind her. She couldn't hide from them, they were too close behind. Her only hope was to find a defensive position from which to fight.

Dhalin! She sent the thought out as wide and loud as possible. She'd never tried to contact Dhalin this way before, but if Dhalin could put her voice in Geriel's head and hear her thoughts, then maybe it would work.

Geriel, climb up the mountain. A voice she wasn't familiar with, but it had to be a dragon. She changed direction, her legs burning, lungs screaming. She was slowing. Branches scratched her face and tore at her clothes.

Move right. There're some rocks you can use for cover. I'm almost there. Others are coming to help.

She ran harder. Through the trees was more light. A large grey rock appeared and her lungs strained as she burst out of the forest onto the hard, rocky ground.

A deep bellowing roar echoed through the mountain

and Geriel flinched even as she recognised the dragon's call. Behind her, shouts of fear. As she scrambled up the rock and ducked behind one balanced atop it, a sandy brown dragon swooped over her. Riltien.

She peeked out from behind the rock. Scorched earth and trees, smoke wafting from the ground and reaching her nose. The Bonamese soldiers had stopped, taken cover behind the trees.

You have no right to be here. The same voice bellowed in her mind and the Bonamese clutched their ears.

Geriel gasped sucking in deep lungfuls of air. The rock she stood on was three metres off the ground with a sharp drop to the ground below, and then she'd have a wide-open sprint to the trees behind. If Riltien kept the soldiers focused on him, she might be able to slip away.

This area is the dragon sanctuary, declared so by the Emperor Xue. You may not be here without permission. The dragon landed on the rock Geriel hid behind.

"The emperor ordered us to search the area after we received a report Rhoran were here." A man stepped out from behind the trees, dressed in red like a few of the other soldiers, but with black epaulettes which marked him as the man in charge. The other soldiers aimed their arrows at Riltien. She couldn't leave him here alone, he was too vulnerable even if he could breathe fire. She'd wait until reinforcements arrived. She notched an arrow to her bow and breathed deeply, to control the shake in her arms.

She is here with our permission, Prince Kun. She seeks a cure for an illness in her tribe.

So that was Kun. His expression didn't change. "We wanted to protect the villagers, and ensure the Rhoran didn't invade your sanctuary."

Then you should have come directly to us and we would have told you the truth.

A movement to the side of Kun. A soldier in red pulled back his bowstring.

"Look out!" Geriel fired her arrow as the soldier released his. Riltien roared as the arrow hit his wing. The soldier who fired fell down dead.

Kun hesitated and ordered. "Hold your fire."

Leave this place. Riltien hunched down, his wing wrapped around his chest.

Geriel stepped out from behind the rock, her own arrow drawn. "You're breaking the treaty, Kun." She pointed her arrow directly at him.

He glared at her. "What do you know of it?"

"Every Rhoran knows the contents of the treaty your father signed with our khan." She paused. "Leave now before you damage the emperor's honour further."

She could feel the pain emanating from Riltien, but she couldn't help him from here. *Can you climb down to me? I might be able to heal you.*

Remove the arrow. The dragon let out a breath of fire, bathing the soldiers in it, and as they ducked for cover, he clambered down the rock next to Geriel. He let out another round of flames and then she pulled the arrow straight out, the barb ripping more tissue. She'd never tried to heal a dragon before. Placing her hand over the wound she visualised the waterfall, keeping her eyes open to track the soldiers, and then poured her healing energy into the dragon. The wound closed and dizziness made her head spin. She lifted her bow again, but it was twice as heavy.

The others are close. Riltien flapped his wings and then roared. *You have defiled the treaty. Leave now before my kin arrive.*

"Kill the girl," Kun ordered. "She invaded Chungson."

Geriel's heart leapt as she fired three arrows in quick succession, hitting each man she aimed at. Riltien took to the air, leaving her behind. Geriel ducked behind the rock as soldiers returned fire.

They had to cross open ground to get to her, unless they circled around using the forest as cover. She glanced to her right, noted a man moving that way and fired at him. How many were there? She'd counted about a dozen and she only had twenty arrows left in her quiver. She couldn't afford to miss.

A shadow loomed overhead and there was a bellow of rage as three dragons, flying in formation, swooped and breathed fire on the soldiers. A scream of pain and Geriel peeked out from behind the rock. One man rolled on the ground covered in flames and the rest hid behind trees.

You should have learnt from your last encounter with dragons, Kun.

Kun glared at Geriel. "Retreat," he yelled.

Footsteps crashed to her right and she spun as both Jie and Chinua ran towards her, bows drawn. No. Not now. They could get hurt and Kun would recognise them both.

"Over here," she yelled.

Chinua ran to her, but Jie continued, his face full of rage, his eyes locked on Kun.

"Are you all right?" Chinua asked.

She nodded.

"Jie." Shock raced across Kun's face, followed by rage. "You're supposed to be dead."

"Come and fight me you coward." Jie stopped in the middle of the clearing.

Fear made her skin hot. Was he trying to get himself killed? The other soldiers were already aiming at him. "Jie, take cover."

He ignored her.

"Idiot," Chinua grumbled and stepped out from behind the rock, going to stand beside Jie. Geriel clambered down and took his other side, her arrow notched.

Leave. The three dragons landed on top of the boulder.

Kun stared at them for a long moment, hatred on his face and then backed away. "Fall back."

Geriel waited, muscles tense, arrow ready until Riltien said, *They have gone.*

She sighed, relaxing the bow and replacing the arrow in her quiver.

"What in God's name were you thinking?" Jie demanded, whirling on her.

She blinked.

"You shouldn't have gone out alone. You could have been killed."

Anger replaced her fear. "I can take care of myself."

"Obviously not. You're lucky the dragons heard you." Jie turned to Riltien. "Thank you."

The dragon nodded. *We should have sensed them.* He huffed out a breath. *One of our elders died today and we are distracted, grieving.*

"I'm so sorry," Geriel said. "Thank you for your help. If there's anything we can do…"

There isn't. Thank you for healing me. He took to the air.

"What happened?" Chinua asked as they headed back towards camp.

"I heard someone coming and hid. Kun had set up a search of the area after news reached him that a Rhoran was spotted in the area." She glanced at Jie. "The child who saw me must have said something."

He grunted.

"I thought I'd got away, but I ran into one, killed

him and then another spotted me. I had to run. Riltien led me here."

Chinua placed a hand on her shoulder. "Are you all right?"

She nodded. She couldn't think about the men she'd killed yet. That could wait until she was alone. "I need to continue searching for plants."

Jie shook his head. "Not today. Kun has left, but now he's seen us, he won't give up. We need to move."

"He knows the dragons have given us permission."

"That might not matter."

Her body flushed in panic. "We can't go. The cure is somewhere in these mountains." Her pulse fluttered.

"We have no choice."

Geriel looked at Chinua to back her up, but instead he said to Jie, "You and Kun have a history?"

"Yes."

She waited for him to elaborate. Nothing. "What is it?"

"Kun blamed me for starting a mud fight which made his father beat him. When Bao died, he blamed me for that as well." He held some branches back so they could walk through. "Since then, whenever I returned to the palace, he made it clear I wasn't welcome."

"So now he's seen you alive?" Geriel asked.

"He won't stop searching for us now he knows I'm involved." He sighed. "The dragons might keep him away for a short while, but not for long."

This was her fault. If she'd waited for Dhalin, she would have been warned about the Bonamese soldiers. She couldn't find a cure if she was constantly dodging Kun's men.

"What can we do?" Chinua asked.

"I need to warn Bao and Wei. We'll need to leave. If

Kun sees them, our whole plan will be ruined."

Geriel wanted to be sick.

Her pride might have not only cost her the cure, but also threatened their end goal to defeat the emperor and live in peace.

Jie was right.

She was weak.

Chapter 11

Geriel's mind whirled the whole way back to the camp. Would Kun really ignore the dragon's orders and continue up the mountain? It didn't matter, they couldn't risk staying in case he did. Which meant the Chungson soldiers had to leave as well. She was so stupid. She shouldn't have let Jie rile her, shouldn't have been so stubborn, shouldn't have panicked about sleeping in.

This was all her fault.

She may have condemned her people to death, and risked the people of Chungson as well. If the soldiers were discovered, the emperor would surely strike quickly to put down any hint of rebellion.

She followed Jie and Chinua out of the trees, into the meadow. Dhalin raced up to her. *We must talk.*

The urgency in her tone filled Geriel's stomach with dread. "Is there news? Are more people dead?"

Calm yourself. Come to Uranchim's camp.

Jie nodded goodbye, and he and Chinua hurried towards the command tent.

Geriel lengthened her stride across the meadow after Dhalin, her heart racing. What had gone wrong now?

Uranchim sat at his campfire stirring something in a pot, the rest of his camp packed. A smile lit his face as she walked up. Hope raised its head. "What's happening?"

He held out his arm. "Check me."

Her heart squeezed and she held her breath as she connected with him and searched his blood for the curse. Sucking in air, she checked again, not willing to believe the clarity of his blood. Finally, her skin hot, she said, "You're clear. What did you take?"

"The tolui paste."

The one she had knocked over. She could barely breathe. She'd done it. She'd found a cure. "We need to get more, send it to Amslan." Before Kun had time to regroup.

Uranchim nodded. "Where did you find it?"

Fear pierced her. She'd gathered so many plants over the past few days she couldn't remember. Where was her book? She dug into the bag which still hung over her shoulder.

The high pasture.

Relief filled her and she nodded her thanks to Dhalin. The high pasture was further away from Kun and his men, it would give them some time. "We need to go now."

"I'll pack Chinua's things if you do yours."

She nodded. "I'll tell Jie."

Her heart raced as she ran back to the camp. They'd finally found a cure. Her head was giddy. If she, Uranchim and Chinua continued to climb the mountain, they'd avoid Kun and his men and when they were done, they'd find a different way down the mountain. Uranchim and Chinua could harvest and she'd make the paste which took a few hours. They wouldn't need a lot for each person. And if Falin continued to fly the cure to the tribes, the Rhoran could be cured in only a few days. Then they'd join the Chungson and defeat the emperor.

In only a few days her mission would be over and she'd return to her tribe and teach the healers everything she had learnt. She ignored the twinge of sadness as she thought of Jie. Her duty was to her tribe.

She strode through camp, straight to the command tent, and found Jie, Bao, Wei and Chinua debating inside.

"We can't let Kun find us," Wei said. "If he knows we're working with you, he'll attack Chungson and Anming is heading for the imperial palace as we speak. It's too dangerous. They'll kill him."

"We have to stay until we find a cure," Chinua argued.

Geriel grinned. "I've found one!" For the first time in a moon, no tension rested on her shoulders.

They all turned to her and Jie's eyes widened. "What?"

"Uranchim is cured. The plant we need is further up the mountains near the dragon's breeding ground."

"Thank Qadan." Chinua swept Geriel into a hug, squeezing the air out of her. Her laugh stuck in her chest and she pushed him away.

"That changes everything," Jie said.

Bao nodded. "We pack up camp," he said. "The Chungson can return to their barracks. Geriel and Chinua can gather the cure and when the Rhoran are healed, we can implement the next stage of our plan."

"Where will you go?" Jie asked.

"With Geriel. I should meet with the khan before we go into battle."

Wei nodded. "Jie should go with you as well. If Kun finds him with us, it will be dangerous to us all."

Geriel's heart jumped as Jie agreed.

"I'll get word to Anming," Wei said. "Let's pack camp."

Chinua pulled her towards the door. "Come on. There's no time to lose."

She grinned.

Finally she was getting somewhere, finally they had real hope. Finally, she'd succeeded.

An hour later most of the camp had been packed and soldiers began leaving in small groups in the hope they wouldn't attract Kun's attention. All were under orders to say they were on a training exercise if questioned—it was the truth anyway. Riltien monitored Kun's location and would warn the groups if they got too near.

Geriel had the spare mounts packed and Khulan saddled. Lien hadn't taken her extra mount when she'd left, so there would be a spare for Jie and Bao, though hopefully they wouldn't be required to ride fast. Geriel tapped a beat on her thigh as she waited with Chinua and Uranchim while Bao and Jie said their final words to Wei. How long did it take to say goodbye?

"Is it wise to bring them with us?" Chinua asked. "We don't know Jie's not secretly working for the emperor."

Kew snorted. *He's not.*

Chinua wasn't forgiving of those who had wronged him, and Jie had led the attack on the Rhoran camp. Chinua hadn't had a chance to get to know the man.

Geriel squeezed his hand. "Kew and Dhalin both vouch for him." Chinua meant well. "I trust him too."

Chinua snorted. "I've seen the way he looks at you. I'm not sure you're the best judge."

Heat flooded her cheeks. "I don't know what you're talking about." She cleared her throat. "Neither of them can stay with the Chungson. If Kun sees them, they'll both be killed."

"They're our allies now," Uranchim added. Chinua grunted.

When Bao and Jie walked over, Geriel handed them the reins for their horses. "Let's go."

The more distance they put between the camp, the better. And she had to find the tolui plant.

They travelled most of the day, staying silent, relying on Dhalin to lead them to the meadow and warn them if anyone was nearby.

Kun and his men are in a village, Kew said as evening fell. *Wei's men continue to travel through the night. They hope to reach the barracks before morning.*

Geriel sighed. It was one less worry. "How far are we from the meadow?"

Not far.

Twenty minutes later the meadow opened in front of them. It was smaller than the lower meadow but held a quiet serenity the other had lacked. A few birds fluttered about in the dusky light.

You may camp on this edge, Dhalin said. *At no stage may you wander off alone. These are our breeding grounds and there are babies nearby. They are unused to humans and may get scared although we have warned them you will be here.*

"May we start gathering the tolui?" Geriel asked.

Leave it for the morning.

Frustration burned inside her. They were so close. But she could be banished for disrespecting the dragons' wishes. Kew rubbed against her leg and sent her waves of sympathy.

Geriel erected her tent between Uranchim and Chinua and scanned each man to ensure everyone was still clear.

"How do you know you don't have the curse?" Jie

asked.

"Dhalin checks me."

He frowned. "You've taken quite a risk."

"I'm a healer, it's part of the role." She smiled at him. "Are we setting a watch?"

Chinua nodded. "Do you want to take the first one?"

"It's not necessary for her to guard," Jie said. "She will be busy tomorrow making the paste."

She frowned. "I can do a couple of hours just like you can."

There is no need for a watch, Kew said. *We always stand guard. No one will sneak up on you here.*

The men exchanged glances. They were unused to relying on others. Even for Geriel, the idea of not setting a sentry made her stomach swirl. She shook her head. The dragons had far better senses and were familiar with the area. This was their home and they were protecting their babies. She couldn't have a better guard. She ate dinner as the men discussed where they would go next. She didn't care as long as they stayed long enough to help her gather the cure. Then she'd travel from camp to camp making sure everyone was clear.

She finished eating and stood. "I'm going to sleep. Wake me if you need me to stand guard." She didn't wait for their permission and Kew accompanied her back to her tent and settled on the ground next to her bed.

"Thank you for your help, Kew."

Kew snorted. *You are my family. I will always help you.*

Geriel stroked Kew's scaly skin. "Do you enjoy it here?"

It was strange at first, but yes, I do. Though I'm constantly tired with the challenge of learning, the worst thing is I miss Lien and your family.

"They miss you too." Her heart ached as she remembered Saran. How were her own family faring? She'd had no news from her tribe. She prayed to Qadan, resisting the urge to get up and start hunting for the tolui. She had to respect the dragons' rules and hopefully they would transport the cure she made in the morning.

She closed her eyes but still the images of her loved ones swarmed around her head.

It was some time before she fell asleep.

~*~

In the morning she woke as the sun peeked above the horizon. Kew still snored beside her, little puffs of smoke coming out of her nose. Geriel smiled and rose, gathering her knife and a bag before leaving her tent. The fire had died down during the night and no one else was up. Mist covered the meadow, hiding any plants in a blanket of white and she pulled her coat tighter around her. It was so quiet, not even the birds had woken yet.

A thwomp, thwomp broke the silence and Riltien appeared through the mist, landing just outside the camp. She walked to him. "Good morning. May I start gathering the plant?"

He nodded. *Know my kin are not happy about you being here. They worry Kun will follow you. We still have many funeral rites to complete for our elder and your presence is disruptive. You should work quickly because I can't guarantee how long you will be allowed to stay.*

Geriel's heart lurched. "Thank you for the warning."

She hurried to Chinua and Uranchim's tents and called, "It's time to get up." A groan inside. "Don't go back to sleep, Chinua, time is short." She crossed to Jie and Bao's tent as Jie strode out, his sword in his hand and Bao right behind him.

"What's wrong?"

Always ready to fight. What kind of life was that? "Riltien tells me the dragons are not happy with us being here. He can't guarantee how long we can stay."

Jie nodded. "Show us what you need us to collect."

Now he was willing to obey her orders. She took the soldiers into the field, her eyes scanning the misty ground, and found the plant. "This is it." She took her knife from her belt. "I need the flowers and the stems. Leave some base so it can regrow." She demonstrated what she meant as she cut the plant close to the ground. The warriors got to work, and after she'd ensured they were doing it correctly, she returned to camp with Uranchim. She stoked the fire, adding a few branches to it and then showed him how to grind the plant and make the paste.

"It breaks down into such a small amount," Uranchim commented.

She nodded. The quantity of fresh plant made about a quarter of the volume in paste. Luckily, they needed only a small amount to cure the disease.

They worked all day, the warriors bringing full bags of tolui for Uranchim and Geriel to cook. Kew wandered through the meadow making sure no one ventured too close to the nests. Though Geriel couldn't see the baby dragons, a high-pitched chirp came from them every now and again as the babies called to their mothers.

At midday, when Geriel had enough cure to send to the Adhan tribe, Kew called Falin. Geriel sealed it in a waterproof container and wrote instructions.

"It shouldn't take more than a few hours to get results," she said as she gave the precious cure to Falin.

"Can you wait, so we are certain it worked for everyone?"

Falin nodded. *I will be back as soon as I can.*

Mid-afternoon, Riltien landed near the camp. *Kun is on the move. He is climbing into the mountain and is not far from where you were camped yesterday. They are armed with flying sticks and are prepared for us.*

Meaning the dragons would be in danger if they attacked. Not good. It would be obvious more than a few people had camped there from the disturbed ground in the meadow. How would Kun respond?

My kin are debating whether you can stay past the day.

She gasped. "Please. We must. We've found the cure."

I have sent some dragons to search for the plant in other areas. I will tell you if we find any. He flew away. There was no compromise in his tone. They were running out of time.

Geriel glanced at Uranchim. "You keep cooking. I'll help gather the plant."

He nodded. "Tell the others to hurry."

She ran across the meadow to Chinua and explained the situation.

"Did Riltien say how many men Kun had?"

"No." It was still several hours climb from the training meadow, but if the dragons let them stay, Kun might still reach them.

She strode to where Jie was on the other side of the meadow and relayed the news.

"We must hope the dragons can find more of this plant elsewhere," he said. "Kun will not give up searching for us. He has a point to prove to his father."

Geriel frowned. "What do you mean?"

"Anming mentioned the emperor was not pleased when Kun returned empty-handed from Rhora.

Together with Lien telling Xue that Fen wasn't his daughter, it has cast a shadow over Kun's parentage. He's lucky he looks so much like his father otherwise he'd already be dead. Anming's sources say the empress has been sent to the summer palace which means she is out of favour. If she wasn't Kun's mother as well, she would have been killed, not banished for her affair."

If Kun's whole position was under threat, he would be a vicious fighter.

Jie placed a hand on her arm, his touch light. "We will get this cure to your people one way or another."

She wished she could have as much faith. "Thank you."

She left him to tell Bao the news and then continued to gather the plants, moving through the meadow, her movements fast. By late afternoon her back ached, but she'd reached the far side. Cut plants littered the ground. They had taken everything they could from the meadow.

Walking back to camp, she counted the bags. Would there be enough?

Twice during the afternoon Kew had called other dragons to take batches of the cure to different tribes. A third of her people may already be healing. She had to remind herself of that.

Uranchim glanced up. "Is that it?"

She nodded. "We've collected everything we can."

My kin are still looking for other crops, Kew said.

"Please thank them for us," she said. "Without them we would be far worse off." She took a bowl and a bag of tolui and started grinding the plant.

"What now?" Chinua asked.

She handed him another bowl. "Now we prepare while we wait for news on Kun."

"We should be ready to leave," Jie said.

She nodded. Perhaps the dragons would be less concerned if they saw they weren't planning to stay long. "You and Bao pack the camp."

"Yes, healer." Bao grinned and winked at her as he obeyed her order.

Heat rushed to her cheeks. She hadn't even thought about telling them what to do.

The sun sank low in the sky. Falin should return soon with news from the Adhan tribe. Geriel prayed the cure would work on everyone as successfully as it had on Uranchim.

Three pots cooked over the fire, each at a different state of readiness. As they finished cooking, Uranchim packed them and Kew called another dragon to deliver it. They finished the three batches before Riltien landed, his posture stiff, his colour grey.

Bad news.

The elders have decided. They ask you to leave this land immediately and not to return.

Nausea welled in her stomach. They had two more bags of tolui to cook and she didn't want to wait. Not that it mattered. It wouldn't be enough for every tribe. Hers would not get the cure, not while they had Amslan and Jochi to help them.

"Where are Kun and his men?" Jie asked.

They have stopped in the lower meadow where you camped. I have ordered them not to go any further, but they will not listen. I fear there will be a battle and my kin will be injured.

Geriel shook her head. It wasn't right. "There must be something we can do to help. You've done so much for us."

You can leave, immediately. He shook his wings. *Kew is to stay with you. She will contact us if required. I will send word through her if we find more of the plant.*

Maybe they had enough. If they found somewhere

safe to cook the remaining paste, she could then go home, help Amslan with their people. She nodded.

"Do we have enough of the cure?" Chinua asked.

"I don't know."

"Then where shall we go?" Jie looked at her.

Everyone waited for her answer. "Why are you asking me?"

"Because we need the Rhoran to fight Xue," Jie said. "And without a cure, we don't have our army." He smiled at her. "Lien tasked you with finding the cure."

Nausea welled in her stomach. She was in charge. Bless the ancestors. She could do this. "We can't go back the way we came without risking running into Kun."

The elders do not wish you to see more of our sanctuary, Riltien interrupted. *You will have to return the way you came.* She could feel his sympathy.

"Then we go back, avoiding the lower meadow." The plant they needed grew at altitude. It would be wise to try and find more while they were here. "I am not familiar with the area. Are there more mountains we can search, that aren't the dragon sanctuary?"

Bao nodded. "The Barrier Mountains are towards the great desert."

"How far?"

"A quarter moon maybe."

Too far. "We need to find somewhere safe, somewhere we can make the remaining cure." She glanced at Riltien. "Will the dragons still carry it?"

He shook his head. *No. Kun's presence has reminded our elders of the fear they faced not so long ago from men. They do not wish to have anything to do with you.*

Sadness flooded her. "I am sorry for the trouble we've caused you." She glanced at the four men. They still needed more of the cure. "Do you know the way to these mountains?"

"I do," Jie said. "I was stationed in the desert for many years."

"Then maybe you can take me there?" She turned to Uranchim and Chinua. "When we get safely past Kun, you'll take the remaining bags, make the cure and then take it to the remaining tribes. I will join you when I've found enough for everyone."

Chinua opened his mouth, but she couldn't bear to hear his doubts. "Let's go."

The warriors moved to their horses, while Uranchim and Geriel wiped the bowls and put out the fire.

"You've done well, Geriel," Uranchim said. "Your father would be proud."

Her heart twisted. If he was still alive. She hadn't done enough, and not nearly fast enough.

The sun sank towards the horizon as they made their way down the mountain.

Kun's men have set up camp in the lower meadow, Kew said.

If they were lucky, they could slip past at night without being noticed. Though it would be hard with the horses, the uneven terrain and the pitch black that would fall as soon as the sun had gone to bed. They couldn't risk using any light.

They rode out, Kew leading the way, providing details of the ground ahead. Little moonlight filtered through the branches and each step was a mystery. Without any reference points, time dragged indeterminably. Geriel leaned close to Khulan's neck to avoid stray branches, and her ears strained for sounds.

No one spoke. The horses' hooves rustled through the leaf litter, and the forest made its night-time sounds; birds of prey, the squeals of the hunted or rustlings of small creatures in the undergrowth. Maybe those sounds would cover the horses' steps.

Sometime towards midnight, Kew called a halt. *We are close to the lower meadow. We must go around. It is rockier, but I sense no guards outside the meadow.*

How are you? Geriel asked. Kew had been leading them all night, constantly scanning the surroundings. She had to be exhausted.

Tired, but it's not far now.

Geriel sighed. As soon as they were past Kun, she'd breathe a little easier. They'd travel down the trail they'd used on their way up the mountain.

She adjusted her quiver on her hip and readied her bow. It was comforting having her weapons in hand. The horses moved slowly and Geriel fought the desire to squeeze her legs and urge Khulan faster.

The sounds underfoot changed as they encountered rock, and the hooves made more of a clopping sound. She winced, holding her breath, straining for evidence the guards had heard them. She didn't know how far away the camp was. It was lighter here, the trees further apart and she could make out the shadow of Uranchim in front of her.

Suddenly a shrill squeal pierced the air and the horse in front of her went down, Uranchim thrown clear.

Her heart raced as she leapt off Khulan. Uranchim's horse continued to scream.

He's broken his ankle, Kew said.

She had to heal it before the Bonamese heard, but already people shouted close by. She ran to the horse, but Jie pushed her out of the way, plunging his sword into the horse's chest.

She gasped.

The horse fell silent.

"See to Uranchim," Jie commanded.

The man lay groaning on the ground and the shouts

were coming closer.

They had to move.

"Uranchim, where are you hurt?"

"Shoulder," he said. "Get me on a horse first. It's fine until we're safe."

Chinua had already brought one of their spare horses to him and he and Jie helped Uranchim on.

"Wait! The cure is in my saddle bags," Uranchim said.

They're getting closer. The whole camp has been roused.

Geriel lunged for the saddle bags, struggling with the tie to get them off.

"We have to go," Jie said, trying to pull her away.

"Not without the cure," she said. "Go, I'll catch up." She yanked and the tie finally gave way. Grabbing the bags, she flung them over Khulan's saddle. Chinua and Uranchim were already moving, and through the trees light glowed.

"Mount up," she ordered Jie as she swung onto Khulan. Her horse needed no urging to move and they plunged into the darkness of the forest again. Behind them voices yelled as they discovered the dead horse.

They wouldn't stop there.

The trail's this way. Kew took them further from the camp and they came to a path which led down, wide enough so a little more light filtered through. In front, Chinua increased his pace. Far too fast in the darkness. Geriel was basically blind as she clung onto Khulan, trusting her horse to be sure-footed. She glanced behind. Light bobbed on the path. Jie was at the rear. Any attack could hit him.

More men ahead. Kew's frantic thought pierced her mind and she whirled around. No light but Kew showed her an image of men waiting on either side of the trail. They were trapped.

"Stay low," Chinua called and kicked his horse faster. They cantered down the path, Kew struggling to keep up with their pace, and Geriel readied her bow. "I've got right." She couldn't see what she was firing at, but she had to hope her arrows would be enough to make the soldiers keep their heads down.

"Left," Chinua called.

Jump!

The call came only moments before Chinua's horse leapt into the air in front of her. Uranchim's followed suit and Geriel had only a second to prepare herself as Khulan jumped over something which lay across the path. She glanced behind, as Bao shouted. As if on a signal, sticks of light lit the trail. Geriel blinked, desperately trying to adjust to the brightness.

Bao's horse had cleared the obstacle, but Bao had fallen to the side, clinging to the saddle, an arrow protruding from his back. Something whizzed past Geriel and she turned her attention to the forest, firing off multiple arrows in quick succession. She glanced back.

Bao had pulled himself back into the saddle and was slumped over his horse's neck.

How many men did Kun have with him? How much further until they cleared the soldiers?

They couldn't have far. Kew would have sensed if there'd been a huge party of Bonamese soldiers waiting for them. Unless she was too tired.

As if in the far distance, Kew said, *Clear.*

Chinua slowed a little and yelled, "Everyone all right?"

"My horse has been shot," Uranchim said.

"I'm fine," Geriel called, "but Bao's been shot." She slowed Khulan, slipped from her back and patted her rump to keep her moving. She hurried to Bao and grabbed his hand, scanned him and winced. The arrow had pierced his lung and he was struggling to breathe.

Fear and panic washed through her. She had to heal him. He was the only way they would stop the emperor, and Lien would be devastated if he died. The responsibility smothered her as she leapt onto his horse behind him. "We need to get the arrow out," she told Jie, who rode beside her.

More shouts behind them. The enemy was following.

Taking the arrow out would cause more damage, but it was the only way. She had to be quick. She drew up her waterfall and then said, "One, two, three!"

They yanked out the arrow and Bao screamed. Blood poured over her hands, warm and slick as she covered the wound. Too much blood. Too fast. She couldn't stop it.

An arrow whizzed past her ear.

"Move!" Jie yelled.

She kicked Bao's horse faster, one hand holding Bao upright and the other hand covering his injury. She tried to block out the sounds of the horses' hooves thundering over the ground, but the occasional jolt as the horse misstepped wrecked her visualisation. The calm waterfall was an impossibility. With desperation and brute strength, she dragged her power from the well. Lung first. She focused, knitting the tissue together and Bao's breathing became a little easier.

Now the other injuries. So much muscle and tendon damage, so much blood covering her body. She exhaled, forcing his body to heal, her panic yelling at her to heal him, heal him, heal him.

Her head swirled and she swayed, catching herself before she fell. She clenched Bao tighter, gripping with her knees. Slowly, so incredibly slowly, his body healed, repairing the damage from the arrow. Her well ran lower and lower until she had only a cup left in it and still his wound bled.

She gasped. One more push. Saving his life was more important than retaining her gift. It had to be done. She scooped up the last cupful and poured it into his wound. The bleeding stopped.

She slumped against Bao, her energy spent.

Chapter 12

Geriel's grip on Bao weakened. No matter how much she ordered her fingers to clench, they wouldn't. Slowly she slid sideways, tilting towards the ground rushing past below her. She couldn't fall. Not now, but she was helpless to prevent it. Her body wouldn't respond to her mind. Bao reached back with one arm, pushed her back, leaving his arm there as a guard.

"Hold on," he yelled.

She couldn't. Even speaking was too much effort. She leaned against him as the horses continued their race down the mountain in the dark.

The thunder of hooves became her mantra. Hold on, hold on, hold on. At least Bao sat upright now, fully recovered, but his touch did little to help her. Her whole body was limp, her mind refused to focus, and the jolt of the horse caused her hands to fall from his waist.

"Jie, take her!" Bao's yell sounded so far away, as if he was in a cave. His horse slowed and hands grabbed her waist, pulling her sideways. She couldn't resist, couldn't do anything to help or to stop it. And then she was on a different horse, Jie behind her, his arms around her, holding her in place.

"What have you done?" he growled in her ear.

His anger stirred indignation. "Healed…" she managed to say.

"You've hurt yourself more," he said. "Put yourself in danger, you foolish woman."

She wanted to retort, wanted to tell him she wasn't foolish, that she'd done what was best for her tribe, but the words wouldn't come. Instead she closed her eyes, and darkness found her.

"Wake up, Geriel." The voice pierced Geriel's consciousness. Rough hands shook her, and she opened her eyes. Her head spun, light stabbing her vision and she blinked several times.

Daylight, she was on a horse, but not her own, and a warm body cradled her.

"Wake up." Another shake and she inhaled, recognising Jie's scent.

"I'm awake," she croaked, her mouth dry. She licked her lips and swallowed as her mind struggled to remember.

"Bless the ancestors." The prayer was so heartfelt that Geriel blinked, twisted to look at him. Concern shone in his eyes.

"What happened?"

"You used too much energy healing Bao. You've been unconscious for hours."

Ahead of her rode Chinua, Uranchim and Bao. They'd been attacked by Kun and his men. "Where are we?"

"Almost at the bottom of the mountain. We've hopefully put enough distance between ourselves and Kun, but we need to change horses."

"Where's Kew?"

"Somewhere behind us."

Geriel's heart squeezed. She hoped Kew was safe. There hadn't been time for her to mount a horse.

"Let me down and I'll ride Khulan."

Jie called a halt and as he dismounted, she slumped forward without his body to support her. She dug deep for some energy, clutched the saddle, but her fingers refused to cooperate. Desperately she tried to stop her slide, but it was no use, she fell right into Jie's arms, her face pressed against his chest. Embarrassment flooded her. She hadn't fallen off a horse since she was a child.

"You're not strong enough to ride by yourself." Jie held her upright against him.

How mortifying. She braced her legs and straightened, but her legs were like noodles, limp and wobbly. She gritted her teeth, tried harder, but without his support she'd be in a heap on the ground. She sighed. "You're right. Help me on Khulan. She can carry both of us."

Uranchim hurried over with some dried meat. "Eat this."

She took the food, but holding it was difficult. She managed to get it in her mouth and chewed slowly.

"Are you all right?" Uranchim asked.

She nodded. Hopefully all she needed was rest. Swallowing, she said, "What about you? You injured your shoulder."

"I'll survive. I've chewed some ground root for the pain."

If she hadn't been so weak, she could have healed him.

"Let's keep going," Chinua said.

Jie helped her onto her horse, then they continued down the mountain. She wanted to ask whether Kun still followed them, but what did it matter? They had to keep moving. She leaned back, nestled in Jie's arms.

"Rest now," he murmured. "I've got you."

She was too tired to disagree and his strong arms around her gave her comfort. Almost against her volition, her eyes closed and she fell asleep.

The sun was at its peak when she woke next, though the trees shaded them from most of its rays. The ground around them was flat. They'd made it off the mountain. Jie's arms tightened around her. "How are you?"

"Tired." Too tired to care she was still wrapped in his arms, still unable to ride by herself. Her stomach rumbled. "And hungry."

A rustle and then he handed her some meat. "Eat this."

"Thank you." Before she bit into it, she asked, "Where are we?"

"On the road heading towards Rhora," he said. "Uranchim hopes Falin will come to us. He was supposed to report back after taking the cure to the Adhan tribe."

She straightened. That's right. She'd forgotten all about it. "Any word from Kew?"

"Not yet. Chinua believes she'll catch us. Apparently, she found Lien both times they were separated, so she should find us as well."

Geriel finished the meat and Jie handed her some more. She smiled. She must have worried him for him to be taking such good care of her. "How is Bao?"

"Alive," he said. "You saved his life."

She nodded. That's what she did. Which reminded her of the plants they still needed to make into a paste. "Can we stop for a while? Make more of the cure?"

He shook his head. "Not yet. We don't know how

far away Kun is. Until Falin or Kew arrive, we've got to keep moving. We're outnumbered and we can't risk Bao's life again."

"What about the lives of my people?" she demanded.

His chuckle vibrated against her. "You have your spark back."

His laugh soothed her anger, but she still wanted an answer. As she opened her mouth to continue arguing a shadow crossed over them. Falin circled overhead before he came to land in front of them, right in the middle of the crossroads they'd just reached.

Jie reined in Khulan.

"How did it go?" Uranchim demanded.

You distracted Kun and his men from the sanctuary. They are now following you rather than invading further. We thank you.

Jie grunted as Uranchim asked, "What about the cure?"

Falin was silent for a long moment. *It healed many people.*

Geriel's stomach dropped. "But not all?"

He shook his head. *It had no effect on those who are advanced in the disease or where the disease is contained, but the container is large.*

"How many?" Chinua asked.

Two-thirds of the tribe are now clear. I don't know about the other tribes.

Geriel slumped, closing her eyes. She'd been so close. Many of her people were still suffering and hoping for a cure.

Jie squeezed her thigh. "You will find a cure which heals everyone," he murmured.

His confidence and light touch warmed her, but she didn't deserve such faith.

"We still have more plants to prepare," Uranchim

said. "We must help those we can."

"We don't have time to stop," Jie said. "Kun is coming after us."

"This is where we split up," Geriel said. "Uranchim, you can make the paste without me. Take the plants and ride hard for Rhora. Kun shouldn't follow you."

"We still need to find a permanent cure," he said.

She nodded. Her original plan had been to gather more tolui in the mountains bordering the desert, but she also needed a treatment that healed everyone. "I'll continue to gather plants on our way to the Barrier Mountains." There had to be more plants, something they hadn't seen before.

"You have no one to test the cures on, and no dragon to take the potions," he protested.

She glanced at Falin.

I will discuss with my kin. Now Kun has left the mountain, they may agree to help again.

"Thank you."

"How many men does Kun have with him?" Jie asked.

About five score.

A hundred men to their four. They couldn't afford for Kun to catch them.

"Kun's soldiers are elite fighters," Bao said. "Trained in multiple forms of combat."

Chinua nodded. "They were fierce when they attacked us earlier this year. If we can't outrun them, we'll need more men."

Could they risk asking the Adhan tribe for warriors? If they weren't all cured, it might spread the disease further.

"We need to make it to the desert outpost," Jie said. "They are loyal to the true emperor; they will fight Kun."

"Can you guarantee it?" Bao asked.

Jie nodded. "If they see you're alive, they will fight."

Geriel's priority had to be finding the cure, not fighting Kun's men. "I'll go on alone," she said. "The rest of you can lead Kun to the desert outpost while I find a cure."

"No!" Four voices replied together.

She stiffened but before she could protest, Jie said, "Kun's men aren't the only dangers in the mountains and the road to the desert outpost is the fastest way to where you want to go. If Kun follows us that far, we can defeat him and then you can find your cure."

"A battle could take days or moons and we can't afford the delay," she said.

"Yes, but weak as you are, you can't fight us, and we're all in agreement you can't go alone," Jie said and the other men nodded.

"We could ask the Danil tribe for help," Chinua suggested. "None of them were infected by the curse. They could meet us at the desert outpost and can help fight Kun and his men."

It still didn't address the issue of finding a cure. "Will Batzorig send his men?" Geriel asked.

Chinua nodded. "I can be convincing."

"How long will it take to get them?" Bao asked. "We don't have a lot of time."

"I can get fresh horses on the way from the other tribes," he said. "Where is the desert station?"

Jie told him.

"I'll meet you there in a quarter moon."

Jie's eyebrows raised. "That quickly?"

Chinua grinned. "We travel light and fast when required."

"All right," Jie said. "Uranchim returns to his tribe to make the paste and send it to those who still need it.

Chinua rides to Danil for help and will meet us in the desert. Bao, Geriel and I will travel directly there and continue to search for a cure on the way." He squeezed her waist. "Do you agree?"

She didn't like it, but they were right about the potential for her to run into trouble alone. She sighed. "I agree."

Chinua glanced at her. "Have you recovered from healing Bao?"

No. Her mind was still foggy, her limbs weak. It was her own fault for panicking, for forgetting everything Dhalin had taught her. She was too scared to test her gift. She would let herself rest, refill and try tomorrow. "I will be fine."

He narrowed his eyes.

She asked Falin, "Can we send word to Lien and Anming?"

Not without risking the emperor discovering the dragons are helping. He might decide to attack our sanctuary.

She turned to Bao. "What about a message?"

He shook his head. "It's too risky. Kun can order any messenger to hand over the letter to him."

"Wei will get word to them that we left," Jie said.

Lien would assume they'd return home, would think they'd found a cure. She could endanger herself by returning to the tribe. Geriel's skin prickled. There was nothing she could do about it. "Do you know where Kew is?"

You are travelling too fast for her. She has been ordered to return to the mountains.

Geriel hoped Kew would make it safely back to the sanctuary. "Let's move." She shifted to dismount and Jie's hands tightened around her.

"Stay with me until nightfall," he said. "You should rest while you can."

Chinua nodded. "He's right, Geriel. You need to find another cure."

Her chest squeezed at the reminder. Exhaustion and fear swirled around her and she was still too weak to confront either. She sighed. "All right." Resting against Jie was a little too comforting.

Chinua gave his spare mount to Jie. "I'll get a fresh horse at the Adhan tribe." Which meant they each had a spare horse. They would need them to outrun Kun.

As Uranchim and Chinua turned north, Geriel mounted one of the spare horses and Jie mounted behind her.

Safe travels. Falin took to the sky and Jie kicked their horse into a canter.

There was still a long way to go.

~*~

Geriel slept on and off during the afternoon and into the night. She slowly came to, feeling a light caress on her thigh. Warmth flooded her as she realised it was Jie's hand and she straightened, her head banging his chin.

He coughed and pulled his hand back. "You're awake."

She swallowed, itching for some distance from him. She couldn't think with him so close. "Where are we?"

"Close to the border," he said. "We'll ride parallel to it."

"And Kun?"

"There's been no sign of him," Bao answered. "He has more men, so he shouldn't be able to keep up with us." He yawned loudly.

"You both need rest." It must have been days since they'd last slept.

"We thought we'd stop for a couple of hours when

you next woke," Jie said. "Can you stand guard?"

"Of course." Though her limbs were stiff, she should feel better when she dismounted.

Jie directed his horse off the road and into the forest. They found a small clearing, tethered their horses and then Jie and Bao unrolled their beds.

Geriel stretched, enjoying the pull of her muscles. She had control of them now. She wasn't as weak. "I'll see to the horses."

Jie nodded. "Wake us before midnight."

Geriel relaxed as both men lay down and she turned her attention to the horses. There was plenty of grass for them to graze, so she took the brushes out of her saddle bag and brushed the horses which hadn't been ridden first. The normal task soothed her and a sweet scent tickled her nose. She followed it and found a tubular purple flower. She picked the flower and added it to her bag to check when she was feeling better.

As she finished brushing the spare horses, she transferred the saddles to them and brushed the horses they had been riding, all the while keeping her senses tuned to her surroundings. They were far enough from the road that the horses' occasional snorts shouldn't be heard.

With the horses cared for, she stretched again. Exhaustion no longer haunted her, but her energy wasn't high. She ate some more dried meat, but lighting a fire to make a tonic was too risky. Kun's soldiers would need to rest at some stage too, but they could also be pushing on, trying to catch them.

She frowned. What was Kun's obsession with Jie? It seemed odd he would continue to pursue them. Though if he considered it a matter of honour, then it made more sense. Lien had held honour in high regard when she'd first arrived in Rhora. Maybe it was a

Bonamese thing.

Unless Kun had caught sight of Bao… Then he would never stop. Bao threatened Kun's place in the palace. If Bao defeated the emperor, Kun would no longer be heir.

She moved around their temporary campsite. It was too dark to make out any more than shapes on the ground around her. She brushed her fingertips against the leaves of a bush, but didn't connect to it. Fear held her hostage. She had definitely used too much of her gift healing Bao, she remembered scooping the last cupful. She wasn't ready to face the possibility she'd condemned the rest of her people to death by forgetting everything the dragons had taught her. She needed to rest, in hope it would refill. Tomorrow was soon enough to try again.

Still her mind wouldn't let her ignore the concern. It looped through the possibilities. If she'd lost her gift, she couldn't test the plants, couldn't find a cure. If she couldn't find a cure, up to a third of her people could die. If a third of her people died, they would be vulnerable to the emperor's further attacks.

She gritted her teeth, took long slow breaths the way Lien had taught her. Calm was what she needed right now. She would visualise her waterfall, reconnect with the image and see what happened.

Crack.

Geriel whirled around to face the sound, her bow drawn. She moved back against a tree, blending in with its shadow and slowly scanned the darkness for movement. Jie and Bao were dark mounds on the ground, relatively easy to distinguish, and the six horses tied up showed it was a campsite.

More soft crunches as whatever or whoever it was moved through the forest, skirting the camp. Geriel turned with it, still scanning for other movement in case it was a decoy. A gentle breeze brushed her face. They were downwind of whatever it was, but it hardly mattered. The thing must know they were there. The horses shifted, heads up, alert and one whinnied. If only she had her father's ability to communicate with them, then she might know what she was dealing with.

Stepping away from the tree to wake Bao and Jie would make herself a target and she'd lose the element of surprise.

The bush on the other side of the clearing rustled. She took aim.

A head poked out of the bushes, low to the ground. Some sort of animal, but smaller than a wolf or leopard. She strained her eyes, hoping to get a clearer picture.

It stepped through the bushes and stood looking at the sleeping men. It was on all fours like a cat but its tail was longer. She didn't know much about the animals of this region. She shifted forward, bow still raised and the animal turned to her, its tail erect, body alert.

"Go," Geriel murmured. "I don't want to kill you."

Jie sat bolt upright in bed and lunged for his sword. "What?"

The animal fled.

Geriel winced as she stepped away from the tree. "You sleep lightly." It was impressive how quickly he'd reacted. "We had a four-legged visitor but I'm not sure what it was. I didn't want to kill it."

He sighed, sheathed his sword. "What time is it?"

"You can sleep for another hour or so."

Bao groaned. "We're awake now. We might as well go."

Guilt filled her. "Sorry. I shouldn't have said anything."

"Better than being attacked," Jie said.

Bao stood and stretched.

"Any other problems?" Jie asked.

"No, it was quiet."

"Good. Do you want to ride with me again?"

She did want to ride with him, liked the feel of his arms around her, but it wasn't smart. They'd ride faster if they both had a horse. "I'll be fine on Khulan."

They mounted and Jie led the way back to the road. They walked side-by-side, Geriel in the middle as if she needed protecting. Bao should be between them. He was the most valuable.

When the sun rose a few hours later, they stopped to eat.

Bao winced as he dismounted, holding his back where the arrow had pierced him.

Concern filled her. "Are you all right?"

"It hurts a bit." He took his hand away. Blood covered it and his face was pale.

Her heart stopped. "Let me look." She hurried to him, pulled up his tunic. The wound had split open and blood oozed out. She sucked in a breath. She'd thought she'd healed him fully.

She had to heal him now. Closing her eyes, she breathed deeply, visualising the waterfall. Gently she reached out to connect with Bao.

Nothing.

Her throat closed and fear prickled her skin. Don't panic. Bao needs you.

She tried again. No connection, not even a slither of his consciousness. Gritting her teeth, she tried forcing her consciousness into him, but it didn't work. The waterfall was full of air not water and her hand was covered in Bao's blood.

"What's wrong?" Bao asked.

"Your wound has reopened."

Jie wandered over and hissed when he saw the injury. "Can you heal it?"

"No." She blinked the tears away. They couldn't know. It might still come back. It had only been a day. "I'm ah… a little tired still."

He frowned at her, examining her face a little too closely. She turned away. "Let me get a thread and some bandages. I can stitch it."

She went to her saddlebags, took a deep breath as she found the things she needed. She'd used a lot of energy healing Bao the first time. She was still tired, and they'd been travelling non-stop.

All her well-intentioned thoughts were drowned out by the one that wailed, You've lost your gift!

"Do you need a hand?" Jie's question broke through her thoughts.

"No." Even without her gift she could stitch Bao's wound, dress it properly. Having an injury would disadvantage him, but as long as the wound wasn't too deep, he should be fine. She closed her eyes. She had no way to tell whether it was only the surface wound that had split, or whether it went deeper.

She could do nothing about anything deeper.

Quickly she made Bao sit and gave him some ground root to chew on. "It will block some pain."

Bao grimaced as he chewed on the bitter-tasting root. Jie stood over her, too close, watching her. "Can you see to the horses?" she asked. "They need to be brushed."

He gave her a long look and then went to do as she asked.

She threaded the needle, her hand shaking. Carefully she wiped away the blood and examined the wound. It didn't look too deep, which hopefully meant the rest of the injury was staying healed. She stitched his skin together and then cleaned the wound again, adding some cleansing paste to it, before winding a bandage around his chest. "How do you feel?"

He spat out the root. "I'll survive."

She prayed he was right. She tidied her things, and then helped Jie finish brushing the horses. As Bao turned his attention to making breakfast, she said, "I'm going to look for plants."

"Don't go far," Bao said.

"I'll go with you." Jie walked over.

No, she needed to be alone. "Better if you guard Bao," she said. "If Kun catches us, he will be the target."

Jie scowled. "Bao can look after himself."

"And so can I." She didn't wait for his response. She snatched her bow and quiver from her horse and strode into the forest, needing to be as far away from them as possible.

She hurried, but still reviewed the plants she passed. Nothing new, nothing she hadn't already tried. When she was far enough away from the camp, she stopped, sank to the ground beneath a tree and pulled her knees to her chest.

Qadan's mercy. She couldn't have lost her gift, she couldn't afford to.

Her body shook and her chest ached as tears welled in her eyes. She was useless without her gift. Her people were relying on her and she'd let them down, all because she couldn't control herself, couldn't master her gift. Her stupidity had a terrifying cost. Dhalin and Falin had tried to teach her.

She had failed them.

Failed her whole tribe.

Burying her face in her knees, she sobbed, the fear, the loathing, the despair welling. How could she face

Lien or any of her family again?

Perhaps she should never return. She wasn't worthy to be called Rhoran.

"You won't find many plants looking at your knees."

She gasped, looked up through her tears at Jie.

Of course he couldn't leave her alone. Of course he had to see her at her most vulnerable.

His expression changed to one of sympathy and he crouched next to her, pulled her into his arms.

She clung to him, unable to resist his kindness, needing someone to hold her for a moment and soothe her pain. Needing Jie to hold her.

"What's wrong?"

No. She couldn't tell him. Best he think she was upset for some other reason. "I miss my family."

Jie pulled away from her, his eyes flat. "Don't lie to me, Geriel."

Guilt hit hard, stopping her from denying it.

He brushed her loose hair back from her face. "You've always been honest with me. Don't change now. I like your honesty, your willingness to stand up for yourself." His thumb caressed her cheek. "Trust me. Tell me what is really wrong."

When he looked at her like that, so intense, so sincere, she couldn't deny him. She wanted to tell him, wanted to share her life with him. "I can't heal Bao."

His smile was small. "You already did," he said. "You saved his life." He shrugged. "You may not have used your gift to heal the last bit, but you still stitched him."

She shook her head. He didn't understand. "No, I can't connect to him, to any of the plants around me." She took a long, shuddery breath. "I've lost my gift."

Jie's mouth dropped open. "Are you sure?" She glared at him and his smile was quick. "Of course you are." He sighed. "How do you get it back?"

"I don't think I can."

"But what about the cure…" The dawning realisation slowly crossed his face. "Oh." He squeezed her. "We'll figure something out." He was silent for a moment. "Maybe Dhalin knows of a way."

"We've had no contact from her," Geriel said. Besides, she'd never heard of someone who had lost the gift being able to retrieve it again.

"Then we do it the normal way—through trial and error. We collect plants and send them back to the tribes."

They'd done enough of that already. If only the tolui had cured everyone.

"Hey." He tilted her head so she had to look at him. "I have faith in you. You will find a cure." The earnest expression on his face made her want to believe. "You're an exceptional woman, Geriel."

Her heart skipped a beat. He thought she was exceptional?

"You're not alone in this. We'll help you any way we can."

She shifted. "Why are you being so nice? I don't deserve it. I've failed my people."

He shook his head. "You only fail when you give up and I won't let you." Jie looked deep into her eyes. "And I'm being nice because I like you, Geriel. A lot."

Oh. The intensity in his eyes left her in no doubt about what he meant. Her lips parted. But now wasn't the right time to explore their feelings. There was too much at stake. "I like you too—when you're not bossing me about."

He laughed, his eyes lighting up, and the sound made her forget her troubles for a moment. "That's one of the things I like most about you—the way you say what you mean."

"I'm Rhoran," she said. "We're taught to speak our minds."

"I look forward to meeting the people who taught you."

Her stomach dropped and she pulled away. "I don't know whether Father is still alive," she said. "He was infected." She climbed to her feet. She couldn't sit here feeling sorry for herself, or wishing Jie would kiss her. She had to find another cure.

Jie stood, placed a hand on her arm to stop her from walking away. "I'm sorry. We'll find the cure." He brushed a kiss against her cheek, his lips soft and warm. "I am yours to command."

She closed her eyes briefly. His faith in her and his willingness to follow her gave her strength while also adding pressure for her to succeed.

He slipped his hand into hers. "Come. Let's get back to Bao. Perhaps rest is all you need."

She hoped that was the case, but she'd always been able to feel the presence of her gift before. She let him lead her back to the camp.

And prayed to Qadan for a miracle.

Chapter 13

When they next stopped for a rest it was nearly nightfall. They'd ridden hard, only stopping to change horses and for Geriel to check Bao's wound. No blood came through the bandages so at least the constant pace wasn't making it worse. Jie led them off the main road into the forest.

"We all need some sleep," he said. "We'll get a couple of hours now."

As she dismounted, she asked, "Can I make a small campfire? I want to heat some tea for Bao to make sure his wound doesn't get infected."

Jie nodded. "There's a river nearby. I'll get us some fresh water."

She worked quickly, building the fire while Bao took care of the horses. When Jie returned with their flasks, she heated some water and added the leaves Bao needed. "I'll take the first watch," she said. "I need to make some tea for myself as well."

Jie studied her and then nodded. "Wake me in a couple of hours."

She handed Bao his tea. "Careful, it's hot. Drink it all and then get some rest."

"Thank you, Geriel."

She smiled at him and returned to the fire, adding the restorative herbs to the boiling water. Hopefully it would give her more strength, allow her to find her gift. After the tea had steeped for long enough, she put out the fire, monitoring it to make sure all the embers had died, and then sipped her drink as she cared for the horses and kept watch.

Something nudged against Geriel's mind. She frowned. It was similar to the way Kew used to communicate with her before she'd learnt how to mind speak. Geriel opened to it and Kew's voice came through.

I am coming.

Geriel turned towards the mountains. *Where are you?*

The foothills. Took a shortcut.

Aren't you supposed to be staying with the dragons?

My family needs me more.

Geriel smiled at the love and determination coming through. It would be good to have Kew with them again. *How far away are you?*

Will be there by morning if you wait.

Could they afford to wait? *Can you tell where Kun and his men are?*

A pause. *Not yet. I'm too far away. I can only find you, because I know your mind so well.*

Geriel glanced at the sleeping forms of Jie and Bao. They'd been riding for days. Some further rest would do them good and when Kew joined them, she could warn them if Kun approached. *We'll wait.*

Thank you.

Geriel placed her cup with her things. The tea had given her a boost of energy, but would it be enough for her to access her gift? Her skin prickled. Only one way to find out. She brushed her fingers against the leaves of a nearby bamboo. The gentle shush of the wind through the leaves was similar to the waterfall. She focused on the sound, regulating her breathing, and visualised the waterfall. At first nothing happened and then gradually something glimmered in the depths of the pool. Her gift.

She reached out, connected with it and then brushed the properties of the bamboo. The connection was weak, but it was there.

Geriel let the visualisation go, her mind a little clearer. Her gift was still there. A little more rest and she'd try again tomorrow, test if she could heal Bao's injury properly.

The night grew late and Geriel's eyes became heavy. She should wake Jie for his turn to stand guard. He and Bao could do a couple of hours each and then hopefully Kew would arrive. She squatted next to Jie but before she could say anything, he clasped her hand. She gasped.

"I'm awake." He sat, his head level to hers and then glanced at the sky. "It's close to midnight. You were supposed to wake me earlier than this."

"There's been a change of plan," she said. "Kew communicated with me. She asked us to wait here until morning when she'll arrive."

"I thought she had to stay." His hand still held hers, and his thumb rubbed the back of it.

Geriel swallowed hard. "She wants to help us."

"I'm not sure waiting is wise."

She wasn't either. "Kun and his men have to sleep at some stage too."

Jie nodded. "But he can send messengers ahead. People will be looking for us."

Her muscles tightened. Would they have to fight the whole way to the mountains? "Kew can warn us if people are a threat."

His fingertips brushed her cheek. "I don't like relying on things I don't understand. We don't know how reliable the dragons are. They didn't warn us Kun had arrived."

"They were grieving the loss of an elder. Besides, Bao needs more rest to heal properly and you need more sleep."

She could make out the curve of his smile in the moonlight. "*Tián xīn*, a soldier's life is full of sleepless nights."

She wasn't sure exactly what *tián xīn* meant, but it sounded sweet. "Stand guard for a few hours," she said. "Then we can ask how far away Kew is."

He paused before nodding. "All right. Rest now." He kissed her cheek and warmth filled her. She shifted to her bedroll and lay down.

What was she supposed to do with this heavy, shiny, happy feeling inside of her? Now wasn't the time to lose her heart over someone. Too much was at stake.

And he wasn't even Rhoran.

Jie made a circuit of their small camp, alert and wary. He would protect her. She'd worry about her feelings another time. Her eyes closed and she drifted off to sleep.

I am here. Don't shoot me.

Kew's words pierced Geriel's dreams and she woke. The sky was the purple of pre-dawn. Bao stood guard and Jie sat up from his bed next to hers.

Rustling sounded through the forest and Kew communicated again. *Almost there.*

Bao kept his bow pointed towards the noise, but his arms were relaxed. Kew burst into the clearing, panting, and he relaxed his hold.

"Are you all right?" Geriel asked.

Tired. She plonked herself next to Geriel.

Jie handed them both some dried meat. "How long do you need to rest?"

I can rest on one of the horses.

He blinked and Geriel laughed. "The horses generally don't mind her. She's ridden them before."

"Good," he said. "We should get moving. Do you know where Kun is?"

Kew snorted out a breath. *Give me a second.*

Geriel packed her bed and readied the horses while Kew rested. Then Kew sat bolt upright.

They are close. Less than a league away.

The words spurred everyone to action. Bao mounted, Jie tied his bed to his horse and Geriel checked the spare mounts. "Can you communicate with the horses now?" she asked Kew. Last time her father had acted as interpreter for Kew and the horses.

Yes.

Moments later they were all mounted, Kew using her limited flying ability to hover over the horse's back and settle.

"Let's go," Jie said.

They rode hard for several hours, swapping horses when needed. Occasionally they skirted towns, moving through the forest so the villagers didn't notice them. It slowed them, but would hopefully put Kun off their trail.

At midday Bao handed out food while Kew, who had slept for much of the journey, went into the forest to find her own meat.

"How much further is it to your outpost?" Geriel asked.

"Days still," Jie answered.

If they continued to ride at this pace, she wouldn't

have time to search for a cure. But they couldn't let Kun catch them either. She'd scanned the foliage as they rode, looking for anything different, but it was all flora she recognised.

"We need to ask Kew how much ground we've gained," Bao said.

"We should also replenish our stock of arrows," Jie said. "We don't want to have to fight hand-to-hand if Kun catches us."

He was right. She only had a few arrows left in her quiver. "What's ahead of us?"

Jie frowned. "There's a border outpost not far away and I was friendly with the captain. There should only be a few men still stationed there, since they're no longer building the wall." He paused. "They'll definitely have arrows and our food is running low."

"It's a big risk." Geriel's stomach swirled. "If Kun sent a messenger ahead, he might have reached there by now."

"Captain Zhong is an opportunist, so he might ignore any message from Kun if I can convince him things are about to change."

Bao shook his head. "We can't all go. Geriel would cause an outcry because she's Rhoran and you're a wanted man," he said. "But no one knows me."

"You're too valuable," Jie said. "If something goes wrong, we can't afford to lose you."

"It's not safe for you either," Geriel said. "We should just keep moving. We might be able to get arrows in a village."

"Not of a decent quality," Jie said. "I can also discover any news. If the emperor's planning something, word would have reached the border outpost, even if it's simply to prepare for further orders."

"Can we trust the captain?" Bao asked.

"He didn't like being stationed all the way out here," Jie said. "But as I said, he'll do whatever he thinks will advance him. If he knows there's about to be a coup, he'll support whoever he thinks is the winning side."

"And if word has reached him that you need to be stopped?" Geriel asked.

"Then you ride on without me. Some of my men will recognise Bao. They'll follow him."

Unacceptable. "No. Rhoran don't leave men behind."

"I'm not Rhoran."

"But I am." Geriel glared at him. "We'll wait for an hour on the other side of the outpost and then we'll come for you."

"No—"

"Yes." It wasn't up for discussion. She wouldn't fail him like she'd failed everyone else.

Bao nodded. "I don't like you going, but you're right. We need more provisions and the border outpost can provide them. You can't be longer than an hour though."

Kew returned with a spring in her step.

"Have you eaten?" Geriel asked.

Yes.

"Where are Kun's men?" Bao asked.

They are too far behind for me to sense.

"How far can you sense?"

Several leagues.

Good news. She glanced at Jie. "So we agree you get arrows and food, and then leave as soon as possible?"

Jie inclined his head. Geriel nudged Khulan into a walk. "Let's go."

It wasn't long before Kew sensed the outpost, and she led Geriel and Bao into the forest, with Jie staying on the road. Geriel glanced back at him, nerves humming across her skin. "Safe journey."

He nodded. "I'll see you soon."

She hoped so. She wasn't leaving without him.

They travelled through the forest, using small trails which were perhaps used by the soldiers hunting for fresh meat, or else people from the nearby village. Kew ordered them to stop a couple of times, but they didn't meet any people. Geriel tucked her braid into her tunic and covered her head with a scarf so at first glance it wouldn't be obvious she was Rhoran. Eventually Kew announced they could wait where they were for Jie.

They were surrounded by trees but there was enough of a clearing for them all to fit. Geriel glanced at the sun. One hour. She wouldn't give him more. Not with Kun so close behind them.

Rather than sitting still and fretting, she dismounted. "Bao, can you take care of the horses? I'm going to look for plants."

He nodded. "Don't wander far."

I'll keep watch, Kew said.

Geriel wandered into the forest, gathering a few unfamiliar plants. She followed the gurgling sounds to a stream where she filled their water flasks, and then gathered some plants which grew on the edge.

Nerves prickled her skin. Time to try her gift again. The restorative tea she'd had last night had helped. Closing her eyes, she reached for her gift, brushed her fingers over the thin leaves and reached her consciousness out to the plant, but still the gift glimmered out of her reach.

Defeated, she dropped her hand.

What is wrong? Kew lay on the ground nearby, resting.

"I can't access my gift."

Kew sent her compassion. *I will ask Dhalin when I next see her. We should head back.*

She was right. It was close to an hour since Jie had left them, but when she returned to Bao, Jie wasn't there. "Can you sense him?" she asked Kew.

A pause. *He is in no danger. He tells me he will leave shortly.*

Geriel let out a breath. "Tell him to hurry."

Kew snorted. *He says to be patient.*

"Where's Kun?" Bao asked.

Kew was silent for a moment. *I can't sense him.* Her top lip curled. *Something is strange.*

Geriel's muscles tightened. "What is?"

There are many more people in the outpost than when Jie first arrived.

"How many?" Bao demanded.

More than five score.

"Kun?"

There are so many thoughts. It is difficult to distinguish one from another. The anxiety in Kew's thoughts was clear. She'd had a hard few days.

"We should go." Geriel strode to her horse.

"We don't know what we're facing yet." Bao grabbed her arm. "If Jie is safe and we ride in there, we'll cause more trouble."

He was right, but she didn't like it. "Should we move closer?"

Wait. I am talking to Jie.

Geriel gritted her teeth and paced while Kew was silent.

Suddenly Kew snorted and smoke came out of her nose.

"What is it?" Geriel asked.

He wants us to leave. He's trying to hide his thoughts from me. Something is wrong. I need to get closer.

Geriel swung onto Khulan. "We'll leave the spare horses here."

Bao nodded. "How close do you need to get?"

This way.

Geriel checked her knives were in place, moved her quiver so it was next to her thigh, and mentally prepared herself. Her stomach was lead. If Jie wanted them to leave, then he'd been captured.

And there was no way she was leaving him behind.

~*~

Kew moved through the forest ahead of them, the faint rustle of her footsteps leading them. Geriel yearned to ask for updates, but she kept her mouth closed, her thoughts within. It would only distract Kew. If there were hundreds of people in the outpost, finding Jie would be difficult.

Stop.

Geriel reined in Khulan as Kew moved back to them.

Kun is there. I don't know how he travelled so fast. I should have been paying better attention.

"Has he found Jie?"

Yes. They are preparing something. Jie is behind bars.

She exchanged a glance with Bao. "How do we get him out?" She had no idea how the outpost was laid out, no clue what would be inside.

Bao hesitated. "He said to leave him."

"You can. I won't." She glared at him. "Could you pretend to be a soldier and bring me in?"

He shook his head. "It won't work. Kun knows about you." He paused. "And I can't afford Kun to recognise me."

Geriel gritted her teeth. Jie would do anything for him. "I won't do nothing!"

"I know." He turned to Kew. "How many guards are on the gate?"

Three.

He dismounted, gestured for Geriel to do the same. They walked forward until the formidable walls of the outpost appeared in the distance. Bao took a stick from the ground. "I once accompanied Anming on a tour of the border. All outposts have the same configuration." He drew a square. "Gates at either end, watch towers on the corners and buildings built out from the walls which don't have gates. Upstairs are barracks and downstairs are the prison and eating quarters. There's a big central square. Jie's likely to be in the prison here." He stabbed at the ground.

"So I need to get past the guards, into the prison, free Jie and escape without anyone raising an alarm?" An impossibility. The walls shut them in, locked their escape routes. Give her a camp on the steppes any day over this.

Geriel shifted forward to peer through the trees. A caravan moved towards the outpost. Their horses were a mixture of Rhoran and lesser breeds, but their loose, baggy clothing identified them as traders from across the mountains. Some of the women wore head scarfs covering the lower half of their faces. Perfect. "I'll enter with them." She could figure out her next step after she was inside.

"Your clothes are too Rhoran." Bao retrieved his spare set of clothes from his horse. "Change into this."

She looked at him. "I have long hair and breasts. No one will mistake me for a man."

"You might pass as a villager," he said. "It's not unheard of for people on the border to mix with Rhoran."

She took the clothes and quickly changed. She

whirled to get Khulan, and Bao grabbed her arm. His eyes were haunted. "I can't go with you."

She nodded. "Return to the spare horses. When we escape, it's likely to be at a run." She glanced at Kew. "Will you be able to hear my thoughts when I'm inside?"

Yes.

"Stay with Bao. Tell him what's going on and when to be ready. I'll be back as soon as I can."

Her muscles were tight as she paused with her hands on Khulan's saddle. Rhoran horses were in high demand with traders. Their stamina and strength were unparalleled by any other breed of horse. It might give her an advantage. She mounted Bao's horse instead which was one of the spare Rhoran mounts. "Take Khulan."

She kicked the horse into a trot to catch up with the travellers, nodding a greeting at the man who guarded the rear and he smiled at her.

"That's a nice horse you've got there," he said in Bonamese.

Hope lifted her. She nodded. "He carries me where I need to go."

"How much do you want for it?"

She smiled. "He's not for sale." Her father had once taught her to never appear overeager when negotiating with traders.

"Everything's for sale. Name your price. We've got some lovely things from across the mountains."

Her pulse beat fast. "How would I travel anywhere without a horse?"

"I will swap you for mine."

The bay horse he rode was a good specimen—not a Rhoran horse, but its steps were sure and its coat healthy. It would be fast in short bursts, and that's all she needed it for.

They were getting closer to the gates. She nudged her horse closer to his. "My horse is worth far more than yours."

He grinned. "Then name your price."

She glanced at the outpost again. She didn't have much time. She lowered her voice. "I want your headscarf and one for myself," she began. "And I want your help getting me into the outpost without detection."

His eyes widened.

"Once inside, I want you to find the other Rhoran horse inside and bring it to where we tether our horses. Then you will transfer my saddlebags to your horse, and if required, you will create a diversion for me when I leave."

The man's eyes became shrewd. He glanced at where the front of the caravan had already stopped outside the gates. "That sounds like a lot of trouble for one horse."

"Not for you. If I get caught, you deny knowledge and you get both Rhoran horses."

He scratched his chin. "Or I could tell the guard you're trying to sneak in and get both horses anyway."

Her heart stopped. "You do that and you'll never trade in Rhora again."

"Who will know?"

I will. Kew's voice sounded in Geriel's mind and the man gaped. *I will tell the khan you betrayed Geriel and he will put a price on your head.*

"What?" The man's face went pale.

The guard at the gate was moving along the caravan, checking it. They were running out of time. "Do you agree?"

He nodded. "But I'll only create a diversion as long as suspicion doesn't fall on me or my people."

"Agreed." She held out her hand and he shook it.

"Which gate do you plan to leave from?"

"This one."

"Come with me." He led her through the group of traders, handing her two head scarfs, and they stopped behind one of the wagons, out of sight of the guards while he tied one in place so only her eyes were showing.

The caravan started moving again as they were granted access.

Geriel let out a quiet breath. *Kew, tell Jie I'm coming for him.*

Silence and then Kew said, *He says don't. Kun is with him. He's being beaten.*

Geriel touched her sabre. *How many men are with him? Just Kun. He's asking about the Rhoran.*

At least he didn't know about Bao.

Geriel nudged her horse forward and the man put his hand out, stopping her.

"Stick with me."

They stayed in the middle of the group and she kept her head down, her muscles tight as she moved past the guard and then she was inside the outpost. Walls surrounded her in every direction and her breath came in pants. Trapped. She prayed for the never-ending sky on the steppes.

"Don't panic." The man patted her hand. "Can you see the horse you want?"

She scanned the yard. The traders were already setting up their market stalls for the soldiers and men were coming out of the barracks. Over on the far side, the gates stood open and Jie's horse was tied to a railing nearby, several quivers of arrows tied to the saddle. "The brown horse by the other gate."

The man glanced in that direction as he dismounted.

"A fine specimen. I don't suppose you want to swap him as well?"

She smiled. "No." She untied her saddle bags, taking a wrapped package from her medicine bag and tucking it into a pouch on her belt. Then she handed the bags to him.

"Pity," he said. "If it's the prison you're after, it's that building there." He nodded towards the building near the well.

She gasped.

"Not many other reasons for you to sneak in here." He grinned and gave her two water flasks. "Go fill them."

She nodded her thanks and moved towards the well. Her shoulders were tight and she waited for a shout of alarm, or for someone to grab her shoulder, but it didn't happen.

Geriel resisted the urge to look around, check for anyone watching her.

"Where are you going?" The sharp order in Bonamese made Geriel jump.

She turned to the soldier on her right and held up the water flasks. "Water." She did her best to mimic the trader's accent. Behind the cloth she gritted her teeth, itching to reach for her knives.

Finally, the soldier grunted. "Be quick."

She nodded and hurried to the well. Quickly she filled the flasks, raising her eyes to scan the yard. Soldiers dressed in grey were already congregating by the market stalls. Others dressed in black—Kun's men—had come to the doors of nearby buildings but when they'd seen what was happening, they went back inside, probably to rest after their hard ride. The trader she'd bargained with was already across by the other gate, untying Jie's horse. No one questioned him. The soldiers were too interested in the market stalls. It might have been moons since they'd had contact with outsiders and the traders always carried exotic items.

Geriel half-filled the flasks so they weren't too heavy. The building the trader had pointed out to her was only a few steps away and two grey-clothed soldiers sat at a table, framed by the open door. She unwrapped the package and palmed the paste it contained, glad her scarf helped block the scent.

Here goes. She walked slowly, carrying the water flasks in front of her as if she'd been ordered to fetch water. Nerves swarmed in her stomach as she reached the door. With a deep breath she walked in.

"What are you doing here?" one man demanded.

"Good sirs, we have come from afar to show you our wares." She held up the flask as if it contained wonders. "Why don't you join us outside?"

One soldier studied her. "We're working."

"On such a fine day? Such a shame. Perhaps I can offer you a drink?" She glided towards them.

"Nice of someone to think of us," the other man said.

Geriel clenched her teeth. She had to be fast. She moved between them, using her body to block what she was doing and as she filled one soldier's cup, she pressed the paste against the other soldier's nose. He had no time to react. The paste was fast acting and he slumped, knocking over his glass.

"What have you—?"

She didn't give the other soldier the chance to finish his question. She shoved the paste at him and in seconds, he too was unconscious. Quickly she strode to the door and closed it. Then she grabbed the rope hanging on the wall and tied the men, stuffing gags in their mouths in case they woke too quickly.

Kew, how many men are with Jie?

Two of Kun's men are outside the room where he's being kept.

There was only one door off this room and she had no excuse to open it. The Bonamese soldiers wouldn't be fooled by her. If only she hadn't left her bow with her horse. She cracked open the door and discovered a large hallway with another door at the end and two guards outside.

She had one chance to get this right.

She prayed to Dzhambul, God of war and hunting, and centred herself. Then she opened the door wide, releasing her knives in quick succession, and rushed forward, drawing her sabre. The first knife hit its target but the second soldier had time to duck and he yelled as the knife embedded in his shoulder. Damn. She lashed out, sliced his arm as he reached for his sword and then followed it with an upswing across his neck. He groaned and slumped to the ground, blood pouring from his wounds.

They were both dead. Her throat closed. She listened for any signs of alarm. Nothing, but no noise from beyond the door either. Kun had to have heard her, he had to be waiting.

Tell Jie I'm outside. She retrieved her knives from the dead bodies.

Jie says to go. Kun is inside and is ready for you.

It couldn't be helped. A bow rested against the wall, a quiver full of arrows next to it. She grinned and grabbed it, testing the bow quickly to feel its flex. It was bigger than what she was used to but it would do.

Kun might kill Jie if she wasn't fast. She braced herself and flung open the door. It took a second for her to register what was inside. Jie tied to a chair, his face bloody and beaten, Kun standing behind him with a knife to his throat.

Kun laughed. "Your rescue party is a single woman? They obviously don't care much about you."

Geriel drew her arrow, pointed it directly at Kun's heart. "Let him go." Her hands shook.

"One yell from me and this whole room will be full of soldiers," Kun said.

Her blood pounded in her veins. There had to be something that would keep him quiet. Only one thing came to mind. "And one word from me and they'll know the true heir is alive."

Kun's face blanched and he stepped back, the knife moving from Jie's neck. "What?"

Jie groaned.

Geriel fired and the arrow hit Kun's shoulder. He stumbled back, fell to the ground. She ran to him, shoved the paste in his face. She couldn't kill him. He'd been kind to Lien during her time at the palace and perhaps Lien could convince him to support Bao. His eyes closed. Then she whirled to Jie and cut the ties on his wrists. His tunic was covered in blood.

"What have you done?" he whispered.

Guilt stabbed her. "What I had to do to get you out." She cut the ties on his ankles.

He tried to push her away. "Go," he whispered. "You can't carry me out."

"I'm not leaving you." She'd come this far, she'd killed those men. But Kun had done a lot of damage in the short time he'd been with Jie. And she couldn't heal him, no longer had her gift. She wrapped her arm around Jie's waist, placed her shoulder under his armpit and helped him to his feet. He groaned and stumbled, his weight pulling her forward and they almost crashed into the wall. There was no way they'd make it across the yard to where she'd left the horses without someone stopping them.

She had to heal him, had to reach her gift.

She pulled him through the doorway and locked the door behind them. Jie leaned against the wall, gasping. Sending prayers to Qadan, she closed her eyes, visualised the waterfall. The shushing roar of water filled her ears and she almost felt the spray on her face. She reached out to the glimmer of power at its edges. This was her gift, her value to her tribe, to her people. She refused to accept it was gone. Not when she needed it. With determination she drew it towards herself, embracing it. Then she connected to Jie.

Pain, a whole lot of pain. She gasped, scanning him, finding the worst affected areas. She healed his internal bleeding first. Broken fingers could wait, but the agony in his legs couldn't. She swept over it, taking away as much pain as possible. She released her gift, a little more energised, but she didn't want to overdo it. Couldn't risk making a mistake and being too exhausted to walk.

"Better?" she asked.

"Some."

She'd try again when they got to the next room. Placing her arm around his waist, she partially carried him along the hallway to the smaller room where the two guards sat slumped on their chairs. Using the water she'd brought, she cleaned Jie's face.

He pushed her away. "Leave me, Geriel. You need to go."

"No," Geriel hissed. "Stop protesting and start helping." She held a cup to his lips and he sipped it. Then she stripped off the tunic of one of the unconscious soldiers. "Put this on." She handed it to him and then dragged the pants from the soldier.

Jie coughed, maybe an attempt at a laugh as he took the pants from her. While he dressed, she peered out of the window. Most of the soldiers were with the traders, browsing their wares. Several of Kun's men were more alert. They strolled around the yard, constantly scanning the area. They would certainly notice a stumbling Chungson soldier.

She returned to Jie and visualised her waterfall again. Her gift shimmered in the water, but it was faint. She had to have faith. She drew it closer and connected with Jie. Still so much pain. His head next, so he could think clearly. She brushed the aches away, her body trembling.

Jie pulled away. "Enough. I will be fine." He took a step towards the door and stumbled.

No, he wouldn't.

There had to be something in the room that could help them. A few swords lined the wall, but fighting their way out of here would only end in their deaths. Some bottles sat on the shelves and she hurried over. Nothing was written on the outside so she cautiously sniffed each one. Rice wine. Perfect. She grabbed the bottle and returned to Jie. "You need to pretend you're drunk," she said. "I'll pour some of this over you and you need to take a sip." It might help his pain. She held the bottle to his lips and he did as she asked. "How do I say, he's had too much to drink in Bonamese?"

Jie told her and she repeated it. Then she poured the rest of the rice wine onto his clothes. He coughed at the stench and her eyes watered. It was the best she could do.

She peered out the window again. No one was looking their way. She adjusted her head scarf to ensure it still covered most of her face. "Let's go."

He pressed heavily against her as she closed the door behind them and took the few steps back to the well. He leaned against the stone as she bent to draw more water, her eyes on the courtyard. Jie's horse was next to the horse she'd swapped with the trader. She could do with his help now. *Kew, can you find the man who helped me? Ask him to come over to us.*

No response. Had something happened to Kew?

People would stop her if she brought the horses to Jie, so they had to walk. He slurred something loudly in Bonamese that Geriel didn't understand. She glanced up and he shifted her scarf down, his lips meeting hers, kissing her. She froze. Why was Jie kissing her here?

A loud voice next to her swore. "Drunk at this time," the man said. "And already availing himself to the traders' wares." The derision was clear.

"The whole outpost needs better training," someone replied.

Jie was protecting them. She slid her arms around his waist, pulling him closer and kissed him back. His lips were firm, warm and ever so nice, though he tasted like rice wine and blood, reminding her he was injured. She softened her kisses, sliding her tongue over his lips. He groaned—either in pleasure or pain—and she stepped back, her heart racing.

Movement caught her attention as the soldiers turned towards the prison. They had very little time.

Someone called to them and they stopped to talk.

"We need to go," she whispered, her heart still beating fast. She shifted, placing her shoulder back under Jie's arm.

"You better not be giving out kisses for free."

Geriel jumped as the trader hefted Jie from the other side.

Relief filled her. "Thank you."

With them both sharing Jie's weight, they reached the horses in no time.

Jie lunged for his horse, still looking like he was

drunk. After a couple of attempts, he swung himself into the saddle.

"Go." She slapped his horse on the rump and it trotted towards the gate, Jie clinging to it.

She grabbed the trader's horse as the soldiers reached the prison entrance.

"Take your own." The trader handed her the reins. "I don't want to be caught in this."

Her saddlebags were already back on it. Bless his ancestors. She mounted. "When you're finished in Chungson, go to the Erseg tribe. Tell the Khan Temur Geriel promised you two of Sukh's finest horses for helping her escape."

He grinned and nodded.

"Close the gates!" someone roared.

No time. She kicked her horse and he lunged forward. People in front of them scattered. Jie was already through the gates, riding hard, though he glanced back at her. Soldiers looked around, confused, but a couple reacted quickly, running to the gates as she charged for it. Slowly the doors swung shut. She grabbed her bow and fired fast, hitting the men at the gate, yet the doors still moved. She ran out of arrows and bent over her horse's neck, urging him faster. Almost there.

Something hard hit her, knocking her forward onto her horse's neck. She gasped as pain shot through her, making her dizzy. She hung on, gritting her teeth as she cleared the outpost. More arrows flew around her and her horse screamed as one hit him. Ahead of her, Jie had stopped, was waiting for her.

"Go!" She waved one hand and pain ricocheted through her back. Damn it. The arrow in her back moved with every step of her horse, twisting and tearing. Warmth poured down her back. She was bleeding heavily.

Kew!

Some villagers saw me and I had to run. With Bao.

Meet us on the road. We'll be there soon.

Behind her the soldiers were already giving chase. She yanked out the arrow stuck in her horse's shoulder and it bucked a little at the pain. She gritted her teeth and clung to the saddle. Jie wasn't far ahead of her. He wasn't riding hard. Was he too injured?

Before she could ask, Bao crashed onto the road in front of them, Kew riding one of the horses.

She glanced behind. The soldiers were keeping pace.

She drew level with Jie. He clung to his horse, his body jerking with every step. He couldn't keep up this pace for long and she needed the arrow in her back removed. *Kew, is there anywhere we can hide?*

I don't know. Frustration and despair came through.

"Bao, do you know this area?"

"We'll reach the edge of the forest soon."

"Then what?"

"The steppes."

Home. She grinned. They'd find somewhere to hide on the steppes.

The arrow shifted in her back, sending searing hot pain through her. She squeezed her eyes shut. Ignore it. Jie needed her. Closing her eyes, she breathed in the waterfall and again a glimmer of her gift was at the edges of her reach. She used the water to pull it forward, stretching for it. Her mind brushed it, drawing it in and she reached for Jie's arm. The arrow dug deeper and she winced, pulling back. "Jie, reach out to me."

He opened his eyes and his mouth dropped open. "You've been shot."

"Yes. Give me your arm."

He did as she asked and she connected, this time fixing his broken fingers and the further aches in his legs. He needed to grip the horse.

He snatched his hand back. "Conserve your energy."

She would be useless if she had to fight with an arrow in her back. Jie and Bao had to be at full strength. Dizziness rushed through her and she swayed, gripping her horse with her thighs. She was losing too much blood.

Ahead, the trees fell away and the world opened into the grassland of the steppes. She inhaled deeply as the tension of being constantly surrounded fell away. She urged her horse faster and glanced back. The soldiers had fallen behind a little. Their horses weren't as fit as Rhoran stock.

She scanned the horizon, noting the undulations, the dips and mounds. That way. She could lose the soldiers there.

Her body slumped against her horse's neck, too tired to hold it upright. *Kew, we need to go this way.* She sent a visualisation of the path she'd chosen.

"Geriel!" Jie rode next to her, more alert, more upright.

"Follow Kew," she said.

It was harder and harder to focus. She closed her eyes, hugged her horse, trusting it to keep up with the others, to follow Kew's lead. The pain captured her focus, any misstep or jerk of her horse sending more agony through her. She reached over her shoulder, tried to put pressure around the wound, but the action unbalanced her.

They rode over the first hill and she glanced back. No more Bonamese.

Kew led them up the next hill and through its valley, turning west again and then over the next hill heading north. At the top of the next hill Geriel glanced back. The Bonamese had disappeared, but there was an obvious trail of hoof prints for them to follow. *Slow down and spread out.* It took too much energy to speak aloud, but Kew told the others. They cantered through the valley and their hoof prints blended better. They continued for another half an hour, Geriel clinging on hard before Kew said, *I cannot sense them any longer.*

"We need to stop," Jie said. "Geriel needs help."

She didn't deny it and pulled her horse to a halt.

Jie dismounted looking far more alert than he had, though he winced as he walked towards her. He helped her down and she collapsed onto the ground. Bao grabbed her medicine bag and hurried over. "How bad is it?"

"She's lost a lot of blood."

Geriel wanted to reassure him, but it was too much effort. *Horses.* The horses needed to cool down after such a hard run.

She wants you to look after the horses.

"After we've seen to her," Jie said. "This is going to hurt." He pulled out the arrow and the pain pierced her soul. Blackness claimed her.

Chapter 14

Geriel smelled dirt, grass and horses. The scent of the steppes. Home. She opened her eyes and lifted her head, wincing at the pain in her shoulder. She lay on her stomach on the ground.

"You're awake." The relief in Jie's voice was evident.

She slowly sat, the effort almost more than she could handle. She'd been shot escaping the outpost. She'd managed to heal some of Jie's injuries before succumbing to her own. No wonder she was exhausted. "How long was I out?"

"Long enough for us to clean, stitch and bandage the wound," he said.

"Thank you." Both Bao and Jie stood over her and Kew rubbed against her side. The rest of the steppe was empty, but Kun's men would be out there somewhere. "We should keep moving."

Jie reached for her hand and helped her to her feet. "Can you manage it?"

"Yes." They had to keep moving, had to get back to the mountains so she could find a cure. Then they could stop Xue.

I'm sorry, Kew said. *I failed you. My skills are not strong.*

Geriel squatted next to Kew. "You are a wonderful guide. You need rest too. None of us blame you." She hugged the dragon.

Bao handed her a freshly made dumpling. Jie must have bought food at the outpost before he'd been arrested.

"Kew tried to contact Dhalin to heal you, but either we're too far away, or she's not answering," Bao said.

I need to watch you heal cuts, Kew said. *Then I might be able to help.*

It didn't matter. She'd survive. "How are you?" she asked Jie.

"Sore, but I'll manage."

She turned to her horse and gasped. He still wore his saddle and was lathered in sweat. Geriel whirled around. "You didn't take care of the horses!"

Jie raised his eyebrows. "We were more concerned about your survival."

She shook her head. "You should have been more worried about them. Without them we'll never get far. Quickly, we need to brush them." The sun was low in the sky and the day would be cooling soon. She brushed Khulan and transferred the saddle to her, before brushing the horse that had carried her. She cleaned its arrow wound, but it didn't require stitches.

Kew turned black. *Kun's men are getting closer.*

Geriel mounted Khulan. "Let's take it slow at first." She didn't have the energy for anything faster. "Tell us if they are catching up."

Kew nodded as she fluttered onto a horse's back.

Geriel led the way, her grip loose on Khulan's reins. She inhaled deeply, wishing she could get energy from air alone. Her eyelids drooped, but then she straightened, wincing at the pain. A communication marker in front of her pointed towards the Gertan tribe. She couldn't lead them there with people still ill. She turned more west, and eventually angled south back towards the Chungson border. As night fell, she stopped so they could eat.

"How far away are Kun's men?" Bao asked.

I can no longer sense them.

"Geriel needs to rest," Jie said. "Can we afford to?"

"I'm fine." She brushed Khulan, her movements slow and small, exhaustion her constant companion again.

Jie took the brush from her and led her away from the horses, pushing her gently to the ground. "You're not. I'll take care of the horses, you eat."

"You were injured too."

"You healed the worst of it," he said. "I can handle bruises and pain."

"We need to talk about what happened." Bao handed her some food and then went to care for his own horse. "Jie?"

He nodded. "It was easy to get inside the outpost." He continued to brush. "I told Zhong about the failed attack on Rhora and that I was returning to my outpost. He agreed to give me food and arrows in exchange for news from Bonam." Jie shook his head. "He knew little of the treaty Xue signed, but had heard of Fen's death. That information came with the order to ready his troops, but he hasn't heard anything since."

"He didn't know Kun was after you?" Geriel asked.

"No."

"When did Kun arrive?" Bao asked.

"As I was about to leave. Zhong stopped me when he saw Kun, said I should wait to meet him. Then Kun spotted me and it was too late to escape. He dragged me into the prison and beat me. He wanted to know why I was still alive, what I was doing in the Chungson mountains, how many Rhoran were there. I tried to convince him I was alone, but he didn't believe me, knew I had some sort of agreement with the Rhoran."

Bao moved on to the next horse. "What happened to him?"

"Geriel shot him."

Bao's eyebrows raised. "Is he dead?"

"He shouldn't be," Geriel said. "I shot him in the shoulder and they discovered him quickly."

"I'm glad. He was a sweet child," Bao said.

Jie grunted. "From all reports, Xue beat that out of him."

Geriel glanced at him. "What do you mean?"

"The emperor doesn't abide weakness, and the empress wanted her son to be heir. Between the two of them, Kun was brutally moulded into shape."

"That's awful!"

Jie nodded. "But another reason he will protect his father's claim to the throne."

Geriel winced, guilt stirring her stomach, making what she'd eaten protest. "I told Kun you were alive."

"What?" Bao demanded.

"Jie was nearly unconscious in the chair and Kun held a knife to his throat. He was going to call his soldiers." She sighed. "So I told him if he shouted for his guards, I would tell them the true heir was alive. He was so shocked he stepped away from Jie and I shot him."

Bao swore.

"I'm sorry. It was the only thing I could think of."

"Did you mention Bao's name?" Jie asked.

"No."

"That's something I guess." Bao sighed.

Jie glared at him and squatted, placing a hand on her knee. "You saved my life."

She nodded. "I should have found another way."

"He held a knife to my throat."

"It's done now," Bao said. "He doesn't know if you're lying or where I am, or what I'll do. The uncertainty will make him wary."

Jie grinned. "It will, won't it?"

She really liked his smile.

He stood and walked back to the horse he was brushing. "So how did you get into the outpost, Geriel?"

"The traders smuggled me in." She told her story. "When I can, I'll send word to Temur to honour the trader's request."

"He deserves it." Jie moved on to the final horse. "So you can access your gift again?"

"Only a little." A rejuvenating tea would help, but they had nothing to start a fire with. The horse dung was too damp.

Kew sat next to her. *I can heat the water.*

Of course. She tried to climb to her feet, but her legs refused to hold her.

"What do you need?" Jie asked.

"A cup, some water and my satchel with teas."

He brought them over and she poured the liquid into the cup. Kew breathed fire on it, warming it slowly until it boiled. Geriel added the tea. "Thank you."

You're welcome.

When the tea had steeped, she sipped it, the liquid warming her insides and giving her a boost of energy. Jie and Bao joined her once the horses were taken care of for the day and they all ate.

"Do we stay here tonight?" Bao asked.

Geriel felt so much safer on the steppes, but it wasn't getting them closer to the desert, or to the plants which might hold a cure.

"Let's get a few hours' sleep," Jie said. "We can reassess at midnight."

I'll stand watch.

Geriel stroked Kew's hard scaly skin. "You've been running hard all day."

"And you didn't notice Kun's men approaching the outpost," Bao said.

Kew snorted. *There were many thoughts, many voices at the outpost and around the village. It was hard to distinguish where everyone was.*

Geriel glared at Bao. "We couldn't have rescued Jie without Kew."

"Are we near any Rhoran tribes?" Bao asked.

"Even if we were, we can't go," Jie said. "They're still infected by the curse and if they see Geriel, they may want her to stay."

He was right. If she hadn't almost drained all her gift she would have insisted on stopping, and helping, but she couldn't even heal Jie's and Bao's remaining injuries.

"All right. I'll take the first watch," Bao said.

"Let me check your wound first," Geriel said. They'd been riding hard all day and it might have been damaged.

"Don't use any healing," Jie ordered as Bao lifted his top.

The skin around the stitches was red, but they hadn't pulled too much. She didn't bother even trying to find her gift. Bao was in no danger. "It looks fine."

Bao covered himself again and then Geriel rolled out her bed. She definitely needed sleep. Hopefully she would feel better when she woke for her watch.

~*~

The next few days passed in a haze of riding. They

crossed back into Chungson and the land around them grew drier and drier. There were few plants for Geriel to test, but she gathered what she could, using her gift sparingly to check their properties.

Geriel pushed the horses as hard as she dared. When they stopped to rest, she and Kew discussed how to regain full access to her gift. Kew had paid attention to the way she healed, had listened to her and Dhalin talk, but neither of them came up with a solution. Occasionally a dragon flew far overhead, but they never stopped, never tried to communicate with Geriel or Kew. They had essentially been cut off from the rest of the world. Geriel prayed Uranchim had made it back to his tribe safely and that Chinua was mobilising the Danil tribe. He should have reached them by now.

Both Chinua and Uranchim knew where they were headed, so they would send news.

The mountain range took up more of the horizon as they drew nearer over the long hot days and cold nights. On the fifth day after leaving the dragon sanctuary, Jie said, "We should reach the desert outpost by the end of the day."

"Will Kun have reached it before us?" Bao asked.

Jie shook his head. "He was injured, and his men can't keep the pace we have. Even if he sent a message, there aren't many places along the road where a messenger can get a fresh horse."

"Will your men still be loyal to you?" Geriel asked.

"I hope so."

She embraced the tension settling on her shoulders. It was an almost constant presence now. "Kew and I could hang back in case you need rescuing again."

He shook his head. "If a patrol sees you, they may attack."

She could outrun a patrol easily enough.

"We should stick together," Bao said. "Do the patrols come and go at specific times?"

Jie nodded. "They usually leave at sunrise and they head in different directions to cover the border."

So from here out they needed to be watchful for patrols as well.

Towards mid-afternoon the outpost finally came into view. It seemed to nestle at the bottom of the mountain, but as they grew closer Geriel realised the outpost was still a league or so from the base. Like the previous outpost, this was a large square walled building with towers on the corners. A few figures were atop the walls, but the surrounding dry plain was empty.

Geriel pursed her lips. "We're on Rhoran horses. Will they attack if we approach?"

"They shouldn't without provocation," Jie said.

A party approaches behind us.

Geriel twisted as a dozen riders dressed in grey tunics cantered towards them. Chungson soldiers, but were they with Kun? "What do we do?" She checked her knives, moved her quiver into position.

Jie squinted at the group. "They look like one of the patrols. Kew can you get a sense of who they are?"

They're excited to come across some travellers. Several of them have been bored by the patrol.

"Let's wait until they are closer," Jie said. "I might recognise them."

"Kew, if we speak to them, can you tell us if they're telling the truth?" Geriel asked.

Yes.

Geriel glanced towards the outpost. The gates opened and a group rode out. "More are coming." They would be trapped between them. "If they're hostile, we ride for the mountains." She couldn't risk being caught.

She still had a cure to find. She swung the bow off her back.

"Put it back, Geriel," Jie said. "They'll see it as a sign of aggression."

"They're herding us between them." Still she replaced her bow and slipped her knives into her hands.

The groups reached them at the same time and the lead rider of the patrol called, "Halt!" He eyed Kew warily.

Kew puffed out her chest and snorted smoke.

Jie smiled. "Is this any way to greet your captain, Ru?"

The man's mouth dropped open. "Captain Jie? You're alive?" He frowned at Geriel. "Did you capture the Rhoran woman when you attacked their camp?"

Geriel coughed in disbelief as Jie shook his head. "I have much to tell you. What news have you had from Bonam?"

"We get little news out here, but we thought you were dead."

True.

"I'm not that easy to kill. Can we talk in the outpost?"

Ru ordered the men at ease and Jie rode next to him. The other outpost soldiers circled them, blocking off any escape. Geriel shifted closer to Bao. If necessary, she could charge those three men and it would give them enough of a gap to ride towards the mountains.

She couldn't hear Jie's conversation, but Kew had dismounted and trotted next to him, occasionally affirming the truth of what Ru said. Promising.

"Didn't think I'd see the captain with a filthy Rhoran whore," one soldier muttered.

Geriel tightened her hold on the knives. She should have expected she wouldn't be welcome here. Well she wasn't staying. As soon as Jie and Bao were safe, she would head into the mountains to find a cure.

"The captain always has his reasons," another said. His loyalty was comforting. After a few moments, she studied both men. She'd avoid the one glaring at her. How many others agreed with his sentiment, but were too professional to show it?

They reached the outpost and rode through the wide wooden gates. Geriel's skin crawled. She'd only just escaped a place like this. In fact it was identical, a large open courtyard with gates at either end and buildings on both sides. Even the well was in the same place. Why did they insist on living enclosed by clay brick?

Soldiers in the towers watched them enter, a couple with bows drawn until Ru called, "Captain Jie has returned."

The soldiers cheered and flocked around, all wanting to greet him. Jie dismounted, calling out greetings and Geriel scanned those closest to him. No one appeared unhappy. She lifted her gaze to check those on the watch towers. All observed the courtyard, but no one raised a weapon.

Geriel directed Khulan away from the crowd and dismounted, tying her horse and the spare mounts to the railing outside the stables. They had carried them far and fast and deserved a long brush and good food. They might not have long to rest.

Bao joined her. "He's certainly popular."

It said a lot about his leadership style. "I'm glad. We need loyalty at the moment."

The sun sank low in the sky. She would give the horses a proper rest tonight and then travel into the mountains in the morning.

Jie strode over. "Come, Ru has refreshments upstairs."

She glanced at him. "I'll take care of the horses first."

He waved a hand. "The men can do that."

How could he still not understand how important the horses were to their success? They'd enabled them to escape Kun twice and carried them hundreds of leagues. They deserved to be cared for properly. "I'd prefer to do it myself." She glanced at Bao. "You go. You both have much to discuss. Take Kew with you so she can ensure Ru is telling the truth." It would be nice to have some time to herself.

Jie frowned, but called over an older soldier with flecks of grey in his hair. "Tadashi, watch Geriel for me. When she's finished with the horses, bring her upstairs."

"Yes, sir." Tadashi saluted and as Jie and Bao walked away, he scowled at her.

Geriel sighed. Jie should be more careful with his words. He'd said watch like she had to be guarded. Turning to Tadashi, she asked, "Is there somewhere we can store our tack?"

He blinked. "You speak Bonamese."

She nodded.

"Where did you learn?"

"My sister taught me." Perhaps mentioning Lien's name would gain her some trust, if not respect. "You might know her as State Princess Lien. She is married to our Khan."

His eyes narrowed. "How is the princess your sister?"

"My family adopted her when she came to Rhora. Certain traditions needed to be carried out for the wedding and it was too far to return to the imperial palace."

He nodded thoughtfully and his whole demeanour

shifted from hostility to curiosity. "I worked at the imperial palace when the princess was young. I spent time guarding her brother." Sadness crossed his face. "I was… surprised to hear she was wedded to the khan. Is she well?" Hope widened his eyes.

Jie had said his men were loyal to the true emperor. Geriel smiled. "She is. She has been welcomed into our tribe and is one of our leaders." She finished brushing Khulan. "Where can I leave our horses?"

"This way."

She followed him to the building opposite the prison. It had wide doors, but Khulan pulled back when Geriel went to lead her in. "It's all right." Geriel stroked her nose. "It's just for a short while."

"What's wrong?" Tadashi asked.

"Our horses have never been inside a building." She understood Khulan's reluctance. Nearby was a fenced off area containing targets, probably used for training. "Can I leave them in there for the night?"

Tadashi frowned. "I'll have to ask the captain."

"All right. I'll leave her here while you do." She tied the reins over the post.

Tadashi hesitated and then stopped a soldier coming out of the stable. "Go ask the captain if the horses can be left in the training yard. They won't go inside the stable."

The man nodded and hurried away.

Geriel returned to the other horses and took another set of brushes out and handed them to Tadashi. "While you're here, you might as well help."

He puffed out his chest and glared at her as if affronted by the fact she was giving him orders.

Of course. She was back to the expectation women did what they were told. She sighed. "Please. It will be much quicker if you help."

"All right." He moved to the horse next to her. "How did you end up with the captain?"

She couldn't tell him that story. If word spread she'd been around people who had the Traders' Curse they would run her out of here. "It's a long and boring story," she said. "Jie speaks fondly of his time here. How long have you been stationed in the desert?"

"Eighteen years."

Since Lien's father had died.

Tadashi glanced at her. "How long have you been with the captain?"

"A while. Do you patrol into the mountains?" Maybe he could tell her what plants grew there.

"Sometimes. Are you staying long?"

She grimaced at his short answers and then laughed. They were both trying to get information from each other. "It is up to Jie to tell you his story. I am a healer and I'm searching for new plants which could help my tribe."

He grunted. "Don't know much about plants except what's in the infirmary."

"You have an infirmary?"

He nodded towards a door next to the stable. "Dai's in charge."

Geriel longed to go there now, discover if Dai knew of a cure, but she had to finish the horses.

"Tadashi," a man called. "Both captains say it's fine for the horses to be left in the training yard."

Tadashi raised a hand in acknowledgement, and Geriel moved the horses she'd finished brushing into the pen.

"Looks like you've been in a fight," Tadashi said when she came back. He pointed to the arrow wound on the horse he brushed. Geriel nodded and examined the wound. She'd cleaned it each day and it had almost healed.

When they finished brushing, Tadashi showed her where to store their tack and then said, "I'll take you to the captain now."

"Thank you."

The sun had dipped below the horizon, but light clung to the day. Some men lit lanterns which hung around the buildings and others trained with swords. The rich smell of roasting meat floated out of one of the nearby buildings and Geriel inhaled deeply. It had been a while since she'd eaten. Upstairs, they walked past several dorm rooms full of beds before they came to the room at the end. Tadashi knocked on the door and Ru's voice called, "Enter."

Jie, Bao and Ru sat around a table drinking tea and Kew lay by Jie's side. Jie smiled at her. "Are the horses cared for?"

She nodded. "Tadashi was kind enough to help me." She sat on the spare seat next to Jie and Ru gasped, horror crossing his face. What had she done wrong now?

"Geriel is our equal," Jie said. "She is a healer who has saved both of our lives and has a place at our table always."

Ru cleared his throat. "A female healer is unusual."

"Not in Rhora." Geriel smiled though she was too tired to deal with small-minded prejudices today. She longed to return to Rhora where she was accepted for who she was.

"Tadashi, is something wrong?" Jie asked.

The soldier still stood by the door, his mouth open and his skin a shade paler as he stared at Bao.

"Tadashi, you look like you've seen a ghost," Ru said.

Kew shifted. *He recognises Bao.*

Of course. If he'd guarded him as a boy, he would be familiar with the prince.

"Close your mouth and shut the door," Jie barked.

Tadashi jumped and did what he was told.

Geriel tensed. Was it still safe for them here? Had Jie told Ru who Bao was?

Tadashi took a step closer, still staring at Bao.

Bao smiled. "It's good to see you again, Tadashi."

The man's eyes glistened. "Prince Bao?" he whispered.

Bao and Jie both nodded.

"But... you died!"

"Obviously not," Ru said.

The poor man looked as if he was going to faint. He fell to the ground and kowtowed, his forehead touching the ground.

"There's no need for that, Tadashi," Bao said.

Geriel stood and helped him to his feet, leading him to her chair. "Please sit." His skin was like ice. She pressed him into her seat and then took another chair from behind Ru's desk and carried it to the table.

"The story you know is false," Jie told him. "Emperor Huang and his wife were murdered by Minister Ying. Only Bao escaped with the help of the dragon, Manalin."

"I remember the dragon." The colour was coming back into the man's face as Geriel poured him a cup of tea.

"Manalin took Bao to Chungson because the emperor believed his brother had desires for the throne," Jie continued. "Lord Anming's father didn't know who to trust and then Xue invaded Chungson and forced them to become vassals. They decided to bide their time until Bao was older."

"But even now we don't know who to trust," Bao

said. "It's been almost twenty years and most accept Xue as the true emperor. We weren't certain we'd have enough support to take back the throne."

Geriel could see Tadashi's mind clicking back into motion. "What's changed?"

"The emperor made a mistake." Jie's smile with lethal. "He married Princess Lien to the Rhoran Khan and now we have their support."

Tadashi shook his head. "The Rhoran are barbarians. Our people will not accept them on our land."

Geriel shifted, ready to defend her people.

"It is temporary," Bao assured him. "When I am emperor, I will correct the misperceptions about our neighbours."

"Can they be trusted?"

"Can you?" Geriel replied. "In the past eighteen years the Bonamese have invaded and stolen our land, kidnapped our people and spread lies about our deeds. We respond only when we are attacked first."

Tadashi pressed his lips together.

"The emperor's latest atrocity was sending goods infected with the Traders' Curse as part of the reparations," she continued. "Over half my people are ill and dying."

Jie swore and shot her a look that clearly said shut up. Both Ru and Tadashi leaned back.

So he hadn't mentioned that bit.

"Then how can they help?" Ru asked.

She glanced at Jie before responding. "I've been searching for a cure. We've found plants which slow the spread, and some which cure it if it's caught early, but nothing to stop advanced infection."

"You should talk to our healer," Ru said.

Jie frowned. "We don't have a healer."

"We do now. One of the men showed an interest and when the last group of traders came through he brought several books on the topic." Ru shrugged. "I figured it wouldn't hurt to have someone who knew more than basic healing."

Geriel's heart skipped a beat. "Can you take me to him now?"

Ru glanced at Jie, who nodded. "Tadashi, take her to Dai and then return."

I'll come with you, Kew said.

"Of course." Tadashi saluted and after he stood, he bowed low to Bao. "It is a pleasure to see you alive."

Bao smiled and Jie said, "Keep it to yourself for now. Be quick. We have a lot to discuss."

Night had fallen, but enough lanterns lit the way. They passed soldiers in the corridor and each one jolted when they saw Geriel and Kew.

Are they more concerned about you or me? Geriel asked.

Kew snorted. *You.*

Perhaps their fear would give her a measure of safety.

Tadashi took them into the infirmary. A young man about Geriel's age sat at the wooden table, a book open in front of him and a bowl of noodles to the side.

"Greetings, Dai," Tadashi said.

Dai didn't look up.

Tadashi cleared his throat. "Dai!" Dai jumped, spilling his bowl. He swore, grabbed the book and lifted it out of harm's way.

"What?" He glared at Tadashi and then stood up fast, knocking over his chair, and stared at both Geriel and Kew. "What's going on?"

"Captain Jie has returned with some friends. This is Geriel of Rhora and the dragon, Kew."

Dai stayed where he was, the dislike clear in his eyes.

His father was killed in the raid on the Rhoran camp. He does not like you.

Not a good start. She inclined her head, tried to remember what Lien had told her about Bonamese etiquette. "It is good to meet you, Dai."

He said nothing.

"Geriel is a healer and would like to read the books you bought from the traders," Tadashi said.

Dai hugged the book closer to his chest.

"Captain's orders."

Dai scowled and then he sucked in a breath and his gaze darted to Kew.

"Did Kew speak to you?" Geriel asked. "It can be a little disconcerting the first time."

Dai nodded. "Does it do it a lot?"

"She speaks when she has something to say."

Dai placed the book back on the table, took a cloth and cleaned his mess, his posture a little less tense.

"I need to return upstairs," Tadashi said. "Will you be fine here?"

"I'm sure Dai and I can work something out," Geriel said. And if not, it wouldn't be too hard to overpower him and tie him up.

Dai nodded and Tadashi left.

Geriel stayed where she was, a few steps inside the room. "Kew tells me your father died during the raid on our camp."

He flinched and moved away from her. "I'm not certain. We never received word back."

She ached for him, but at least she could give him some closure. "I'm very sorry," she said. "The only person to survive was Jie. He was fortunate Princess Lien recognised him and begged for his life."

His mouth dropped open. "Everyone else died?"

"Yes. The attack was unprovoked. We couldn't

afford for the soldiers to regroup and attack again."

He shook his head. "The Rhoran stole something from the emperor. The soldiers were to get it back."

How many lies had Xue told? "The Rhoran rescued some of their people who had been taken prisoner," she said. "The emperor then attacked Lien, our khan and the party they were with."

"How do you know this?" he demanded.

"Lien told me." She had to connect with him in order to read the book he held. "When the Bonamese attacked, I watched friends and family die. I had to fight to survive."

His posture relaxed a little. He took a step closer to the table. "The emperor should never have ordered the attack. It was suicide."

She nodded. "Too many innocent people on both sides died that day."

Surprise showed in his eyes. "You are right." He swallowed hard and then gestured to a chair. "What do you know about healing?"

She moved closer, placed her hands on the back of the chair opposite him. "I have trained as a healer since I was twelve," she said. "But I am always eager to learn more."

"Then you probably know more than me. I'm not sure if there will be anything useful for you in these books." He placed the book on the table and pushed it over to her. Then he took two more thick bound books from the shelves.

Her heart skipped a beat. So much knowledge at her fingers. Would there be a cure between the pages?

"I am looking for a cure," she said. "The emperor infected my people with a disease known as Traders' Curse." She described the symptoms. "It's killing my people."

Dai placed the books on the table. "Why would he do that?"

"He couldn't defeat us in battle, so he had to try some other way."

He frowned. "That's dishonourable."

These people and their honour. Still, she nodded. "We must find a cure quickly."

"I haven't had a chance to read all the books yet," he said. "I'm not good at reading and the words are unfamiliar to me. I haven't got to infectious diseases yet."

"Perhaps we can look together."

He nodded and opened one of the books.

Geriel examined the one in front of her. It was leather-bound and the title had been carved into it—Potions and lotions. The first page read, Collected by Nooshin Ghanooni and translated by Nasim Ghanooni. Her heart beat faster. They were names from across the mountains. There could be all sorts of cures in here that she had never heard of.

Her hand shook as she turned the first page.

Chapter 15

The candle had burned low by the time Geriel finished the first book. She'd had to force herself not to read every word although the information was fascinating. Instead she reviewed the disease or ailment the potion was to cure and then continued. But every so often she would recognise an ailment and read what cure was recommended. Some of the plants had different names but the beautiful drawings included in the book showed what they were. After she had found a cure for the curse, she would return to copy these books. They would make a valuable addition to Rhora's knowledge.

The door opened and the candles flickered as the cold air swept in along with Jie and Bao. "Have you found anything?" Jie placed a plate of food in front of her.

"Not yet." The meaty fragrance tickled her nose and she inhaled deeply, her stomach rumbling. She'd forgotten all about dinner.

"My apologies for not bringing food earlier. I got caught up," Jie said.

"So did I." She pushed the book away so nothing spilled on it. "Thank you."

Dai glanced up, and hurriedly stood, saluting.

"At ease," Jie said. "It's good to see you again, Dai."

"And you, sir. Geriel tells me you fought with my father."

Sadness crossed Jie's face. "I did. He fought and died bravely."

"Thank you, sir." Dai glanced at Geriel. "She explained what happened."

Jie nodded. "Those books must contain some fascinating information."

"They do." Geriel smiled. "I would like to take a copy for our tribe." She stretched out the kinks in her back, wincing at the pain. "So far, I haven't found anything pertaining to the curse but there are another two books to read." Dai was only a quarter of the way through his book.

"It's getting late. Ru has arranged a bed for you in his office."

She shook her head. "I'd like to continue reading."

"The books will be here when you wake," he said.

Perhaps he'd forgotten the urgency. "Every hour I delay, more of my people die," she retorted. "Our journey has delayed us enough."

Dai yawned. "With your permission, Captain, I will retire. I can help again in the morning." He stood.

Jie nodded and Dai bowed and left the room.

Dai might need sleep, but she didn't, not yet. There was too much knowledge to take in. "Could you get me another candle, Jie?"

Jie growled in displeasure. "You need to rest."

"Save your breath, Jie," Bao said. "I recognise her stubborn expression. Get her the candles and either help her, or leave her be." He winked at her.

Geriel grinned. "Thank you, Bao."

Jie sighed. "I'll be right back."

Bao slid into the chair Dai had vacated and examined the book. "This must have cost a fortune."

She had no idea how much the books were worth. "Traders often barter items rather than selling them," Geriel said.

"I'll have to ask Ru what they bartered with, because an outpost like this wouldn't have the coin." Bao flicked through a couple of pages. "What are you looking for?"

"Anything that mentions a disease that easily spreads from person to person. Also any cures for pustules, rashes and scabs."

"OK. I'll start where Dai left off."

Should she tell him not to bother? She would read the book whether he did or not. There was too much at stake to leave it to someone with no experience of healing, or someone who couldn't read very well—though she was sure Bao was well read at least.

Jie returned, a gust of cold wind coming in with him. He lit another lantern and the extra light made the pages much easier to read. "What can I do?"

"There are only these two books left," Geriel told him. "You might as well go to sleep."

Bao pushed back his chair. "You can take this one," he said. "My brain is too tired to make sense of it."

"Don't bother," she said. "I'll need to read it anyway."

Jie stared at her. "I'll help."

A little thrill swept through her. Having him there made her feel less alone, less like she was Rhora's only hope. "Go ahead."

Bao bid them goodnight and left. Kew snored quietly under the table. This was the first time they'd been alone since she'd rescued him. They'd never discussed the kiss at the outpost. Though now wasn't the right time either. Too much work to do.

"Have you found anything?" Jie asked as he sat.

"A lot of really valuable information," she said. "Just nothing to do with the curse yet."

"What should I be looking for?"

She explained and aside from the rasp of pages, silence settled in the room.

Geriel's head swam with words; so many ailments, diseases, plants and cures. They all jumbled around in her head and as it grew late, she forgot what fit where. She pushed her chair back, rubbed her eyes.

"Anything?" Jie asked.

She shook her head, frustration filling her. "It's fascinating, but nothing is relevant."

Understanding crossed his face. "Perhaps it's time for a break."

She stood, stretching her arms to the ceiling, feeling the pull of her muscles and she winced as the arrow wound ached. She ran through one of the patterns Lien had taught her, punching, blocking and kicking to loosen her muscles.

"Where did you learn that?" Jie asked.

"From Lien."

"It shouldn't still surprise me she knows these things, or that you do." He shook his head. "It's hard to ignore years of conditioning telling me women are gentle creatures who need protecting."

She smiled. "In Rhora, everyone learns to protect themselves, whether it be from animal attack, the weather or a fellow man. We're not all experts, but we know enough. It's how we held you at bay until our warriors returned from the hunt."

Jie grimaced. "I was horrified when I realised the camp was mostly women and children," he confessed. "I nearly ordered the retreat right then."

She studied him. "Why didn't you?"

"My second-in-command disliked me, wanted to be in charge. If I'd ordered the retreat, he would have killed me and continued the attack anyway. And then your warriors returned and it was too late." He shook his head. "The mass of horses thundering towards us was one of the most terrifying things I've seen in my life."

"From your point of view," she said. "I'd never been so happy to see anyone—particularly Lien."

Regret filled his eyes. "I am so sorry for the pain I've caused your people." He stood, walked over so he was only a foot away. "I don't want to hurt you ever again."

He was too close. It was hard to think when he was only a step away and looking at her with such focus.

He held her hand. "I admire you, Geriel. Your bravery, strength and intelligence."

Her breath caught in her throat. She wished the situation was different, wished she could take the time to explore this attraction between them. All she'd ever wanted in a man was understanding and support. "Thank you."

Kew snorted, the noise loud in the otherwise silence and Geriel jumped. The dragon watched them both with one eye open and a flush of pink to her skin. Blood rushed to Geriel's face and she stepped away from Jie. She cleared her throat. "We should continue reading."

He sent Kew a bemused look and nodded.

The words on the pages in front of her meant nothing as she stared at them, waiting for Jie to sit back down. She didn't know how to deal with him. He was older than her, probably well versed in relationships with the opposite sex. The only times she'd flirted with boys had been at the tribal gatherings once a year and this year there'd been far greater concerns than finding a husband. She'd always thought marrying would prevent her from travelling as she'd dreamed, but she wasn't sure what it would be like with Jie.

She sighed and focused on the words. Nothing could happen until she found a cure.

"I've found something!"

Jie's words startled her and then the meaning sank in. Her heart jumped. "Show me." She leapt up and went around the table to peer over his shoulder. The page described a disease similar to the curse. She scanned the lists of medications tried and results from each one. Then there was a drawing of a tiny yellow flower with a bulbous root. The root contained the properties that would kill the disease. "Do you recognise this plant?"

He shook his head and kept reading. "It says it's found in the Barrier Mountains and flowers at the beginning of summer."

Which meant it had probably stopped flowering by now, and might have reduced back to its bulb. They might not find it without digging up the whole mountain. Despair filled her. "We might be too late for this season."

"Let me ask my men tomorrow," Jie said. "They go into the mountains to hunt and might have seen it."

She hoped so. She reread the page and then frowned, flicking the book closed. Infections and Diseases. "This is one of the first pages of the book."

"I finished the book and decided to review what Dai had read. He's not the strongest reader."

Strong reader or not, if he couldn't comprehend this, then there had been no point him reading any of the book. Had he purposefully not told her, or had the pages stuck together and he'd missed it?

She wouldn't worry about it now. She still had to finish the rest of her book. She turned back to her chair.

"Geriel, this is good news," Jie said.

She shook her head. "I can't get my hopes up. Not until we've found the actual plant. I need to keep looking for options."

"What you need is sleep." He grabbed her hand, tugged her back around and stood. "You've been working hard for three-quarters of a moon now. You almost lost your gift, and it's not back at full strength yet, is it?"

She shook her head. No matter what she tried it was always at the edges of her reach.

He ran a thumb over the back of her hand. "Then go and rest."

"But I need to read the rest of these books."

"I will do it," he said. "I know what I'm looking for and by the time you wake, I will have finished."

She stared at him. "You need to sleep too."

"I am used to long periods of little rest." He smiled. "Besides, you're more important than I am right now. It's your skills we need, your knowledge."

His argument was persuasive, particularly because her eyes were heavy and she was having trouble focusing.

"There's a bed in here," he continued. "You can sleep there and if I find something, I'll wake you."

The bed had probably had many an injured man on it, but the blankets looked clean. "Do you promise to wake me as soon as you find anything relevant?"

His lips quirked. "Does the morning count as soon?"

She couldn't help smiling. "No. The moment you find something."

"All right. I promise." He led her to the bed. "Sleep well, *tián xīn*."

She slid her shoes off and lay down. Jie stood over her and for the first time in days she felt completely safe. "Wake me if you find anything," she said again.

"I will," he promised.

She closed her eyes and fell asleep.

~*~

"Geriel, I've finished. Time to wake up." Jie's gentle caress on her arm pulled Geriel out of sleep. She blinked at him and then glanced towards the table. The candles in the lanterns were almost out and the books on the table were closed.

"You didn't find anything else?" She sat up.

He shook his head. "Just the meadow flower. We'll ask the men about it in a couple of hours when the sun rises, but you can't stay here for the rest of the night. You should go upstairs to Ru's office."

"Where will you sleep?"

"I have a bed in the barracks."

She stood and yawned. For so many nights she'd slept with him nearby, it would be strange to be alone.

I'll stay with you.

She blinked. Under the table Kew stretched and yawned. She'd forgotten about the dragon. "Shall we go?" She picked up the book with the cure in it. She prayed to Qadan the plant was still flowering.

"You're taking it with you?"

"I can't afford to lose it now."

"I'll get you some paper to copy it onto tomorrow."

They walked outside. A cold chill settled on Geriel's shoulders and she hugged her arms around her. Her jacket was still in her saddlebags. Far above them, the stars shone brightly. Most of the outpost slept but there was movement at the towers and the quiet murmur of voices. Jie showed her upstairs into Ru's office where a bed had been made up.

"Lock the door after me." He showed her the piece of wood which could barricade the door.

She frowned. "Am I not safe here?"

"I won't risk it. Some men may have a problem with you being Rhoran and some may simply seek you out because they haven't had female company in a while."

She was under no illusions what he meant by that. "I'll sleep with my knives in reach."

He smiled. "Good idea."

I can protect us too.

"I hope you don't have to." He left and she slid the wood into place. Then she checked the bedding in case someone had left her a nasty surprise. It was clear. Only a few more hours of night and she would travel into the mountains to find the flower which held the cure.

And would save her tribe.

The outpost woke early. Shouted orders and the heavy footsteps of men outside the room made it impossible for Geriel to sleep past dawn. She wandered to the window. From here she viewed the courtyard below. The men carried out their routines—some carried water from the well into one of the buildings, others washed themselves, and some were saddling horses in preparation for their patrol.

She didn't recognise anyone and she couldn't walk into the barracks searching for Jie or Bao. It would be considered improper and it was best if she remembered the differences between her culture and this one. Kew stretched and yawned.

"Can you tell if Jie or Bao are awake?"

Let me check.

Geriel poured herself a glass of water from the jug on Ru's desk.

Someone tapped sharply on the door.

She turned. That might be Jie now.

It's not.

Lien glanced at Kew. She slipped her knives back into her belt and muscles tight, she opened the door. The Chungson soldier stepped back, his eyes widening and his hand reaching for his sword. "Barbarian!"

"Wait." She stumbled back, putting the table between her and the man as he brandished his weapon. "I'm a friend." Her heart thumped as she withdrew her knives, ready for his attack.

"Where is Captain Ru?" the soldier demanded.

"He's not here."

Kew stalked towards the man and growled.

The soldier gaped, took a step back, lowered his sword a little. "Who are you? What are you doing here?"

Geriel took in his dusty uniform and messed up hair. "Have you just arrived?" Her fingers tightened on the handles of her blades.

"That's none of your business."

Footsteps pounded down the corridor and Bao arrived, puffing. "She's a friend."

"She's Rhoran," the soldier growled.

Bao swallowed hard. "You have a message for Ru?"

The soldier nodded.

"I can take you to him." He gestured down the hallway.

The soldier's eyes narrowed, but he moved out of the office and waited for Bao.

Bao turned to Geriel. "You'd better come with me too."

Yes, she didn't want any more misunderstandings.

"Where's Jie?"

"Still asleep I think."

He must be exhausted from last night if he could sleep through the racket. She hoped he continued to sleep.

Geriel followed Bao and the soldier down the stairs and across the courtyard. Both Ru and Jie exited the dining hall as they approached. The soldier saluted. "An urgent message from the emperor."

Geriel's heart stopped. If this soldier was loyal to Xue, they couldn't let him leave.

"Thank you." Ru unrolled the paper he was handed and read it. His face showed no reaction. Then he looked up and smiled. "I need to write my response. Please take time to eat and rest while you're here." He called Tadashi over. "Show this messenger to the dining hall and see he has everything he needs."

Tadashi nodded and the messenger glanced at Geriel again before following the man across the courtyard.

The moment he left, Ru's expression darkened. "We've got trouble. Come with me."

They returned to Ru's office and when the door closed behind them, Jie asked, "What does it say?"

"The message is from Prince Kun, warning of an impostor claiming to be the true heir to the throne. They are searching for him now, but he's travelling with a Rhoran woman and a deserter—you."

"Did he say what to do if you found us?" Jie asked.

"I'm to send word immediately and the emperor will send his forces to deal with it."

"Are you going to respond?" Geriel asked. "The messenger has already seen me, and I mentioned Jie's name when talking to Bao." She had to learn to be more careful with her words. She wasn't used to being unable to trust everyone around her.

"If I don't respond, Kun will realise you're here," Ru said. "Normally I'd send the same messenger with my response, but I can't."

"So what do we do?" she asked.

"We need to talk to the soldiers," Jie said. "If we have their support, we can protect Bao."

"And if you don't?"

"Then we'll need to leave."

She couldn't keep running from Kun. "We found a cure for the curse last night," she said. "That must be our priority. If I can find it and get it to the tribes, the Rhoran can protect Bao until we come up with a plan. It will take Kun time to amass an army, won't it?"

"I don't know what resources he has," Jie said.

Bao cleared his throat. "I must start gathering supporters. The men here were either my father's men, or have crossed Xue. If I can't get them to support me, then I have little chance with the rest of my people. The outpost can hold off the hundred men Kun has with him until Chinua arrives with the Danil tribe."

She didn't like the idea of him and Jie staying here, waiting to be found. "You should come into the mountains with me." Geriel showed Ru the picture of the flower she was after. "Do you know where I can find this?"

He studied it. "There's a meadow in the mountains not far from here. The men use it as a base when they're hunting. I think I've seen it there."

Her heart raced. "Then we go there now," she said. "We'll gather the cure and get it to the Rhoran tribes."

"How?" Jie asked. "The dragons aren't helping us anymore."

I will keep trying to contact them, Kew said.

"And if they won't help, I'll take it," Geriel said.

Bao shook his head. "I can't go. I must convince

these men to follow me."

Geriel let out a breath. "Then I go alone."

"No!" Jie said.

Frustration welled in her. "I can't stay here. I might be the only one who can save my people and Bao needs the Rhoran to defeat Xue."

Jie scowled and opened his mouth when Bao said, "She's right. Can we send some men with her?"

"Kew can go with you," Jie said.

She shook her head. "No. Kew needs to stay here and help you figure out who you can trust. If the men turn on you, then you'll all die." She couldn't bear it.

"How about Dai?" Ru said. "He has an interest in healing and he knows where the meadow is."

"I don't need a chaperone," Geriel said.

"You need someone to guard you while you sleep," Bao said.

She wasn't certain Dai was someone she wanted guarding her.

I will check his intentions before you leave.

Ru nodded. "Get your mount ready, Geriel and I'll speak to Dai."

Her heart raced. She was so close to the cure. "Do you have any paper so I can take a copy of this?"

He retrieved a piece from his drawer and handed her a quill.

"Let me," Jie said, taking the paper. "You get ready and I'll bring the copy down when it's done."

"Thank you." Geriel hurried to the training yard where the horses were, Kew following her. The idea of leaving Jie and Bao here didn't sit well with her, especially with Kun still a threat and having no guarantee how the soldiers would react.

The soldiers are talking. The messenger is spreading word of what Kun's message said.

She froze. "What's the reaction?"

Some hope it is true, hope Xue can be disposed of, some don't believe it and a few want to ride out with word you're here.

"Tell Ru." She saddled Khulan and then one of the spare horses for Dai. The Rhoran horses had better stamina than any the Chungson had. As she worked, men ran to the gates, closing them and standing guard.

A lump formed in her throat. Trapped.

Had Ru given the order for the gates to be shut?

Soldiers stopped each other in the courtyard to speak in hushed tones and some glanced at her.

Not good.

She swung her bow onto her back and made sure her quiver was within reach.

The loud clang of a bell made Geriel jump and Khulan skittered.

"Gather for orders!" The cry went out.

The soldiers hurried into the courtyard, some still holding food. Jie trotted down the steps with a piece of paper in his hand and Ru brought Dai over. "You'll take orders from Geriel while you're with her," Ru said.

Dai frowned. "Yes, sir."

Ru turned to her. "Wait by the gate. We can't open them until we know who is loyal."

She sighed, relief filling her and handed Dai the reins of the horse she'd saddled. He mounted and rode to the gate.

Jie handed her the paper. "Be watchful of wolves," he said, a slight smile on his face. "And be quick. I don't like sending you alone."

"Dai will be with me."

"Has Kew checked him?"

"I don't know."

"I'll get her to." He squeezed her hand. "Take care." He joined Ru, Bao and Kew.

Geriel let out a breath and took two more horses and led them and Khulan over to the large gate.

Kew glanced at her. *Dai doesn't like that he has to take orders from you, but he will.*

Geriel nodded. She would be unwise to trust him too much.

Ru spoke quietly to Jie and Bao before standing on top of a wagon on one side of the courtyard. Kew and Jie moved into the crowd as he spoke. "We've received word from the emperor," he called and the crowd went silent. "I need to put together a team for the task, so if Captain Jie taps you on the shoulder, please go into the infirmary."

Jie made his way through the crowd, tapping men on the shoulder whenever Kew turned black.

Geriel smiled. They were isolating the people loyal to Xue. About a dozen men walked into the infirmary, the last being the messenger who had brought the news. Tadashi shut the door and several men joined him to guard it. He nodded to Ru.

"For eighteen years, Chungson has been a vassal of Bonam, no longer able to make our own decisions, or live the way we want to live. Many of you have discussed your dissatisfaction about this to me and in fact, most of us are here because at some time or another, we have displeased the emperor. This outpost has been our punishment."

The soldiers murmured, glancing at each other. Unease crept along Geriel's skin and she studied Dai. His focus was on Ru.

"I received word from the emperor today. He tells me an impostor has appeared claiming to be Prince Bao, the true heir to the throne."

Gasps and a few cheers.

"If we find him, we are to turn him over to the

emperor," Ru said.

One man jeered.

"I know for a fact, the rumour is true," Ru continued. "Prince Bao did survive the attack on his family, only the attack wasn't by the Rhoran as we were told, but by men loyal to our current emperor."

Shouts of outrage.

Kew walked through the men and growled at one along the edge, puffing out smoke. Tadashi strode over and grabbed his arm. The man fought back, shouting and two more men helped to restrain him.

Jie stepped up next to Ru. "You all know the emperor recalled me to the palace several moons ago. It was to lead an unprovoked attack on Rhora. All my men were slaughtered and the only reason I am alive today is because State Princess Lien recognised me. She had been wed to the Rhoran Khan." More rumblings. "While I was in the camp she told me she'd been informed that her brother was still alive. She asked me to authenticate the claim. I grew up with Prince Bao and Princess Lien before I became a soldier."

"Captain Jie has long stood up for us, and treated us like comrades," Ru added.

In front of Geriel, the men nodded.

"I travelled to where Bao was living and I asked him questions only he could answer, secrets we had shared with each other as children," Jie continued. "I confirmed he is who he says he is, the rightful emperor of Bonam."

"Given that the so-called impostor is actually the true Prince Bao," Ru said, "how do you feel about this order? Do we obey, or do we resist?"

"Resist," someone yelled.

"Resist," another agreed.

"Where is he now?" someone yelled.

Bao stepped onto the platform. "Here."

The soldiers roared their approval and Ru gestured for quiet. "Some of our number don't believe, and we've taken the opportunity to restrain them. We will need help to place them into the holding cells for now. But we have a bigger problem. We must respond to the emperor's message and yet we cannot send the same messenger back. Prince Kun knows Captain Jie is with Bao and that Jie was stationed here. We suspect he will bring forces here to stop us. We must make plans—do we fight, or do we run?"

Geriel shifted in her saddle. The soldiers completely supported Bao. He and Jie would be safe here. Time to leave. She waved at Ru and he nodded. "Open the gate to let Geriel and Dai out," he called.

Her gaze caught on Jie's and he mouthed, Be careful.

She nodded and rode through the gate. He had his mission for his people.

She had hers.

Chapter 16

Dai was a competent horseman and they rode fast across the desert towards the mountain, swapping horses when required. There was no time for conversation for which Geriel was glad. She didn't know what to say to him, wasn't entirely sure she could trust him. But that didn't matter, she could handle Dai. She wasn't defenceless. By nightfall they were high in the foothills and Dai called a halt.

"It's best if we camp here tonight," he said. "Snow leopards and wolves hunt these areas."

"Will they attack?" she asked.

"If we keep the fire burning, they should leave us alone."

She glanced up the mountain, not wanting to stop. "How much further is the meadow?"

"We should reach it by mid-morning."

Her heart raced. Not far to go. "Can't we reach there tonight?"

He shook his head. "It's safer in the daylight."

Frustration welled in her. They were so close. She prayed to Qadan the bulb would indeed be the cure they needed. Far above circled a dragon.

She sent out a thought as loudly as she could. *Please send word to Falin or Dhalin. I need to speak with them.*

The dragon continued to circle, not responding.

She sighed. Without a dragon taking the cure to the tribes, she wouldn't know if it was the right one. She might be wasting her time collecting it. She dismounted and took care of the horses while Dai collected wood for the fire. From here the desert stretched out sparse and sandy, with red sand dunes in the distance. Desolate and empty. Directly in front lay the outpost, a small dark square. How were Jie and Bao? What preparations were they making for Kun's arrival? Or had they changed their minds and were making plans to leave? Her gaze moved beyond the outpost to the steppes in the far distance. No tribes were visible from here, but they wouldn't be more than a couple of days' ride away.

"How many bulbs do we need?" Dai asked.

His voice startled her and she moved to where he was laying the fire. "I'm not certain. It depends on the size." She brushed her hands together. "The bulbs need to be pulped and then the juice is drunk. The book suggests patients only need a spoonful."

"At least it's not a difficult preparation." He smiled.

He was right. She should be focusing on the positives.

As the fire crackled to life, Dai asked, "How well do you know Prince Bao?"

"I have known him for almost a half moon."

Dai added another stick to the fire, a frown on his face. "Is he a good man?"

Geriel hesitated. It was only natural he'd have questions about the man who would become his new emperor, but would her opinion count for much? "I believe so. He does not see Rhora as the enemy. I hope we will finally have peace between our countries."

He was silent as he got food from their saddlebags and handed Geriel a package of rice with some mutton. "Doesn't Emperor Xue want that?"

"Not in my experience. All he wants is power and land. He has warred with Rhora since he came to rule, blamed Emperor Huang's death on us. Bao wants peace, and his rightful title."

"How can you be so sure?" The words were defiant, angry.

Geriel reminded herself his father had been killed in the attack on Rhora. He possibly had other family he cared about, others whose safety could be threatened. "His sister, Lien is Rhora's tribal mother, and he is close to her. I don't see him going to war with her." She ate some of her meal. "After his parents were killed, he grew up as a servant, so he knows how difficult it is when you don't have power or wealth."

Dai's eyes widened. "He was a servant?"

Inwardly she winced, but she nodded. It was best he didn't know where Bao had been for the past eighteen years. Neither Jie nor Ru had mentioned Anming's name.

Dai grunted. "Maybe he will understand."

She understood his concerns. A soldier had little say over his life. Serving a power-hungry man like Xue wouldn't be easy.

They finished eating and Geriel stood. "I'll take first watch."

Dai frowned at her. "Do you know how?"

She bit back a sigh. Constantly having to prove herself was wearisome. "Yes. Staying awake and watching for predators is not difficult."

"And if someone comes?"

"I can use a bow and arrow. All Rhoran are taught

to hunt and fight." Though it would be easy to prove herself to him, she didn't want him understanding her skills. She might need the element of surprise.

"All right." He blew out a breath. "No wonder my father never stood a chance."

Her heart squeezed. "I'm sorry for your loss."

He shrugged, not looking at her.

She adjusted the knives in her belt. "Get some sleep. We've got another long day ahead of us tomorrow."

He rolled out his bed and Geriel checked the horses before looping around their small campsite. The plants here were similar to those in the dragon sanctuary and the noises of the forest were now familiar. She stayed away from the glow of the fire, the light enough to ruin her night vision, though the moon was large tonight. It shone over the desert and thousands of stars brightened the sky. Even with her uncertainty about Dai, it was far more pleasant to be outside with a view over the desert and the steppes, than to be inside the walls of the outpost.

The night grew cold and she pulled on her jacket, holding it close to her body.

Her stomach twisted into knots as she thought about what tomorrow would bring. Was she really this close to finding an actual cure? Could all her people be well by the end of the quarter moon?

She prayed for it.

For the first time in days she allowed herself to think of her family. Were her father and Shuren still alive? How was Jochi coping with being a healer? Had anyone else been infected?

She squeezed her eyes closed. It was possible she'd have answers to all her questions soon when she took the cure home.

Then what would her life bring?

For all her dreams of exploring the world, she hadn't considered she would be the odd one out, looked upon with distrust or stared at as an oddity. She'd had enough of that with the Chungson men and again at the outpost. Would she be considered the enemy everywhere she went?

Dai snorted in his sleep. How did he view her? She didn't want to hurt him. She'd already killed far more people than she ever wanted to. Their deaths weighed heavily on her soul. They were at war. More people would die before it was over, before Bao reclaimed his throne. It was kill or be killed and she wanted to live.

She would keep her guard up around Dai although Jie never would have sent him with her if he didn't trust him.

But Jie saw her as Geriel, whereas to most everyone else she was Rhoran first. And that might make all the difference.

She sighed. Nothing she could do about it now. The cure was her priority.

If only she could get a message to the dragons.

Dhalin, are you out there?

If the dragons helped them again, her people would heal so much faster. She held her breath, but no response came. What had she been expecting? Even Kew had been told to return to the dragon sanctuary and stop communication with them. She hoped Kew's refusal wasn't going to cause trouble for her.

When the moon began to sink towards the horizon again, it was time to wake Dai for his shift. The idea of sleeping while he stood over her made her skin crawl, but she needed rest so she had enough energy to dig up the cure tomorrow. She checked the horses again, but they were fine.

No more excuses.

She gently nudged Dai's foot with her own. "Dai, it's your turn to stand guard."

The man woke with a start, sitting bolt upright and reaching for his sword. She stepped back. "Dai, it's Geriel."

He huffed out a breath and ran a hand over his face. "My turn?"

"Yes."

"Anything unusual?"

"No, it's been quiet." She rolled out her bed close to where the horses were and climbed in fully dressed. "Wake me as soon as it's light."

"Will do." He got to his feet, strapped his sword to his waist and moved away from the fire. He made a loop of the campsite and then settled in a spot next to a tree.

Geriel's eyes grew heavy and they closed of their own accord.

She sighed, and let herself sleep.

~*~

Only a couple of hours after they left their camp site the next morning they wandered into a meadow about half the size of the field Geriel had camped in with the Chungson.

"This is it," Dai said.

Geriel scanned the ground for the tiny yellow flowers. There were grasses and purple, pink and red flowers but no yellow ones. Nothing even close. "Are you sure?"

"Yes. It's beautiful in spring and early summer."

Her heart fell. She dismounted, leaving Khulan and the spare horses near the trees, and walked through the meadow, her gaze moving back and forth.

Dai joined her and knelt on the ground, digging in

the dirt. After a few minutes he held up two small bulbs. "See!"

She took them from him. They looked similar in shape to the bulb in the drawing but she had to test if this was indeed the right plant and not some other bulb which shared the meadow. Her stomach swirled as she visualised the waterfall and brushed the gift lying at the bottom of the deep pool the waterfall ran into. She teased it forward and scanned the properties of both bulbs. One felt like the description in the book, the other had vastly different properties. They were two separate plants.

Her head spun with the effort and tears welled in her eyes. She gritted her teeth. She would have to scan every bulb they found but already her head hurt from using a tiny amount of gift.

She threw the wrong bulb away.

"Hey. What did you do that for?"

"They're different." She held up the correct bulb. "This is the one we want." She slipped it into her bag.

"How can you tell?"

She pressed her lips together. She shouldn't tell him about her gift. "They look different. Let's make a pile and then we can sort through them." One thing at a time.

He returned to the horses to get the shovel.

Geriel joined him, taking a few items from her bags. How much juice would she get from a bulb this size? Carefully she crushed it, pressing on the soft flesh, squeezing all the liquid from the bulb. By the time it had been reduced to a small ball of pulp, she had perhaps two sips of liquid in the container. She read the notes Bao had copied for her.

A bulb this size should be enough to cure one person.

She needed hundreds.

Not letting the task overwhelm her, she crossed to where Dai was digging, already with a small pile of bulbs next to him. "How about we take turns?" Geriel said. "You dig and I'll gather the bulbs and then when you tire, I'll dig."

He nodded.

The bulbs were located a hand span under the earth and the soil was dense and damp. In no time, Geriel's hands were filthy, but at least the bags were filling quickly. By midday they had two sacks full.

She stretched her back and said, "Let's take a short break to eat." Geriel carried the sacks to the stream which ran alongside the meadow. She washed her hands.

A squeal made her jump and spin around. Not far away, Dai picked up a marmot he'd killed.

She let out a breath. At least they would have fresh meat.

She left him to make the fire and skin the animal. She had to sort the bulbs.

She sat cross-legged on the bank with one bag beside her. Dhalin had taught her that her gift was not as limited as she'd thought. Confidence was what she needed, belief she hadn't lost her gift, that she could find it, reconnect to it and the waterfall which gave it strength. Focus.

The water gurgled and shushed as it ran past her, occasionally splashing, but mostly following the path it had flowed for hundreds of years. It was only three yards wide, not very deep, and it was fiercely cold, the water coming from the snow-capped mountains above. In a few more months the snow would travel down the mountain and coat the meadow, freeze the stream.

She inhaled dampness and flowers, grass and dirt,

and closed her eyes, letting her senses guide her. The gurgles and shushes grew louder as she focused on them, picturing the water flow in her mind's eye, smelling the meadow all around her. She reached for her gift, but it was so far down at the bottom of the pool it was impossible to reach.

No. There had to be a way.

Swirling the water, she made a whirlpool, but the gift stayed at the centre of it instead of moving upwards. She reversed the flow, visualised it flowing up with the swirl and it shifted, catching the current and drifting towards her.

Elation filled her as the gift circled to the surface and she embraced it, drawing it into her and reaching for the bulbs. She scanned the first bulb, letting the whirlpool settle and with it the gift drained back to the bottom.

No!

She huffed out a breath and began the visualisation again, drawing the gift back to the top and this time, she kept the whirlpool moving as she reached for the next bulb. She scanned it with difficulty, the effort of keeping part of her thoughts on swirling the water and the rest on checking the properties of the bulb akin to hopping up and down and rubbing her belly.

She managed to scan three bulbs before she had to let the visualisation go. Opening her eyes, she panted.

"Are you all right?" Dai asked, handing her some cooked marmot.

She nodded though it was not the truth. Two whole bags of bulbs sat in front of her. They might as well have been mountains. Using this method would exhaust her.

But she couldn't send bulbs that would do nothing back to the camp. Tears pricked her eyes. She was useless. She'd finally found the cure and she was failing her people yet again.

Dai's eyes widened as he stared behind her and he stumbled back, grabbing his sword. "Dragon!"

Geriel spun around, heart pounding and recognised Dhalin coming in to land. Relief filled her and she placed a hand on Dai's arm. "Stop. Dhalin is a friend."

Dai lowered his sword, but didn't sheath it as Dhalin walked to Geriel.

I got your message you wanted to see me.

Geriel's chest expanded and tears pricked her eyes. Dhalin could help her. Everything would be OK. *Yes. We found a cure. It's the bulb of this flower.* She pictured the plant in her mind.

Dhalin nodded. *There are many such bulbs in this meadow.*

And many other bulbs as well.

You can study them like you studied the other plants.

Geriel's chest tightened. *I can't access my gift easily anymore. I used too much healing Bao when he was shot.*

Nonsense. We've told you. You can't use too much.

Watch. Geriel tried reaching for the gift at the bottom of the pool.

Why is it at the bottom? Where is your waterfall stream?

It fell there after healing Bao.

Then take it out again. It's your visualisation.

She shook her head. *I can't.*

You can, and you must. What you need is faith in yourself, Geriel. We can't give it to you.

A lump formed in her throat. *It's not that easy.*

What are you afraid of?

She stepped back. *Nothing.*

That's not true. If you weren't afraid, you could access your gift.

Geriel closed her eyes, reached down deep and

revealed her secret. *What if I fail?*

She felt Dhalin's confusion. *By not doing, you fail. Why choose the certainty of failure over the possibility of success?*

She shook her head, trying to deny her words and found she couldn't. Dhalin was right. How had Geriel not seen it before? She'd hidden behind her perceived lack of talent in case she couldn't live up to people's expectations. Better she have fewer expectations.

Dhalin smiled. *Try again.*

She closed her eyes, visualised her waterfall and instead of keeping her gift in a lump at the bottom, she dissolved it into the water, dispersing it throughout and then let it flow upwards into the stream above the waterfall. It was lighter, less dense but at the same time more abundant. This time when she reached for a bulb, she only had to brush it to tell whether it was the correct bulb or not. She sorted them quickly into two piles, the meadow flower bulb the more plentiful. She grinned. *Thank you.*

Remember to have faith in yourself. Dhalin shook her wings. *I must go. The elders didn't want me to come.*

Wait! Please, could I ask one last thing? I've only read that this bulb is the cure. I need to get it to the nearest tribe for confirmation as soon as possible.

Dhalin hesitated. *The elders are worried about our sanctuary. The emperor could easily go back on his word if he sees us helping you.*

If you help us, we will defeat the emperor and you will be safe.

Dhalin snorted. *Until the next emperor decides we have something they need.*

Bao isn't like that.

No, but his children might be.

She couldn't deny it. The future wasn't certain. *Just this one bag,* she pleaded. *If it works, tell them to send riders to us for more of the cure and we'll disperse it to the other tribes.*

Dhalin was silent. Finally she said, *I will carry one bag, and confirm if it works. Then I will return home.*

Relief overwhelmed her. *Thank you.* Quickly she placed the bulbs back into the bags and tied them so they didn't fall out. Then she explained to Dhalin how to prepare the bulb and how much to use. Geriel handed Dhalin the bag and winced as the arrow wound pulled.

You are hurt.

I was shot rescuing Jie.

Let me. Dhalin placed her front foot on Geriel's arm and after a soft probing, the pain vanished.

Thank you.

The dragon nodded. *I'll be back by nightfall.*

Geriel waved as Dhalin took off, rising into the sky with the bag in her claws, and winged her way towards the steppes.

"Wow," Dai breathed.

Geriel jumped and turned back to the soldier. She'd forgotten about him. "You saw Kew at the outpost."

"But she's not as big as that one. She doesn't fly, doesn't give off the same presence."

"She was raised in the imperial palace, not with other dragons."

"How come the dragons are helping you?"

Geriel hesitated. "When we defeated the emperor's army, part of the treaty declared the dragon's breeding grounds a sanctuary and forbid men from entering it. The dragons were forced from their lands when the emperor stole eggs from them."

Dai shook his head. "Rhora seems to be more involved in our business than we have been told."

"Only through necessity." She moved away from the river. "We need to keep digging." Now she could access her gift, she could check the bulbs as she went and leave the incorrect ones in the ground where they were. They made their way across the meadow, trying to leave much of the ground as they found it and by late afternoon they had filled another two bags.

Dhalin returned, landing not far from where they worked. Geriel brushed the dirt from her hands and walked over to her, her heart beating fast. "Did it cure them?"

Dhalin nodded. *The healer made a batch and fed it to those who were ill. While the pox has not disappeared immediately, the disease is gone from their bodies.*

Tears blurred her vision and her chest swelled. She'd done it. She'd found the cure.

The healer believes she will only need half the bag to cure her tribe, so she's sending the rest on to the next tribe. When I explained the dragons couldn't carry the cure, she sent several riders to the outpost. They should arrive in a day or so.

It meant she had at most another day to collect the bulbs, before returning to the outpost to give the cure to the riders. *Thank you.*

Dhalin inclined her head. *I am pleased you have found a cure. We wish you well in your battle with the emperor.*

We will send word when it is done.

If you need help, ask us. After some time has passed, my kin may be willing to help again.

I will. She hesitated and then asked, *Did Lien return?*

We have not heard from her or any of Anming's people.

Geriel frowned. By now there should have been some news—unless Lien had been captured. It didn't bear thinking about.

Take care, and remember your gift is always with you.

She smiled. *Thank you. Send my regards to Falin and the others.*

Dhalin flew away and Dai said, "Should we set up camp now?"

Geriel shook her head. "We need to continue for as long as we can. It will take a day to return to the outpost and we need to have enough bulbs to cure the remaining seven tribes."

"How many are infected?"

"I don't know. It could be hundreds still." They had to fill at least another bag and they were halfway across the meadow. It went against everything she'd been taught to take everything available. She had to leave some bulbs behind so they could continue to grow and populate, otherwise the next time they had an outbreak of the curse, they would be just as helpless.

"We should get back to work then." He picked up his shovel.

The sun had long since sunk below the horizon when Geriel called it a day. Dai had made a torch to light their way, but even it was growing dim. Her hands were filthy, her fingers sore from prying the bulbs out of the ground but they'd filled another bag. She hoped it would be enough. She washed her hands in the stream and then checked the horses. The meadow was a good source of water and food, and they seemed content.

Dai lit a fire and they spread their beds out beside it.

Geriel stretched her back. "I think we have enough," she told Dai. "We can return to the outpost as soon as it is light."

"Your people will survive?"

"Yes." Joy filled her. She had done it. She had found the cure. Now she needed to get it back to her people. Though she wanted to leave immediately, a few wolves had howled last night and another breakneck race down a mountain at night was not what she wanted.

After they finished eating, Dai said, "I'll take the first watch."

Geriel was too tired to disagree. "Thank you." She checked the horses again and then lay down and fell asleep.

Chapter 17

The odour of burning plants tickled Geriel's nose, bringing her back to consciousness. As she woke, she noted the crackle of flames and the increased heat coming from the fire. She opened her eyes, squinted at the bright light dancing in the fire Dai had lit. Why was it so bright? She blinked a couple of times. The flames circled a large lump in the middle. What was that?

She turned away to allow her eyes to adjust as Dai carried a sack of bulbs towards the fire.

"Dai?" She sat as he glanced at her, anger in his eyes and then he threw the bag of bulbs onto the flames.

"No!" She leapt up, her legs tangling in her blankets in her rush. She stumbled to the fire, reaching in to grab the bag, the flames scorching her skin. She gritted her teeth and yanked the bag out, throwing it onto the ground and swatting the flames. "What are you doing?" She spun around. He had the third bag in his hand, swinging it towards the fire. She leapt, hitting him hard, tackling him to the ground. The bag fell from his hand, spilling open.

He punched her and pain shot through her cheek, bringing tears to her eyes and making her dizzy. She fought back, pinning him to the ground. "Dai, what's going on?" She grunted as he freed one hand and hit her again.

"The Rhoran don't deserve to survive," he spat. "They killed my father, killed my uncle and brother. They're murderous barbarians. They don't deserve happiness."

Her breath caught in her throat at his vitriol. "They were attacked by the emperor." She captured his hand, twisting it back.

"They didn't have to kill everyone!" he snarled.

And yet he was sentencing her people to death by destroying the bulbs. Fury rose in her, matching his anger. There would be no reasoning with him. She had to restrain him, couldn't let him destroy any more bulbs.

He bucked, dislodging her and rolling. She rolled with him, got him into a wrestling hold she'd used many times in the past, bending his arm back. "Give up."

His yelp of pain pierced her anger. He was grieving for his family.

It wouldn't take much to dislocate his elbow. "Stop struggling."

"No," he growled. "I won't be beaten by a Rhoran woman."

She squeezed her eyes closed, applying more pressure and he screamed as his elbow popped out of joint. He continued to struggle and Geriel cringed at his pain. "I don't want to hurt you further."

"I need to destroy those bulbs."

No. She shifted, using his pain against him and wrapped her arm around his neck, squeezing. He fell limp and she stood, moving both bags of bulbs out of his reach. He floundered, trying to move, as she grabbed rope from her pack and the paste she'd used at the outpost. She held the paste over his nose and he stopped moving.

Unconscious.

Quickly she tied his feet together and then she healed his elbow before tying his hands behind his back. She patted him, checking for hidden weapons, but he was clear.

With his eyes closed he looked peaceful. But he'd tried to destroy her people.

Her heart still pounding, she turned to the fire. There was no saving the bag in the middle of the flames. The smell of burnt bulb was thick and noxious.

Her chest squeezed. She'd been so close to being done.

The smoke coming from the bag she'd rescued caught her attention.

No time to grieve. Picking it up, she hurried to the stream and submerged it in the water. The icy cold water soothed the burns on her own arm.

Had the fire damaged the bulbs' properties? Would they be useless?

After a few minutes, she withdrew the sack from the stream and scanned a couple. Their properties were different, they'd been heated, reducing the fluid and making them useless.

Despair threatened to overwhelm her.

She breathed deeply. One step at a time. She returned to the fire, ensured Dai was still unconscious and then tipped the bulbs out. She scanned each one, throwing the useless ones back over the meadow. Maybe they would still grow next year. By the time she finished, she had half a bag. Dai had destroyed half of their bulbs. She moved them to a stronger bag and then gathered the bulbs that had fallen out of the third bag, and retied it.

She needed more.

She checked Dai's ties to ensure they were still tight, though when he woke he might shuffle his way towards the cure. She couldn't afford to put out the fire, not with the wild animals around. Instead she packed her things, saddled two of the horses and tied the bags of bulbs to Khulan.

Leaving Dai by the fire, she led all the horses across the meadow to where they'd finished digging that evening and tethered them nearby. The moon was full, bathing the meadow in enough light for her to see. As soon as she'd replenished the cure, she would leave. She kept her bow and arrows close to her, took the shovel from their pack and began to dig.

About half an hour later, Dai grunted and then yelled. "Help! Someone help me." All the noise might attract not only four-legged creatures, but two-legged ones as well. Geriel strode back to him, anger simmering in her belly.

His eyes widened. "You're still here. What are you going to do to me?" He shrank away from her. The fury was gone leaving a scared boy.

Pity filled her, but not enough to trust him. "I won't let you go until I've replaced the bulbs you destroyed."

"But you will let me go?"

"I don't know." It went against what she believed to harm a person, but he was a threat.

He swore and struggled against the ropes. There was nothing sharp nearby he could use to get free. Though there was the fire.

She sighed. She had hoped to keep it alight, but the risk was too great. Quickly she retrieved a water flask from the horses and doused the flames. "Go to sleep," she told him. "I'll wake you before I leave."

He continued to struggle as she walked away. She couldn't stand guard and dig for bulbs and the plants were the priority. With the horses saddled and ready to go, she could escape before he got close enough to do any damage. She returned to the patch, keeping an eye on Dai while digging and scanning the bulbs. Her arm throbbed from the burn despite the ointment she'd rubbed on it and made it harder to concentrate on the waterfall. She stopped for a moment, re-centred herself and then continued, digging quickly. At least she'd had an hour's sleep before she'd been woken.

By the time the sky lightened, she had replaced the burnt bulbs and was almost at the end of the meadow. She prayed she had enough. She had to leave some behind to repopulate.

She tied the bag to Khulan and stretched, yawning as she did so.

"Argh!" The yell came from Dai.

Geriel checked the saddles were cinched tightly and led the horses to Dai. He looked at her, noticed the horses were ready to go. "You found enough bulbs?"

She nodded and got some food out of her bag. What was she going to do with him? She studied him as she ate.

"I'm sorry." He shifted to a seated position.

She swallowed. "What were you planning to do to me after you'd destroyed the bulbs?"

He shrugged. "I hadn't got that far."

She gritted her teeth. At least he was being honest. Maybe his anger would fade if he understood the whole truth of that day. "Your father and the Bonamese soldiers attacked our camp on the day of the Great Hunt," she said. "All of our warriors and hunters were gone. The only ones left in the camp were the elderly, children and a few women."

Dai's eyes widened.

"We were fortunate my sister went riding and spotted the soldiers. We had time to call back our warriors. If she hadn't, half my people may have been killed." She held some meat in front of his mouth and he took it, chewing slowly. "The soldiers who survived the first attack didn't leave Rhora. They regrouped, waiting for another opportunity to attack. We couldn't ignore them. Jie told me the emperor ordered them not to return until they were successful and to disobey the order would mean death."

Dai grimaced. "You're saying the only way my father would have survived was if they defeated the Rhoran?"

She nodded. "All the tribes were gathered together for the khan's wedding. The small group of Bonamese men faced our entire people."

"Then the emperor is to blame," he said quickly. "Will you untie me?"

She almost laughed. "No." She didn't believe him.

She sighed. If she left him here, he could free himself and go straight to Prince Kun and tell him everything. But she couldn't kill him when her life wasn't in danger. She understood the hatred that had made him act the way he had. "I'll take you with me," she said. "I'll untie your legs so you can ride, but if you attack me or run, I will kill you." Jie and Bao could decide on his punishment.

"Where are you going?"

She ignored his question. "Do you agree?"

He nodded.

She cut the ties around his feet, her muscles tense, and stepped back, out of his reach. She swapped her knife for her bow and pointed an arrow at him. Dai rotated his ankles and then got to his feet.

"There's a boulder by the stream you can use to

mount."

He scowled and moved to it. He struggled to mount with his hands still tied behind his back, but after he had, Geriel took his reins. She tugged the bags to ensure they were secure and then rode down the mountain.

At first Dai swayed alarmingly, unable to get his balance, but then he settled into the rhythm. It was faster going downhill, though she paced the horses, not wanting them to misstep in the dawn light, or for her to lose her way. When they left the forest and moved into the foothills, the plain stretched out before them, the outpost clearly visible. In the far distance beyond it, a dark mass moved closer, far larger than a few riders coming for the cure. She studied it. It was coming from the northern ranges. Perhaps it was Chinua with the Danil riders.

She increased her pace and not long after midday she spotted a small group of riders far out on the steppes coming from the north-east. Her heart leapt. They could be the riders coming for the cure.

As she scanned, a movement further east caught her attention. Her breath stopped.

An army. Hundreds, maybe thousands of Bonamese soldiers marched on the outpost. How had Kun marshalled so many people in such a short time? She estimated the distance. She might reach the outpost before the army, but the Rhoran riders wouldn't.

She had to get the cure to them.

She kicked Khulan into a canter. Dai yelped and lurched to the side of his horse. "Grip with your knees," she called as she slowed Khulan again. "Centre yourself." She waited until he righted himself and then kicked her horse into a canter again. This time he stayed more central though he swayed all over the place.

Damn him.

She definitely wouldn't make it in time if she had to worry about Dai's ability to ride, but she couldn't risk him going straight to Kun. She dismounted. "Get off." She pulled him off the horse and he landed hard on the ground.

"What are you doing?" Dai shrieked.

She cut the ties on his hands. "You can walk the rest of the way." She slung her bow onto her back, tied the quiver to her belt and mounted one of the spare horses, not bothering with the saddle and kicked him into a gallop. She tore down the mountain and across the plains, the hard dirt and spindly grass, her tension transferring to the horse and pushing him faster. The spare horses kept up and the bags of bulbs bounced against Khulan's saddle.

Please don't let them fall.

As she rode closer, the Rhoran riders appeared again on the plain before her. The second they noticed the Bonamese army, they kicked their horses into a gallop. Would they make it? If she got caught by Kun's army, her people would be dead.

She checked the distance. Mounted men broke away from the main body of Bonamese soldiers and galloped towards the outpost, to head her off. There weren't enough men in the outpost to protect her, and keeping Bao safe behind the walls would be their priority.

The distance decreased. Half a league… a quarter. Her horse breathed heavily but still pushed hard. She could make out the seven Rhoran riders coming towards her but the Bonamese cavalry had at least fifty men in it. And they were gaining fast.

Archers lined the wall of the outpost. She'd come within shooting distance of them and she hoped Jie or Bao were up there and had given orders not to shoot her.

Not far now.

The Rhoran riders turned, heading towards the Bonamese cavalry—buying her some time. Most of the cavalry changed direction, heading for them, but about a dozen continued to head her off. The thundering hooves were the beat to her mantra. Not far now, not far now. She took her bow off her back, readied the first arrow. As soon as the rider came within range she shot and hit him in the chest. He reeled back, but didn't fall off. They were wearing leather armour, but the arrow must have pierced it.

She ducked as one of the others returned fire and then she continued to shoot until she ran out of arrows. Whistling, she slowed her horse as Khulan ran alongside her and Geriel leapt onto her horse's back, grabbing more arrows from the spare quiver and firing them.

The archers on top of the outpost were firing too and she moved closer to the wall to draw the Bonamese into their range.

The Rhoran riders had engaged the Bonamese but Geriel was too busy ducking arrows to pay any attention to the fight. She had to get past and then keep riding and hope the Rhoran riders followed her.

The bulbs, the cure was vital.

She hit three riders in quick succession and they fell off their horses. Another two fell, hit by outpost archers. She raced past the gates, using her last arrows and then lowered her head and urged Khulan faster. Her only chance now was to outrun them, and if anyone could, it was Khulan.

Geriel stayed low, reducing her target and the spare horses behind her gave her some protection. She whistled again, loud and piercing, and the Rhoran broke away from the fight, riding around to join her. Then they were with her, forming a wall around her, defending her as they rode flat out across the steppes. She recognised Naran, the head healer of the tribe and a few men who had attended Lien's martial arts classes with her. Around her were yells and screams but she didn't stop. One of the riders urged his horse to the front and gestured for her to follow. He knew this area better than she did. He'd lead them away from the Bonamese.

She followed, occasionally glancing behind. They were definitely gaining ground, the Bonamese falling back. They rode between and around hills and Geriel recognised the land she'd travelled only a few days ago. Finally someone shouted and the rider ahead slowed.

Geriel turned to find only five men behind her. One was missing. Her heart clenched, but they couldn't afford to go back yet and recover his body. The cure was paramount.

They continued at a canter for a few more minutes before slowing to a walk. The horses heaved with the exhaustion and she stroked Khulan. "Thank you."

"What happened, Geriel?" the healer, Naran asked.

"Prince Kun must have got word Bao and Jie are at the outpost." Were they still alive? "We need to send warriors to help defend it."

"Where's the cure?" Naran asked.

Geriel tapped the bags on her saddle. "Here. Did Dhalin explain how to prepare it?"

Naran nodded. "Everyone we gave it to has had a remarkable recovery."

Relief swept away her fear. "We need to get it to the rest of the tribes." She dismounted, split the bulbs into seven smaller bags and handed them out amongst the riders as they took care of their horses.

"What about you?" Naran asked. "Aren't you taking some to a tribe?"

She froze. She hadn't even considered it. "No, I need to help the outpost." Jie and Kew were there. "If Bao dies, there's no one to take over from the emperor." As her breath calmed from the ride her mind raced. How could she defeat Kun? She brushed Khulan, murmuring her thanks.

"They gave us this curse!" one of the warriors said. "Why should we help them?"

"Temur promised to help defeat Xue, promised to put Bao back on the throne. To keep his promise, we must help the outpost."

"We shouldn't involve ourselves in their affairs."

Anger coursed through her veins. "Both Bao and Jie have saved my life. Without them, I wouldn't have found a cure." She drew herself up. "Naran, are we close to your tribe? Can you get more warriors from there?"

"Yes. I'll send them. Maybe you should wait for them?"

She shook her head. "I need to find the Danil tribe and warn them," she said. "They're heading for the outpost." She mounted Khulan again. "Safe travels."

"May Dzhambul ride with you," Naran said and then the riders split up, travelling in different directions to deliver the cure.

Geriel took a deep breath and let it out. She had done it. She had found the cure and delivered it to her people. But she wasn't finished yet.

She had another battle to fight. She needed to rescue those who had helped her. Those she'd come to care for.

She nudged Khulan into a gallop and headed north.

~*~

Geriel rode as fast as she dared towards where she'd seen the mass of riders. They couldn't be too far. She stopped every so often to listen and eventually heard the soft rumble of horses. Kicking Khulan into a canter, she rode towards the sound, her heart racing. Kun would have reached the outpost by now. Jie would be fighting. Would the outpost survive the onslaught?

She knew nothing about siege warfare.

The rumble became louder and as she crested a hill, the Danil warriors spread out below her. Her heart leapt. She scanned the group of three hundred or more and found Batzorig and Chinua towards the front. One of the warriors spotted her and let out a cry. She whistled a response and headed towards them.

Chinua and Batzorig broke off and met her halfway. "What are you doing here?" Chinua demanded. "Where are Bao and Jie?"

She raised a hand to calm him. "Kun has attacked the outpost with about a thousand men. Jie, Kew and Bao are all inside."

"What about the cure?"

She smiled. "I found it. Riders from the Gertan tribe are distributing it to the other tribes now."

"The dragons wouldn't help?"

She shook her head. "No. Dhalin took a batch to one tribe, but she couldn't help any further."

"So we're expecting a battle when we arrive?" Batzorig said.

"Yes. I only just made it through. Some of their cavalry followed us but we lost them. We might come across them still searching, or they might have returned to the outpost."

Batzorig scowled. "I knew we should have killed Kun when we had the chance. How many on horseback?"

"About fifty."

"We'll deal with them first."

"I've asked Naran to send more warriors from the Gertan camp."

"They're cured?" Chinua asked.

"Yes." She turned to Batzorig. "You'll see what you're up against when we get to the desert plain. It's flat the whole way to the outpost."

"All right." He kicked his horse into a gallop.

It was mid-afternoon when the outpost appeared before them in the distance. Kun's army was still trying to get in, swarming around the outside.

Geriel breathed a sigh of relief. Jie should still be safe.

Batzorig gestured for the warriors to stop and prepare as he examined the battlefield. He waved Geriel over. "Tell me about the outpost."

She described the layout and the land around it. The hard-packed dirt shouldn't give the horses any trouble. When Batzorig was satisfied, she restocked her arrows from the supplies.

"What are you doing?" Chinua asked.

"Preparing," she replied.

He shook his head. "You can't fight. You're needed as a healer."

"I need to be able to defend myself." She could fight as well as the next warrior, but Chinua was right. It was her responsibility to heal any injured.

Despite her success on the mountain, nerves swirled in her stomach as the Rhoran moved to the rear of Kun's army to attack from behind. They would be caught between the outpost and the Rhoran.

As they drew closer there were shouts of alarm. A few Bonamese soldiers ran, only to be shot by their own people. The price of cowardice.

A horse grazed next to a lone body out on the plain. She slowed Khulan and let the warriors charge ahead. It could be the Rhoran rider who'd fallen. She rode fast towards him, her bow and arrow ready in case he was the enemy, and then relaxed when she recognised his clothing. He was Rhoran. She scanned her surroundings and then dismounted. An arrow protruded from his back and his arm was bent at the wrong angle. She checked his pulse.

Still alive.

She took a deep breath and connected to him, letting the waterfall flow around her. The arrow had embedded deeply, and had torn muscles and tendons. There was a lot of pain and blood. She pulled the arrow out, using her gift to heal the wound. The warrior groaned. Good. He was awake.

"This is going to hurt." She realigned the bones in his arm and he screamed in pain. She winced.

Geriel, behind you! Kew's frantic cry sounded loud in her head and Geriel looked up, straight at a group of Bonamese riders coming from the steppes.

Her heart leapt. "Get up!" She poured her gift into the warrior's arm, pushing it to heal and when it was, she grabbed her bow and arrow from her saddle and sent arrows flying. The man clambered to his feet, whistled for his horse, stumbling a little. If he could mount his horse and ride, he'd have a chance.

She leapt onto Khulan, keeping herself between the Rhoran warrior and the approaching men as he mounted. They were getting closer, but weren't firing on her. Maybe they'd run out of arrows.

Finally the warrior was mounted and she kicked Khulan into a gallop, racing back towards the Danil warriors, the now healed man riding with her.

She rode hard, her heart pounding in her chest as

she checked behind. They were falling back but the dozen or so men were focused on her. She whistled loudly and a couple of Rhoran warriors at the rear of the pack turned. They shouted and rode towards her.

Thank Dzhambul.

Soon they passed her and engaged the Bonamese.

Geriel slowed, studying the man she'd healed. He clung to the saddle of his horse, his face pale. He needed rest, not to fight, he'd lost a lot of blood. "Stay with me," she called.

He nodded.

The Rhoran encircled the bulk of the Bonamese soldiers, pushing them towards the outpost; shouts and screams punctuated the day. The clash of sword and sabre rang out. Behind her, the Rhoran warriors had made short work of the Bonamese cavalry and had returned to the main battle. She scanned the area, looking for people who needed her help.

As the wave of Rhoran riders passed through the Bonamese, bodies were left in their wake. Most were Bonamese, but some were Rhoran. Were they still alive? "Can you guard me?" she called to the warrior.

"Yes."

She approached the battlefield, hand on her sabre, ready to fight and scanned the bodies on the ground. Some moved and moaned and as she grew closer her eyes widened. These weren't soldiers. They wore the garb of peasants and no armour. Kun must have ordered them to fight despite being unequipped and untrained.

She couldn't let them die.

Dismounting, she approached the first man.

"He's Bonamese," her guard called.

"He's hurt," she replied.

The injured man's eyes shot open and he cringed

away from her. "Don't kill me, I'm just a Chungson farmer."

Her heart squeezed. "I won't. I want to heal you." She shifted his weapon away from him and lay a hand on his arm. He'd been stabbed. She drew from her waterfall and healed him with little effort.

His hand went to his stomach and he stared at her. "What did you do?"

She smiled. "I healed you." She scanned the field. So many bodies lying there, some groaning, some dead. "Help me find others who are injured. This was not your fight and you shouldn't be punished for it."

"Thank you," he whispered and began to search.

Geriel went from person to person, some Rhoran, some peasants and healed them. Those she healed in turn helped to protect her and to search for those still alive.

The Rhoran who were too weak to return to battle gathered their dead while the battle raged a hundred yards away. A man groaned and she turned around. He wore the red uniform of Kun's guard.

She thought of Dai's father. He had simply been following orders.

One way to change the Bonamese's opinion was to show she wasn't a barbarian. She had the skills to help this man, and she should. She knelt and the man's eyes opened.

"Don't be afraid. I'm here to heal you."

The man growled and swung his right hand, a knife glistening in it. She lurched back and the tip sliced her forearm. Pain shot through her and her guard yelled and stabbed the Bonamese soldier in the chest. Geriel shifted away from him, holding her arm, squeezing her eyes closed. Foolish. Not everyone wanted what she did.

She prodded the wound.

"Are you all right?" her guard called.

"Yes. Get me a bandage from my saddle."

One of the Chungson peasants ran to fetch it. About two dozen men searched the battlefield, men she'd healed, and she wasn't exhausted. Maybe finally she'd learnt how to use her gift properly.

The battle had stalled, not getting any closer to the wall and from where she was, she couldn't see why. It was too dangerous for her to get any closer, but men dragged bodies towards her for her to heal.

"Why are you doing this?" one of the peasants she'd just healed demanded. "The Rhoran are killers."

"No. We defend our land. The Bonamese have been attacking us since Emperor Xue came to power." She studied the dirt on his face. She had to appeal to a shared experience. "We want to stop him, but you don't deserve to be caught in the middle. We want to protect you and allow you to farm in peace."

The man was silent as she moved on to the next person and then he said, "I am the elder of my village. How can we help you?"

Her breath caught. Perhaps she could do more than just heal. Perhaps she could make allies. "Let's discuss that after the battle has ended." She would have to ask Bao how best to use them.

Geriel mounted Khulan to get a better view of the battle. Men stood at the corner towers of the outpost firing arrows and others strode along the ramparts at the top of the wall preparing something.

The Rhoran fought at the edges of the army, moving slowly inward. In the middle of the Bonamese group was Kun, easily recognisable by the way half a dozen men surrounded him, protecting him.

She drew an arrow, stood on Khulan's back to get a

better angle. Fighters moved in and out of the way. She prayed to Dzhambul and the soldier guarding Kun shifted to the left giving her a clear shot. She released the arrow.

It flew straight, heading for his heart. Then at the last second, the guard shifted back and the arrow pierced his chest. He fell, landing on Kun, taking him down with him. Shouts of panic and one of the guards spotted her, returned fire.

Goat dung.

She leapt back into the saddle and kicked Khulan, moving out of range.

Then Kew's voice shouted frantically in her head. *Jie's been shot!*

Chapter 18

Fast images accompanied Kew's words; Jie lying on the brick walkway, an arrow in his chest, dangerously close to his heart.

Geriel gasped as Kew's panic punched her. Fear ripped through her. She had to get inside the outpost. Had to save him. She scanned the battle, looking for a way in.

Too many fighters stood between her and the gate on this side. She wouldn't make it. Maybe the other gate was clear. *Is there fighting by the western gate?*

Yes.

How many people?

A hundred.

It was possible if she could get the Rhoran to help. *Soldiers or peasants?*

Both.

She yelled to the Rhoran men she'd healed. "Get your horses." They reacted immediately to the order, mounting. They weren't in the best shape but they'd provide the distraction she needed. She found the Chungson elder and rode towards him. "I need your help." She stretched out her arm, he grabbed it, and she swung him onto Khulan behind her. Then she kicked Khulan into a gallop, rounding the army, and headed for the western gate. As she passed, Chinua called some men to him and joined her.

"You need to get inside," he yelled.

"Yes." Kew must have told him. She twisted to the man behind her. "I need you to convince the peasants to surrender," she called. "If they run, we won't chase them."

Chinua's eyes widened when he saw the elder.

"The Bonamese will shoot us," the elder yelled.

"We'll protect you."

Chinua nodded.

"I'll try," the elder said.

They rode down the side wall and around the corner where a hundred men fought. Several grappling hooks had been secured to the ramparts and a couple of men climbed the wall. That was her way in. She shot the closest soldier and he fell with a scream, landing hard on his back. "Cover me," she called to Chinua and headed for the still dangling rope. At the top of the ramparts, Tadashi was trying to dislodge it. "Tadashi!" she bellowed.

He glanced down and she grabbed the rope, hauling herself out of the saddle. Her arms burned but she climbed, bracing her feet against the wall as the Bonamese had done.

Below her the village elder yelled, "Run. Don't fight for the Bonamese. Save yourselves."

An arrow hit the wall right by her hand and she flinched.

Faster.

The rope wobbled. Above her Tadashi and another soldier pulled her up. She moved quickly as more arrows hit the walls around her. She looked down at the

Chungson farmers running away and the Rhoran herding the remaining Bonamese soldiers around the side of wall, back towards the main battle.

It was a long way to the ground.

Her hands slipped on the rope, burning her palms. She gripped tighter, gritting her teeth and paused for a second to breathe. Almost there.

She kept climbing, ignoring the pain, praying Jie was still alive.

He is. Hurry. I can't heal him properly.

At Kew's urging she pushed herself harder. Finally she reached the top and Tadashi helped her over. "Where's Jie?"

"This way."

She ran along the ramparts to the other gate where Bao and Kew were crouched next to Jie. Jie's skin was pale, the arrow still sticking out of his chest and blood dribbling out of his mouth. "Move!"

Her order made men scatter and she knelt on the ground next to Jie, placed her hand on his arm. "Stay with me."

"Geriel." It was barely a whisper.

"Don't talk."

She closed her eyes, connected with him and horror flooded her body. The arrow had pierced his heart and blood filled the cavity. She couldn't heal it. It was her father's injury all over again. She needed Amslan.

Why did the men she loved get hurt all the time?

You can heal it. Kew said. *Have faith. Remember your waterfall.*

The certainty in Kew's voice broke through Geriel's panic and she realised Kew was also connected to Jie, slowing his blood, watching what she was doing.

They had both learnt so much more in the past few moons. Geriel could do this. She wouldn't let Jie die.

Her hands shook as she visualised her waterfall and drew her gift to her. Bleeding first. She worked quickly, sealing the interior tears. The arrow plugged the worst of them and she would have to be fast when it was removed. She drew more of her gift, letting it flow through her and fix all his injuries. Jie's breathing became less laboured. "We need to remove the arrow."

Bao held Jie's other hand. "Now?"

"When I say."

He got into position to pull and she reconnected with Jie, drawing the gift towards her, ready to seal the hole the arrow would leave. As she had all she could hold, she said, "Now."

Bao pulled the arrow and warm blood spurted out at her. She covered the hole with her hand, focusing the gift on it. Her hand was slick with blood, so much blood, squirting fast. She frantically dragged more gift to her and it ran out.

No, no, no.

She pressed her hands over the wound to stop the blood flow as she desperately searched for more gift, but couldn't visualise her waterfall. All she saw was Jie's life draining away.

She sobbed as she fought for more.

Calm! Kew's shout added to her fears. *Geriel, relaxation and calm will work better than force and fear.*

Part of her brain acknowledged Kew's words and while her pulse raced, she slowed her breathing, relaxed her mind. The waterfall, the shush and roar, gentle and powerful, never-ending source of her gift. She pictured Jie smiling at her, brushing a kiss against her cheek and she calmed further, reaching and finding her gift, directing it towards his wound.

It flowed through her, finding the injury, repairing it as if it was nothing more than a scratch. His heart beat slowly but without difficulty and she continued to heal the tissue along the entry wound. Finally she opened her eyes and sat back.

Jie's eyes were closed and she checked his pulse. Strong.

She sighed, relief pouring through her.

"How is he?" Bao asked.

Tears pricked her eyes. "He'll live." She wanted to fling her arms around Jie and hug him, never let him go.

"Thank you, Geriel." Bao hugged her.

She smiled. "He needs rest. He lost a lot of blood. Can you find him a bed and someone to watch him?"

"Of course." Bao lifted Jie's torso and Geriel shifted so Tadashi could carry Jie's legs. They carried him down the stairs to the infirmary and Geriel glanced over the wall.

Only about two hundred Bonamese were left and now instead of attacking the outpost, they gathered around Kun, protecting him. "Will he surrender?" she asked Ru.

"If he wants to live."

Kew rubbed against Geriel's leg. Geriel squatted and hugged her. "Thank you. I couldn't have healed him without you."

Yes, you could have. You need to remember what Dhalin taught you and trust yourself.

Geriel smiled. "It's not as easy as it sounds."

I know. Kun is afraid of failing too.

She blinked. "Can you talk to him?"

Yes.

"Tell him to surrender and we'll let him live."

Kew was silent for a moment. *He doesn't believe me.*

"Tell him I'll get the Rhoran to retreat and then he can surrender." She waited.

He agrees.

"Ask Chinua to sound the retreat."

Moments later a horn split the air and the Rhoran retreated, riding back towards the steppes. Bodies littered the ground and Kun stood in the middle of his men.

"Throw down your weapons," she yelled to Kun.

He glared at her.

You promised.

He said something to his men and they threw their weapons to the ground. The men in the outpost cheered.

Ru yelled to his men in the courtyard, "Get ready to open the gates."

"Ask Chinua to return and ensure the Bonamese are disarmed," Geriel said to Kew.

Chinua broke off from the retreating Rhoran with some men and they cautiously approached Kun. Geriel picked up a nearby bow and arrow and waited for any sign Kun would go back on his word.

Chinua yelled orders and the Bonamese split into smaller groups.

"Have you got enough room to imprison them?" Geriel asked.

Ru shook his head. "I don't know what we'll do with them all."

"We need to put a guard on Bao and Jie," she said. "They will be the target if any of the Bonamese get free."

He nodded. "We'll guard most of them outside the outpost and just bring Kun inside."

A good idea. "The Rhoran will help. I'll speak to Batzorig myself." A groan in the courtyard caught her attention. "I need to see to the injured." She strode downstairs and into the infirmary. Jie lay on one of the beds and a couple of soldiers were tending to others who had been shot. "How is he?"

Bao glanced at her. "He woke briefly and the colour in his face is better."

She touched Jie's arm. He slept as his body worked to replace the blood he'd lost, but he was in no danger. She smiled and then turned to the injured soldiers. "Let me." She nudged aside the soldier who was doing a rough job of stitching the wound and placed her hand over it. In moments he was healed and she moved to the next one.

"How?"

Bao answered. "She has a gift."

When Geriel had healed the second man she asked, "Are there any other injured?"

"Not inside."

She said to Bao, "I'll go outside and help where I can. Fetch me if you need me."

Outside the infirmary, Kew joined her and they continued to the gate where Ru was organising his men.

"Guard her," Ru commanded and three men surrounded her. "Open the gates!"

The ground was strewn with bodies and the bulk of the Rhoran were already making their way through, collecting their dead. "Can you lead me to the worst injured?" she asked Kew.

Of course.

She hurried through the battlefield healing Rhoran, Chungson and Bonamese alike, her gift flowing in a never-ending stream. She moved close to where Ru spoke to the Chungson elder she had healed.

"The prince ordered us to join him," the elder said. "To refuse was to die."

"We will do what we can to keep Bonam away from Chungson in the future," Ru said. "The true heir to the Bonam throne is inside the outpost and he will stop the emperor."

The elder's jaw dropped. "I wish you luck. If there's anything I can do to help…"

The battle had turned the moment the Chungson farmers and Rhoran began to work together, trusting each other—the Chungson leaving the fight, the Rhoran protecting them. If that continued, they would all be stronger.

"You could report rumours and troop movements to us," Geriel said. "I can arrange a communication system between you and Rhora."

The man nodded. "Of course."

"We'll be in touch," Ru said. "Take one of our carts for your dead and take your men home."

"Thank you." The elder handed Khulan's reins to Geriel.

She smiled. "Travel safely."

"Thank you again for saving my life." He grinned. "My wife and children will be happy to see me." He walked off.

Geriel's heart swelled. Perhaps this was a new beginning.

Chinua gestured to her.

"How did we fare?" she asked.

"Six dead, about two dozen injured, but you've already healed most of them. We've gathered the others together if you've got time now."

"Of course." She moved to her people. Some had been stabbed, others shot, but nothing was life-threatening. She healed each person, thanking them for coming to her aid. When she finished, Batzorig joined her.

"What now?" he asked.

"Come into the outpost with me. We need to discuss the future with Jie and Bao."

Batzorig tilted his head to the side as he studied her. "You've become a leader, Geriel. Temur and Sukh will be proud of you."

Her heart squeezed. Still no news from either of them. "Thank you."

Batzorig nodded. "I'll get my men to guard the Bonamese." He grinned. "It's becoming a habit."

She smiled, though all the death was devastating. Xue needed to be defeated once and for all and they needed to do it soon, before he had a chance to gather more men to him. She scanned the battlefield. Bonamese soldiers were all that were left. "We should gather their dead."

"Let them do it," he grunted.

Kun was still surrounded by his men. His face was covered in dirt, and blood seeped through his tunic at his shoulder. Was that where she'd shot him at the outpost? Any stitches would have come apart when he fought. She walked to him. "You may gather your dead."

He glared at her. "I don't take orders from a Rhoran whore."

She raised her eyebrows. "I didn't order you, I gave you permission. If you don't want to honour the men who died for you, it's your decision."

Ru walked over. "Are you done out here?"

"I am, if none of these men need me." One soldier cradled his arm, his face pale. "I'm a healer. Do you want me to help you?"

He glanced at Kun.

"Women can't heal," Kun sneered.

He is scared and ashamed. He has failed the emperor again.

Kun glared at her, defiance on his face. He hid his fear well.

"Unless you brought a healer with you, I'm your

only option," Geriel said.

The soldier shifted forward and another soldier grabbed his injured arm to stop him. The man yelped.

Geriel waited as the indecision flashed across Kun's face.

"Do what you can," he said.

The soldier hurried towards her and she gently touched his arm. It was broken in two places and he also had a concussion. "Sit. This is going to hurt." She squatted on the ground next to him and handed him a cloth to bite on. Her guards stood in a ring around her, protecting her from attack.

"Count to three."

When he got to two, she realigned his arm, and he screamed. She poured her gift into him, healing the bone and then gently healing his head. When she opened her eyes, he was staring at her.

"What did you do?" He moved his arm back and forth, fear and awe in his eyes.

She got to her feet, offered him a hand up. "I healed you." She turned back to Kun's men. "Is anyone else injured?"

"Witch!" one of the men cried and lunged forward.

Geriel braced herself as one of her guards intercepted her attacker and pinned him to the ground.

Her heart raced. "I am no witch. I'm a healer. Is there anyone else who needs my help?" She nodded to Kun's shoulder.

A couple of Kun's men stepped in front of him. Loyalty.

The man whose arm she had healed walked over to his prince. "Look. It doesn't hurt."

After a moment's hesitation, two soldiers stepped forward and she healed their gashes. Then Kun stepped up to her. His injury was older, and a little infected. She had done this to him. "I'm sorry." He flinched as she touched him, but then held still.

He said nothing.

Ru waited for her to finish and then said, "We'll take Kun inside."

Kun moved forward, waving his guards away. "Stay here, gather our dead, rest. I'll return when I can."

Batzorig and Ru walked by his side. As Geriel followed them, a Bonamese soldier grabbed her arm. She whirled back, hand raised to defend herself, heart thumping, but he let go quickly and simply said, "Thank you."

She relaxed. This was a start to understanding each other, to better relations. She nodded and returned to the outpost.

~*~

The lanterns were lit in the courtyard and men moved about, some cleaning weapons, others collecting arrows and still more doing the everyday tasks like preparing dinner and looking after the horses. No wasting time grieving. There would be time for that later. The Chungson would be strong allies.

As Ru led Kun towards the stairs, she said, "I'll check the infirmary." She wanted to see Jie.

Ru nodded. "Tell them we'll be in my office."

Tadashi guarded the infirmary and stood aside to let her in.

Jie sat in bed, a bowl of food in his hands, talking to Bao. His face had regained some of its colour and his eyes were alert. He wore a clean set of clothes. The last remaining tension left her.

His eyes lit up. "Geriel. Are you all right?"

She smiled at him. "I'm pleased to see you awake."

"You saved my life."

Letting him die had never been an option.

Bao shifted out of the way as she approached Jie's bed and sat. She resisted the urge to hug him, putting her healer training first, and laid a hand on his arm. "You need to rest for a couple of days." Her throat closed as she remembered how close she'd come to losing him. She flung her arms around him, pulling him close. "Don't you ever get shot again."

His arms wrapped around her. "I don't plan to," he murmured.

Bao cleared his throat and Geriel let go of Jie, her face flaming. Be professional. She shifted away, but Jie captured her hand in his and held on.

"What's happening out there?" he asked.

"Kun has surrendered and is with Ru in his office," she said. "The Chungson peasants have been sent home, but expressed interest in helping us defeat Xue, and the Rhoran are guarding the remaining Bonamese soldiers."

"I expected more injured to come to the infirmary," Bao said.

"I healed everyone on the battlefield," she told him.

Jie studied her. "You don't look fatigued."

She smiled. "I believe I have finally mastered my gift."

He squeezed her hand. "I am glad."

"We should meet with Kun," Bao said.

Jie nodded and shifted to get up.

Geriel stopped him. "You're not strong enough yet."

He raised an eyebrow. "I can walk just fine. I'm not being left out of these discussions."

She glanced at Bao, but she wasn't getting any support from him. "If you feel the slightest bit dizzy, you need to rest."

"Agreed."

Geriel moved so he could stand. "Take care on the stairs."

"You should come with us. This has been your fight too." Jie held out a hand to her.

Her heart warmed. "All right." She slipped her arm around his waist, both to support him, and to be near him. Bao held the door open for them.

A few soldiers called greetings as they walked across the courtyard. The gates had been closed again so they could monitor who came in and out. It would be easy to mistake a Bonamese soldier for an outpost soldier and there was still a chance someone might attempt to kill Bao.

Tadashi fell into step beside them as did another soldier. Kew trotted over from where she'd been lying near the well, resting.

I'm glad to see you well, Jie.

He smiled. "Thank you for keeping me alive until Geriel arrived."

Kew flushed blue. *I am learning.*

At Ru's door, Jie let go of Geriel and stood straight. He needed to be a picture of strength and power in front of Kun. He pushed the door open and walked in, greeting those inside.

Geriel followed him. Kun sat on a chair on one side of the room and Ru, Batzorig and Chinua sat facing him.

"I'll guard the door," Tadashi said.

Jie sat on one of the spare chairs and Kun glared at him, hatred in every muscle, not even sparing a glance for Geriel, Bao or Kew.

"I won't negotiate with him," Kun growled.

"You have no choice," Jie replied, a slight smile on his face.

Geriel rolled her eyes. They weren't going to get

anywhere if the two of them couldn't play nicely. She opened her mouth to speak as Bao said, "You two used to be friends."

Kun whirled on him. "Who the hell are you to say…" The blood drained from his face and his mouth dropped open.

"Hello, cousin," Bao said. "It's been a long time."

"Bao?" he whispered. He glanced at Kew as if wanting confirmation. The dragon nodded.

"How?" He shook his head. "I thought you were dead. How are you not dead?" The confusion and something else—hope?—in his voice surprised Geriel.

Bao's expression softened. "When Ying attacked us, Manalin saved me."

Kun frowned. "Ying? No, the Rhoran attacked you."

Jie laughed. "You can't still believe the lie your father told you."

Kun glared at him. "My father grieved when his brother died."

"Not for long. He quickly took power and started changing things."

"What would you know about it?" Kun snapped. "You were a child like me."

Jie bristled. "My family was thrown out of the palace because we challenged the details of the emperor's death. Two attempts were made on my father's life."

Kun sat back, his eyes wide, shaking his head.

Geriel frowned. He couldn't be that naive. *How does he feel?* she asked Kew.

He suspected his father was not as noble as he believed, but he didn't want confirmation. Even now he's trying to justify Xue's actions.

Kun's gaze went to Bao, then to Jie and back to Bao again. "Where have you been all these years?"

"Somewhere safe," Bao responded. "I couldn't let

your father know I was alive in case he tried to kill me again."

Kun scowled. "How do I know anything you say is true? You might be an impostor."

Lien had been the same when she'd arrived at the camp—reaching for excuses, trying to justify Xue's actions.

Bao pulled up a chair and sat. "You confided something to me on your ninth birthday," he said. "Do you remember what it was?"

Kun leaned back, glanced at the others and then nodded once.

"I never told a soul. Shall I repeat it now?"

Kun clenched his jaw and his eye twitched. Finally he breathed out in defeat. "Go on."

"You wished my father was yours."

Pain creased Kun's face and Geriel's heart went out to him. If his childhood had been anything like Lien's, it had been loveless and lonely.

"Now do you believe I am who I say I am?" Bao asked.

"How do I know you didn't tell Jie?"

"I promised you I wouldn't."

Kun scanned the people before him, resting only for a second on each person's face before returning to Bao. He sighed. "I believe you."

Kew flushed green.

Kun flinched. "What happens now?"

"I'm taking back my throne," Bao replied.

"The emperor won't give up easily," Kun said.

Geriel frowned. "Are you turning on your father this quickly?" Where was his loyalty?

Kun narrowed his eyes. "My father has done things I've disagreed with for a long time. The recent invasion of Rhora was one of them. Your khan and Lien could have killed me then, but they didn't and I am grateful for it."

Batzorig grunted. "And yet you still attacked the outpost and tried to stop Geriel from delivering the cure to the curse to us."

"What curse?"

"Your father infected the reparations he sent us with Traders' Curse," Geriel told him. "It has killed many of my people and we were in the dragon sanctuary searching for a cure when you attacked us the first time."

Kun paled. "That's why you were there?" he asked. "We received word Chungson was planning a coup and soldiers were training in the mountains with the Rhoran."

She exchanged a glance with Jie. No need for Kun to know the whole truth, but someone had betrayed them. "The cure is being taken to the tribes as we speak." She could only hope it was in time.

Kun glanced at her. "I assume Rhora supports Bao's claim to the throne."

Geriel nodded. "Lien vouches for him and we want the fighting between our two countries to end."

"Lien knows Bao is alive?"

Bao nodded. "I recently sent word to her. She accompanied Geriel to the mountains to meet with me."

"Where is she?"

"I do not know."

Geriel studied Kun. He was being far more forthcoming than she expected, particularly with the antagonism he had shown her. She wasn't quite ready to trust him, no matter what Kew said.

Kun reached for a glass of water and winced as he did so.

"Are you hurt?" Geriel thought she'd healed him.

He glared at Chinua. "I fell on a fist."

She cast an exasperated look at Chinua. "Really?"

He shrugged. "He was the enemy."

Geriel rolled her eyes and placed a hand on Kun's arm. From the damage, it appeared he'd fallen on multiple fists. She took away the pain and healed the bruises. When she moved back, Kun said, "How do you do that?"

"It's my gift."

He frowned. "Like Lien is fast?"

"Yes."

He pursed his lips. "That could be very valuable. If you and Lien were fighting together, one killing the enemies and one healing the allies, you'd be unstoppable."

"Which is why we protected her when she went onto the battlefield," Ru said.

Geriel bit her lip. She'd never considered herself as powerful as Lien, but it was true she'd mastered her gift. Maybe it did make her powerful.

Before Kun asked anything further, Jie asked, "What do you know about your father's invasion of Rhora?"

Kun scowled. "He wanted some mythical artefact. Thought it would grant everyone the gift of speed."

"Where do you believe the gift comes from?" Geriel asked.

"God. Though why he chose so many women for it, I don't know."

The Bonamese still didn't know the gift was passed down through the mother, which was probably for the best. "Women are as capable as men."

"Maybe in Rhora." Kun touched his shoulder. "I didn't expect you to shoot so well."

"Neither did I at first." Jie smiled at her. "But Geriel

is capable in many ways."

Her heart warmed. To hear his praise in public meant a lot.

"She is one of our best," Chinua said.

"Will you support us to overthrow your father?" Batzorig asked.

Only a slight hesitation. "I will do what I can."

It wasn't the rousing declaration Geriel had hoped for and the Bonamese had a way of twisting words.

"Stealth won't work," Kun said. "My father knows about the rumour Bao is alive."

"So he'll be expecting us," Batzorig said.

Kun nodded. "If Father knows I was defeated, he won't trust me. He might even send me away, but as his only male heir, he won't kill me yet."

Bonamese politics were not pretty.

"He knows Rhoran were seen in the mountains so he'll expect Rhora to help Bao," Kun continued. "Though he may not know a cure for the curse has been found."

"We'll have to keep it quiet," Jie said. "I think the only ones who know are in this room."

Geriel shook her head. "Dai knows too." Her muscles tensed. "Did anyone see if Dai made it back to the outpost?"

"What happened to him?" Ru asked.

"I left him behind when I saw the Bonamese army approaching. He couldn't ride fast enough." She hesitated. "He also destroyed the first bags of bulbs we collected. He didn't want the Rhoran to survive."

Jie's mouth dropped open. "Did he hurt you?"

"No. He threw the bulbs into the fire, but I woke in time to save most of them. Then I tied him up and finished collecting them on my own."

I'm sorry. I didn't sense his intentions.

"I don't think he'd made up his mind," Geriel replied.

"We'll find and question him," Jie said. "We also need to decide what to do with the men who still support the emperor." He turned to Kun. "Will your soldiers support you?"

"I don't know. Some are loyal to me, but many got their positions from Father."

"Geriel impressed many by healing all who fought," Ru said. "My men are a lot less suspicious of her and the Rhoran who fought for the outpost."

Kun frowned. "Yes, but my men lost, so won't be quite as forgiving."

Did that include Kun?

Chinua spoke up. "Kun shouldn't be a part of these discussions. We can tell him what he needs to know later."

"Kew has vouched for him," Bao said.

"And Kew makes mistakes when she is tired. She spent a lot of time helping us communicate with each other during the battle."

Kew slunk down. *Chinua is right.*

You'll get stronger, Geriel told her.

Chinua stood. "I'll take him out."

"No more hitting," Geriel told him.

Chinua pulled a face. "Yes, healer."

They waited a few minutes for Chinua to return. "Tadashi is guarding him. Where were we?"

"Xue will be expecting something. We need to work out how to get more support in Bonam and its vassal states," Bao said.

"And how to ensure it doesn't seem like the Rhoran are invading," Jie added.

"Perhaps we start with words and deeds," Geriel said. "Tell them what we want to accomplish and show them the Rhoran aren't the monsters they think we are. We could start with the men here by holding funerals for all the men who died."

Bao nodded. "It's a good idea. We need cohesion between us first. We don't have the men—or women—to fight Xue right now. Not until the Rhoran are cured and we can speak with the other vassal states to discover whether they are also unhappy about Bonamese rule."

"I'll tell my men to prepare for the funerals tomorrow." Ru went to the door to speak with the soldier outside.

Geriel glanced at Chinua and Batzorig. "We should send word to Temur and Lien and call a tribal council."

"I can send riders," Batzorig said. "Where shall we meet?"

"How about the treaty grounds?" Geriel said. They were close to the border and each tribe would have to travel a similar distance.

Bao nodded. "We can all meet there."

"What about the curse?" Jie asked. "Without the dragons, how do we know the cure worked on everyone? We could spread it further."

"I can examine everyone who arrives," Geriel said. "And afterwards I can travel from tribe to tribe and check."

"What do we do with Kun and his men?" Chinua asked.

"Take them with us," Bao said. "We can't afford them giving the emperor too much information. The less he knows, the better."

"We should disarm them," Jie said. "Someone may hope to curry favour with Xue by killing you."

Batzorig nodded. "We'll keep them separate from the rest."

It made sense but, "Won't that make it more difficult to show them we're not barbarians, that we want the same thing—to live in peace?"

"Then we keep a guard around Bao," Batzorig said. "When we guarded the Bonamese after the last battle, we got to know them. Some remained antagonistic, but many were friendly, and relieved to be alive."

They talked logistics for many more hours and by the time they were done it was late. Geriel's head spun with information and exhaustion clouded her mind. She'd barely slept in two days. As they called it a night, she got to her feet, stumbling a little. Jie caught her, wrapping his arm around her waist. "You need sleep," he murmured.

She nodded. Now she didn't have to worry about any threats, she wanted to sleep out on the steppes with the rest of her people. She crossed to the door and Jie tugged her back.

"Thank you again for saving my life." His eyes captured hers and his fingers caressed her palm.

"I almost didn't, I was so scared," she said.

"Tadashi tells me you scaled the wall to get to me. I would have liked to have seen it."

Around them people said goodnight, but she only had eyes for Jie. "Well don't hurt yourself again just to see it." Her skin prickled at the idea of him dying.

"I won't. You're my hero, Geriel."

Her breath caught in her throat.

"I don't know whether we'll be able to spend much time together in the next few moons, but afterwards… maybe we can."

"I'd like that." She yawned so wide her jaw hurt and blood rushed to her cheeks as Jie laughed.

"I'll leave you to get some sleep."

She shook her head and gestured to the door. "No

need. I'm coming with you."

"Aren't you sleeping in here?"

"I'd prefer to sleep on the steppes."

His expression was incredulous. "But you have a comfortable bed here."

She smiled. "I prefer nature around me."

He hesitated. "I can't go with you. I need to protect Bao."

"I don't need your protection. I'll be safe with my people."

Chinua poked his head back into the room. "Are you two coming?"

She nodded and followed him out.

As the gate opened to let them out, Jie pulled her back. "I'll see you in the morning." He brushed a kiss against the back of her hand. "Sleep well."

"I will."

The smile stayed on her face long after she'd gone to sleep.

Chapter 19

In the morning, Ru gathered all the men outside the outpost. Each group—Bonamese, Rhoran and Chungson—stood separate to the other, sharing uneasy glances towards the people who'd been their enemy the day before. Chinua stood on top of a wagon next to Ru and Kun to translate what was said to the Rhoran. Geriel stayed with her people, watchful for any sign someone could take offence and act out.

Ru cleared his throat. "Thank you all for the way you fought yesterday. Your bravery should be commended, though I'm sorry we were fighting each other. We had a discussion with Prince Kun last night and reached a truce." He gestured for Kun to take over.

Around Geriel people mumbled. Kew travelled through the crowd again and Geriel studied her changing colours. Most people were uncertain, but not antagonistic. "When I heard rumours someone was claiming to be the true heir to my father's throne I was furious. I thought my cousin, Prince Bao had died eighteen years ago, and I had grieved for him and his parents." He scanned the crowd. "Then after our defeat I was brought inside the outpost and I met with the man." He motioned for Bao to join him and placed a hand on Bao's shoulder. "I have come to the conclusion this man is who he says he is, First Prince Bao, true heir to the Bonamese throne."

Gasps went through the crowd and voices lifted in excitement.

"We will journey with Bao and protect him until we reach the imperial palace," he continued.

Geriel studied Kun's men. Most appeared shocked, but not unhappy. It would be foolish to expect everyone to embrace the change though. Some men might be loyal to the emperor, and be reluctant to disobey him. They needed to be wary, needed to protect Bao, and watch Kun himself. She still didn't trust him.

Bao stepped forward and as he spoke, Geriel moved through the crowd, listening to whispers, studying faces. Some men nodded to her and others smiled. No longer did she have to endure cold stares.

Someone wants to kill Bao. Kew's voice was loud and Geriel flinched, spinning around to the wagon. Jie had already moved next to Bao and was scanning the crowd while Bao continued to talk.

Who?

I can't tell. There are too many thoughts. He has a knife.

Geriel continued moving through the crowd towards Bao, her gaze on people's hands. Nothing stood out to her.

Bao finished his speech and she strode towards the wagon. She met Jie's gaze and shook her head at his question. She hadn't seen anyone. The wagon had been chocked on blocks to form a flat platform, and as she approached, a man stepped forward and knocked the blocks out of the way.

Bao flailed his arms as the wagon jolted to the

ground.

Geriel grabbed the soldier's shoulder and he twisted. Dai.

He roared and lunged forward to stab Bao with the knife he held. Geriel pulled his shoulder back and swept his legs out from under him so he fell to the ground. She followed him down, ready to pin him and he lashed out at her.

Pain shot through her as the knife plunged into her chest. She grabbed his hand, trying to stop the momentum, her breath catching in agony.

"Geriel!" Jie's cry was faint as her mind roared in pain.

She gasped, but air was not her friend. She collapsed to the ground as bodies pushed in front of her, grabbing Dai and pulling him away. Geriel lay on her back with the knife still in her chest, her hands clutching the hilt, trying to stop the blood flow. She recognised the searing pain from so many others she had healed. The blade was deep in her chest, had pierced a lung. There wasn't anyone here who could heal her. She bit back the fear. Others had survived being stabbed, without the use of her gift. She could too.

Jie dropped to his knees beside her, eyes wide, hand going to the knife, tears in his eyes. "Hold on, Geriel."

"We need to get her inside," Tadashi said and between the two of them, they picked her up and carried her inside the infirmary.

Geriel gritted her teeth as the movement shifted the knife and her throat closed. The urge to panic was strong, but she pictured her waterfall. She'd never been able to heal herself, but with her newfound skills, maybe she could.

They lay her on a bed and she closed her eyes to

focus.

"Geriel, no, don't close your eyes." The terror in Jie's voice was clear.

"Trying…" she swallowed. Forming words was torture. "Heal myself."

"Can you do that?" He gripped her hand.

"Maybe." She closed her eyes again and reached for her waterfall. The gift came easily to her, but it was hard to focus. Normally she pulled from herself and into someone else, but pulling now just drained her. She couldn't do it.

She opened her eyes. "Tell family… I love them."

"No," Jie growled, his expression fierce. "You'll tell them yourself." He glanced over his shoulder. "Get me a healer," he bellowed.

A Bonamese soldier rushed in with Bao and Kun. "Let me see her."

The pain was excruciating. The blood pumped out of her body as each breath squeezed out her lungs. It was bad. And if she was going to die, she wanted to be honest with Jie. Her fingers curled around his hand and his attention was immediately back on her. "Love you."

His eyes widened, but before Jie could respond, the healer pushed him aside. He reached to pull out the knife, but suddenly he yelped and sprang back. The smell of smoke was strong as Kew slipped close to Geriel's bed. *I can do this.*

She sounded a little uncertain.

You can.

Kew snorted, placing one paw on Geriel's arm and her nose against her chest. *Pull the knife out.*

Jie did as she asked and white-hot pain flashed through Geriel.

~*~

It was dark. Only a faint flicker of candlelight shone through the window and Geriel blinked. Where was she? Why did her chest hurt so much? Gingerly she shifted and a voice said, "Geriel?"

"Jie?"

A flash of a flint and then a candle was lit. Jie sat on a makeshift bed on the floor, holding a candle and Kew lay next to him.

She frowned. "What are you doing there?"

His eyes glistened. "How are you?" He touched her arm, interlaced their fingers.

The concern in his eyes warmed her. "Sore." She touched her chest, struggling to clear her mind. The last thing she remembered was Kun and Bao talking in the courtyard. "What happened?"

Dai stabbed you.

"Kew healed your lungs and some of the wound and then one of Kun's soldiers stitched you."

It came back to her now. The agonising pain, the fear. Kew being uncertain herself. "Thank you," she croaked and then swallowed.

Jie hurried to the table to get her a drink.

You scared me. If I hadn't watched you heal so many people, I wouldn't have known what to do. Kew nudged her leg.

Dhalin will be impressed. Her thoughts were foggy and she fought through it.

Kew snorted, but flushed blue.

Jie brought Geriel a cup and helped her to sip it and then she lay down again, too exhausted to hold herself upright. "Is Bao all right?"

"He's fine and Dai is locked away." Jie brushed her hair off her face. "When I think I sent you away with him…"

Her stomach cramped. "How long have I been unconscious?"

"About eighteen hours," Jie replied. "Can I get you something to eat?" His eyes were bloodshot and dirt streaked his face.

She nodded and he hurried to the table to get some food. This was a different side to Jie than she'd seen before. "Are you all right?"

He turned back to her, his hands shaking around a bowl of rice. "You almost died, Geriel. I've never been so terrified in my entire life."

Her heart did a funny little flip. "I'm fine."

He shook his head as if he didn't quite believe it. "You shouldn't have got in the way."

She raised an eyebrow. "I saved Bao's life."

"By risking your own. You could have saved him after he'd been stabbed."

Kew snorted and Geriel laughed, the movement pulling her stitches and making her wince. "He might have killed Bao instantly," she said. "I can't bring people back from the dead."

He handed her the bowl and helped her up, sitting behind her so she could lean on him. His hands rested on either side of her, cocooning her. "You should return to your tribe immediately so you can heal properly."

Geriel frowned. "We're all travelling together to the treaty ground."

He shook his head. "You should go straight home. Someone else may be unhappy about our alliance."

"Dai was after Bao not me. I just got in the way."

A growl came from his throat. "It was foolish. I was helpless to stop it." His voice caught.

She reminded herself he'd been scared. "We agreed I would go to the treaty grounds with you and Bao. Besides, my tribe lives past the treaty grounds, so I have to go that way."

He scowled. "Then go to a closer tribe to heal. It's too dangerous."

Annoyance began to push her understanding aside. "Then I guess you won't be going either."

"It's my job to protect Bao."

"And it's my job to protect my people and ensure they are all cured." She handed him back the empty bowl and winced as she shifted away from him.

He cares for you.

And I love him. But I'm not stopping him from doing what he's trained to do. And she'd told him she loved him before she fell unconscious. Heat rushed to her cheeks. She'd definitely thought she was dying.

Kew puffed out smoke and nudged Jie, then went to the door. *I need some fresh air.*

Jie let her out and turned back to Geriel, his face screwed up in confusion and frustration. "I want to protect you." He sat next to her again, brushed his thumb over her cheek. "You don't need me to, and it's one of the things I admire about you, but it doesn't stop the urge."

She revelled in his touch and smiled. "I worry about you too, but I know you're capable."

He sighed. "After I discovered Bao was alive, I had a clear goal, to return him to the throne. But since meeting you I find my loyalty is split. For a moment after you'd been stabbed, I wished it had been Bao. I can't afford to be so distracted."

Anger simmered. "So this is my fault?"

"Yes." He shook his head. "No… I never thought I could feel this way about someone."

She was tired of all the talk. "And what way is that?"

He opened his mouth and then closed it again.

Why was it so hard for him to admit how he felt? After nearly dying she wasn't interested in hiding her feelings. "Jie, I love you, but I'm not a woman who needs to be protected. I won't conform to the Bonamese idea of a perfect and protected woman."

He opened his mouth and closed it again, tapping his fingers on his thighs. "I was dedicated to my life as a soldier, determined not to marry."

She tilted her head to the side. "Why not?"

"A soldier is away for months, sometimes years at a time. It isn't fair to the ones he leaves at home. I can't give you what you want."

She raised an eyebrow. "What do I want?"

"A home on the steppes. I have to stay with Bao, I have to see him back on the throne."

The pain in her chest wasn't from the knife. "Why in Qadan's name would you think that?" He didn't understand her at all. "What I want is to be challenged, I want to argue and debate, I want a partner." She hadn't thought past finding a cure for the curse, but after the discussions with Kun, she knew something else she wanted. "I want to be part of putting Bao back on his throne too."

Jie shook his head, pressed his lips together. "I've already said it's too dangerous."

She was tired of this conversation. "That's not your decision to make." She turned her back on him. "Good night, Jie."

He was silent for a long moment and then sighed and blew out the candle.

She stared at the darkness, tears welling in her eyes. He still didn't see her as an equal, still didn't respect her enough. And as much as she loved him, she wouldn't settle for anything less.

Chapter 20

They left the outpost the next day, heading for the treaty grounds, leaving only a dozen men behind in case travellers wandered that way. The rest of the outpost soldiers joined Kun's men and Batzorig's warriors and they travelled north-east together. Geriel spent the first few days riding with her people after Jie had argued she should stay with the nearest Rhoran tribe. Fortunately Chinua and Batzorig had backed her and pointed out she was needed to ensure all who arrived at the treaty ground were clear of the curse. To that end, Batzorig had sent riders ahead to each of the tribes to spread the news of Kun's defeat and ask them to meet.

On the second day, Geriel and Kew slipped away from the main group and continued to the Gertan tribe to ensure they were all cured. She told only Batzorig and Chinua, not wanting to argue with Jie or be forced to travel with a guard.

Her heart lifted as she approached the camp. People moved around outside, doing normal everyday things. She was greeted warmly and after speaking to the healers, they arranged for her to scan each person. With her new control on her gift it took only a few hours.

The whole tribe was clear.

The remaining fear hovering over her disappeared. She'd done it. She'd saved her people. She prayed the cure had reached her own tribe in time to save her father and Shuren.

The tribal khan and spiritual leader of the Gertan joined her and she caught up with the mismatched group the next morning. Jie's glare sliced through her, but he hadn't said a word about her going on her own. In fact he avoided her completely, spending most of his days riding with the other leaders discussing matters. She was no longer invited to take part and Kun was often absent too.

Each nation kept themselves separate for the first couple of days of travel, but slowly, in the evening when they stopped for the night, they had begun to mingle. The groups watched each other train and while there was a language barrier to overcome, the language of fighting was universal. They began to swap tips through those who spoke both languages.

For a couple of hours each day, Bao rode with Kun and Kew told Geriel they were catching up. It gave Geriel hope that Kun was in fact willing to step aside.

For Geriel the journey was both physically and emotionally painful. Every muscle in her body seemed connected to her stab wound and it pulled and stretched as she rode. Jie stayed with his men when he wasn't planning with the other leaders, and she wouldn't approach him again. She'd made her feelings clear. If he couldn't accept her for who she was, then they'd never have a relationship. It had taken her long enough to embrace her gift and her power and she wasn't turning her back on it.

Riding with her people comforted her. With them she wasn't lesser for being female, she was simply

Geriel, healer and warrior.

One night, soon after she'd visited the Gertan tribe, Jie came to speak with Batzorig and Chinua. He was only a few yards away and yet he ignored her, his posture straight, his gaze not wavering from the men he spoke to.

Geriel sighed. "I thought he was different," she said to Kew.

He is. He's Bonamese. Remember how reserved Lien was when we arrived in Rhora?

Kew was right. It had taken time for Lien to shake off her sensibilities. Like Lien, Jie now had conflicting loyalties. He had to work his way through them. She wouldn't pine over Jie. She would demonstrate her worth.

From then on she spent time speaking with soldiers in each of the different groups and soon she was equally welcomed by the Bonamese and Chungson. Many of them were still alive because of her and they wanted to learn more about her gift.

Mid-morning a half moon later, their strange party reached the treaty grounds. A couple of yurts had already been set up and people walked around, but from a distance it was difficult to see which tribe it was.

Geriel rode to the front of the group where the men had stopped.

"We should send a few people ahead," Bao was saying. "So they know we're friendly, and don't think we're coming to attack."

Chinua nodded. "Batzorig and I will go."

Geriel shook her head and nudged Khulan forward. They forgot so quickly. "You can't," she said. "I need to make sure whoever is there no longer has the curse."

"You're not going alone," Jie growled.

Anger flared. He still didn't understand. Her people

wouldn't hurt her. Before she could retort, Kew said, *I'll go with her.*

Geriel's anger faded. Jie wouldn't argue with Kew. "Let's go."

They rode forward and the sentry rode out to greet them. She grinned. "Uranchim! What are you doing here?"

"I wanted to be the first to thank you and congratulate you on finding the cure. All my tribe are now healthy and well."

"That's wonderful." Her chest swelled. "I will check everyone just in case, before the others come."

Uranchim held out his arm and as she connected to him, he said, "That's quite a mixture of people you're riding with."

He was still clear. "Yes," she agreed. "Who else is here?" she asked as they rode towards the camp.

"Our new leader, Ganbold and some of our elders."

Geriel's heart pinched, feeling Muunokhoi's loss. She swallowed hard. "I'll examine them and then introduce you to the others."

She walked into the yurt, her eyes adjusting to the dimmer light and she inhaled deeply. It was like coming home. The central fire, the curtains segmenting the room into personal and public spaces and the few faces she recognised from past tribal gatherings.

Geriel greeted each person and scanned them. All were clear of the curse and healthy. "We have much news to share," she said. "Let me fetch my group."

I've already told them, Kew said.

She walked outside to the large marquee. Batzorig and Chinua greeted Uranchim and Geriel made the introductions. At Kun's name, Uranchim stepped back in shock, his hand reaching for his sabre. "He attacked us."

Geriel nodded. "It's a long story, one that should wait until everyone arrives."

As the day wore on, members of the different tribes arrived. Geriel rode out to check them all before they were allowed into the treaty grounds. Towards evening only one tribe hadn't yet arrived. Her own.

She stared in the direction they should be coming from, hoping it would make them appear. Kew came to stand next to her.

Can you sense them? Geriel asked.

They will be here by nightfall.

Who would be coming? Temur most certainly, and Lien if she'd safely returned from Bonam. None of the other tribes had any news about her. Solongo should be there as well as their spiritual adviser.

Kew grumbled and her skin turned black.

Geriel drew her sabre. "What's wrong?"

Amslan needs your help.

"Which way?" Geriel whistled for Khulan.

Kew projected the location to her and Geriel mounted her horse.

"Geriel!" Jie yelled.

"I'll be back." She didn't wait for his response. She kicked Khulan into a gallop and rode hard across the steppes, following Kew's directions. She clenched her teeth at the pain in her chest. Soon a party of five appeared ahead of her. Her heart sang with joy as she recognised Lien and her father, then Temur and Solongo, but one figure was slumped over his saddle. Amslan. As she drew closer, she saw his skin was pale, almost grey and his eyes were closed.

"Thank Qadan you're here," Temur said.

"What happened?" Geriel smiled at her father as she moved Khulan next to Amslan.

"He's been like this for a half moon. Trying to keep

the curse at bay has exhausted him," Lien said.

"I'm glad to see you safe, sister," Geriel said as she transferred to Amslan's horse, placing her arms around him and her hands on his. He didn't move.

She closed her eyes, scanned his body. She couldn't sense any injury, but his mind pulsed strangely. She hadn't dealt with injuries of the mind before.

The familiar tension threatened to overwhelm her and she shut it off. It had no place here. She could heal Amslan. She opened her eyes. Sukh had dismounted and was brushing the sweat from Khulan. "Thank you, Father."

His smile lit up her heart. "You're welcome, Child."

She held out her hand. "Come here. Let me check you all before we go any further."

One-by-one she scanned each person and pronounced them clear of the curse. She turned her attention back to Amslan. "Lead us to camp," she told Temur, pointing in the direction she'd come. "This might take a while."

Temur's eyes widened and Geriel cringed, realising she'd just ordered her khan. She'd deal with the repercussions later. Amslan needed her. She closed her eyes, connecting again with him. First she sent a flow of gift through his body to energise him. It didn't appear as if he'd eaten in days. Then she pictured her waterfall and gently connected with his mind. There were no thoughts, no spark of consciousness. Her heart leapt and concern pooled in her stomach but she didn't let it take hold. *Amslan.*

Nothing.

Softly she spread the gift through his mind like a silk cloth floating to the ground. *Amslan.*

A tiny flicker of something.

She concentrated on it, keeping the gift flowing all

around his mind. *Amslan, you need to come back.*

A stronger pulse this time. She smiled. *You've had your rest. You've saved our tribe. Now you can focus on you.*

She felt his groan, but whether it was also audible to those around them she didn't know. *That's it. Embrace the gift I'm giving you. Let yourself heal.*

The one point of consciousness grew larger and she shifted her thoughts back to allow it room, as she fed it the gift. It moved so slowly, millimetre by millimetre and she continued to coax him out.

Finally after an age, he said, *Geriel?*

Her heart lifted. *Yes. Welcome back. How do you feel?*

So tired. I lost my gift.

I can help you find it again, she said. *But first I need you to come out of your stupor.*

What happened? Why are you here?

Temur brought you to me. We are gathering to discuss our next move against Xue.

Anger emanated from him. *He needs to die for what he did.*

You can't argue for that if you're not awake. The threat motivated him and his consciousness pushed forward, leaving Geriel only a small amount of space. *Take it slowly now. Don't overdo it.* She fed him more of the gift.

You're so much stronger.

Yes. Can you manage?

She felt his assent and pulled away from his mind, then his body and opened her eyes. She blinked. The light was dim, not dusk but dawn. They were back at the treaty grounds and she still sat behind Amslan on his horse but every muscle in her body ached. She stretched, wincing as her stab wound and muscles pulled.

"Geriel." The relief in Jie's voice was clear and she looked down. He stood there, eyes wide and next to him were Lien, Temur and Sukh.

"Is everyone all right? How long have I been here?"

"All night," Lien answered.

No wonder she was sore.

"How's Amslan?" Temur asked.

"He should wake soon."

Sukh grinned at her. "You have grown, my child."

His smile filled her with such joy. He was alive and well and here with her. She nodded. "Could you help me down? I don't think I can move."

Temur held Amslan steady as both Jie and Sukh helped her to the ground. It took a moment for her legs to strengthen and Jie's hands tightened on her arms. "You did it again," he growled. "I didn't think you would wake."

Geriel stepped away and glared at him.

"You should have more faith in my daughter," Sukh said, stroking her back.

Jie's eyes widened. "Your daughter?"

His shock made her smile. "Hasn't anyone done the introductions yet?"

"He was a little too frantic." Her father hugged her.

She inhaled deeply, squeezing him back. He smelled like horses and home. Tears made her vision blurry. "I am relieved to see you well."

"I have you and Amslan to thank for that."

"How are Shuren and Jochi?"

"All your family are well and send their love. Jochi has grown into his responsibilities. He was a big help to Amslan."

At his name, Amslan opened his eyes and groaned. Temur and Lien both held him steady. "What's going on?" His gaze found Geriel's. "You were in my head."

She nodded. "How are you?"

"Tired."

"We'll find you a bed and some food," Lien said.

"You've missed a bit, brother," Temur said. "But we'll fill you in when you've rested."

He gazed around the camp. When he noticed the Bonamese, he yelled and reached for his sabre, which was thankfully not there. Lien stepped in front of his horse. "They're not our enemy, Amslan."

He frowned, his hand slowly lowering. "I must have missed a lot."

"Let me help you," Temur said and Amslan gingerly dismounted. Temur and Lien led him away leaving Geriel with Jie and Sukh.

She stretched gently, hoping she could walk. "Father, this is Lien's friend, Jie."

Jie bowed low. "It is an honour to meet you."

Sukh nodded a greeting. "You're the one we sent to Chungson?"

"Yes."

"It seems you've got to know my daughter quite well." His tone wasn't critical, but it demanded an explanation.

Geriel winced. She hadn't prepared herself for their meeting, hadn't expected her father to come with Temur.

"That's right, sir," Jie answered, his posture stiff. "I admire her greatly."

Admire. It wasn't the word she wanted him to use. "I'm sure we can discuss this more at a later time," Geriel said. Over by the marquee, Solongo was setting out cushions and preparing drinks. "The tribal council must be starting soon."

"We were waiting for you, Child," her father said.

"I need some food and then I'll be ready."

"Don't you need rest?" he asked.

Not if it gave her father and Jie a chance to speak

alone. "No. I'm feeling quite energised." Her stiff muscles were another matter, but healing Amslan hadn't been difficult. She shuffled to the marquee, her steps becoming easier as her muscles loosened. People began to join them.

"Geriel, it's good to see you." Solongo hugged her.

Geriel closed her eyes. Before she'd left camp, seeing the spiritual leader was a reminder she was meant to marry. Now she was relieved to see her alive. "And you." She took some cheese from the table and ate. Temur and Lien were the last to arrive and Amslan was with them.

"He insisted," Lien said before Geriel could ask.

Amslan glared at her, daring her to disagree. She swallowed her smile. Some things never changed.

Temur cleared his throat. "I'd like to thank you all for coming at such short notice and to welcome you here. This is the first time our three countries have come together in a long time." Everyone raised their cups in acknowledgement. "Much has happened and I think it best if Geriel starts the story."

Geriel's breath caught in her throat. She was a healer not a leader. "Perhaps our Tribal Mother should explain."

Lien shook her head. "This is your story, sister."

Everyone watched her intently, waiting. Jie nodded in encouragement. She could do this. "It all started when Tuya identified Berke's sickness as the Traders' Curse." She briefly explained what had happened on their journey to the dragon sanctuary, how the dragons had helped them and then about Kun's attack. She neglected to mention the Chungson soldiers training there. Kun didn't need to know everything. She took a sip of water as a few people glared at Kun. "We escaped and made our way to the outpost on the edge of the desert where Jie had previously been stationed. There Jie found reference to the meadow flower in a book." She continued her story, talking about finding the bulbs, the attack on the outpost and Kun's subsequent surrender and shock at discovering Bao was still alive. "We then called this tribal council."

Sukh squeezed her hand. "I am so proud of you, Child."

Geriel ducked her head, her cheeks warm and then remembered something. "I promised a trader two of our finest horses for helping me rescue Jie."

Sukh smiled. "He can have ten for saving my daughter."

Temur nodded.

The trader would be pleased. She glanced to her sister. "Now it's your turn. I'd like to know what happened to Lien."

Chinua glanced at Kun. "Perhaps it's best Kun doesn't hear this," he said. "He may feel it necessary to tell his father how easy it is to sneak into the imperial palace." They hadn't told him about Anming's involvement yet. The less he knew, the safer Anming's sister would be.

Kun scowled. "I thought we were allies."

"You're yet to prove yourself," Chinua said.

Temur nodded. "Chinua's right. This isn't relevant to what you need to know."

Lien stood. "Don't be upset, cousin. It took time for the Rhoran to trust me as well." She accompanied him away from the marquee to where Tadashi spoke to one of the Rhoran warriors. When she returned she said, "My plan was to go to the imperial palace to search for a reference to the cure. Anming was there to negotiate the betrothal of his sister, Lady Daiyu to Prince Kun." She sipped her mare's milk.

"I dressed as one of his guards and that night I sneaked into the library to discover hundreds of books on healing. I went through them quickly, but by the end of the night there were still so many left." She glanced at Geriel. "I had no idea there was so much information." She shifted on her pillow. "The next night was the same and on the third day Xue announced we needed to leave as he was expecting other guests. The betrothal had been arranged and there was no excuse for us to stay. I stole two of the books before we left, but they didn't contain the information we needed." She smiled at Bao. "I will return them."

He inclined his head.

"We travelled back to the dragon sanctuary but met with Wei before we got there and he told us about Kun. I then travelled back to camp and Anming returned home."

Temur took over. "Now my people have been healed, we need to address the problem of the emperor. Bao is the true heir and Kun says he supports his claim."

"We would be unwise to trust him at his word, no matter what Kew thinks," Lien said. "Xue has a way of getting into your head, convincing you he is right. Kun might change his mind when he gets back to the palace."

"Is Xue likely to abdicate?" Temur asked.

"No. He will dispute Bao's claim."

"Then we will need to fight," Bao said.

Temur nodded.

"Anming has sent some of his most trusted men to the neighbouring states," Lien said. "They will discover whether those states wish to remain vassals of Bonam, or whether they will fight with us."

"How many did he believe will fight?" Temur asked.

"At least two."

"What was the final outcome from the curse?" Temur asked.

Geriel stiffened. She didn't want to know.

One by one, the leaders of each tribe reported the number of dead, their role in the tribe and how many had been weakened and were still recovering from the pox.

As each person spoke, Geriel sank lower and lower in her seat. So many dead. Mostly children and the elderly but some of their finest warriors and craftspeople as well. She hadn't found the cure fast enough.

Sukh squeezed her hand. "Without you, many more would have died."

Amslan nodded. "Each potion the dragons brought us helped to some degree. The cloud flower halted it in its tracks. Without that we would have lost so many more."

When each tribe had said their numbers, Temur said, "We should have almost a full contingent of warriors ready to fight if all the tribes agree."

"The emperor needs to be stopped," Batzorig said. "He has killed too many of our people."

The others nodded in agreement.

"Is he likely to strike us again?" Solongo asked. "With our warriors away, our families will be more vulnerable."

"We can make arrangements," Temur said.

Uranchim spoke. "If we are going to gather en-masse, Geriel should check each person to ensure they have no trace of the curse."

Amslan shook his head. "It's not possible. She'll be exhausted before she does half a tribe."

Geriel smiled at him. "I learnt some things from the

dragons," she said. "I can do it, though it might take me a few days."

His eyes widened. "We need to talk later."

She nodded.

Discussions continued until mid-afternoon. Finally, Temur summarised what they had agreed. "Geriel will travel to each tribe, checking they are clear, after which the warriors will travel here," he said. "The rest of our people will travel inland, away from the border and group together for safety. Bao will return to Anming's palace and they will wait for word of which states will support our fight. Kew will return to the dragon sanctuary and ask for their support." He paused. "We will send Kun back to the imperial palace and he will work to convince people Bao is the true heir. He doesn't know enough of our plan to be dangerous. All he can do is confirm Bao is alive. Perhaps he can convince his father to step down."

They all knew it was unlikely.

Temur dismissed them.

Geriel got to her feet and stretched. The Adhan tribe was the closest and she could probably reach them by the end of the day if she left now. Jie walked towards her, but someone touched her arm and she turned to Amslan.

"Can we talk?" His face was still pale and sweat beaded on his brow. He needed more rest.

"Yes." When he stumbled, she took his arm, sending him healing as she helped him to one of the yurts. Kew joined them and Amslan glowered the whole way. "I'm not used to our roles being reversed."

She grinned. "You did tell me I had a lot to learn." She settled him onto one of the beds and handed him some food. "How are you feeling?"

"Like I could sleep for days." He studied her.

"You're much more confident. What really happened?"

She went into detail about Dhalin and Falin training her, explained about the waterfall and about thinking she had lost her gift. When she was finished, Amslan said, "Let me try." He touched her hand and then frowned. "You're hurt. Did someone stab you?"

"Yes." Before she could stop him, the fierce heat of healing hit her and the pain in her chest faded. She yanked her hand away. "You're not strong enough to heal."

He swayed. "I just did."

You didn't use your waterfall though.

Amslan blinked. "I'm not used to you talking yet, Kew."

She flashed her teeth at him in a grin.

"You need to rest and not use your gift until you're fully healed," Geriel told him.

"Who's giving orders now?" he grumbled. "I won't use it unless it's necessary."

"Only if it's life-threatening," Geriel said. It was pointless to argue with him, but she said, "I'll tell Lien what you can and can't do."

He huffed like a child having his favourite toy taken away.

She got to her feet. "I need to prepare for my journey."

"I should go with you," he said.

She touched his hand, felt his fatigue. "It took me some time to learn how to connect with my waterfall and it didn't always work," she said. "You need to rest first. Return to our tribe and practise when you're feeling better. Then you can check them."

He nodded. "Yes, healer."

She laughed, her heart light. "Rest now." She left the yurt and immediately spotted Jie across the camp. He moved towards her.

"Child, may I have a word?"

She jumped and turned to her father. "Of course."

He steered her away from the others. "It seems you have grown in more than one way since you've been gone," he said. "Tell me, what are your feelings for Jie?"

She stopped walking, stared at him.

He laughed. "Come now, Child. I see the way he looks at you and I see you looking at him."

Her face flushed. "I love him."

"Have you told him?"

She nodded.

"And how does he feel about you?"

She sighed. "He says he cares for me."

Sukh frowned. "If he cannot admit how he feels, he is not brave enough for you."

"I know, but do you remember what Lien was like when she first arrived? She told us showing emotions was a sign of weakness amongst the Bonamese."

He grunted. "You will both need to make compromises if you are to be together," he said. "You may have to live inside walls, or he may have to learn how to live on the steppes."

She hadn't thought any further than her feelings for Jie. Hadn't considered what life would be like after Xue was stopped. She'd always wanted to see the world, but to rarely return to the steppes was another issue entirely. She glanced around the camp. The soldiers and warriors intermingled and Jie spoke to Lien and Temur though his gaze found hers.

"Do you think I'm foolish?"

He shook his head. "You've always known what you wanted, Geriel. I trust your judgement and Lien also speaks highly of Jie." He smiled. "Though I would like some time alone with him before I leave."

She grinned. "Yes, Father."

"Now, your love has been frustrated enough today. It's time he got to speak with you." Sukh kissed her cheek. "No matter what happens, you will always have a home with us."

She blinked back the tears. The knowledge gave her strength.

As Sukh left, Jie interrupted whatever Lien was saying and strode towards Geriel. Her pulse increased. He looked exhausted, but determined. Was he going to tell her off again?

"When was the last time you slept?" she asked him.

He ran a hand through his hair. "Night before last."

No wonder he looked tired. "You should rest then."

He shook his head. "Not yet. I need to talk to you." He hesitated, glancing at the people moving around them. "Can we go for a walk?"

"Of course." They walked away from the camp, out along the steppes. She held her face up to the sun's warm rays, enjoying the lack of shade and the wide-open spaces.

"You're happy here," Jie said, his tone dull.

"Yes. The steppes are my home."

He stopped walking. "We should go back." His whole expression closed, locked behind the Bonamese shell.

Frustration and anger welled in her. "You brought me here to say something, Jie, so say it. Don't presume you know what my response will be."

His forehead wrinkled, a crack in his façade. "I can't ask it of you."

"Why not?"

"Because I don't want you to be unhappy."

She growled. "What's making me unhappy is your inability to talk to me, to tell me how you feel."

His eyes widened and he stepped back, distancing himself.

Her heart hurt, but she swallowed hard. This wouldn't ever work, but she'd make it clear it wasn't through her lack of trying. "I've told you I love you. I want a partnership with you." She placed her hands on her hips and challenged him. "So tell me, what do you want?"

A brief smile crossed his lips, but concern filled his eyes. "You, Geriel. I want you more than I've ever wanted anything, and it terrifies me."

Some of the hurt eased. "Do you love me?"

He nodded. "Of course. So much, but we come from such different worlds."

Joy washed the rest of the hurt away. "That doesn't matter." She turned him to face the camp. "Look. Our worlds are mixing without conflict right now." On the far side of the camp, Batzorig was teaching the Bonamese and Chungson soldiers how to wrestle. She wasn't fooling herself though. "There will be challenges and compromises, but I want you in my life."

He slipped his hand into hers. "Will your family accept me?"

"Father has already given his blessing, though he wishes to speak to you alone before you leave."

Jie straightened. "Of course."

Geriel wrapped her arms around his waist. "Does that mean you want me in your life as well?"

He pulled her close, brushed her hair off her face. "Yes. I would be honoured if you would agree to be my wife."

Her breath caught and she smiled. "I will be your wife, your healer, your protector and your partner."

He grinned, the expression lighting his face. "Agreed." He glanced to the camp. "I would very much like to kiss you now."

Her heart skipped a beat. "I won't stop you."

"It's not appropriate in public," he said, his regret clear.

She chuckled. "Perhaps in Bonam it's not, but you're in Rhora now." She tilted her head. "And we like to show our emotions."

His face flushed, but he smiled. "I'm going to enjoy learning about your culture." Then his lips met hers and Geriel knew whatever happened, they'd work through it together.

Chapter 21

Geriel woke as the sun rose above the horizon. Next to her lay Jie, still asleep. She smiled. Although he'd been offered a bed in one of the yurts, he'd refused, choosing instead to sleep next to her, out in the open, on their travel beds. Now his face was unlined, no troubles haunting him. She shifted as the soldiers around her stirred. Clouds filled the sky, giving the morning a dull, grey light. The season was beginning to turn, heading towards winter. It would still be another couple of months before the snow set in, but they needed to act against Xue quickly before it did.

Quietly so not to disturb Jie, she got up and walked to the communal fire. Out on the steppes a short distance away, Lien and Temur were doing morning patterns and nearby the horses grazed, Sukh wandering through them, checking their wellbeing. She breathed deeply, inhaling the peace, the smell of home.

She would have at least another moon on the steppes, reviewing the tribes, making sure they were all healed. She would introduce Jie to their way of life. He was too well known to accompany Bao back to Chungson, so Jie had insisted he would travel with her.

She took the bowl of rice Chinua handed her with a smile.

"Are we leaving soon?" Chinua asked. He would travel with them as a chaperone.

She glanced at the still sleeping Jie. "When Jie wakes. He's not slept much over the past few days."

Chinua was silent a moment. "I wish you well, Geriel. I don't believe making a life with Jie will be easy. You both have commitments to your own people."

She nodded. "I know. We'll work it out." Arms slipped around her waist, hugging her and Jie said, "You're up early."

Love filled her heart. "We should go soon." Now Jie had admitted how he felt, he was embracing the Rhoran way of showing affection. She liked it.

"Yeah, we've been waiting for the lazy Bonamese to wake." Chinua grinned.

Jie stiffened for a moment and then realised Chinua was teasing him. "You'll have to wait a little longer. I need to speak with Sukh." He scanned the people who were already up.

"He's by the horses." Geriel pointed.

Jie squeezed her hand. "I'll be back soon. Do you want to pack?"

He walked across to her father, confidence in his steps. She clutched her hands together. Though her father had given her his approval, she still wasn't sure what would happen.

Jie bowed to Sukh. Her father didn't smile as Jie spoke, though he nodded a couple of times. She couldn't hear a word they said.

"Relax, Geriel. Everything will be fine," Chinua said.

"What's wrong?" Lien asked, coming to the fire.

"Jie is talking to Father," Geriel replied, not looking away from the men she loved.

Lien's arm wrapped around Geriel's waist. "He will give his permission," she murmured. "He asked Bao, Ru and me about Jie at length last night."

Geriel turned to her and frowned. "When?"

"After you and Jie had gone to sleep." She smiled. "He's looking out for you." She nudged Geriel and nodded to the horses. "Look, they're coming now."

Jie walked beside her father and he was smiling.

Sukh greeted her formally. "Daughter, this man Jie requests your hand in marriage. He has no horses, but he has other wealth and I believe he will be able to support you. What say you of the request?"

Geriel's heart jumped. Her father was following the traditions of their people. She straightened. "I believe I can support him, even if he cannot support me. I accept his request of marriage."

Sukh inclined his head and then took her hand and placed it on Jie's. "Then I agree to this betrothal. I shall speak to Solongo about an auspicious date for the wedding."

Geriel didn't want to wait. "Can we not marry before we leave this morning? Then Chinua won't need to chaperone us."

Sukh shook his head. "Your mother would be devastated if she missed your wedding, and Jie's family may also wish to take part."

Jie kissed her hand. "Your father is right. You deserve to follow your traditions. Perhaps we can have two weddings—one here in Rhora and, when it is safe for me to return to Bonam, we can marry again there."

She sighed. Perhaps there was no rush. They would at least be together. "All right."

"I will speak with Solongo." Sukh hugged her and then left.

"I'm so happy for you both," Lien said, squeezing

Geriel tightly.

Chinua grunted in agreement and then turned to Jie. "Geriel is like a sister to me. I'd threaten to kill you if you hurt her, but she's capable of doing it herself." He grinned. "But know I'll be watching you."

Jie smiled. "You won't need to make good on any threats. Geriel is my life."

She wouldn't get tired of hearing that. She handed him some food. "You eat while I pack," she said. "That way we'll be ready to go when Father returns."

She had just finished when Sukh and Solongo approached them and with them were Lien, Temur and Bao.

"I have spoken with the Gods," Solongo announced. "They have chosen a date one moon hence."

"It will give you enough time to go to each of the tribes and return home," Lien said.

"Your mother and I will arrange the wedding," Sukh told her.

Geriel glanced at Jie. "Would you like your parents to come?" She didn't know much about them.

He shook his head. "The risk is too great for them. They will be watched, but I look forward to the day when I can introduce you to them."

They gathered their things, and as they approached the horses, Sukh led a chestnut gelding over to them. "You need a good horse if you're going to keep up with Geriel." He handed the reins to Jie. "He is one of my best and will serve you well on your journey."

Geriel's heart squeezed. It was a clear sign of his acceptance of Jie. He'd been saving the horse for someone special.

Jie stared at him. "Thank you. He's magnificent."

"Geriel will teach you how to care for him

properly." He paused. "I expect you to care for my daughter as well."

Jie straightened. "Always."

"Good." Sukh turned to Geriel. "Safe travels, Child."

"Thank you." Geriel threw her arms around her father, squeezed him. "I will see you in a moon."

"Are we ready?" Chinua rode up.

"Almost." Geriel finished saddling Khulan, checking she had everything she needed.

"Swift travels," Lien said as Geriel mounted.

Her betrothed looked majestic on his new horse. "Ready?"

"Always."

"Let's go." She nudged Khulan into a trot. Life wouldn't be normal until Xue was defeated, but in a way she was grateful to him. He'd forced her to confront her fears. By infecting Rhora, he'd forced her to master her gift and he'd brought Jie into her life.

He'd made her far more powerful.

And it would be his downfall.

Thank you for reading!

I hope you enjoyed the book. It would be lovely if you could leave a review wherever you bought it, because I enjoy finding out what you thought of the story and it helps others decide whether they want to read the book.

Acknowledgements

I had a lot of fun writing The Healer's Curse, though when I wrote it I had no idea that the world would soon see a deadly highly infectious virus spread through it forcing people into quarantine and isolation on a global scale. I want to acknowledge all the doctors, nurses and other health care professionals who worked tirelessly, risking their own health, to care for those who were ill and dying. Thank you. For them, caring for others is part of their everyday life and they don't get nearly enough praise and acknowledgement for what they do.

I would also like to thank my publishing crew, Ann Harth, Teena Raffa-Mulligan, Lana Pecherczyk and Shona Husk, with an additional thanks to Shuree Tumursukh who helped with the pronunciations for The Assassin's Gift audiobook and Sura Siu who narrated it.

The Servant's Grace

The Emperor's Conspiracy #3

A tyrannical ruler. A hidden heir. Can a simple handmaiden save her realm from doom?

Lady's maid Shan works for a privileged family, though she longs to see all servants treated fairly. But when she's caught with equality propaganda, no favours can keep her from execution. With no other way to save herself, Shan reveals her ability to turn invisible and agrees to a risky mission spying on the emperor.

Slipping through the palace corridors to collect evidence of the callous monarch's plans, Shan discovers the true heir to the throne may be alive. But with attempts on her mistress's life and the emperor determined to root out any plot against him, even her power to vanish might not be enough to save her.

Can a lowly servant become the key to saving an empire from a bloodthirsty despot?

The Servant's Grace is the thrilling conclusion to the Emperor's Conspiracy fantasy series. If you like determined heroines, high-stakes espionage, and epic power struggles, then you'll love Claire Leggett's action-packed finale.

Buy *The Servant's Grace* for the final battle against tyranny today!